The
LOST BOYS
of
BARLOWE
THEATER

Books by Jaime Jo Wright

The LOST BOYS *of* BARLOWE THEATER

JAIME JO WRIGHT

BETHANYHOUSE
a division of Baker Publishing Group
Minneapolis, Minnesota

© 2023 by Jaime Sundsmo

Published by Bethany House Publishers
Minneapolis, Minnesota
www.bethanyhouse.com

Bethany House Publishers is a division of
Baker Publishing Group, Grand Rapids, Michigan

Printed in the United States of America

Library of Congress Cataloging-in-Publication Data
Names: Wright, Jaime Jo, author.
Title: The lost boys of Barlowe Theater / Jaime Jo Wright.
Description: Minneapolis, Minnesota : Bethany House Publishers, a division of
    Baker Publishing Group, 2023.
Identifiers: LCCN 2023018333 | ISBN 9780764241444 (paperback) | ISBN
    9780764242212 (casebound) | ISBN 9781493443734 (ebook)
Subjects: LCGFT: Christian fiction. | Detective and mystery fiction. | Novels.
Classification: LCC PS3623.R5388 L67 2023 | DDC 813/.6—dc23/eng/20230612
LC record available at https://lccn.loc.gov/2023018333

Scripture quotations are from the King James Version of the Bible.

Author is represented by Books & Such Literary Agency.

Baker Publishing Group publications use paper produced from sustainable forestry
practices and post-consumer waste whenever possible.

23 24 25 26 27 28 29   7 6 5 4 3 2 1

1

Greta Mercy

OCTOBER 1915
KIPPER'S GROVE, WISCONSIN

Sometimes death came quietly. A phantom swooping in and siphoning the last remnant of a soul from one's body, leaving behind a shell of a person who once was and would never be again. Other times, death decided that dramatics coupled with terror were its preferred method of delivery. Tonight, that was the chosen form death took.

Screams echoed throughout the theater's golden, embellished auditorium and drifted upward to the domed, hand-painted ceiling, where Putti flew as angelic, childlike spirits over the mass of onlookers.

A shoulder rammed into Greta's arm as a husky man, far too large for the narrow seats, pushed his way past her toward the center aisle.

"Let me pass!" he barked. Urgency spurred him forward. "I'm a doctor, let me pass!"

The vaudeville lights on either side of the stage boasted letters *a* through *g*, with the *g* lit and distinct over the other letters.

"I'm letter *g*!" The doctor shouted while those in front of him jostled to the side or hurried ahead to move out of his way. Doctors were assigned specific letters from the vaudeville lights, and if they were lit, a doctor was needed—either at home, on call, or in the vicinity.

The vicinity was here. It was now.

Onlookers continued to gasp and protest. Women in beautiful silks and satins hurried to the back to find respite in the upstairs ladies' room. Men in evening wear catapulted over seats and to the floor on the far left of the auditorium.

Greta was frozen in place, her seat having flipped up against its back so she could move. But her eyes were fixed with horror on the scene unfolding. They lifted to one of the box seats above the floor, where men, including the doctor, were congregating en masse. The gilded box was a flurry of activity. A man embraced a woman, who fought and clawed at his hold. Her screams had many onlookers staring at her, including the performer in her violet gown and befeathered hair. Moments before, her vocals had swirled around them all in a cadence of beauty and refined music. Now, her mouth was open, her face pale, her entire pose aghast. She had captured an enthralled audience, all whose gazes toward the stage had kept them from seeing what Greta had seen. Greta, who shouldn't have been here to begin with. She didn't belong with the pomp and circumstance, the heady scent of perfume and cologne, which made her mind thick and her eyes wander. They'd wandered to the box seat, and she'd witnessed what no one else had. The white hands stretching, reaching over the side, dangling . . .

"It was a *child*!" The horrified cry slipped for the third time from Greta's lips. She could hear herself screaming and was unable to stop. Her screams had ripped through the performance as the child in a white nightdress plummeted into the shadows of the floor's obscure corner.

The woman in the box seat had been pulled from view, its red velvet curtain shut swiftly.

"It was a baby!" Greta rasped out as horror strangled her.

"Greta. It's all right." The reassuring voice of her friend, Eleanor Boyd, as well as the comforting grip on Greta's arm finally stilled her.

Greta focused again on her friend—her wealthy friend who should not be her friend at all.

Eleanor's blue eyes were round with fear that must mirror Greta's own. Her blond curls swept upward and were twisted with pearls. Her dress was a baby-blue silk. Any other moment, Greta would have soaked in the awe that tonight she, Greta Boyd, who could barely keep her family fed and clothed, was sitting among the elite, pretending to be one of them. But now? It hardly mattered. The borrowed corset that tucked in her waistline, the aged but wearable pink dress she had borrowed from Eleanor, and even the gloves she wore on her dry, cracked hands—none of them mattered now.

"What happened? What did you see?" Eleanor clutched at Greta's arm.

Greta couldn't reply. The sheer magnitude of the moment, the honor of being in the audience of the Barlowe Theater had been overwhelming . . . until she'd seen it. The *baby* launched over the side of the box seat. Like a cherub from the mural above, it had taken flight before it disappeared.

Greta's knees gave out, and she fell to where her seat should have been had it not folded in on itself. Her hip struck the polished wood arm.

"Greta!" Eleanor reached for her.

Greta felt Eleanor's brother on her other side, grabbing for her waist to give her support. But it was too late. She had collapsed to the narrow walkway between the seats. Her knees hit the carpeted floor.

Was she the only person who had seen death's swift visitation tonight? The only one who had witnessed its evil intent as it ripped the babe forcefully from its mother's arms?

It wouldn't survive. It could not. The fall was too far, too great.

Death had decided to match the theater's reputation for drama and awe. Greta couldn't tear her gaze from where she'd seen the small form disappear on its way to its resting place on the floor of the Barlowe Theater.

The babe had slipped. No, it had been *tossed*. Its mother's screams still echoed from the hallway beyond the curtain. Those in the crowd cried "Accident," "Traumatic mishap," and other such things. But Greta knew differently. She had known before she came tonight, and she should have stayed away.

Barlowe Theater was not a place that brought joy and entertainment, as was its supposed purpose. No, it had already taken lives in the construction of it, tortured the ones who dared stand in its way, and now it was hunting those innocents who had happened into the shadows of its deadly interior. The theater was cursed.

Kit Boyd

OCTOBER, PRESENT DAY
KIPPER'S GROVE, WISCONSIN

Death stuck with a place. Once the blood had seeped into the carpet, the flooring, the walls, it stayed there, long after the stains were removed. They were the testament to lives robbed of their rightful journey through time. Cut short. Obliterated. Bludgeoned into nonexistence. Smothered by the grave, burrowed into by the worms—

"Hey!"

Fingers snapped in front of Kit Boyd's face, and she startled out of her staring into the dark, narrow stairwell that led beneath the stage of the Barlowe Theater.

"Get with it, bruh." The fingers snapped again. Kit looked up at the taller man beside her. He was overweight and smelled like pizza, but he had a nice face. His name was Tom, they'd told her, the crew from the TV show *Psychic and the Skeptic*.

"Sorry." Kit offered him a wince. She'd paused on the first concrete step while her best friend, Madison, the psychic medium, Heather Grant, and the skeptic investigator, Evan Fischer, disappeared into the bowels of the theater. Tom the cameraman was held back by her hesitation. She gave him a warning look, though the theater's darkness in the midnight atmosphere probably hid most of her expression. "You *do* know people died here . . . have disappeared here."

"That's the point." Tom waved her forward, the camera on his shoulder blinking a red light. "But I need to catch them on film if I can, and you're in my way."

Fabulous. She was on camera. That would probably make the show too. Kit Boyd, the quirky sidekick to Madison Farrington, the historical activist, the beauty, the granddaughter of the town's ambitious CEO of all things expansion, modern, and money-making.

"Hello?" There was definite irritation in Tom's voice.

"I'm *going*! I'm going." Kit hurried down the steps. She'd taken them many times before. Anyone who was native to Kipper's Grove, Wisconsin, had grown up in the Barlowe Theater at one point or another. Dancers had tapped and glided across its stage in recitals, high school glee clubs with dreams of Broadway had warbled off-key through its hall, and the local theater guild had put on such plays as *Arsenic and Old Lace* and *The Music Man*. Kit hadn't been in any of those. Instead, she was the one backstage handing bottles of water to the performers, smiling and cracking jokes to encourage the stage-frozen little six-year-old dressed in a yellow tutu with glitter on her cheeks.

"Oh, *c'mon*!" Tom hissed, his irritation past the point of being hidden. How he'd gotten behind her anyway was a faux pas for filming. He was supposed to stick close to the stars of the show, Heather and Evan. And boy, did those two get along famously—*not*.

"Whew!" Kit wheezed under her breath, not caring if Tom heard. "I'd try to avoid those two if you could."

"Yeah, well, I have a job to do." Tom squeezed past Kit as she hugged the cement-block wall at the bottom of the stairs to let him through. He elbowed her arm and didn't bother to apologize. He probably felt as if she owed him that luxury. The luxury of being annoyed.

Okay, fine. She did.

If she was being honest, Kit wasn't a fan of the Barlowe Theater past dark. Which was the cliché of all theaters built just after the turn of the century. It was dark. Haunted. The place was like a tomb. Crank up some vaudeville music and the place became a literal haunted house of horrors for Halloween. And Kit hated Halloween. The darkness, the Gothic look and feel, Halloween was for morbid people who thought Edgar Allan Poe was romantic in his mystery and lore instead of macabre and bleak. Hadn't he died questionably? She'd heard a podcast once that claimed the poet might have been murdered, contrary to the popular belief that his death had been the result of some fatal malady undiagnosed.

Kit shook her head to clear her thoughts. Mom said cobwebs couldn't possibly gather in her head because she had too many ideas. Mom was right. Kit would never be accused of having an underactive imagination.

A finger jabbed into the back of her shoulder.

"Stop it!" Kit spun to glare at the offender.

No one was there.

Her skin began crawling. "Gahhhhhh!" She waved her hands wildly at the unseen ghost finger. Probably her imagination, but whatever. She had let Madison sucker her into a ghost hunt for the popular ghost-hunting television show. This was her penance? Getting poked by an elusive spirit?

"Sorry, God." Kit mumbled an apology to the Almighty, who was probably rolling His eyes at their attempts to mess with the spirit world. But this was Madison. She believed *anything* was possible. Kit had been raised to believe that this type of *anything* was probably demonic. There had to be a middle ground. Hadn't there?

Kit hurried around the corner, stubbing her toe on a bolt that rose half an inch up from the floor. Dampness and time had warped the theater's floor, making it uneven. She leaned against the wall, rubbing her bare toe. Flip-flops on a ghost hunt. Bad idea.

She looked around—well, as best as she could. The basement was dark, as were the dressing rooms to her right, sized like prison cells. The short hall to her left leading directly below the stage was also dark.

"Hello, darkness," Kit crooned quietly, craning her neck to peer ahead. "Hello?" she tried again, this time louder.

No answer.

"Seriously, someone?" Kit was beginning to share Tom the cameraman's annoyance now. Two argumentative television stars, her best friend, and a cameraman didn't just vanish within minutes. The basement wasn't *that* huge.

But it was Barlowe Theater.

"*Tom?*" Kit hissed, daring a few steps into the dank blackness. "Madison?"

Again, no one answered. The only light was a flickering bulb that had to be a wattage short of worth having at all.

It buzzed too. Of course it did. If this stunt was for show dramatics . . .

"Madison!" Kit shouted. In the ten years since they'd graduated high school, she had followed this woman around. She was owed some loyalty in return. "If this is for ratings, it's unkind of you!" Kit yelled. Her words echoed back at her.

"Madis—"

Light slammed into her face, blinding Kit. She raised her hands as the flashlight's beam collided with her eyes.

"They're gone!" It was Tom.

Kit could see the whites of his eyes just beyond the flashlight he swung around wildly.

"What do you mean?" Kit tried to take captive Tom's arm as he flooded the hallway with the light, then a dressing room, then the ceiling. His camera wasn't on his shoulder.

He wasn't filming.

Kit's throat tightened. Okay, that wasn't a good sign. "Where's Madison?"

Tom swung the light back in Kit's face. "Where's Evan? Where's Heather? Where's my *team*?" His voice shook with undisguised concern, turning fast into panic. "How big is this place?"

"Not *that* big." Kit pushed past him. Concerned now. This had gone too far. Madison and her harebrained schemes to keep her own grandfather from ruining the historic downtown. Make it famous, she said. Put it on TV, she said. Make viewers defend Kipper's Grove, she said. "Madison!" Kit shouted, anxiousness seeping into her voice. "Stop this! It's not funny!"

Tom's light bounced on the floor in front of them as Kit spun around and marched back toward him. She shoved past his husky chest and down the short passage to the door leading under the stage. Her fingers curled around the doorknob, its old mechanics making it wobbly beneath her grip.

Kit jerked it open.

She fell back with a shriek, colliding with Tom, who had come way too close behind her.

Heather, the medium from the show, stood stock-still facing them. Her eyes were wide and unfocused, her skin white in the flashlight's glow.

"She's gone." Heather's monotone voice filtered through the passage.

Kit words were stolen from her as her stomach dropped.

"Who's gone?" Tom demanded.

"Madison." Evan Fischer, the cohost, the skeptic, and the all-around grumpy hero of the show strode past his partner. Heather's expression didn't waver as her eyes remained fixated on . . . whatever she was staring at in the spirit world beyond. "Madison's gone."

Evan left less than a few inches between his face and Kit's as he bent his six-foot frame down to meet her five-foot-four one. "Where is she?"

"I don't kn—"

"Where. Is. She?" He cut off Kit's answer as unsatisfactory.

Her breaths came shorter, faster. She could feel Tom behind her. She was sandwiched between him and Evan, with Heather staring into the great abyss.

"I told you. I don't know." Kit heard the quaver in her voice. She shoved her trembling hands into her pockets.

"She's gone." Evan slapped the wall, glaring at Tom, who was speechless. "Is this a scam? A stunt?"

Kit couldn't answer. Of course, the show would think it was a ploy by Madison. A publicity ploy. But it went deeper than that. Far deeper. Kit sagged against the wall, the air not reaching her lungs as it should.

She prayed then. Prayed that Madison really was messing with them. That she had simply gone too far ahead beneath the stage and left them behind.

But the theater was hungry, and everyone in Kipper's Grove knew it was only a matter of time before this hunger added to the stories of death and spirits. That's how the theater was, after all. Drama. Suspense. And the unearthly way that such things drifted through its rafters.

2

Greta

"Please, I am fine." Greta made the pretense of dusting off her dress—no, Eleanor's dress—if only to avoid Eleanor and her brother Oscar's concerned expressions. She still felt woozy, and she also felt foolish. Foolish for drawing attention when the events of tonight were nothing at all about her.

"Greta, darling, I—" Eleanor bit off her words as Greta lifted her eyes and beseeched her to be silent. Eleanor didn't understand, but she pressed her lips together and exchanged looks with Oscar that Greta couldn't interpret.

No. Eleanor and Oscar wouldn't understand. Greta looked about her. The audience was dissipating from the theater in a respectful, solemn manner, even though the authorities were standing guard at the doors with grim faces, there to manage any potential chaos.

With the evening cut short, wealthy guests from out of town were being escorted to the train station where they could catch a train for the two-hour trip back to their homes in the capital city of Madison. They were the ones who should be here, after

17

all, basking in the opulent architecture Mr. Barlowe and his wife had financed in Kipper's Grove. The Barlowes had been faithful to the small town, imagining the place to be as important as the surrounding, much larger cities.

It didn't matter. The Barlowes. The wealthy out-of-towners. The social elite of Kipper's Grove, which included the banker and his wife, investors in the railroad, and Eleanor's family who were simply from old money. Money going back to Boston that had made its way through Eleanor's father all the way to Wisconsin. Politics. Investments. No one knew exactly how Mr. Boyd made his money, but they all knew he had money. Lots of it. Enough that he hobnobbed with Mr. Barlowe himself, who not only had gifted Kipper's Grove with their own theater that mimicked French architecture but also spent most of his money on Chicago's edifices, which would one day, in Eleanor's parroted words from her father, "touch the clouds."

Greta simply did not belong. Eleanor was her dearest friend, generous to a fault. Even Oscar, who Greta knew less but admired equally, was a gentleman when many in his station wouldn't bestow such kindness on her. Yet their world was not *her* world. What she lived was only in their nightmares, whereas what they lived was in Greta's dreams. So tonight she should not have bore witness to what she'd seen. The traumatic event had touched both worlds and would mark all attendees. For Greta, it merely emphasized what was already deeply buried within her. That feeling. That awful, gut-twisting foreboding as she stared up at the marquee and its golden frame, and as she stood in the glow of the electric lamps that spilled from the doorway of the theater and lit the walk.

"Greta?"

Eleanor's light touch on Greta's bare arm between her glove and the sleeve, its rose-colored tassels tickling her skin, competed for her attention.

"Greta, are you all right?"

"I can't be all right. Not here." Greta felt faint again, black shutters crowding the edges of her vision.

"Go fetch our driver," she heard Eleanor instruct Oscar.

She focused on Oscar's retreating form, weaving his way through the throng, his arm outstretched in a wave at a carriage not far down the block. His evening wear was trim, stylish, his hat perched on his neatly combed dark hair. He wore round-rimmed glasses. He was lean, not strong, yet he was brilliant. Perhaps that made up for his not being particularly handsome. At least she didn't think he was.

"Greta."

Once again, Eleanor's voice broke into Greta's cloudy thoughts. It helped to focus on Oscar. On anything other than this place.

"Come with me." Eleanor's gentle prodding steered Greta from the main entrance down the sidewalk, where she tucked Greta under the lamplight of an iron post. "I never should have brought you here. It wasn't sensitive of me."

"It's not your fault," Greta breathed. "How were you to know what would happen?" She needed to get herself under control. She couldn't allow her angst, her horror, her *grief* to spread to Eleanor, as if ungratefulness were the only payment Greta could offer the Boyds for their generosity. She was Eleanor's childhood playmate, only because Greta's mother had been a maid in the Boyd mansion that abutted the Barlowes' yard. Their homes had been dubbed the *Royal B Crest* by the people of Kipper's Grove. The two families overlooked the valley below, the windows of their storied mansions rising like beacons of economic hope for the small town.

Greta had grown up in their shadow, while Eleanor had grown up in their light. But they had grown up together, and Eleanor was of the firm belief that nothing in adulthood should change them. And Eleanor dreamed, while Greta was a realist. She had to be. Her parents had died two years ago and left Greta and her older brother, Gerard, to care for their four younger brothers. But now it was just Greta. Alone. Ever since this horrid theater had stolen Gerard from her too. He'd fallen from the scaffolding, they'd told her. He'd been helping set the crown molding during the theater's construction, finished a mere six months ago. He was dead—the theater had taken him from her. In fact, it had taken several men during the fast and intense construction. But Gerard was her brother. Her constant.

"I never should have brought you here," Eleanor said. "After your brother, I should have known better."

"Don't fault yourself," Greta replied, trying to reassure her friend. No one could have imagined a mother would drop her baby from a box seat. Or that the theater floor would swallow the baby as if hungry to take further life. Where was Mr. Barlowe? He must shut the place down!

An irrational insistence built within Greta. Yes, the theater should be closed for the safety of the community! Only it wouldn't be. It couldn't be. It had costs *thousands* to construct. All in plain view of the acreage on the outskirts of Kipper's Grove that Barlowe hoped to detract attention from. The poorhouse, more politely referred to as Grove House, the place where they sent the riffraff of the area. The patients with minds that had gone awry, or widows with no money to support their children, bankrupt farmers, and even old folks dying of ailments no doctor could cure.

Grove House was where Greta was scrambling to avoid being sent. Her and her remaining four younger brothers. But Evelyn didn't know this. She couldn't. Greta would never tell her. She would play the part of Eleanor's childhood playmate, dress in Eleanor's clothes, and be appreciative of her friend's charity. She would do all that for Eleanor because Greta knew that in Eleanor's way, she wanted to bless Greta, even pamper her. It was heartwarming as well, if not a little terrible.

The carriage pulled to a stop in front of the lamppost. The

team of chestnut horses clomped their hooves against the brick street. One of them snorted. Oscar Boyd hopped from the innards of the carriage and beckoned them forward. Eleanor led the way, taking her brother's hand, gathering the sleek, lacy folds of her evening gown and climbing inside.

Greta hesitated.

Oscar extended his hand to her, as if that would convince her to accept his courteous gesture. Like the lady she wasn't.

Greta shook her head and backed away a step. She noted the frown on Oscar's angular face.

"Miss Mercy?"

"Thank you, Mr. Boyd, but I . . . I think I would prefer to walk home."

His brow furrowed. "I could hardly allow that, Miss Mercy."

She ignored his concern. "No, I am sorry. Sorry to have inconvenienced you with my histrionics." Greta tugged at her elbow-length gloves, pulling her fingers from them. "These are Eleanor's. Tell her I shall return the dress as well just as soon as I'm able."

"Greta!" Eleanor leaned from inside the carriage, her beautiful features highlighted by the streetlamp. "You mustn't walk home!"

Greta shoved the gloves into Oscar's hand, ignoring his bewildered expression. "I-I'm so sorry, Eleanor. Mr. Boyd." Whirling, Greta surged ahead down the sidewalk, ignoring Eleanor's call. Tears could not be held back any longer. Tonight had been a night of death. She was far too much of a companion to death of late, and more than ever it reminded Greta that her brothers relied on her now. *Her.* Attending fancy shows and masquerading as someone she wasn't helped them not even a little. Worse, being reminded of the boys' vulnerability spurred Greta into a run.

She hoisted the silken skirts of Eleanor's dress, hurrying down the sidewalk toward home. Toward the south side of town where the pretty homes slowly melted into ill-kempt streets, small houses that tilted on their foundations, boxlike and worthless.

The only thing of value in this part of Kipper's Grove were her brothers, who were everything to Greta. The death tonight—the death of an innocent—stabbed Greta with the fierce reality of her circumstances. She must keep her brothers alive and free from the poorhouse. There was no time for play, or death would continue to harass them. With illness, or hunger, or with one of the boys having to take on a job that included danger merely to help feed them.

Tonight, the Barlowe Theater had taught her another horrible lesson. The innocent would always suffer at the hands of those who paraded in pomp and ignored the lesser ones suffering in their shadow.

She would not be that to her brothers. Despite Eleanor's kindness, no more would she flirt with the Boyds' wealth.

Greta ignored the hair that slipped from her chignon down the side of her face.

She couldn't. The loss of Gerard and her parents had already been a price she'd not wanted to pay for nothing in return. That wasn't entirely true. She had received in return, only it was sorrow, poverty, and the death of her own hopes for a future. She would not risk her brothers' futures. The harsh truth was that sometimes God chose to bless others, and other times He allowed the wages of sin to run rampant and uncontrolled. She was left to wade through the chaos alone. For her brothers.

Leo met her at the door, his eyes eager, his face plastered with dirt and filth from not having bathed or washed in a few days.

Greta pushed past her fourteen-year-old brother. "Leo, you need to wash your face and your hands."

His eyebrows drew together in a fascinated and unbelieving expression. "Did I hear right? Someone tossed a baby over the box at the theater?"

"*Tossed* is hardly an appropriate word, Leo. Are the boys in bed?" Greta skirted the question, feeling conspicuous in Eleanor's dress next to her brother's ratty clothes. She glanced back at the door as Leo closed it. The front porch had long since unattached itself and tipped to the side, ripping from the main roof. It had left a hole above the doorframe that Leo had attempted to seal with newspaper stuffed into the gap and a piece of tin he'd pilfered from somewhere. But Greta could still feel the autumn chill seeping into the room. The small stove in the corner was cold, its rusted pipe not snapping as its metal adjusted to the hotter temperature. "You let the fire go out?"

Greta shifted her attention to the dark room beyond. A mattress lay on the floor, where she saw the sleeping forms of her other brothers.

Leo hurried to a pail next to the stove. It had kindling in it, but there was no coal or additional firewood. "I figured we'd be okay tonight without a fire."

"Oh." Greta nodded. He was right. Conserve. Conserve and stop being a ninny. "Keep your back turned," she instructed. Leo did as he was asked and stood facing the wall. Greta made fast work of struggling out of Eleanor's dress. Then the corset, which was no small feat. She stood in her undergarments and reached for her gray cotton apron dress that hung from a peg on the wall.

"You almost done?" Leo was impatient for his sister to finish dressing.

"Yes." Greta hurried to button the dress.

"So?" Leo pressed.

"So what?" Greta struggled with a broken button that didn't want to cooperate.

"Did a baby get killed tonight?"

"Leo!" Greta reared her head up.

Leo shrugged. "What? That's the word on the street."

News traveled quickly in Kipper's Grove, but on the south side it became oh so much crasser. Here, the ugliness of life was simply . . . life. They would all die. Whether as an infant or as an elderly person, it would happen. There was no mincing words.

"Yes." She nodded and returned to buttoning her dress, no longer caring that Leo could see her shift underneath.

"Gosh." Leo curled his lip in a wince.

"And I don't want to talk about it any further." She was firm.

Leo searched her face. "Yeah. Okay. I get it." And he did. Greta knew he was remembering that day—the day one of the construction workers from the theater had arrived at the sagging front door and told them the awful news.

"So, what's—?" Leo's question was cut short by a loud, urgent knock on the door.

Greta felt a gust of chilling emotion, and she froze. Leo shot her a questioning glance, then headed for the door. A policeman stood on the other side, his mustache thick, his dark eyes somber.

"Is this the Mercy residence?" His voice was deep and sounded like gravel.

Greta met his eyes and was comforted only briefly by the gentleness she saw there.

"Yeah," Leo answered.

"I'm Officer Hargrove. John Hargrove." The offering of his first name was merely a peace offering. Greta sensed it, grappling for a hold on the back of a rickety ladder chair. She recounted the boys she'd seen in bed in the next room. Cecil, Alvin, Virgil . . . there were three forms. With Leo here, all were accounted for. She had no other family to lose.

"Miss Mercy, we were informed you witnessed tonight's events at the theater. Is that true?"

Oh. Of course. She felt ashamed she was so relieved. That

a mother had lost her infant was a tragedy beyond words, and yet now that she was home with the boys, Greta was beginning to find her foundation once more. "Yes. I did, Officer."

Hargrove scanned the room. She knew what he saw and the questions that would come to mind. How could someone like her afford to attend a premiere event? Who had she attended with?

"Is there a problem?" Leo stepped in front of Greta. His lanky body was taller than her by an inch, but his voice still cracked with the onset of manhood.

The officer redirected his gaze to Leo. Man to man. Greta appreciated that. "No, son. I just have some questions for your sister."

"It were an accident, wasn't it?" Leo pressed.

"Questions are standard," Officer Hargrove responded.

"Ask the rich folk next to her then. My sister didn't do anything."

"Leo." Greta laid a hand on Leo's shoulder.

"I'm not implying your sister is in trouble," Officer Hargrove responded. "There's just been some conflicting reports, so we need to hear as many accounts of what happened as we can. Miss Boyd and her brother gave a statement tonight and indicated you were with them, and you were quite upset at the scene?"

The officer's brown eyes met Greta's. He had long lashes with a dark shadow around his jaw. There was no question he was strong, his shoulders square, his neck and chest hinting at the muscles beneath his uniform.

"She was upset 'cause my brother died there a few months ago." Leo's words had a bite to them. "Now this. Whaddya expect Greta to be like? All la-di-da?"

"Leo!" Greta squeezed her brother's shoulder sharply. He dodged her grip and glowered at her. She turned to Officer Hargrove. "Yes. I was there tonight when—" she squelched a sob—"when the babe fell."

Officer Hargrove had an inscrutable look on his face. "The babe. Mm-hmm. And did you witness the child falling?"

Greta wanted to close her eyes against the scene that threatened to replay itself over and over again. Instead, she mustered her courage, ignoring the way Leo had ducked from her grip and was glaring next to her.

"Yes. The mother stood up and then just . . . well, it appeared as though she . . . she . . ."

"She what?" Office Hargrove encouraged.

"Well, it looked almost as if the woman *flung* the baby. Flung it over the balcony." This time, the sob catching in Greta's throat was audible. She pressed her fingers to her lips.

"And you saw the baby fall?"

The question was merely reworded from before. Greta nodded.

"Okay." Hargrove glanced at Leo, then shifted his weight to his other leg. "Then what happened?"

Greta eyed him quizzically. "Well, the doctor—he was sitting in our row—was summoned by the stage lights. And there was panic. Everyone was crying and scrambling."

"And what did you do?"

Greta frowned. She could remember, but she didn't understand why her personal reaction to the baby's plummet over the balcony had any influence on the situation. She answered anyway. "I-I cried out. Eleanor was horrified as well. You can ask her."

"We did" was the officer's response.

"And then I felt faint. Mr. Boyd, Eleanor's brother, tried to catch me. He helped me and Eleanor make our way out of the auditorium onto the street."

"Did you see the baby after it fell?"

Greta glanced at Leo, whose countenance was darkening by the moment, and she couldn't understand why. The officer meant no harm or insult. "No. I-I mean there were too many people. They were gathering where the child had fallen. There was a woman, who was hysterical. I thought I saw someone pull her away. After that, I saw nothing more. We merely focused on exiting the theater."

"Why the questions?" Leo interrupted.

Officer Hargrove caught Greta's eye, and he looked almost apologetic. He rolled his lips together in resignation, and his broad chest rose in a subtle sigh. "The problem is, Miss Mercy, that there wasn't a babe. No one fell from the balcony. In fact, no one was *in* those seats tonight."

Greta's breath caught in her chest, and she stared at the officer. Leo snorted. Officer Hargrove didn't change his expression. Leo stopped his laugh of derision and gave Greta a sideways glance. Everything in her quailed at the attention. She wrapped her arms around herself, shaking her head. "No. No, that's not possible. I *saw* it. I saw it happen!"

Officer Hargrove held up a calming hand. "This is why I'm here. Folks in attendance said you stood up in the middle of the program and screamed. The chaos was in fact caused by your insistence that a baby had been thrown from the balcony."

"Eleanor saw it too!" Greta almost shouted in eagerness to defend herself, to defend what she'd seen.

Hargrove's intake of breath was riddled with hesitation. "Miss Boyd and Mr. Boyd both indicated they didn't see it but only responded to your claims. As did the doctor in attendance and the other attendees."

"They *summoned* the doctor! On the letter board!"

"Standard protocol in an emergency, Miss Mercy."

"Are you sayin' my sister is looney?" Leo interjected. His lanky frame stepped in front of Greta. "Huh? If she saw a baby fall, she wouldn't make that sorta thing up."

"I would never say that about your sister or anyone. I believe you that your sister has no ill intentions," Officer Hargrove tried to reassure them. "But there was no baby. No one was injured at the theater tonight. There were no witnesses except to your sister's outburst and the subsequent panic to save a would-be infant. Your sister's . . . Miss Mercy's outburst *caused* the panic. She was believed, and people rushed to the aid of the child, but there was no child. There was no woman in the box seat."

Greta's legs wobbled, weakness flooding through them. Officer Hargrove noticed, and he leaped forward, yanking out a chair from the table and urging her onto it.

He was closer to her now, and she could smell the warm scents of citrus and cinnamon on his skin. "Miss Mercy?" His voice was soothing. Greta lifted her eyes and met the officer's. He held her gaze for a moment and then continued, "We're not sure what you saw tonight, but the Barlowe family is considering pressing charges for the disruption of the performance."

"Pressing charges!" Leo shouted.

Greta felt the cold, clammy wave of faintness wash over her.

"Disturbing the peace," Officer Hargrove supplied, his watchful eyes not leaving Greta's face.

"I didn't mean it," Greta whispered. She hadn't meant to be disruptive. Eleanor had said nothing to shush her—or had she? No, she'd inquired about the baby as well. And Oscar had gone along with her. There'd been no reprimand.

She leveled her words on the officer, not waiting to interpret the expression of pity or tolerance or whatever it was on his handsome face.

"I saw a baby fall, Office Hargrove. I did not make it up."

Officer Hargrove gave a deep sigh, and his response stilled Greta to her core. "Then where is it? Where's this baby that no one has claimed, no one can find, and no one saw? Where, Miss Mercy?"

3

Kit

"Is this some kind of *joke*?" Al Farrington charged into the office of the Barlowe Theater. All the lights were on. LED lights, which were the kind that made Kit's eyes hurt.

She huddled on a chair in the corner next to Tom the cameraman, who might become her new best friend after tonight since he had gotten past his annoyance and offered her comradeship—and a stick of cinnamon gum. She chewed it, allowing the spicy tingle to awaken her senses. Chewing was something to do while they waited.

Cops searched the theater. Lights were on in every room of the place. A disgruntled Evan Fischer stood at the far end of the room, his sports jacket shoved back, his hands on his hips. He spoke in a firm, animated tone to a detective. She couldn't hear what he was saying.

Heather Grant, the medium, sat calmly in a chair not far away from them. She was in deep conversation with the show's manager, who looked like he'd been jerked out of his hotel room bed not long after finishing a bottle of gin. His eyes were

29

red-rimmed. He must not have expected to be at the filming tonight.

Al Farrington's blustery presence announced more trouble. Kit chewed on her gum more urgently now. Al was Madison's grandfather. He thought he owned Kipper's Grove—well, he practically did—and the fact that Madison had been here at all tonight had to have his undies in a bunch.

Kit bit back a smile at the thought. Probably silk boxers. That had to be the type of underwear Mr. Al Farrington wore. He was in his seventies but looked—and acted—like a soap star. Did anyone watch soaps anymore? Kit directed her attention to the older man's face. By sheer genetics he was definitely Madison's grandfather. They looked a lot alike. They were just very different as to convictions and beliefs. Al would have razed the entire block of historical buildings in exchange for his modern apartment complexes that really could bring in far more than a struggling theater no one really used much anymore. But Madison was anti-modern influence, anti-progress, and mostly anti-her grandfather. Kit knew it went deeper than just business and history—it was family history. Dysfunction and aggression mixed with grudges for nameless past wrongs that now had become the fabric of the Farrington family.

"Kit!" On spotting her, Mr. Farrington bellowed.

Kit shrank into her chair. Fabulous. As if she had any control over what Madison did or where she went. The fact that Madison was still missing was eating away at Kit's insides, and she'd be darned if she let Al Farrington bully her into anything.

"Kit!" he rumbled again.

"Yes, Mr. Farrington?" Kit jumped to her feet as if he were a four-star general and she a recruit.

"Where is my granddaughter? Tell us, and stop this nonsense before it gets out of hand." His blue eyes were sharp like Madison's, intelligent and commanding, his white hair combed back from his forehead, with expensive-looking glasses perched on a straight nose. He wore tailored pants and a pressed Oxford shirt with the sleeves rolled up to his forearms. Kit could only imagine the hearts of the widowed older ladies—and divorced older ladies—he'd broken in his wake.

Al snapped his fingers in Kit's face. "Stop your daydreaming, Kit, and answer me. What is going on?"

"Sir." An officer approached them. "Are you Mr. Farrington?"

"Of course I am." Al didn't remove his skewering glare from Kit's face. "And I'm sure if you question this young lady, we will have everything cleared up shortly."

Young lady. As if she wasn't on the short stick and downward slide to thirty. Al had a way of making her feel as if she were eleven years old and had just ridden her bike through the petunias in the front garden.

"Al, I don't know . . ." she started. She'd been on a first-name basis with him since she'd met Madison in grade school. Madison called her grandfather "Al," so Kit merely followed suit. As she did with everything Madison did.

"Don't give me that nonsense!" Al waved her off.

All eyes were turning on them. Kit glanced down at Tom, who lifted his eyebrows in an affected expression that implied he wouldn't be getting involved more than he already was.

"This was Madison's harebrained scheme, wasn't it? Bring in publicity? Shut me down. The little—"

"Mr. Harrington." Detective Seamans stepped in and rescued Kit. She plopped back down onto her chair. Detective Seamans was the same age as Kit's own father—late fifties—and a deacon in her church. She took comfort he was here, even though he did nothing to acknowledge their personal connection. "Your granddaughter is missing. We have officers searching the theater as we speak."

"I can see that," Al growled. "It's *these* folks"—he swept his arm toward Evan Fischer and Heather Grant—"*ghost* hunters? Madison brought in *ghost* hunters?"

"It's her right to," Detective Seamans concluded firmly. "She's head of the Friends of Barlowe Theater Guild. If they want to have the theater featured, they can."

"She's trying to sabotage me—typical of Madison."

Detective Seamans's jaw twitched, and Kit could tell he was fast losing patience with Farrington. "That's between you and your granddaughter, Mr. Farrington. But right now, her safety is our primary concern."

"Precisely." Al spun and glared down at her. "Where's my granddaughter?"

"I don't know." The floor could open and swallow her at any moment now.

"What do you mean, you don't know?" For the first time, a glimmer of concern reflected in Al's eyes.

"Just that." Kit garnered courage. "I don't know where she is."

The sound of footsteps drew their attention. Evan Fischer strode toward them. He barely looked at Kit. She was all right with that. He was intimidating, not just because he looked peeved but also because he was "hot." Madison's observation, Kit was quick to remind herself. Madison had taken one look at the real-life Evan Fischer early this evening and elbowed Kit with a "Holy *wow*, he's mine!" Of course he was. Kit was no competition for Madison.

Now Evan entered the fray. He was none too happy either. "Miss Farrington was leading our party through that maze of hallways below the theater. She turned a corner and vanished. I believe it was in what she called the 'boiler room'?"

"A maze of hallways?" Kit inserted, confused. There were only three hallways.

"Fine." Evan waved her off. "A labyrinth of hallways, then."

Nope. She didn't like Evan Fischer.

Detective Seamans held up his hands, palms facing out. "Okay, folks. We're going to need all your statements and your cooperation. Until Madison is found and all this gets straight-ened out, please keep your opinions on the situation to your-selves. We merely need the facts."

"The fact is," Al said, "Madison is probably in hiding on purpose. Or in cahoots with this show to make it appear she's vanished and thus raise the show's ratings."

Evan shook his head. "We don't coerce situations for the sake of viewers."

"No?" Al retorted. "I thought that's what everyone in Hol-lywood did?"

"We're not from Hollywood," Evan argued.

"Stop!" Detective Seamans glared at the men.

Kit and Tom exchanged glances.

"I want you all to have a seat," Detective Seamans ordered. "You too, Mr. Farrington. Let's get this sorted out."

She unlocked the door to her apartment, relishing in the lock's click. Her body hurt. Every joint and muscle. But it wasn't fair to Madison if she fell onto her couch in a deep sleep. Four a.m. and Madison was still missing. Nothing had been "sorted out," and the police had found no evidence of where Madison had vanished to. The whole ordeal was surreal.

Kit tossed her keys into a basket on a small table just inside the door. She dropped her bag to the ground and bent so she was eye level to the half wall that divided the front entrance and the kitchen. Her ant farm was perched there. The six-by-nine plexiglass container showed a maze of tunnels with busy farm ants hauling tiny pieces of lettuce she'd fed them yesterday to their food stores. One ant had a fellow dead one hoisted on its back and was depositing it in their graveyard at the far left.

Madison had always accused Kit of being a bit odd—her

fascination with the insect world and all. Kit admitted to having the regret of a misguided young adult who'd listened to the educators in her life, who'd told her to follow pursuits more fitting for her skill set. Communications. That was a noble degree, and far more marketable than an entomologist. At least to a smalltown high school counselor who couldn't see any future in entomology.

Kit distracted her frayed nerves as she watched her ants, then swept her gaze over a shadow box she'd created in her early twenties: butterflies of the Midwest. Mounted with care. Labeled. The little yellow-headed pins held them to the mounting board by their thoraxes.

She tapped the glass lightly with her fingertip, addressing her high school counselor who had long since moved away, "I could have been in forensic science. I could have pursued the study of larvae to help determine time of death on crime victims."

Kit paused. Madison was probably right. She was a bit odd.

A lump grew in her throat, caused by exhaustion and worry. She could see Madison's excitement from earlier yesterday as the time drew near to meet the staff of the show.

"Ghost hunters, Kit!" Madison had practically sang. *"With promotion from being on the show, Kipper's Grove will gain notoriety and the theater can be spared the unappreciative greed of Al Farrington."*

It had been a crusade perhaps, maybe even an overdramatic one, but that was Madison. Kit was the quirky, insect-loving sidekick, Madison the beautiful zealot whose sunshine and passion attracted everyone. Including the producers of an otherwise hard-to-book show.

Heaving a sigh riddled with worry, Kit padded across the tan carpeting into the kitchen and retrieved a glass of water.

"Where are you, Madi?" Her mutter into the silent apartment was met with more silence, the kind that reminded her of the theater. After all the doors had been closed, the lights had

34

gone out, and it stood in stillness. Enveloped in the history of its secrets. When no one was about, did the ghosts really come out to play? Many of the locals said they did. Several claimed to have seen them—or heard them—including Madison.

Shivering, Kit set her water glass on the counter and hurried to her room, where she stripped from her clothes that Madison had picked out for her to wear during filming. The yellow blouse over jeans was not normally something she would have chosen, but Madison insisted. Now, Kit tugged on a cotton T-shirt with a logo of a local coffee shop on the front. She rubbed her hand under her nose, sniffing. Tears were unwelcome, and so were the tempestuous emotions. A call to her mom would help. Mom grounded her in ways no one else did. Kit retrieved her phone from her bag that she'd dropped in the entryway. She and her mom were close. Her parents knew her inside and out, and even though she was nearing the end of her twenties, was unmarried and had never really dated, Mom had never acted like Kit was missing out on some magical equation of Christian female purpose. It was okay to be single. It was okay to love bugs—

A knock on the door startled Kit, and she yelped, ramming her elbow into the wall and dropping her phone. Scrambling to pick it up, she pressed her eye against the peephole in the door. An elongated version of Evan Fischer stared back at her. The skeptic from the show. The one who thought the whole thing was a crock, and Madison had pulled some disappearing act simply to boost the show's interest in her cause to bring publicity to the theater.

"Hello?" She opened the door because she could trust a television personality, right? On second thought, Kit propped her foot behind the door as a deterrent should Evan Fischer be a villain who had somehow harmed Madison. Her foot would definitely deter the six-foot-tall man with his muscled physique. Definitely.

His blue eyes smoldered, his ashy-blond hair long in front and short in back. Probably a two-hundred-dollar haircut designed to make him look scruffy but professionally chic all at the same time. His beard was more of a goatee, as his chiseled jawline was sketchy in the whisker department.

"How'd you know where I live?" she asked.

"We need to talk." Evan's hands were shoved in the pockets of his jeans. He'd shed his sports jacket and now wore a white T-shirt.

"We do?" Kit's voice squeaked in honor of his blatant good looks and the aversion to being the focus of his attention.

"Can I come in?" He motioned with his hand.

Kit stepped back. "I-I guess?"

Evan's eyebrow raised at her questioning acceptance of his appearance at her door, but he stepped inside anyway.

Closing the door behind him, Kit pointed awkwardly at the living room that was directly off the kitchen with a half wall dividing them. Evan took a few steps, glanced at her ant farm, paused, made an uninterpretable face, and continued in. He left a soft wake of bay rum and nutmeg behind him. Kit secretly inhaled, reveling in the scent. Gosh, he smelled good.

Evan sank onto a stuffed chair covered by a cream linen fabric. He picked up a wire statuette of a cricket, studied it, then set it back on the side table. With a little grunt of dismissal toward the cricket, he looked at Kit and said, "We need to talk about Madison."

Kit sat opposite him on her dark blue couch. She grabbed a yellow throw pillow and hugged it while leveling her eyes on him. "I'll do anything I can to find Madi."

Evan leaned forward, resting his elbows on his knees, spearing her with his icy blues. "What is she up to?"

"I don't like what you're implying." Kit gulped. She wasn't great at being direct, but then she also didn't appreciate people who asserted anything negative about those she was closest to.

For all sakes and purposes, Madison was family. Evan had no right to imply Madison was scheming.

An eyebrow raised above one eye. "I'm not implying anything. I'm just asking."

"You asked what she was up to . . ."

Evan scowled. "Listen, I'm not nice when I'm being played. What's the story?"

Kit bristled. "No one is playing *you.*" Madison didn't have a conniving bone in her body, unless it was to thwart her grandfather from ripping down historical landmarks. "Madi wouldn't do that."

"No?"

"No." Kit was firm. *And you can go now,* she added internally, though she hadn't quite mustered the confidence to utter it aloud.

Evan pursed his lips and studied her for a minute. "My producer wants us to stay on—to build Madison's disappearance into the show."

It took Kit a minute to register what he was saying. When it did, she flushed with irritation. "You're going to exploit the fact that she is missing?"

Evan didn't deny it. "They want Heather and me to do our own investigations until Madison is found. She vanished during our walk, and Heather believes her disappearance was influenced by the paranormal."

"A ghost abducted Madison?" Kit's own skepticism resonated in her question.

Evan nodded. "Yeah. That. My producer doesn't care if it was a phantom, or someone real, or if Madison simply ran away and is hiding. It's a show. Insert creepy music, unanswered questions, Heather's visions, my irritation, and you have an epic episode. It'll boost ratings for *Psychic and the Skeptic,* and they're all about ratings." He didn't sound enthused.

"And you're not?" Kit played nervously with the edge of the

pillow. It was hard not to look at him when Evan's eyes were so vivid and stabbing.

"I hold the title of skeptic for a reason. Unfortunately, when I signed on with the show, I was under the impression I would legitimately be debunking the paranormal. Instead, I get to be Heather's sidekick and do all the historical investigations. While I can come up with plenty of explanations, they seem to get debunked by Heather, not the other way around."

Kit didn't know what to say, so she offered him a polite wince of understanding, which he didn't seem to notice.

He rubbed his palms together. "Now, your friend has gone missing, and the show wants to use it to prove that the paranormal *can* reach from the beyond. Heather has implied on many of the shows that various forms can harm and even kill people."

"Kill people." It was her statement of disbelief that seemed to soften Evan's expression. Maybe he was so used to being challenged for his position as a realist and a logistician that he found himself always on the defense.

"Yeah. Get inside people's heads, influence them to do things like . . . well, it doesn't matter what." Evan dragged his fingers through his hair. "Anyway, please tell me it's all a prank, or a plot, or anything that will stop this ridiculous charade. I really don't want to spend time trying to investigate a woman's disappearance to prove the spirit world has that sort of power or to find out it was a giant waste of time because she had her own agenda."

Kit's throat tightened, making it hard for her to speak. "I wish . . . I wish it was just a prank," she croaked.

Evan's countenance darkened. "You really believe it's not?"

Kit shook her head. "No. Madi was genuinely hoping to bring exposure to the theater by being featured on your show. But she's not sneaky enough to create this type of panic. Not to mention, she'd be aware of the consequences, like the impact on law enforcement, on the town, on her family and *me*."

Evan didn't respond. He just studied her for a long moment. Kit shrank back against the couch, pulling the pillow against her chest. He didn't believe the police when they started the search for Madison last night. He obviously was still trying to find a reason to believe it, and that had landed him here. In her apartment. Smelling like a spicy autumn drink in a mug.

"You know, if you're not telling me the truth, I will figure it out."

Well, wasn't that nice of him? Kit narrowed her eyes as her cynical side took offense. "I'm not lying."

"Great." The sudden slap of his palms on his knees made Kit jerk in surprise. Evan launched to his feet. "Come on then."

"What?"

He extended his hand and waved his fingertips, beckoning her to stand as well. "You're going to help me figure out what happened."

"No, I'm not." She'd do anything to find Madison, but not with Evan. Not with cameras following them, documenting them, turning the fright of Madison's disappearance into entertainment. "I won't make a show out of this. I'll work with the police to find Madi. We'll find her without your show."

Evan dropped his hand. His voice lowered into a mesmerizing and patronizing tone. "Mm-hmm. Go ahead and try. As a former detective myself, you won't be invited into their investigation. You'll be questioned, maybe questioned again, and then, unless you make a suspect list, you'll be waiting along with everyone else. For hours. Days. Weeks. Until Madison becomes a Bankers Box in the vault of cold cases."

"Get out." Kit stood, dropping the pillow. Evan Fischer had gone too far.

His eyes flashed. "Get out? What are you going to do on

your own to find your friend? She vanished. What if you vanish too? Assuming you're on the up-and-up, this thing is dark and potentially dangerous. You're going to sniff out what happened by yourself?"

"Well, I won't do any sniffing with you!" Kit bit her tongue. That didn't sound as good as it had in her head.

A wry smile quirked Evan's mouth. "Suit yourself. But I think we could benefit from each other. I have investigative skills, and you know Madison. If we worked together, maybe we could find her before this gets blown into a full-on paranormal investigation or a legit missing-persons case."

"It is a legit case."

"Not technically. She hasn't been missing for over twenty-four hours. The only reason anyone is investigating is because she practically disappeared in front of us. In a normal case, they'd wait to see if she showed up on her own. She's an adult. No law-enforcement agency is going to assume a crime until there's evidence of it."

Evan's straightforward and unemotional delivery of the facts was enough to make Kit want to physically shove him out of her apartment. "She disappeared. That's evidence enough."

Evan offered her a thin-lipped smile. "Sure."

Kit didn't know how to respond, and for a moment there was silence between them.

"Listen," Evan finally said, "I'm just saying, if we team up, we could hopefully put an end to this faster than if we each go it on our own."

Kit hesitated.

"You don't want anything to happen to Madison, do you?"

She met Evan's eyes. "It already has."

He gave a curt nod that caused a strand of hair to tilt over his forehead. "Then let's go find her."

4

Greta

Sleep had been fitful. She'd tossed and turned and been bumped into by her little brother, Virgil, whose naturally scrawny frame was even scrawnier due to a lack of nutrition. Now, Greta raised up on her elbow to look down at her brothers. One bed. Four of them. Leo slept on a cot by the door in the other room. Cecil and Alvin were too old to sleep with their sister and little brother, but it was either that or on the bare floor.

Cecil lay on the far side of the bed. His hair was messy, and there was dirt from yesterday's work still smudged across his cheek. He was twelve, with Alvin only a year behind. But there was an age in Cecil's eyes as his met hers. An age that shouldn't be in the eyes of a young lad.

"We got anythin' for breakfast?" he whispered over the two brothers between them.

Greta grimaced. "We can make pudding."

Cecil fell back on his pillow with a sigh. "I'm sick of corn-meal mush."

"It's what we have."

41

"Callin' it 'pudding' don't make it taste better."

Greta remembered their mother referring to it as "hasty pudding." Mama had grown up in England in the filthy London streets. Coming overseas hadn't treated her any better, and now she was cold in the grave.

Greta sat up and swung her legs over the edge of the bed. Her feet hit the cold floor. There was a chill in the air. Early October could be warm or cool in Wisconsin, but this year it was trending to be cool. Which meant they'd need heat, which meant they'd need coal. Or wood. Winter would shape up to be long. Maybe they *would* be better in the poorhouse . . .

"I'll go make breakfast." Greta cut off her thoughts as Virgil stirred. She glanced at Cecil, whose sullen look made her feel even more guilty than she already did. "I'll add some sugar."

He perked up, and for a moment, Greta felt better. Her brother's happiness was worth a precious tablespoon of sweet.

She changed swiftly behind a small screen in the room's corner. Once finished, she tiptoed into the main room and glanced toward Leo's cot. Empty. Questioning, Greta moved to the window and peered out. It wasn't typical for Leo to leave with no word. Expecting to see him on the rickety porch, Greta frowned when she noted its emptiness.

Drawing in a shuddering breath, she closed her eyes and pressed a hand to her stomach to calm her nerves. She wasn't losing her mind. However, adding anxiety on top of anxiety was going to send her to a certain early death. Like Mama. Now the Barlowe family was furious with her? And the police thought she was addled?

Greta yanked open the front door. "Leo!" she called, then quickly bit her lip. Her shout would wake the neighbors. She looked up and down the street.

"Where's Leo?" Cecil's groggy voice bounced off Greta's back.

"I don't know." Greta shut the flimsy door, pressing her palm to the rough, paint-chipped wood. She looked over her shoulder. "Pudding or Leo?" she asked.

Cecil blew out a sigh that aged him further than his boyish, almost-teenage looks. "I'll make the pudding." He accepted his fate with a grimace.

Greta reached out and cupped his face. His cheek was still soft beneath her hand, whiskers not yet coming in. They stared at each other for a moment. She'd always been closest to Cecil. He understood her. She understood him.

Nodding, Greta reached for her crocheted shawl and wrapped it around her shoulders to ward off the chill of the fall morning. A low fog had settled over the street. The other houses on the street weren't much different from hers. All in the shadow of the train yards, the lumber mill with its paltry wages, and at the farthest outskirts of Kipper's Grove, the poorhouse. Set on its acreage like an estate that was long neglected and now occupied by the lowest of humanity.

Foolishness and guilt spread ugly fingers of nausea through Greta as she hurried down the street, looking in between shacks and small clapboard houses for a glimpse of Leo. She'd been an imbecile to pretend she was something she wasn't. Cavorting with Eleanor Boyd and attending the theater in silks that would never be hers was as ridiculous as pretending Grove House wasn't in their immediate future.

Greta heard the rumble of a train about half a mile from their street. Leo spent too much time near the tracks with his friends. She wasn't even sure what the names of his little gang members were. They caused trouble, she knew that, and occasionally a slab of bacon or an apple pie would wind up on their table. Stolen. From the betters of Kipper's Grove. But how could she return it? Food spoiled, and she didn't know where it came from, so she served it, ignoring the satisfaction on Leo's face. He was providing. In his own way. Especially now that Gerard was dead. Greta couldn't lean on her older brother any longer. It was up to her. And to Leo. And now she envisioned Cecil making hasty pudding—he didn't deserve this burden.

"Leo!" Greta called softly. People were stirring as the morning made them aware of a new day. She waved to a curious neighbor, who was dumping dirty water into a barrel. Odds were, Leo had retreated to the train yards to cavort with his buddies. Part of her wanted to scold him for being so irresponsible, but how could she? Not after she'd irresponsibly left her brothers to attend the opera at Barlowe Theater.

"Ho there!"

The male voice caused Greta to stumble to a stop. She pulled her shawl tighter around her as she saw Mr. Zimmerman hurrying toward her. His clothes were well-worn but clean—Mrs. Zimmerman saw to that. Though his features appeared kind as he approached her, worry marred their creases.

"Have you seen Teddy?" Mr. Zimmerman asked.

She shook her head, matching his concern. "No. I'm looking for Leo also."

Mr. Zimmerman removed his hat and ran a hand over his balding head. "Boy snuck out last night. Hasn't come home. He does that sometimes, but he never misses breakfast."

Greta couldn't ignore the knot growing in her stomach. Leo wasn't that predictable, but still . . . "Have you asked the Christliebs?"

Mr. Zimmerman's countenance darkened. "With their boy being the ringleader? 'Course I did. Fred is missing too."

"I'm sure they're just out causing trouble." Greta hated to admit that, but the truth was no longer something to skirt around.

"Can't tie 'em down, I guess, but we raised Teddy to do better."

An unspoken understanding stretched between Greta and the man in front of her, who had once been friends with her father prior to his death. She wasn't sure what steps to take next, and she knew she was staring at Mr. Zimmerman with a helpless expression.

He blew out a hefty breath. "I'll check down at the station. Make sure they didn't do anything stupid there."

Vandalizing had been happening there lately, and Greta feared it was the work of Leo, Teddy, and Fred.

By midafternoon, Greta knew something was desperately wrong. Leo was a rabble-rouser, yes, but he wasn't completely reckless. He was protective of her, of the boys, and he knew that by nine in the morning, Greta was due to be downtown for her job at Kipper's Laundry and Dry Cleaning. It was hot and difficult work, paid little, made her hands red and raw, but it helped with the bills.

"Come work for *us*!" Eleanor had pled with Greta not long after Greta's mother had taken ill and shortly before she passed. And Greta would have. Only Eleanor's mother saw fit to fill the position with someone else. There had been no explanation for why, and there was no extended offer to Greta for any other positions. Eleanor's apologies meant little, as it wasn't her fault. Mrs. Boyd obviously had her own reasons, and Greta had faith that it was nothing personal, just the way things worked.

While she missed the Boyds and the carefree nature of childhood, necessity drove her to the steamy laundry room. At least it was honest work, cleaning the linens and towels and tablecloths for the various establishments throughout Kipper's Grove and beyond. She reminded herself of that, and the times she was able to see Eleanor, her friend never discouraged or demeaned her. That was what had endeared Greta to the Boyds. After all, they had taken care of her mother as a part of their household staff, allowed Greta to tag along and play with their own daughter. Humility was a rare quality with the wealthy, but the Boyds had displayed such a nature, and so Greta could not hold them at fault.

Leaving the younger lads with Cecil, and having heard nothing from Mr. Zimmerman, Greta hiked into the better part of town. Large maples tinted with brilliant orange leaves competed with oaks and their glorious yellow tones. Here, the houses of Kipper's Grove were pretty. The middle-class was the perfect position and way of life, Greta had concluded. Neither wealthy and pompous nor poverty-stricken, they lived tranquil lives with just enough to make ends meet, give a little to charities, and buy oranges for their children's Christmas stockings.

A confetti of leaves floated through the air and around Greta's feet as she strode down the sidewalk. Today was not the time to covertly peer into windows as she passed by the beautiful family homes. The fog that still hung in the air, the chill that blew through Greta's shawl, and the foreboding sense that something was not right all served to dampen the cheery autumn day.

"Miss Mercy!" A shout from across the street snagged her attention.

Gracious. It was Officer John Hargrove. She was keenly aware of the disarray of her hair, the frayed cuffs of her blouse, and the homemade shawl. Still, it was apparent the officer's attention was not on her appearance. As he jogged across the street, holding up a hand to a passing motorcar, there was a grimness etched into the crevices of his face.

"Miss Mercy," he repeated, coming to a stop in front of her. His police uniform was crisp, dark blue, the buttons polished. His eyes were as warm as they had been the previous night. But they were also shadowed.

"Officer Hargrove," Greta acknowledged.

He swiped his cap from his head in a polite gesture toward her womanhood. "John," Officer Hargrove stated. "Please, call me John."

Greta waited. That was unusual, even for well-acquainted folk, to call a police officer by his first name. Regardless, she dipped her head, though not offering him the same familiarity in return.

John turned his cap in his hands. "I was on my way to your home. Just now. I'm afraid we . . . well, we have a situation."

And there it was. The words she'd expected to hear after the churning in her soul. Greta's expectation of them had been growing. *Situations* were never a good thing. The first one had been followed by news of her father's death five years prior. Pneumonia. The second had been when their mother passed only two years prior after cancer had eaten away at her liver. The third situation involved Gerard. A fall from scaffolding during the construction of Mr. Barlowe's beloved theater as he made his mark in Kipper's Grove for generations to come.

"What is it?" Greta pictured Cecil at home, managing the younger two brothers. God help her if she had to return home with another tragic announcement. She tried to hide the shaking of her hands and the tension in her face, but it was futile.

John reached out and gave her a reassuring touch of his fingertips on her upper arm. "No one has been hurt that we know of. I . . ." He looked down at the cap in his hands, then back at her. "I have two situations. The first is concerning last night's debacle. The Barlowes are pressing charges against you."

"They're what?" Greta reared back.

"And . . ." John glanced over her shoulder and down the walk behind her. Apparently assured they were alone, he continued, "And last night, the theater was broken into."

Greta stared at John wordlessly. The police officer waited for her reaction, but she couldn't provide him with one. She understood what he was implying. At last, she found her voice again. "Leo?"

He nodded. "That is the general belief, yes. He and two

others were seen early this morning in the alleyway behind the theater."

"Teddy and Fred." Greta stated their names as facts, not a question.

"They broke in through the back door by the loading dock, which leads to the rear of the stage." Officer Hargrove—John—studied her for a moment, then added, "But . . . they never exited the theater."

"What do you mean?" Greta wrapped her arms around herself in a protective embrace. Against the cool wind that swept along the sidewalk, against the news of the Barlowes' intent to hold her responsible for their thwarted opera last evening, and against the idea that Leo had committed a crime. "How could anyone possibly know they never left the theater?"

"The man who witnessed the boys breaking in does repairs for the firm who manages the theater. He barred the door your brother and his friends broke into and locked the boys inside the theater. Barred the front entrance too. And then he went to fetch us, the police."

"Is Leo in jail?" Greta squelched the panic rising up within her. She'd have no money to pay for him to be released on bail. No money to pay restitution for the damages. She held her eyes shut for a long moment, pushing back unwanted, burning tears.

"No."

The blunt response made Greta open her eyes. "No?" she echoed.

John replaced his cap on his head. "They're missing. All three boys. We can't find them."

"What do you mean, you can't find them?" Greta tried to comprehend what she was being told. "If they couldn't get out, then they have to be inside."

"We checked everywhere. Under the stage, in the dressing rooms, maintenance closet, the ticket booth, even the attic space where they lower the auditorium chandelier to be cleaned."

"They must have escaped through a window." Yet Greta's simple explanation didn't help to relieve her.

John shook his head. "None of the windows were broken, nor were any of the locks tampered with. "

"Well, they couldn't have just vanished," she argued, adjusting her shawl. "If the boys were locked inside the theater, then they're still there."

John nodded. "Stands to reason. And yet . . ."

"And yet what?"

"And yet they're not there. Miss Mercy, your brother Leo and his friends have disappeared. They've gone missing. Inside Barlowe Theater."

"Then find them—!" Her voice broke, and she took a deep breath to calm herself. "Please, Officer. It can't be that difficult."

"I realize that, but you know the tales." John looked across the street in the theater's direction.

"The tales?" Greta asked.

"Yes, the tales that the theater is cursed."

Greta felt her ire rising to the surface. "Every building where strange things have happened is considered cursed. It's no more cursed than my family is cursed. If anything or anyone should be held responsible, it is God himself. He's already allowed the theater to lay claim to one of my brothers. I will not allow it to do the same to Leo." She bit back her bitterness coupled with fear. God didn't deserve her anger, but someone did—something did. Didn't it?

John's chest rose with a heavy sigh. "We'll find them, Miss Mercy."

"Yes." Greta nodded emphatically. "You will." Then she added in a whisper, "You have to."

5

Kit

"Want one?" Tom extended a stick of gum in her direction.

Kit smiled at the camera operator, who produced gum like a vending machine. Cinnamon again. "Thanks." She took the gum and unwrapped it.

Evan eyed them both in the rearview mirror from the driver's seat of his rented SUV. "We'll swing by the hotel and pick up Heather." The sentence gritted through his tight jaw. Kit could tell it was the last thing he wanted to do. "Then we'll head over to the theater and begin our investigation."

"Cops won't let us in." The fact he had his face turned to look out the window muffled Tom's statement. "I tried to snag some footage this morning and got denied."

"It's not a crime scene," Evan retorted as he made a left turn.

"Yes, it is." Kit sat straighter in the back seat.

"No." Evan shook his head. "It's not. Madison is missing, not murdered. They'll release the place back to its owners as soon as they're finished with their search."

Kit's phone rang, and she tried not to glare at Evan's reflection in the mirror. He was rude. She didn't have to be the same way. Maybe she could re-home some of her ant farm into the man's pants. Yes. That would be far more satisfying. Or perhaps up the ante with fire ants—granted, they weren't native to Wisconsin. She considered her inventory of insect knowledge as she swiped at her phone to answer the call.

"Hello?" She ignored her own vengeful thoughts toward the skeptic.

"Kit, we need you down here ASAP."

"Corey?" The harried voice of her coworker at the local food pantry filled the car. Her day job was an interruption she could do without today. But it was a necessary part of life. She fumbled, trying to get her phone off speaker.

"Someone broke into the pantry last night."

A sickening lump formed inside her chest. The kind that felt like a five-hundred-pound horse had just joined the two-thousand-pound elephant that Madison's missing status had already settled there. "What did they take? Did they break into the safe?" She could picture it under her desk, its pitiful lock mechanism not much of a fortress against a determined thief.

"No." Corey's voice bounced off the interior of the car. Evan and Tom had the decency to stay quiet. "But there was only petty change in there anyway. No, they completely wrecked the place, Kit. All the eggs in the dairy freezer?"

She winced, having a feeling she already knew what had happened.

"Tossed them everywhere. There's legit egg yolk on the flippin' ceiling!"

"Oh no."

"And the produce freezers. Honey, they chucked grapes, peaches, pineapples, and cottage cheese all over the place."

"So they had a party with the donated food?" Kit sank into her seat. Her stress level was growing by the second. The food pantry fed over three hundred and fifty families every Wednesday evening. Grocery bags stuffed by volunteers were handed to those in need as they waited in line for them. People in the community relied on the pantry. Relied on *her*. It was what she'd used her communications degree for. She was the liaison for the pantry at Kipper's Grove.

"Oh, I'm not done," Corey said.

Kit squeezed her eyes closed against his words.

"They ripped all the bread bags open. You know, the *two hundred* paper grocery bags the volunteers filled on Friday? And to top it off, someone had the guts to spray-paint messages on the floor, Kit, in *orange and lime green*. I mean, not even a good color palette."

She ignored that last comment. "Did you call the cops?" Kit could feel Tom's eyes on her and had given up trying to get the call off speaker.

"Yeah. Then I heard about Madison. What the heck is going on?"

Kit swallowed hard. It felt like an attack. It *was* an attack. Madison missing? The food pantry? If anyone were to chart out the three most critical parts of Kit's life, there were two of them right there, with her parents rounding it out.

"I'm not sure," she answered Corey. "We're on our way to the theater to see if we can help in the search for Madi."

"Yeah, yeah, makes sense. But we've been torpedoed, Kit, and I need you here at the pantry. The police are going to have questions. We need to organize a cleanup. You'll have to contact our insurance. The landlord has to be contacted, and you *know* how thrilled he's going to be when he finds out his warehouse was trashed."

That overwhelming feeling of being cornered—no, trapped—was suffocating her fast. Kit summoned the ability to stuff her emotions into a compartment that was manageable. "Corey, can you please just handle it for now? I need to help find Madi. I know it's tough, but really, she's more important."

"Yeah. Sure." The stress in Corey's voice was obvious. The man was in his forties, and the food pantry was his life. He was a gem. She couldn't run the place without him, but she also knew she could rely on him in a pinch. This was more than a pinch.

"I'm sorry, Corey," Kit said. "I'll get over there as soon as I can. I promise."

His sigh was audible.

Kit caught Evan's raised eyebrow in the rearview mirror.

"Okay," Corey agreed, "but let the cops do their thing for Madison, all right? We're going to need you here. Over three hundred folks in Kipper's Grove will be expecting food tomorrow night. I don't know what we're gonna do. Madi wouldn't want the community to suffer on her behalf."

"You're going to just get it done," Evan inserted sternly from the front seat. "Figure it out, man."

Kit's eyes widened. She met Tom's look beside her. He shrugged.

"Pardon me?" Corey said, his offense palpable, directed at the strange voice that had just intruded into their speakerphone conversation.

Kit quickly interceded. "You're right, Corey. Madi wouldn't want things at the pantry to come to a halt. She loves its mission and the Kipper's Grove community. I'll come down as soon as I can. In the meantime, give the police whatever they need, but hold off calling the landlord. I'll do that later." She ended the call with an unconcealed sigh.

"You need to a have a team there so you don't have to do it all yourself." Evan's suggestion might have merit, but it hadn't been invited.

"You try to keep a regular, reliable team of volunteers," she retorted. It was another thing Madison tried to assist with— recruiting volunteers, being a cheerful face for the pantry. There wasn't much more influence than having a Farrington on one's side, and Madison made sure she was always at the important pantry events. Kit's patience was thinner than an icy pond with a milk cow trying to cross it. Pretty soon she was going to turn into Tsunami Kit, and then Evan Fischer would drown in her temper.

Don't do it, Kit. Don't lose your cool.

She could hear her dad's voice reminding her she'd always had a temper from the day they'd brought her home from the adoption agency when she was three weeks old. He'd said she'd screamed and stiffened even in the early days whenever she was pressed beyond her limits. Even now, she could see Mom's cautionary look that told Kit to breathe deep and let God be God.

Maybe God wanted to work through her to slap Evan Fischer silly? Mom didn't think of things like that, but Kit knew for a biblical fact that God didn't always tiptoe around people. He had a few wipe-out-the-enemy scenes in the Old Testament.

And with that thought, Kit blushed in spite of herself. Mom would be furious at her devil-may-care attitude toward another human soul. It was God's place to cast judgment, and it was her place to love.

Kit suppressed the mental conversation she could hear, as well as the vision of Mom's reprimanding look. Even as an adult, a woman could be quelled by her mother with just one glance.

"Annnnd here we are!" Tom's overly energetic announcement sliced the tension as the vehicle pulled into the hotel parking lot.

Kit looked out the window as Heather Grant approached the car. She offered an empathetic smile, her long chestnut hair pulled back into a braid. Kit responded in kind. At least Heather was friendly, even if their philosophies and beliefs were worlds apart.

The passenger door opened, and Heather slid into the front, bringing with her fresh, crisp autumn air and a whiff of cucumber-and-vanilla body lotion. She offered Tom a thin, worried smile, then leveled her gaze on Evan.

55

"It's not good, Evan," she stated.

"What's not good?" He didn't bother to look at his cohost as he pulled out of the parking lot.

"Madison's disappearance. One of them has attached themself to me. They came back to the hotel with me."

One of who? Kit mouthed at Tom, who shook his head.

Evan growled in his throat and said nothing more.

Heather looked at the road ahead of them but didn't hold back her thoughts. "You know what that means, Evan. The energy at the theater is negative. Terrible. I'm going to have to be super careful or I may get sick again."

Evan flicked his turn signal. Kit noticed a muscle in his jaw clenching and unclenching. "Okay" was all he said.

Kit shot Tom another questioning look.

Tom leaned over and whispered, "You don't wanna know."

But she did. She really, truly did. Kit lifted her eyes and met Evan's in the mirror one more time. This time his expression said he was disturbed . . . even a little afraid.

The theater was quiet. Too quiet. The minute Evan pulled the rental car into the diagonal parking lot space in front of the theater, Kit noted the marquee that extended over the main entrance. A booking was listed on it. A reshowing of *Breakfast at Tiffany's* last Thursday night. One of the latest efforts to bring awareness to the theater—and value. Show old movies. Madison said there had been about twenty in attendance. She hadn't expounded on the pessimistic side of the equation in that the elliptical-shaped auditorium sat six hundred.

Heather stood beneath the canopy, fixed in a dead stare. Tom had already exited the car and held his professional-grade video camera, filming her. Footage. This was all about footage.

Irritation flooded Kit as she wrestled her body from the back seat of the car. Some Friday night special of *Psychic and the Skeptic* would air in the near future, and Madison would be its main focus.

Kit slammed the door with intent and would have marched toward Heather and Tom if a strong hand hadn't planted itself against the body of the car in front of her, the man's arm effectively halting her.

She looked up and met Evan's blue eyes.

"Don't." His instruction was clear, his face emotionless.

"You're really going to make a show about Madison's disappearance?" Curse the quaver in her voice. Kit bit her lip and turned to the sky for help. Puffy white clouds. Baby-blue atmosphere. Somewhere beyond was God. She needed strength that wasn't hers to possess or she was going to clock Evan Fischer and make the Old Testament heroes proud and her mother ashamed. Fischer was her Philistine. Lowering her gaze back on Evan, she hoped that ferocity showed in her face. She might be average, but she was unpredictable whenever someone messed with her people. And Madison was her people.

"Ah-ah-ah." Evan's stern scolding stopped her. He leaned closer. "Don't say a word."

"But—"

"Ah!" His eyes held an icy chill. "Stop," he commanded, yet he hadn't raised his voice. In fact, it seemed he'd lowered it to avoid being overheard. "Let Heather do her thing."

"You're filming it," Kit gritted out. "My best friend has vanished, and you're *filming* it!"

"That shouldn't be a surprise to you." Evan hadn't moved his hand from the car, blocking her still from moving forward. She could feel his breath on her nose. "Madison signed a contract with the production company. We have rights to film. There's about fifty pages of fine print outlining every scenario so the show can make use of whatever happens during a walk."

Kit couldn't respond.

"I hate it as much as you, but contracts are contracts. So suck it up, Kitty-cat, and play along.'"

Kitty-cat? He had *not* just called her Kitty-cat.

Evan Fischer wasn't finished. "We all want to find Madison. But is it worth the effort to fight against the show, or is it wiser to use that energy to find Madison?"

He had a point.

Kit swiped at the moisture in her eye. A single tear, but she'd pass it off as something else. "Allergies," she stated.

Evan's expression darkened with doubt.

Kit swallowed back every ounce of worry, exhausted fear, and her halfway sprint into all-out anxiety.

"You may not like what Heather does." Evan glanced over his shoulder at the woman, who still stood like a statue, staring at the theater. "But it's what she does. In this case, it'll get us access to the place—to finding Madison."

"I can't lose her," Kit said, voicing her concern.

Evan's expression gentled, and his next words surprised Kit. "I'm sorry this happened. I really am."

Kit looked away from his penetrating stare that suddenly unnerved her to her core. He didn't need to see into her soul—deeper into the meaning of her declaration of fear, of loss. It was selfish to a degree. At least Kit judged herself as being selfish. She cleared her throat and attempted to explain so she didn't sound so desperate.

"I just want Madi to be all right."

"That's why we're looking for her," Evan assured her.

Kit tried to be content to leave it at that. Evan Fischer couldn't possibly know what it was like to have someone disappear. Leave. To be abandoned. Most people didn't understand how it affected Kit, and most never would. They dismissed it as not applicable 'cause she'd been an infant, but it was the often unacknowledged adoption hangover . . .

"Kit?"

Evan's soft prodding jolted her from her thoughts.

She lifted startled eyes. A mistake. His were narrowed, searching her face, and this time all traces of the cool and aloof ghost debunker were gone. "You're not okay, are you?" His question, which on the surface had so obvious an answer, went deeper than Madison. He was too perceptive.

Kit shook her head. "I'm fine." She pushed off from the car, and Evan finally dropped his arm. She shut the door and did a quick sweep of her fingers through her shoulder-length hair. "It's Madison we need to worry about."

She'd spent twenty-eight years dealing with loss, and not the grieving sort of loss caused by death but the sort that equated to being left alone, wandering, with moments when rescue came into view. But in truth, hope was too terrifying a thing to lose to reach out and grasp it. It was easier to function without it—without expectations. Then, when loss visited, it was a familiar silence. A cold one, but one she'd learned to live with. It was what happened when the one person in the world who was supposed to fight for you—give their all for you—instead just gave you away. That was what it meant to be adopted. Whether as a baby, like Kit had been, or as a foster child, like Corey. Either way, the most important person in their world, their mother, had been lost to them and by her own choosing. Life then became a dark, scary woods they had to navigate. Always wondering if the ones who professed their loyalty and love would really stay, and always convinced their promises were thin, conditional.

Madison had promised to stay. For Kit. She understood Kit's darkest fear—or at least she claimed she did. Which was why her disappearance was beyond unsettling. It was a broken promise, and Kit wanted to believe Madison would never break it unless she'd been forced to. Which made the potential outcome so much worse, and much more terrifying.

6

Skin prickles were a real thing. It might be daylight outside, but the interior lights with the wattage of maybe sixty made the inside of the theater dim. Kit glanced at Evan, who walked beside her. His face was set without expression. She looked ahead at Heather, who led the way, much as she had the previous night during their night walk through the theater.

"Tell me what you see," Tom prompted Heather, aiming the camera lens at her. Her footsteps were silent on the red carpet that lined the hall. The psychic ran her hand along the wall, which was covered in a cream wallpaper with tiny golden pinstripes. The wood finishes were a dark mahogany. The entire theater dripped like blood with hues of red and gold, the remnants of old-money wealth.

"It's quiet here. For now," Heather murmured. She dropped her fingertips from the wall as she approached one of the arched doorways into the auditorium. She stood in its entryway, lifting her face toward the domed ceiling. "There's an energy in this room." Heather took a few steps down the aisle, her hip brushing the vintage wooden frame of a theater seat. She pointed to the immense chandelier in the center of the ceiling, surrounded by murals of hand-painted blue sky and flying cherubim. "It's solemn." Heather glanced at Tom, who nodded his encouragement. It seemed the cameraman also served as her companion, helping to coax from her the visions that only she could see.

Evan hung back, a scowl deepening between his brows. Kit rubbed her bare arms, feeling the tiny bumps on her skin. Everything about this felt wrong. And it seemed like they were twiddling their thumbs, chasing Halloween tales while Madison was only God knew where. And Kit meant that wholeheartedly. Only God *did* know where she was.

Kit was opening her mouth to interrupt this tête-à-tête with the supernatural when Evan's hand on her elbow stopped her. He gave his head a stern shake. She couldn't tell if he was for, against, or impartial to this whole ghost-walk thing. She bit her tongue to keep the peace, but it was getting harder.

"Something happened here . . ." Heather let her words hang. She scanned the balcony seats that jutted out over the floor. The velvet curtains had been tied back, the chairs properly positioned. They were empty. Void. Heather drew a contemplative breath and gestured toward one at the far side of the auditorium to the left of the stage. "I'm seeing a woman. There's screaming. Something about . . ." Heather squinted enough to scrunch her face into a wince of concentration. "Something about a child? Falling." She nodded to herself. "Lots of screaming."

"Do you see who's screaming?" Tom pressed. The red record light on his camera blinked.

Heather shook her head slowly, tucking her hair behind her ear and scooping it off her neck and over her shoulder. "A woman in the crowd? I think she saw the child fall? I'm not sure, but . . . something about a woman in white. A woman—"

A door slammed behind them in the adjacent lobby, echoing across the marble floors and into the hall and auditorium.

Startled, Heather spun around.

Kit grabbed at a chair as if it would somehow save her from the paranormal vision Heather was reciting.

Tom shut off the camera and lowered it. "That's that," he groused.

Evan had zero reaction, yet his eyes sharpened when a shadow cast across the floor, and a man's form entered the archway they'd just come through.

"Who let you in here?" Detective Seamans looked perplexed as he approached them.

Kit relaxed at the sight of him. As if the detective could jar them all back to reality. Their ghost hunting was a deterrent from finding Madison, she was convinced of that.

"The theater guild gave us access," Evan explained. He shook hands with Detective Seamans.

"It's in our contract," Tom added.

Detective Seamans appeared unimpressed.

Kit edged between Tom and Evan. "Have you found Madison?"

The detective settled his gaze on Kit, apology in his eyes. "Unfortunately, no. She hasn't called or contacted you, has she?"

"No." Kit shook her head emphatically. "Her disappearing—it's not like her."

"I know." Detective Seamans did know. Everyone in Kipper's Grove knew Madison, and everyone loved her.

"Do you have any ideas?" Kit didn't care that the three others from the show stood behind her, or that Detective Seamans had thwarted Heather's flirtation with some vision of hers.

Seamans blew out a deep breath. "There's not much I can do at the moment but wait."

"No evidence of a crime, eh?" Evan inserted.

The detective shook his head. "No. And frankly, you all haven't offered us much to follow up on. But I'm glad I found you all here. I need to ask you more questions."

"Absolutely," Evan said.

"Whatever we can do to help," Heather added.

Tom stayed silent, monkeying around with his camera.

Kit leaned against a theater seat, her legs shaky.

"So, Madison was with you last night?" Detective Seamans directed his question at Heather.

She nodded, appearing adequately concerned for Madison. "Yes. And Evan. We had gone ahead. I'm not sure what had kept Tom behind—or Kit."

"Kit was walking slow," Tom said.

Kit shot him a glance. Up until now, she'd been starting to like him. But if he was going opt for a passive insinuation that somehow she was at fault . . .

"It was only a matter of a few minutes," Tom said. He gave Kit a small smile, as if he hoped this might soften his prior accusation. "I got perturbed because—" he lifted the camera to draw attention to it—"camera guy here, I sorta need to be where the action is."

"And the *action* is with you, Ms. Grant. Mr. Fischer." Seamans crossed his arms over his chest. The lines in his face and the graying at his temple made the detective a serious and imposing figure. Perhaps that's what he was going for.

Heather stepped forward, moving next to Kit. She smiled warmly in a way that made her seem endearingly sweet. "Yes, if you can call it that. You see, we do our night walks for me to get a sense of the activity in the buildings we investigate. Sometimes I see people, or spirits—beings who are otherworldly— and sometimes I see remnants of old memories. Energies that communicate unresolved pieces of the past. And souls who haven't passed on."

"You talk to ghosts?" Detective Seamans raised a brow.

Heather bobbed her head. "Well, sort of. Each place varies as to what I see, who I talk to. *If* I talk to anyone, or if I'm merely a witness to happenings that sensitives like myself can see or feel."

"And last night?" Detective Seamans prompted.

Kit shifted her attention to Heather.

"Last night was curiously quiet." Heather's statement hung in the air for a moment. Then she continued, "But after Madison . . . well, it wasn't good."

"What wasn't good?" Another prompt from the detective.

"The energy in this place. I was very uncomfortable. I felt nauseated. I could see—" she exchanged a look with Evan—"I saw a boy."

"A boy?" Seamans repeated.

"That's right," Heather said. "And the boy followed me home."

"He followed you home?" Another parroted phrase from the detective as he interrogated Heather.

"Sometimes a spirit will attach itself to someone they feel might help them—or threaten them. It's happened to me before. They eventually leave, or I help them . . ." It was apparent Heather was struggling to find words to explain her point of view. "But he's not happy. He's angry. In fact, he made me sick."

"He made you sick?" Kit could identify with Detective Seamans's tone of disbelief.

Heather nodded. "A spirit can influence the body physically. It manifests in ways like headaches or joint aches, sometimes nausea, even heart issues."

"I know we went over this last night but tell me again how Madison vanished if she was right beside you." As Seamans shifted his attention to Evan, the detective seemed ready to dismiss the supernatural for something more tangible.

Evan cleared his throat. "We'd gone into the basement and past the dressing rooms. It was dark down there, so I had a flashlight with me. None of us were talking outside of Heather communicating what she was or wasn't seeing or feeling." Evan shot her a glance. "The hallway branches off toward the space beneath the stage. There's a door at the end that was locked. Madison unlocked it and went inside. She mentioned something about finding a light and for us to hold back for a second. We did, and then she just disappeared."

"Did you hear anything? Did she say anything more?" Detective Seamans pressed.

"Nothing. Not even a scuffle." Evan acquiesced to Heather, who had straightened in anticipation of wanting to say something.

"There was a definite heaviness to the air the moment she opened the door. That was when I first saw the boy."

"Okay," said Detective Seamans. "Did you go into the room to look for her?"

"I did." Evan nodded. "Like I told you last night, I went in and called for her. I looked around before going back to get Kit and Tom. I figured Kit might know where Madison went or if there was some other hallway or room we were supposed to follow Madison to."

"Yeah." The detective nodded slowly. "Well, I was hoping maybe you'd recall something fresh this morning."

"I don't," Evan admitted. "The weird thing was, there isn't anywhere to go down there. I mean not that I saw. No doors that lead outside."

"There's a trapdoor to the stage," Kit said.

Detective Seamans grimaced. "I was just thinking about that."

"But wouldn't we have heard it?" Heather asked.

"Possibly." He hefted a sigh and shoved his hands into his pockets. "The fact is, she could've slipped through the trapdoor. And there's a small window at the end of the boiler room just off the storage area below the stage."

"Big enough for Madison to fit through?" Evan inquired.

"Maybe." Detective Seamans shrugged.

"What about the boy?" Heather's question silenced them all for a moment. She looked pointedly at each one of them, landing on Kit.

Kit squirmed. She wanted to like Heather. But there were so many question marks where she was concerned. Authenticity, believability, *plausibility*. And that didn't even branch into the arguments of mixing spiritualism with Christian faith.

"What about the boy?" Detective Seamans responded.

"Like I said, he's angry." Heather was more direct now, her voice firm. "It's possible he influenced Madison to do something."

"What, in a matter of seconds?" Evan's skepticism was undisguised. "So an angry spirit had the ability to influence Madison to disappear? That's a stretch, Heather, even for you."

"You can't discount—"

"I *am* discounting it." Evan's words shut the medium down. Heather's lips tightened into an irritated line.

"Explain to me exactly what your relationship is." Detective Seamans eyed them. "It's apparent you're not on the same plane when it comes to your jobs."

"I'm the show's skeptic, the one responsible for debunking Heather's claims." Evan's eyes narrowed. "In short, I do historical and current research on the buildings we're investigating. Then I try to find reasonable explanations for the activity in the location, provide answers to Heather's claims of potential spirits, and prove that what appears to be a ghost has a human explanation. There's *always* an explanation."

"Oh, is there?" Heather snapped.

Tom broke into the impending argument, his hand held up, palm forward. "All right. So, to summarize before these two pulverize each other, it's like any other ghost-hunting show with the exception that we have an Evan who works at explaining it all away. Like someone exposing a magician's tricks."

"Only these aren't tricks," Heather added sternly.

"Got it." Detective Seamans moved the conversation on. "Did Madison say anything or act a particular way that gave you any reason to believe something wasn't right?"

"No," Evan said.

"No," Heather agreed.

"Not to me," Tom added.

The detective's eyes leveled on Kit. "You've had another issue show up today, haven't you?"

Kit was determined to not get teary-eyed at the gentle look on Detective Seamans's face. It was daunting, the reminder that once she'd stepped outside the theater, she had the pantry's vandalization to deal with.

"I understand this is rough on you, Kit. Is there anything that would lead you to believe that Madison's disappearance and what happened at the pantry are related?"

Kit hugged herself, noting the prickles on her arms had subsided, but the anxiousness inside was only increasing by the moment. "No. Not that they're related."

"But you have suspicions?"

Kit winced. "Madison wanted to save this place from what her grandfather's company had planned for it. Save this area of town from being built up and modernized. She made some people frustrated."

"I know about that."

The detective's acknowledgment encouraged Kit to continue. "She was outspoken about the food pantry's benefits for the community. She helped with our fundraising and volunteer programs. And people *do* get annoyed by the pantry. It's for low-income families, and some would prefer the place not be located so close to the main part of town. I know Al doesn't like Madison's involvement with it, not even as community service. She's a Farrington, and—"

"And there are other endeavors more suited to the Farrington charity," Detective Seamans finished. "I've heard Al give that explanation before about Madison's association with the pantry. There's been a stigma around that area ever since it was used for the poorhouse back in the day. Claims of riffraff being too close to homes with children. As if someone living below the poverty level is predisposed to harming kids."

"It's discrimination," Tom muttered.

"Actually, it's outright discrimination coupled with arguments that the area attracts drugs. We shut down a meth lab in a house near there just last month. So while the prejudice can be based in a social hierarchy, it's also out of genuine concern for safety and community." Detective Seamans drew in a heavy breath, seeming to consider his options. "Is anything ever black and white?"

None of them answered.

Kit considered his argument. She typically focused on those who weren't supportive of the pantry and the negativism toward the stereotypical lower class. But she couldn't argue with the detective about the population the area also drew. She'd seen a tennis shoe hanging by its laces on a phone line just last week. Sign of a meet-up spot for drug dealing.

"All right then." Detective Seamans cleared his throat. "I'm going to have to ask you all to clear out of the theater. I want to search the place in the daylight and see if anything was missed. Meanwhile, if you hear anything from Madison, call me right away, okay?" His instruction was directed toward Kit.

The ghost-hunting team moved ahead, with Kit following. Detective Seamans reached for her to slow her down. His look was cautionary. "I don't know what's going on with them"—he tilted his head in the direction of their retreating forms—"but be careful. I checked into the production company, and it's reputable. Still, I get the feeling they're going to insert themselves for a story."

Kit's stomach twisted into a knot. "Evan already admitted that."

"Yeah." Detective Seamans narrowed his eyes. "And that guy's got a chip on his shoulder. He's out to prove that medium is a load of hooey, and while I can't say I disagree, Fischer seems a tad bit aggressive."

"You think *he* hurt Madison?" Kit ignored the quaver in her voice. She'd let the man into her apartment.

Seamans didn't give her much of a reaction. "It's too soon to say. If it wasn't for your validating the claim Madison disappeared, I'd question whether Madison was ever with them during their walk to begin with."

"She was," Kit affirmed.

"I believe you. I'm just saying . . . be careful."

"I will."

"Oh, and Kit?"

"Yes?"

"Get yourself to the pantry. Corey needs you. It's worse than you think."

7

Greta

It spread like wildfire. Within two days, Kipper's Grove was spinning with the news that three boys had disappeared within the confines of Barlowe Theater. Mr. Zimmerman and the Christliebs joined Greta in a vigil outside the building, for they were refused entrance. Mr. Barlowe had allowed only the police into his theater, and from what Greta had been told, he'd done so grudgingly.

It had been two days since Leo went missing with the other two boys. The news filled the house with dread. For now, their neighbor, Mrs. Welder, had agreed to watch the younger boys, but that was only if Greta promised to provide food for them during the day. *"Don't have enough to feed my own, let alone yours,"* Mrs. Welder had said.

Poverty was its own demon in Kipper's Grove. More than just Greta and the boys lived within the threatening shadow of the poorhouse. Now more than ever, it stretched its dark oppression in Greta's direction. If she didn't work, she couldn't afford to pay their rent. They would end up destitute. That wasn't even accounting for the massive fine that had been given to her for disrupting the night at the theater. Now there was talk that Barlowe wished to level a lawsuit, asking to be paid for any lost wages and profits. He could sue her, but she had nothing to give. Nothing. It was obvious he was displaying his position and power, and Greta was Barlowe's warning to anyone who mistreated his theater.

Greta paced in front of the theater while Mr. Zimmerman banged on the door.

"No one's gonna answer you," his wife moaned. "They don't care about our boys."

"We're not good enough to care about," Mrs. Christlieb added.

It all sounded petty and childish to Greta. Becoming a victim because of one's economic standing might have its merit, but she would not join them on a soapbox to make some point, not while Leo was missing. If the point was their boys weren't being given priority because of their social status as south-end factory workers, that was valid, yet arguing only ostracized people like Mr. Barlowe for showing them any mercy at all. They would engage no new sympathies, especially perched outside of the illustrious theater.

Greta's conclusion was validated as a motorcar pulled up with its white-rimmed tires and polished black runners. Mr. Barlowe. She quailed at the foolishness of being caught here at the theater. Barlowe would blame her. Hold her responsible for rabble-rousing when the original goal had merely been to request access to the theater to see if they could uncover clues as to where the boys might have disappeared to.

Mr. Barlowe was imposing in his own way. His eyes were deep-set and shrewd. His head was covered in a bowler hat, his frame in a tailored suit, and his shoes had been polished to a mirror-like shine.

"What is the meaning of this disturbance?" Barlowe strode toward the families gathered outside his theater. There were only five of them. The parents of Teddy and Fred, and Greta. And yet, from Mr. Barlowe's perspective, the street in front of the theater was busy, and they stood here in tattered clothes. They would detract from the glory of the new building and its boasts of fame and entertainment for those who could afford to make it a social endeavor.

Mr. Zimmerman and Mr. Christlieb swiped their hats from their heads out of respect. Mr. Christlieb gave his wife a look that was clear in directing her to stay silent.

"We're looking for our boys," Mr. Zimmerman informed Mr. Barlowe.

"Ah, yes." Mr. Barlowe looked beyond them to the locked double doors of the theater's entrance. "So it was your rapscallions who broke into my theater last evening?"

"May not have been right," Mr. Christlieb interjected, "and my sincere apologies for that, but now they're missin'. We need to find our boys."

Mr. Barlowe offered them a consoling smile. "Of course. I assure you, if we had any idea as to the boy's whereabouts, we would cooperate fully. The authorities, however, have given the theater a full once-over. Your children are not inside."

"But how'd they get out?" Mr. Zimmerman challenged. "They were barred inside."

Mr. Barlowe sniffed. "If I knew that, then the mystery would be solved, would it not? Trust me, if we find something to assist in the collection of your sons, we will inform the police immediately. But for now, please do me the respect of removing yourselves from my property. We've a show tonight, and I don't need further issues to address from scenes being caused." He turned a cold eye on Greta. "Especially from you. If one of these boys is your relation, he had quite the gall to enter my establishment uninvited after the trouble you caused."

"He is my brother," Greta informed Mr. Barlowe, her voice strained.

73

"Where are your parents? Your father? I should speak with him directly about the behavior of his children."

Greta lifted her chin. "My father passed away. As did my mother. My eldest brother died *here*, sir, during construction of the theater."

"Ahhh!" Recognition passed across Mr. Barlowe's face. "Was he the lad who fell from the scaffolding in the auditorium?"

"Yes, sir." Greta felt the eyes of the Zimmermans and Christliebs on her. She must tread carefully now. Cast no further blame on Mr. Barlowe or she might risk their not receiving any help in finding the boys.

"A pity." Mr. Barlowe clicked his tongue, tugging on the lapels of his jacket. "Such an unfortunate mishap."

"Hardly a mishap," Greta retorted without thinking.

"I apologize." Mr. Barlowe dipped his head. "I meant to say *misstep*. Your brother's misstep off the scaffolding was unfortunate. For all involved."

Mr. Zimmerman stepped between Greta and Mr. Barlowe. Greta attempted to swallow the bile that rose in her throat, both out of fury at Mr. Barlowe's veiled denial of responsibility and grief that had yet to heal from the loss of Gerard.

"Please, sir, all we ask is—"

Mr. Barlowe held up his hand, stopping Mr. Zimmerman. He grew chillier in his demeanor. "*I* ask that you coordinate with the police as to your boys and leave my property at once."

The next few moments were filled with pleas and tears from the Zimmermans and Christliebs. Greta couldn't blame them. She shrank against the theater in paralyzed horror that Mr. Barlowe was so unsympathetic, and that Leo and his friends could so easily and terribly vanish.

Mr. Barlowe's voice rose in determination.

Mr. Zimmerman's arms waved with frantic motions while Mr. Christlieb held the form of his collapsing wife.

A small crowd began to gather, passersby who had heard

the commotion. With the county courthouse directly across the street and filling up the middle square of the block, there were businessmen in suits and ties, lawyers, refined ladies out for strolls along the shops that skirted the square. Carriages and motorcars warred for position on the brick street. The hotel next to the theater welcomed a few of its guests onto its balconies to watch the display forming.

"Leave at once!" Mr. Barlowe bellowed. "I will call the authorities!"

Then the backfiring of a car with its puff of black smoke snagged Greta's attention. A lanky form climbed from the driver's seat. Long arms clad in a brown suit coat waved back and forth to usher away the curious onlookers.

"There's nothing to see, folks, nothing to see," he urged them. They listened reluctantly, moving on but very slowly.

Oscar Boyd, Eleanor's brother, hurried toward her. His ash-colored hair was smoothed back from his forehead, his gold-rimmed glasses emphasizing the intelligence in his eyes. "Greta!" He was almost breathless when he reached her.

Mr. Christlieb was shouting now, his rotund body drawing closer to Mr. Barlowe, and his ruddy cheeks becoming redder.

"Greta, you need to leave here. Now." Oscar's hand grazed her arm.

She couldn't help but stare at him. Dazed, she didn't know what to do or where to go. Home? Without Leo? Why couldn't Mr. Barlowe just allow them to look in the theater for themselves? What if Leo had been caught somewhere, perhaps by a ruffian. Had he been kidnapped? Leo would not have simply run away. He knew she'd been blamed for the other evening's debacle with the falling child, so of course he came to the theater. He would try in his own way to find evidence to clear her from the Barlowes' accusations.

"Greta." Oscar's voice was gentle but urgent as he tugged on her sleeve. "Please. Come now."

The crowd was growing again.

She allowed Oscar to lead her between bystanders and away from the spectacle. Mr. Barlowe's driver was running across the street for help, and the sound of a police whistle filled the air.

Oscar opened the door to his motorcar. "Get in," he coaxed.

Greta slid onto the padded seat. She'd never ridden in a motorcar before. She smelled oil and gasoline. Oscar climbed in on the driver's side after cranking the vehicle into a chugging start. Gears ground as he fought with a long metal stick rising from the floor. The motorcar lurched forward. Oscar shouted at a group of pedestrians, ordering them to get out of the street. They raced away in a puff of exhaust, leaving behind the sound of Mr. Christlieb and Mr. Barlowe arguing with each other.

She sank into the seat, ignoring the blur of sidewalk and trees as the town car moved her faster than she'd ever moved in her life.

Oscar turned onto a side road lined with overhanging maple trees. The park was quiet. It was also a place she rarely came. Greta stared out the window of the Boyds' car and wished she could enjoy the scene. That she could pretend the bushes turning red and the leaves on the trees flirting with burnt orange were as romantic as they appeared. In the distance, two mothers pushed hooded baby carriages. A little boy ran ahead of them in shorts to his knees and wearing a sailor's shirt.

Oscar shut off the car's engine, and silence followed.

Greta wrapped her arms around herself. Her muscles felt numb. "We cannot find them."

"I know," Oscar said calmly.

Greta met his eyes, which reminded her of the color of lentils.

He offered her an empathetic wince that emphasized the slight cleft in his chin. "Eleanor and I heard yesterday morning."

Greta looked away from him toward the mothers, who had paused while the boy scurried around and picked up fallen leaves. "Something dreadful has happened."

"You don't know that." Oscar's words were an attempt to comfort, but instead they rang hollow to her ears.

"I don't even know where to begin to find Leo. I've already forfeited my position at the laundry since I've been out looking for him . . ." Greta stopped. This was none of Oscar's business. He would tell Eleanor. Eleanor would see fit to continue her charity toward Greta, and that simply couldn't be. It couldn't. Growing into young women had brought with it that tentative balance between friendship and the realities of the lives they'd been born into. Eleanor had a good heart, but Greta and her brothers weren't her friend's responsibility to care for. Nor were they the Boyds' responsibility. Greta had no wish to burden them. Her family was hers to care for.

Oscar twisted in his seat. "Perhaps we could inquire at the police station? See if they've had any new developments?"

Greta shook her head. "Officer Hargrove has been kind enough to keep me informed." She recalled the dusky depths of his eyes. On another day, not so long ago, she would have been foolish enough to dream of him as she scrubbed linens. Now? Romanticizing anything in life—even dreaming of something better—felt like a betrayal to her parents, to Gerard, and—

She sucked in a sob and pressed her fingertips to her lips.

"Greta?" Oscar's concern filtered through the space between them.

"I'm so sorry," she whispered. Oscar wasn't unlike his sister. He too had a kind heart. Neither Boyd children seemed affected by their parents' wealth, but Greta knew it was still something to flee from. The wealthy rarely understood the plight of people like her.

Greta fumbled with the door, attempting to open it. She

could walk home from here. She could search the ditches and the back alleys. Lord help her if she found Leo and he was—

"Please stop." Oscar's tone took a decidedly firm note, though he couched it in gentleness. "You'll work yourself up into a tither and then where will Leo be?"

Greta paused. The logic was clear. Oscar was right. Hysterics would do Leo no good now. Her own emotional outburst the other night had cost her more than she could ever repay the Barlowe Theater and . . . She whirled toward Oscar, her gaze colliding with his. "I saw an infant fall the other night. I did."

"I believe you." Oscar nodded, though his face told her he hadn't witnessed it himself. He was being polite, just as he had been that night.

"I'm almost certain my brother went to the theater to try to prove I wasn't seeing things. Creating visions that weren't there. Leo was trying to help me. But someone must have . . . oh, I don't know! I don't know what happened!" Greta couldn't stop her tears, and she hated herself for them. Hated that they only exacerbated the unspoken argument that she wasn't stable. That grief had created in the mind of Greta Mercy a tentative lease on sanity.

"Please." Oscar fished in his coat pocket and came up with a clean handkerchief. He handed it to her while simultaneously pushing his glasses up the bridge of his nose. "I confess, I didn't see what you witnessed while at the theater, but the response was palpable, and I can hardly find it believable that your outcry was the sole reason for the chaos that ensued."

Greta blinked, pondering his explanation. She took the handkerchief and dabbed at her cheeks with it. It smelled like cedarwood. There was a large O embroidered in the corner in a manly navy blue.

"I believe the first thing we must do is piece together what exactly happened at the theater. What did you see?"

"I saw an infant fall from the—"

Oscar held up a hand. "I realize what you believe you saw. I am not saying you're in error either. My point is that sight versus fact *can* indeed be different things. If we can understand what exactly occurred there, then perhaps we'll discover something that led your brother astray in the theater. Perhaps he uncovered something, and he's still out looking. Attempting to compile answers and evidence to relieve you of the responsibility of lost profits the Barlowes have issued against you."

Greta pressed the heels of her hands to her eyes and shook her head. "You speak as though there is a conspiracy, and somehow I stumbled on to it." She locked eyes with Oscar. "How could I possibly mistake an infant falling from a balcony, and how could an *entire theater* of guests not witness its poor form on the auditorium's floor?"

Oscar's lentil eyes darkened, looking a tad greener now than yellow-brown. A strand escaped his carefully combed hair, and for a short moment he had a rakish appearance. Then he pushed the strand back with his hand and became bookish again. "My point, Greta, is that those questions you're asking are not in vain. They demand answers. We must uncover them if we are going to find your brother."

8

"It's like we're spies!" Eleanor's nervous but excited pitch made Greta clutch at her arm. Her fingers meshed with the black muslin of Eleanor's dress, and she was distinctly aware of the mended and patched black cotton she wore herself.

Oscar draped his arm over the steering wheel and peered through the darkness at Eleanor, who was perched between him and Greta. "This isn't the war front, Eleanor. This is Kipper's Grove. Control your excitement."

"But it's *so* exciting!" she tittered in a whisper. Her eyes widened, and Greta could see the whites of them. "Just think! There are women in Germany right now spying on behalf of their nation! They've even printed posters to warn the Navy boys overseas to watch out for those women's wiles."

"You wish to be a German spy?" Disbelief made Oscar's response a pitch higher.

"No, silly, of course not. After they sank the *Lusitania* this spring, why, I—"

"Cease speaking." Oscar's command met its mark, and Eleanor clamped her hand over her mouth. He leaned around his sister and met Greta's eyes. "Are you sure you wish to do this?"

Greta wasn't sure of anything. Desperation was causing her to listen to Oscar against her better wishes. It was causing her to agree to Eleanor joining them when Oscar admitted she had caught him rummaging through old funeral clothes to camouflage himself in the night. She was placing the Boyds in danger now as well, which would be detrimental if they were discovered. It would ruin Eleanor. It would cast shame on the Boyd name. It would be the last straw that kept Greta and the boys from that structure south of town where the poor, the insane, and the unwanted were kept. Of no value to anyone.

And yet . . . Leo. Greta nodded in belated response to Oscar's question. "Yes. Yes, I'm sure."

She could hear him breathe and felt Eleanor groping for her hand.

They spent the next moments with Oscar giving them instructions, and then, before Greta could question herself further, they had exited the town car and were scampering across the street. They darted into the alley behind the theater. The buildings rose two stories, all in a line. The theater had large double barn doors in the back, padlocked and secured even more tightly now that Leo and the boys had successfully found their way inside. There were no windows.

"How do you plan to—?" Eleanor's question was cut short when Oscar pulled bolt cutters from the pack he carried. "Oscar!"

There would be no turning back now. Greta steeled herself for what they were about to do. Were she still alive, her mother would be appalled to know what Greta was up to. Her father? He would understand. Anything for family. No limits. Even breaking and entering.

The lock broke beneath Oscar's tool. The chain rattled as it snaked through the door handles.

"Curse!" Oscar said in whispered panic as he grabbed at the chain to keep it from clattering.

The trio stood in the alley, Oscar balancing the chain in his hand, Eleanor gripping Greta's sleeve. Greta was certain her pallor was ghostly white. Silence invaded the alleyway.

Oscar released the breath he'd been holding and carefully lowered the chain to the ground. He tugged on the door, and it opened. Waving his hand for them to follow, he stepped into the theater's backstage loading area. Eleanor followed. Greta paused, looking over her shoulder down the alley. No one was there. No sound but the crickets. No light but a sliver from the streetlamp half a block away. She slipped through the opening.

A musty smell greeted her, and Greta could tell that this was where backdrops were loaded, repaired, and assembled. The scent of sawdust mingled with the stale air in the windowless room that rose the full height of the theater. Overhead was a black, vaulted ceiling made up of ropes, pulleys, scaffolding, and a platform. The mechanics of the stage. Greta was unimpressed. It all loomed like evil shadows, rising up from the floor and descending from the rafters, demons determined to swallow anyone who lingered after dark. Playing tricks on them, taunting them—

"Greta!" Eleanor's harsh whisper made Greta jump.

She could hardly see her friend in the dark. Oscar waved to them silently, bidding them to come. Greta drew close, her shoulder brushing Eleanor's.

"We need to work swiftly," Oscar said. "We'll search the first floor, and then we'll go to the box seats and the upper sitting and rest areas. If we exhaust those with no clues as to where the boys were lost, then we'll venture to the basement and the dressing rooms."

"What if one of us vanishes?" Eleanor seemed far too hopeful it would happen.

Greta ruined Eleanor's excitement. "Then it means we're more than likely never going to be seen again. My brother has disappeared. His friends are gone. Must you play with death?"

She should feel guilty for speaking to Eleanor in such a way, not to mention the harshness in her reprimand. Eleanor became quiet. Greta understood why, but she also knew it was important that Eleanor see this not as a game to played. This was no adventure. They were breaking the law in hopes of rescuing Leo and the other boys.

"We stay together," Oscar continued. "I have a flashlight, but its battery will not last long—not to mention a light may draw undue attention. So we'll only use it if absolutely necessary."

"Is that Father's flashlight?" Eleanor gave a quick intake of breath. "He'll notice it's missing."

"No, it's mine." Oscar sounded a tad annoyed at his sister. "Now come along."

Greta followed Oscar and Eleanor, their footsteps echoing lightly on the stage. It was painted black and covered a wide expanse with an opening for the orchestra pit. To the right of the pit, Greta could make out the Wurlitzer organ.

"What are we looking for?" Eleanor's question sliced through the stillness.

"Anything that could lead us to the boys," Oscar answered. Greta watched his angular form as he hurried down the steps to the auditorium floor.

"I can't see!" Eleanor whispered.

"Shhh!" Oscar said.

"Why?" Eleanor pointed to the auditorium. "There's no one in here—the seats are all empty."

Neither Oscar nor Greta replied.

Greta peered into the chasm of the theater. With the house-lights turned off, there wasn't much she could see. "I think you may need to use the flashlight." She moved her hand to the next row, trying to maintain her position in the center aisle without stubbing her toes on the seats, which were bolted to the floor. "Oscar, if we can't see anything, how are we going to find Leo?"

Oscar didn't respond. Greta's toe hit a riser in the next row of seats. She stumbled, catching herself on the arm of a seat, nearly falling to the carpeted floor. She could sense the empty void of the domed ceiling above her. There was a tiny musical clinking as the chandelier crystals bumped into one another, as if a small breeze had disturbed their slumber.

"Eleanor?" Greta hissed.

An uncanny stillness was the only response.

Greta straightened and looked around. The fear that she was alone seeped into her blood, chilling it. Trying to control her breaths, she took small ones, though they still sounded terribly loud when she released them.

"Oscar!" Her voice echoed through the auditorium. "Eleanor!"

Greta strained to look up at the box seats. She could see the outline of them jutting out over the floor below. She focused on the box seat that the infant had fallen from, walking toward it into a row of seats.

"Eleanor!" she tried again, hoping perhaps the Boyds had the same inclination to revisit the scene of a few nights before.

Greta could envision that night, that moment with the woman holding the infant, a blanket swaddled around it. The woman had been wearing a white dress with elegant lace, a beautiful evening gown of taste and expense. Then, as if drawn by some irrevocable force, the woman had opened her hands.

Greta gasped at the memory. The babe plummeting toward the floor, its blanket unwinding and floating down after the child. And then all she recalled was her screaming. The ruckus. The lights flashing on. The doctor pressing his fleshy body past her as he attempted to rush to the aid of the infant.

The woman's face. So expressionless, then so horrified. Greta had stared at her, met her gaze in that moment. The shock shared between them was mutual.

A light flickered on and then off, jerking Greta from her remembrance. It was an electric light, a single bulb perched on the wall beneath the box seat.

It flickered again as if it were trying to stay lit but hadn't the energy to.

Greta saw her then. In the brief moment, light stunned her eyes and then faded to blackness. The woman in white. She stood in the box seat again. She wore the same gown. The same haunted expression.

"Ma'am!" Greta didn't bother to subdue her voice. "Ma'am, are you there?"

The auditorium was suddenly dark again. Consumed by the night. It was pure aloneness then. Greta felt it crawling across her skin—

A boy cried out beneath her feet. Then to her left.

Greta whirled. "Leo!"

Banging. Metal on metal. Another cry and then it trailed away as though the boy was running into an oblivion Greta couldn't see. She spun back. "Leo!" she shouted. The name reverberated through the auditorium.

The light flickered again. The woman in white stood directly in front of Greta. Her eyes were black. Her white gown was tattered. Her hair hung in strands around her face, and her cheeks—her pale and papery white cheeks—were wet with tears.

Greta's scream raked her throat.

The light went out. A boy screamed from inside the walls. And she heard the infant cry.

9

Kit

Detective Seamans hadn't been kidding. The food pantry, what used to be the poorhouse back in the day, was covered in slop. Broken eggs, milk, torn paper bags, white bread rolls tossed onto shelves, and bacon splayed into stickmen figures on the floor like body outlines at a crime scene.

Ruin. The word was scrawled in orange spray paint next to one bacon stick figure.

Obsessed. It was painted in lime green with drops where it had dripped over its own bacon person.

The bacon stunk.

Even with the front doors propped open and the back windows wound wide, the place smelled of expired, fatty meat.

"I'll never eat bacon again." Corey gagged. He had the constitution of a kindergartner, but Kit hugged his arm anyway for strength.

"Me neither." She eyed the catastrophe in sheer disgust.

Corey bent his head to look directly at her. Kit was sure there were a few more gray hairs in his goatee and at his temples.

87

He'd lived his life as a bachelor and devoted all his time to this place—like she did. They were the only two paid, albeit poorly paid, employees of the nonprofit. But it was different for Corey. He had come out of the streets of the south side of Kipper's Grove. Low-income housing, his dad having abandoned him, mom a meth addict. Corey had grown up in the nineties listening to ska punk and eating stale Pop-Tarts. He knew what it was like to be in need. This was hurtful to Corey, and especially personal.

Regardless of the ten-year age gap that pushed Corey toward forty and Kit toward thirty, they were kindred spirits. In the *Anne of Green Gables* sense of the word.

Kit met his defeat with a wobbly smile. "We can fix it."

"Sure." Corey planted a platonic kiss on the top of her head. "And pigs can fly."

"Don't be a killjoy," Kit retorted.

"Me?" Corey drew back with a mock look of horror on his face. "Never." He pulled away from Kit and bent to retrieve a stray piece of cardboard slathered in egg yolk. He tossed it into a garbage bin.

The back door slammed. They both looked up as a thin woman wound her way around the mess, her lip curled in disgust at the damage. She wore a stocking cap, her face weathered from hard life and cigarettes, but her sad smile was genuine as she greeted them. "This is astounding," she announced.

"Here to help clean up, Gwen?" Kit winced as she followed Gwen's gaze. She was a loyal volunteer at the pantry and was invaluable to Kit, similarly to Corey, though without quite the amount of affection.

Gwen's expression was one of shameful apology. "I can't." She pointed to the door she'd just come through. "I came to pick up the refrigerated truck. We have donations to pick up from Fletcher's Dairy."

"Oh, that's right!" Kit snapped her fingers and exchanged

glances with Corey. "We need to get this place in order. At least the refrigerators. They said they had over one hundred gallons of milk to donate."

Corey curled his lip and sniffed. "Figures they'd be generous this week."

Kit understood Corey's take on the irony of the situation. Fletcher's Dairy was the largest in the county, owning farms valued at millions. They were a large family with financial backers like Al Farrington—which was why they weren't known to be big donators to the food pantry.

"It was Madison," Gwen piped up. She was wrestling a cigarette from a pack. "She's been hobnobbing with the Fletchers' eldest son, and you know how Madi is." Gwen chuckled, fingering the cigarette like a pointer at a whiteboard. "She'll work her magic, especially if it bites her grandfather in the—" she hesitated—"the backside."

"What is it with those two?" Corey asked.

Kit rolled her eyes and sighed. "The Fletcher Farm isn't particularly concerned about the environment or organics." At least that was what Madi had told her. And it had irked Madi to no end that it was another thing her grandfather was involved with that had the potential to damage something.

"They're farmers, though," Gwen argued. "They're not going to ruin the land when it's their livelihood." She seemed genuinely perplexed as she stuck her unlit cigarette in the corner of her mouth. That was Gwen. She'd wait to light it, but a cigarette in her mouth was her trademark nonetheless.

"It's the chemical sprays," Kit said.

"Most farmers spray their crops," Corey countered.

"It's Madi." Gwen chuckled. "That girl's a firecracker."

Kit couldn't argue with Gwen.

"Anyway," Gwen said, "I need to grab the truck keys and then I'm off. If you need help getting this place in order when I get back, I can see if the guys helping me unload will stay longer."

"Thank you." Kit gave Gwen a quick side hug. The woman didn't have to donate her time. She was what Kit wished more people would be like. Not critical or competitive, but kind and generous and reliable.

Gwen walked toward the back office to fetch the truck keys. Corey shifted toward Kit, his brow furrowed. "Speaking of Madi, has there been any news?"

Kit wrapped her arms around herself now that Corey was too far away to hang on to. Would it be so bad if she just burst into tears? Her eyes hurt from lack of sleep and the attempt to keep the tears at bay. She shook her head, opting for no words for fear if she spoke, that would be the end of her emotional restraint.

Corey wagged his finger in the air. "It's Madi. She'll show up."

"I pray she will!" Kit was serious. Prayer was needed. Maybe she could call her pastor—start a prayer chain. That was an idea! Mom could organize it. Prayer could do wonders in—

"Pray away, Kit, but feet to the ground. Madi would tell you that. Don't focus on her, focus on this place and all the folks who need us."

Kit recalled tearing a piece of paper in two. The ripping and the uneven way it ended up was how she felt right now. She couldn't be in two places at once. She couldn't lift three hundred and fifty hungry people on one arm while sweeping the air with her other for some chance she'd grab hold of Madison and pull her back to them.

"A person just doesn't *vanish* when they step into another room!" Kit stated, her words bouncing off Corey's back as he picked up a dirty dinner roll and lobbed it into the garbage bin.

"Maybe you should ask Madi's grandpa. Mr. Farrington probably whisked her away so she'd get *out* of his way. She's probably flying first class to Fiji right now, while we're wiping up a food crime scene. 'Girl, bring in the CSI 'cause this better not become a serial food slaying.'"

Kit laughed a watery chuckle. Corey's nature was straightforward, funny, and disturbingly sardonic. Unfortunately, none of that could make her feel any better. Not as she stared at the ominous messages and body art made from rotting bacon. Not as she grew more convinced in her gut that something had gone terribly wrong with Madison, and that the theater was a literal house of historical horrors.

Dusk had settled in by the time she and Corey had made a dent in the cleanup efforts. Gwen and her volunteers made it back and unloaded the dairy after which Kit was able to set them to work. She took the opportunity to search the pantry warehouse for Corey. Finding him outside in one of the walk-in freezers, Kit kicked at the orange construction cone that kept the heavy door from closing on him.

Corey hefted a cardboard banana box on top of a five-tier stack of them. He gave her an exasperated look. "Our precious little vandal might not have gotten into the freezer here, but we're short dinner rolls now by about twelve dozen."

Kit didn't respond. She couldn't think. She'd been awake since yesterday. She'd been fielding calls all afternoon for pantry-related issues, the police had contacted her twice, Detective Seamans had called her and asked her to come into the station in the morning to answer more questions, and worst of all, she'd received five voicemails from Madison's grandfather. She'd listened to one, and after managing not to collapse under the authoritative pompousness of his message declaring it was time she and Madison stopped messing around like children and "come up for air," Kit had chosen not to listen to the other messages.

"Earth to Kit!" Corey waved his hand in front of her face.

"Ew." She winced. "You stink."

"Yes, well, rotten eggs will do that to a guy." Corey swept his arm through the air. "I've lost my manly mojo, Kit. Cancel my dates. I'll be single forever."

"I'd be lost if I had to share you with another woman anyway." Kit had zero romantic intentions toward him, but there was an element of anxious truth behind it. Corey was her rock. A big brother. An older cousin. A—

"The way I'm going, honey, you and this place will be the only ones in my life for a long time." Corey's laugh made her feel a bit better, even though Kit gave him a crooked smile of permission.

"You probably *should* find a real woman," Kit admitted, even though she didn't really want him to.

Corey waved her off. "The pantry would get jealous."

Kit's laugh was a weak one.

Corey's demeanor gentled. "Hey, Kit, we've got this. We'll work together and get the pantry back on its feet. It's a setback, that's all. Although a rather creepy one if you consider the bacon-outlined crime scene. Our vandals have a sick sense of humor."

"Corey . . ." Kit hesitated, not sure of what to do or say next.

"Okay." Corey flung an arm around her shoulder, sensing her struggle. "Here's what you're going to do."

Kit waited expectantly. This was the Corey she needed. The guy who gave her instructions and told her what to do. Sometimes she just needed that. She wasn't the leading lady, after all. She was the one who served, who helped, who managed behind the scenes. And tonight? She was sapped of all energy.

"You're going to go home and shower. Because if I stink, then you smell like a skunk had a tête-à-tête with a septic tank."

"Thanks a lot," Kit said.

"Then you're going to get some sleep."

"I don't know if I can sleep."

"Take a sleeping pill or drink some chamomile tea. Melatonin. Heck, have a shot of whiskey. Not all at the same time, though, just to be clear." Corey tipped his head to the side. "Look, you're no good to me here if you're a walking zombie."

"I know." Kit offered a wobbly smile.

"So sleep! Get some food in you too. Then do what you need tomorrow for Madi. They will find her. We will find her. She's our girl as much as she is yours. The pantry needs Madi too, you know. She'll be found, and it'll all be okay."

Corey's promise fell flat.

Kit sniffed. "You don't know that."

Corey wiped away her renegade tear. His voice lowered. "Hear me out when I say this. You need to let the police do what they do best. Find Madison. You're just going to drive yourself nuts otherwise."

"I could maybe put up posters," she said.

Corey swiped another tear from her cheek. "Go home. Better yet, go to your mom and dad's. Curl up with their dog and have a snooze. I'll see you tomorrow."

"My ants need me," Kit protested weakly. "And they don't have a dog."

"Your insects will be fine, weirdo. You need your parents." Corey's words were soft. Kit knew he'd give anything to have the blessing of a solid set of parents to go home to. He gave her a little shove. "Go."

"All right. All right. I'm going."

Gathering her things together, Kit waved goodbye to Corey and slipped into the driver's seat of her car. Minutes later, she pulled onto the highway leading to her parents' home. It was a good idea. Her parents could bring some normalcy to an otherwise surreal day.

Trees whizzed by as the road became a blur. A dried-up cornfield waited to be harvested, and up ahead, a deer bounded across the pavement. As her surroundings grew fuzzy, Kit squeezed her eyes shut in an effort to clear them.

Without warning, her car jerked to the left. Kit grappled for control with the steering wheel, but the car fought against her. The back end on the driver's side dropped lower than the front. Metal scraping on asphalt grated in her ears as the car barreled toward the ditch and the trees that lined it. Kit screamed, stiffening herself for the impending collision.

Her airbag exploded, sending chemical fumes into the car and stealing her breath from her. The crunching of metal emphasized Kit's complete loss of control. Her phone flew off the passenger seat, hitting her in the right cheek. The frame of the vehicle was pushed against Kit's legs.

Stillness followed. That sickening kind of stunned silence after absolute chaos. Pawing at the deflated airbag, she tried to see over and around it, but to no avail. She saw tiny dots of light. Her cheek burned where her phone had smashed into it. What she could see of the country road was that it was deserted. The car's horn honked repeatedly, engaging the pounding in her head with a painful staccato.

Kit struggled to clear the fog from her mind. Her legs and arms were working okay and without serious pain.

She moaned, grappling to stop the car's honking. Fumbling for the car door, Kit managed to open it. She slid from the car and stumbled to her feet, looking around for her phone. Not finding it, she pressed her hands against her knees and bent over, willing herself not to pass out. Once the black shutters cleared from the corners of her eyes, she glanced toward the rear of the car.

Her tire was completely missing. All she could see was the hub where the tire should have been. Had the tire come off? How was that even poss—?

Kit's confusion was interrupted when an SUV approached where she'd careened off the road. Kit managed to stagger from the ditch, waving her arms to flag it down. The SUV slowed, and she noticed the chrome along the rims and the runners. The polished black. The tinted windows. The bright flash of red shirt.

Evan Fischer pulled the vehicle onto the shoulder, flung open his door, and jumped out. He wasn't the one she preferred to play her hero, but car accident victims couldn't be picky.

"Kit!" he exclaimed.

She squinted as Evan's image before her spun in a circle, and then she was happy to bid the ghost hunter skeptic farewell as she collapsed onto the trunk of her car and hit the ground with her knees.

"I got you!" was all Kit heard Evan say before blackness flooded her in the sweet abyss of lost consciousness.

10

Kit grabbed for Evan's arm as the EMTs hefted her into the ambulance. She was strapped to a backboard, her neck secured in a brace.

He pulled away.

"I can't—"

Kit lost her grip as they pushed her gently into the emergency vehicle. She could taste the metallic flavor of blood. Her bottom teeth had almost pierced through her lip from the impact with the airbag. She could smell hot rubber, antiseptic, and nothing at all familiar. Evan Fischer was as close to familiar as Kit had right now, and even through her haze, she knew she had to be in the wrong frame of mind to be grabbing for Evan to comfort her.

"Please . . ." she mumbled through her swollen lip.

"You can ride along if you want," the medic said to Evan, then reached across Kit for something, squatting next to her in the ambulance. "She'll be immobile until we get to X-ray and clear her for a spinal fracture. Might be a comfort for her if you're close by."

Evan said something about his rental vehicle and just being an acquaintance. There was a nod from the medic.

Voices.

The cops were there. Kit could hear them talking in the background, hollow and distant, as though they were at the far end of a tunnel.

"Lost her tire—"

"Lug nuts on the left rear were loose too. Tampered with—" Evan made a comment.

One of the ambulance doors shut, causing Kit to startle. She fought her restraints. "Evan!" Her cry sounded foreign to her ears. Trauma had gotten the best of her.

There was shifting, movement, and then Evan was at her side and crouching by the stretcher. Because of the neck brace, she could see him only out of her peripheral vision. Kit was stuck staring at the roof of the ambulance. She wanted to yell that she hadn't broken her back—she hadn't broken anything. She didn't think she had anyway.

The ambulance doors closed, and the medic pounded on them to indicate they were ready to go.

"I'm sorry," Kit whimpered. She was coherent enough to know that tomorrow she'd regret every tear and every whine she'd allowed Evan to witness. He wasn't her friend—he was barely an acquaintance—and yet the events of the week had shoved them together.

"Don't worry about it." Evan was casual, calm. "I'll call Tom. He and one of the crew will go get my rental."

She hadn't meant she was sorry she'd made him leave his rental on the side of the road. She was sorry he had to witness her like this. Sorry she'd disrupted his schedule and wherever he'd been going. Sorry—

"Do you have any idea who did this?" Evan leaned over her.

Was he really holding her hand or was that the medic? Kit struggled to identify who had her hand clasped between two warm palms.

"You," she whispered. It had to be Evan's hands.

"Me what?" Evan's eyes narrowed.

He went in and out of focus. Kit blinked her eyes rapidly.

"Does she have a concussion?" Evan's question floated over her toward the medic.

A faint rumble of voices. Someone stuffed a wad of gauze between her bottom teeth and lip. A wet cloth dabbed at her cheek and chin.

"Nothing seems broke . . . CT scan for a concussion." The medic's voice came in and out.

She wouldn't end up paralyzed, that was good. Kit's thoughts were muddled. Of course she wasn't paralyzed. She could feel her toes, her knees, her waist . . . "I can feel your hands." She gave Evan a goofy, lopsided smile, at the same time chiding herself for the lack of self-control.

"You gave her something, didn't you?" Evan asked the medic. Then she heard no more.

The ER was slowly coming into focus. The oxygen clampy thing was on her finger. She couldn't remember what it was called, just what it was for. The room was cold, but someone had covered her with a warm cotton blanket that was fast losing its comforting temperature. The ceiling light above her bed had a panel displaying blue butterflies. They were faded but pretty.

"Hey, Kitty-cat."

The deep, unfamiliar voice startled her. Slowly, Kit turned her head to the left to see who was perched in a chair beside her bed. The movement made her head pound with a pain she'd not experienced before.

"Hey, hold still." A hand brushed a strand of hair from her eyes. "You've been going in and out."

Kit winced, closing her eyes. She could feel the IV in her forearm, taped and secured. "What's the IV for?" she mumbled.

"Fluids. Pain meds." Evan leaned back in his chair. "X-rays

came back clear. No breaks. CT scan showed a concussion, but no brain bleeds."

"What a fancy checklist of information." Her sarcasm came out slurred.

He ignored it. "Your parents are on their way here. The hospital finally reached them. And that"—Evan pointed to the IV in her arm—"is the result of their not finding a vein in the normal spot."

She winced again. "I thought you said I was on pain meds."

"You are. Hence your drunken stupor."

"I'm in pain, I'm not drunk."

"You'll wish you were once the meds wear off tomorrow."

"Tomorrow? Why can't I stay on them for weeks and weeks?" Kit heard herself and clamped her mouth shut. She could feel the puffy lower lip. There was a stitch on the inside where her teeth had bitten through.

Evan chuckled. "Yeah, they don't send you home with the IV, Kitty-cat."

"Don't call me Kitty-cat."

"Sure."

"Can I have a drink of something?" Her tongue felt thick.

"Uh, yeah." Evan retrieved a plastic-capped cup with a straw from the wheeled tray at the foot of the bed. He stood over her, staring down with bright blue eyes, his angular cheekbones emphasized by the beard around his chin and mouth.

"You have a goatee." Kit stated the obvious.

"I do. Now shush and drink." Evan held the straw to her lips.

Kit sucked in some iced water, not moving her eyes from his. He was platonically distant in his return stare. Yet his expression was a caring one, and that was unexpected.

When Kit was finished, Evan set the cup back on the tray. "I know you're not with it entirely," he started, sitting back in the chair, "but can you tell me anything about what happened?"

"You probably need to get somewhere." Kit looked around

for a clock. How long had he been here with her? He didn't need to stick around.

"I'm fine," Evan replied. "So, do you remember anything about the accident?"

Kit closed her eyes, willing away the brain fog so she could recall. "I remember the car jerking to the left. I heard a grinding noise—the car felt like it was down-shifting or something."

"It shifted gears?"

"No, like the back of the car literally fell onto the road."

"You lost a tire," Evan supplied.

Kit gave a small snort and then wished she hadn't as it brought a throb of pain. "How does a person lose a tire like that?"

"The lug nuts weren't on it." Evan's eyes sharpened. "Did you recently get your tires changed?"

"No." Kit stared at him, trying to understand the implications of the tire missing its lug nuts. "What does that mean?"

"It means somehow—someone—removed the lug nuts from your tire. When the tire went flying off your car, that's what made you lose control."

"Who would remove the lug nuts?" She felt funny even asking it. Her dad always helped her with tire changes, and she'd taken the car in for an alignment just last year. "Can lug nuts work their way off tires by accident?" Kit asked helplessly.

"Not unless they were put on sloppy to begin with. They could if they hadn't been tightened."

"Dad wouldn't miss something like that," Kit said. A fresh wave of pain radiated through her head.

Evan patted the bed. "You'd better rest now. Your parents should be here soon. The nurse said they'll be releasing you after observation, another hour or so. You'll need to go home with someone."

"Mom and Dad to the rescue." Kit managed a smile.

"In the meantime," Evan added with a frown, "I want to check into a few things."

"What things?" Kit asked.

"What happened was no 'accident'—not with Madison's disappearance and the vandalism at the food pantry."

"This doesn't have anything to do with Madi," Kit argued in a whisper, taut with emotion.

"You know that for a fact?" Evan challenged.

Kit's silence was his answer.

11

The chair Evan Fischer sat on creaked beneath his weight, the wicker frame protesting. Kit eyed him from her reclined position on the love seat opposite him on her parents' screened-in porch. Her entire body ached, and she didn't have the energy to tell Evan to go away. She could ask her mom to do it, but Mom was too nice. It'd hurt her conscience to evict the man who'd rescued her daughter from the accident yesterday. But she wished she could tell him to leave for the simple reason she really wanted him to stay—and that was weird. There had to be some sort of psychological term for what she was feeling. That warm sense of security, however false, when a hero walked into the room. He'd rescued her. He'd sat with her at the hospital. He—

"Earth to Kitty-cat."

Well, that jolted the heroism right out of the man. "What?"

"I was saying, the cops found your tire."

"Oh."

"There's no evidence of a crime being committed, though, any more than it was an accidental oversight by whoever last put the tires on."

"My dad? But that was two months ago." Kit shook her

head. "Dad knows what he's doing. And there's no way I could have driven for two months with an unsecured tire."

Evan nodded. "Right, so we're back to believing it was tampered with."

That was unnerving. Kit tried to adjust her position on the love seat without jiggling her head and arousing the throbbing pain from the concussion. It had subsided to a bearable level for the moment. "I don't have enemies."

"Are you sure?"

"Well, maybe some of the people who are annoyed that the old poorhouse was converted into a food pantry. I think the reality of poverty offends man's ego." Kit offered her wry and unfiltered opinion.

"Maybe. Or it has to do with your relationship with Madison. Her disappearance."

"What, they're jealous I'm friends with her? That doesn't sound stalkerish at all." Kit sank back into her pillow and closed her eyes.

"Does the pantry have cameras? We can watch the footage of the parking lot and maybe see if anyone there tampered with your tire."

"At the pantry?" Kit cracked open an eye. "Who says it was tampered with at the pantry? And no, they don't have cameras. That costs money."

"I'm guessing it was at the pantry since you'd driven there safely, and it was after you left that you had the accident."

Kit opened both eyes. "The only people at the pantry were Corey and me. Gwen was there for a bit, but she soon left in the truck, not to mention she probably wouldn't know how to loosen a lug nut. Doesn't that take a special tool?"

"Not unless your car has a key for them so your tires can't be stolen. Otherwise you'd just need a lug wrench and some brute strength, assuming the lug nuts aren't rusted or stuck. The hubcap would need to be removed too."

"There were some other guys there who helped Gwen unload the milk." Kit tried to recall their faces. Two of them were from church, and one was Madison's friend. "I can't see any of them doing it."

"I didn't say it was someone from the pantry, but *anyone* who knows you, who knows where to find you. It could have been someone who followed you there."

Evan's words were more disconcerting than Kit wanted to let on. She brushed them off with a lackadaisical wave of her hand. "I'm sure it was a coincidence and a fluke."

Evan leaned forward, his elbows on his knees. "In my book, there's no such thing as coincidences. I want to find what links this stuff together, and maybe it will help us find Madison."

Kit felt the warmth flood her once again as she saw Evan through her hero glasses. Which was irritating because he wasn't exactly a nice guy, so she didn't want to like him. He chased ghosts for a living—literally—and he spoke in clipped sentences as if rattling off a list of facts.

But Madison . . .

Kit ran her tongue along the stitch on the inside of her lip. It was nice Evan cared that Madison had vanished. There weren't many people in this world who spent energy on people they didn't have to. Then again, what was in it for him?

"Why do you care so much about finding Madison?" Kit asked.

He appeared genuinely taken aback. "Why wouldn't I care?"

"It's the show, isn't it? They want an angle on Madison's disappearance. To make a story out of it?"

"Wow. Okay." Evan scowled and pulled back in his chair. "That's pretty harsh. And you think *I'm* rude?"

Guilt flooded her that he'd seen through her opinion of him. That warring type of guilt that said she was being too cold and that her protective barriers were going up. She liked her softer side, the side that wanted a hero. The side that believed they existed—and that they stayed. She just didn't believe heroes had longevity. At some point, a person ran out of monopoly with their hero, and then they were abandoned. Unable to pay the emotional, mental, or physical return on their investment? Buh-bye. This was what happened when a girl's birth mother left her behind at the hospital when she was a vulnerable baby. Even if the mother had followed the adoption laws and her story warranted grace because she was a young, pregnant teenager.

It was a hard truth that Kit knew from experience, and only those who'd been adopted or fostered could fully understand it. She reminded herself of this before, and she would remind herself of it again and again until she had protected herself enough not to be surprised when it happened.

Love, loyalty, and heroism came with expiration dates. It was only a matter of time.

The sliding door into the screened porch opened. Kit and Evan had fallen silent, and Kit had traveled deep into herself, visiting those places inside that she argued over. The end of loyalty came with betrayal or rejection. It was a terrible price to pay. And then there was Mom . . .

Kit looked up to see her mom step onto the porch bearing a tray with glasses of apple cider and a plate of apple-cider doughnuts from a local orchard. Mom had always been there. So had Dad. From the moment they'd taken her, just three weeks old, from the arms of her foster family. They had never abandoned her. That was the awful part. Knowing her parents adored her, cherished her, would probably die for her, but at the same time believing there was still something that could make them leave. Something stronger than love. Something that could melt it away and leave in its place just her. Alone. Alone in the big woods.

"Here we are!" Mom announced, oblivious to Kit's tumultuous thoughts.

Evan offered Kit's mom a smile that would have warmed the sun. So he *could* be charming when he wanted to be? Or maybe it was just that Mom had found the source of the man's soft spot. Sugar and apples.

"You deserve the entire plate." Mom set the tray on the glass top of the wicker-framed coffee table between Evan and Kit. "But," she added, grinning at Kit, "don't underestimate my daughter's penchant for doughnuts."

"Mom." Twenty-eight years old and Mom could still embarrass her in front of boys she didn't even like. That was parental talent.

Evan reached for a soft, fresh-baked doughnut. He took a bite, chewed, and swallowed. His eyes brightened. "Mrs. Boyd, you are an amazing baker."

"Please, call me Kris. Actually, I can't take credit—I bought them at the apple orchard this morning. I wanted to spoil you."

"You're doing a fine job of it, but I hardly deserve it."

Mom leaned over and brushed a strand of brown hair from Kit's face. She studied her eyes, looking at Kit's pupils. "You're lucky it was just a concussion. God was watching over you."

Kit nodded.

"Amen," Evan agreed.

Both women swung their gazes toward him, a smile spreading across her mom's face, and perplexity making Kit stare in disbelief.

"You're a praying man?" Mom beamed.

Evan dipped his head. "Yes, ma'am." The quick glance he shot Kit seemed to dare her to fight him on it.

"God bless you. Here." Mom picked up a doughnut and gave it to him. "Have another one."

After she'd exited the porch, Evan and Kit sat in silence. Evan because he was scarfing down his second doughnut, and

Kit because he was such a conundrum, she wasn't sure what to think. Or maybe the accident had done more to her brain than originally thought.

"You confuse me," Kit stated. Might as well get it out in the open. Dancing around it would only make things more tense.

Evan took a drink of apple cider and set the glass back on the tray. "I thought you didn't like me."

"I never said that."

"You didn't have to."

"You pray?"

"Yeah, and I hunt ghosts. Figure that one out." He leaned back in the chair and crossed his right ankle over his left knee.

Kit ignored the doughnuts and the cider. "I'm trying to, but my head hurts too much."

His eyes twinkled back at her. "Then don't try. Just deal with it." His wry tone made Kit give a little snort in response.

"Is that going to be your epitaph when you die?" she asked. "'Just deal with it'?"

He grinned, and it transformed his irritable face into something more good-looking than Kit preferred. "Hey, it'll stop a person from hanging out at my grave."

"You don't want visitors?"

"I don't care one way or the other. I'll be dead, right?" Evan pulled a booklet from his backpack on the floor and thumbed through it. "So I thought we should start here," he said as though they'd been interrupted from a prior conversation.

"Start here for what?" Kit gently massaged the sore muscles on the back of her neck.

"Coincidences, remember? I don't believe in them?"

Kit nodded. It wasn't right to be propped up with pillows, cozy and comfy when Madison was still out there—who knew where? Suffering who knew what?

Evan's thumb held the booklet open, and Kit could see the

title on the cover: *Phantom Seekers of Barlowe Theater*. "That was written way back in the eighties," Kit reminded him.

Evan lifted his azure blue eyes with a look that implied her observation had little relevance. "Ghosts don't pay attention to copyright dates," he quipped.

"I thought you didn't believe in ghosts."

Evan shrugged. "I believe in research."

She sighed. "Fine."

He flipped the booklet open again. "Contrary to popular belief, I'm not totally without feelings, and my *gut* tells me we need to be as vigilant looking into the theater as looking into your accident—and the vandalism at the food pantry. After skimming through this book, I wanted to ask you what you know about the tunnels beneath the theater."

Kit frowned. "There are no tunnels."

"Mrs. Green would beg to differ." He tilted the book in her direction.

"Alpharetta Green wrote that book for tourists to buy during her ghost tours decades ago. She told the public what they wanted to hear." Kit moaned and laid her head back on the pillow, closing her eyes. The weight of the accident, the pantry's vandalism, Madison's disappearance . . . it all was so much.

"Or was it based in truth?" Evan shut the book and tossed it onto the coffee table. "Most ghost stories contain elements of truth. History and real events that capture people's imaginations. Heather seems to think the spirits hang around to hear their stories told. I believe it's that people *want* to see or hear something to substantiate the stories, to keep them alive. Mrs. Green writes that there were rumors of tunnels that led from below the theater to the Barlowe home a block away. Mr. and Mrs. Barlowe could attend the performances and slip through the crowds of the social elite without difficulty."

"I suppose." Kit accepted the theory.

"And if that were true . . ."

Kit opened one eye to find Evan staring at her. "What?"

He shook his head as if she were missing something obvious. "Then it's possible Madison left through one of the tunnels."

Kit's other eye opened, and she stiffened. "But there *are* no tunnels. People have looked and never found them. And why would Madison leave the theater by way of a secret tunnel and tell no one and then remain as if she *disappeared*?"

Evan snapped his fingers. "That's a million-dollar question."

"I don't think anyone's going to pay a million dollars for the answer based on that theory." Though if Kit could, she would. Anything to get her best friend home safely.

"Don't you want to find out, though?" Evan's voice grew serious.

"I want to find Madison. That's what I want."

"What if this is how we do it? Reaching for what seems unreachable?" Evan tapped the booklet with his finger, not taking his eyes off Kit's face.

Kit worked hard at keeping the ever-ready burning of tears at bay. She'd give anything to receive a text from Madison, to learn her best friend had somehow just gotten lost in an unknown tunnel system beneath the theater.

"But that's why they call it 'unreachable,'" she whispered hoarsely.

Evan studied her for a moment before nodding slowly, his lips pressed together in thought. His response, when it came, was disheartening. "So *I'm* the skeptic?"

Kit stared at him. "I'm just trying to be realistic."

"I'm all about being realistic. But that's after all the possibilities have been exhausted. It's what I did as a detective. It's what I do on the show to debunk the paranormal and prove that things have explanations. But first you have to dig—in places where no one else takes the time to. You can line up all the facts, but at some point you have to step out in faith too."

Kit eyed him. "I wouldn't expect someone like you to say something like that."

Evan gave her an apologetic smile. "Sorry to disappoint you. I have faith that there are things we can't see until we look for them."

"Like ghosts?" Kit meant for her challenge to add some humor, to offset the seriousness that had risen between them.

Evan wasn't smiling. Instead, he replied, "Not ghosts. Things of value. With substance. That will change the course of an investigation where no one thought it could be changed. That can change the course of a life even."

"You really *do* like ghost hunting with Heather, don't you?" Realization was dawning on her, and she wasn't sure if she liked what she was uncovering.

Evan looked down at the booklet, then up at Kit. "I like finding out the truth. I don't like abandoning a search. I won't abandon Heather. We don't see eye to eye, but that doesn't mean I'd quit on her. On what she believes she sees or experiences."

"Why then do you try to prove her wrong?"

"I hunt for truth and I never, *never* give up if there is hope."

Kit could relate but on a different level. People had always been that hope to her. Those who came to the pantry, the ones the community didn't see as valuable as others, the people who paraded themselves about as if they were worth everything while inside they felt they were nothing. Her quest was to find that hope in people—their value as God saw them—who were created to be so much more than what life had dealt them. And yet . . .

"What if we run out of hope?" she asked.

12

Greta

Greta rushed outside, pushing open the massive loading-dock door to make room and not caring who saw her as she stumbled into the alleyway. Oscar and Eleanor were nowhere to be seen. The moon was tucked behind a thick layer of clouds, leaving the sky a bluish-black. Behind the theater, the road was narrow and rutted, skirting the back of the hotel next door. All the windows were dark. The world was asleep, except for Greta and the haunting figure she'd left inside the theater.

"What are you doing here?"

The deep, male voice caused Greta to scream. She lashed out with her hands, but the man grabbed her wrists in a firm grasp. Struggling, Greta tried to free herself, the heel of her foot kicking the theater's loading-dock door that had swung completely open. The backstage and loading area were a dark vault of secrets.

"Stop!"

She cried out as her skin pinched beneath the strong grip on her wrists.

113

"Greta?"

The incredulous shock in the man's voice made her still. Awareness flooded her, and she collapsed against the policeman, her hands splayed against his chest. "John! You must help. Oscar, Eleanor—" she gasped for breath—"and the woman in white is inside. I heard a boy shouting, and there was banging from inside the wall. I think it was Leo. I think he's trapped!"

"Greta. Greta!" Officer Hargrove gave her a little shake with his hands on her shoulders. "You must collect yourself."

Greta was trembling now. Her limbs, every muscle in her body, even her head quivered. "I swear on my mother's grave, you must—"

"Greta!" Footsteps on the stage platform stopped them both, the voice from inside the theater echoing into the night.

Greta whirled, though John kept an arm about her shoulder in a protective gesture.

Eleanor burst into the alley, the whites of her eyes enhanced by the reflection of John's flashlight. Oscar followed on her heels.

"Where did you go?" Oscar demanded, concern and urgency making him more forceful than he probably intended.

"Where did *you* both go?" Greta could feel tears trailing down her cheeks.

"Whoa there, all of you." John released her and held up his hand.

Eleanor shrank into her brother, slipping behind him.

The policeman squared his shoulders. "Did you all break into the theater?"

"The ladies had nothing to do with it," Oscar said. "I was the one who cut the lock."

"Why?" John's voice turned sterner.

Greta stepped away from the officer, unsure if he was going to arrest her, save her, or clap them all in irons. "We were trying to find Leo," she breathed. She couldn't allow Oscar and Eleanor to be ruined by this. "Please, John—Officer Hargrove—don't blame the Boyds for this."

John hefted an enormous sigh and extended his arm toward the doors. "You broke in and entered the Barlowe Theater, an upstanding citizen such as yourself, Mr. Boyd? Miss Boyd?" John turned to her next. "And you, Greta. The Barlowes are already holding you responsible for the disturbance at their last showing. How do we explain what you've done tonight?"

"We don't." Eleanor stepped from behind Oscar and ignored the way he grabbed for her. She batted his hand away.

"What do you mean, we don't?" John set his hands on his hips, glowering at her through the darkness. "Miss Boyd, I am a man of the law."

"I realize that. You're also quite adept at fixing things." A charming smile went with Eleanor's voice, even though it was difficult to see in the night.

"I beg your pardon?" John sounded offended.

Greta moved to intervene, but Eleanor held up her hand. "Officer, I met you at the cotillion this last spring. Do you remember?"

He flustered, and Greta frowned, waiting.

"Do you recall that incident with Carlton Jepson? He was being terribly rude to me, and you intervened—as police officers do, as protectors and overseers for the good of the community. Do you also recall taking a turn with Mr. Jepson's cousin?"

John shifted his feet. "Miss Boyd, I—"

"And while you did, I saw you snag your jackknife on Mr. Jepson's motorcar. Just a tiny bit. You chipped off a piece of its glossy black paint."

"Miss Boyd—"

"It *fixed* the problem. It made you—and me, if I'm being honest—feel much better about the entire situation. It was Mr. Jepson's comeuppance, as well as his cousin's, who is quite prissy and unkind."

"That has nothing to do with—" John was interrupted once more as Eleanor sidled close to him, resting her hand on his forearm.

"I can't imagine that a show of temper that results in vandalizing a man's expensive motorcar is legal. Is it? Is the punishment for defacing another's personal property worse if it's committed by an officer of the law?"

"Eleanor." Oscar broke into his sister's not-so-veiled insinuations.

John cleared his throat. Greta noticed he glanced her way, then nervously shuffled his feet again. "It's hardly the same thing as trespassing and—"

"But we didn't steal anything," Eleanor insisted.

"So you say," John countered.

"Search me!" She spread her arms wide.

Oscar lurched forward, pressing Eleanor's arms down at her sides. "All right, that's enough." He nudged Eleanor to the side. "Officer Hargrove, if you need to arrest anyone, please, let it be me. And let the ladies go free."

John expelled a nervous breath, obviously affected by what Eleanor had said. "I-I think I can find a lock to replace this one."

"Thank you, John," Greta said, pressing her fingertips to her lips in gratitude.

He gave her a sideways look. "I'll explain to the Barlowes that I was concerned that Leo was inside."

"You needn't lie on our behalf," Oscar said, his tone firm. He straightened his lankier build with a dignified acceptance of the consequences.

John ignored Oscar and looked at Greta. "You heard a boy inside?"

She nodded. "Yes. I . . ." Oh, how did she explain what she'd seen? The mother of the infant, first in the box seat and then suddenly in front of her? She avoided that and focused solely on the boy. "I heard a banging. In the walls. As if someone were taking a crowbar and hitting a metal pipe. I heard a boy cry out."

"In the walls?" Oscar's repetition wasn't stated out of doubt so much as to confirm he'd heard her correctly.

Greta nodded. "In the walls, yes. Or maybe from under the floor."

"I don't know how that would be possible," John said. "I'll check it out, though." He cleared his throat. "Now that you have . . . reported it to me as responsible citizens."

"Precisely!" Eleanor was beaming with approval. Greta could tell by the lilt in her voice, and by the way John's frame puffed a bit with pride.

"Let's get to it then," John stated. He swept the alleyway with the beam of his flashlight, then aimed it backstage. "This light won't last long, so let's not delay."

They toured the theater while walking behind John, exchanging glances and apprehensive looks. Eleanor clung to Greta's hand so they didn't get separated again, and Oscar took up the rear. Greta hated to admit the thought that ran rampant through her mind. There was little doubt John Hargrove's imposing and powerful physique could take down anyone who might wish them harm, but Oscar? She knew that his courage did not match the image he set forth. He seemed soft in a rich man's sort of way, and with long limbs and a slim build, he didn't inspire nearly as much security behind her.

Even so, they made it through the theater's halls, the second level, a perusal of the box seats, and even a cursory tour beneath the stage and in the dressing rooms. The place was as quiet as a tomb. There were no infant cries, no banging pipes, and no sightings of the woman in white.

"I'm sorry, Gre . . . Miss Mercy," John said with a swift

glance in Oscar's direction. Oscar's gold-wire spectacles reflected the light from John's flashlight, and his eyebrow rose at the familiarity John showed Greta. "Perhaps the banging you heard was just the pipes. Sometimes hot water traveling through can cause a banging noise."

Greta couldn't assuage the disappointment. It made no sense—boys clanging on pipes inside the theater walls—and yet she *had* heard a boy. She had seen what she saw, but to contest it aloud would be to add an exclamation point to the already tenuous ground on which she stood. The mutterings about town were that Greta Mercy had finally slipped over into a world of her own making—after losing two parents and now two brothers.

Greta opened her mouth to protest but was stilled when Oscar's fingertips grazed the back of her hand. "I will see you home."

"But—"

John stepped forward. "I can escort the lady back to her house."

Eleanor sidled between them. "Or perhaps you could see *me* home? I'm quite exhausted and I'm not certain my weary feet could go another step."

"But you and your brother live—"

"Posh! Our house may be blocks away"—Eleanor waved her hand toward Oscar—"but my brother thrives on playing the hero. Let him be one for Greta, as she may be the only young lady who takes him up on his offer."

It wasn't meant to be mean, Greta knew. Eleanor was attempting to be playful and to give Greta and Oscar an opportunity to discuss what had happened tonight—or what *hadn't* happened.

John protested again, this time with a tinge of annoyance in his voice. "Miss Boyd, the south side of Kipper's Grove is seedier than—"

"All the more reason Oscar should escort my dear friend home. I'll know she arrived safely when he returns to our house and can inform me." Eleanor smiled innocently, the beam from John's flashlight growing dimmer by the moment.

"It's fine, John," Greta reassured. Part of her felt a pang of disappointment. There was something about John, about his bearing, that not only made her feel safe but also made her feel . . . valuable.

"If you're comfortable with that, Miss Mercy." John slapped the flashlight against his palm as it flickered. "It is hardly appropriate, but—"

"We're at an impasse," Eleanor concluded. She tucked her arm through John's elbow, the wool of his coat more than likely making her skin itch. Eleanor despised wool, and while Greta would have never had the luxury to make such a distinction, she knew her spoiled friend well enough to read Eleanor's thoughts. "Take care, dear Greta." Eleanor blew a kiss with her free hand, then proceeded to monopolize John's time. The flickering light faded with the couple as they strode away, leaving Oscar and Greta in a completely improper flood of darkness.

"I apologize for everything. Tonight was not at all what I'd hoped." Oscar's formal tone didn't match his haphazard appearance.

"It's all right," Greta heard herself say, even though it wasn't. They'd achieved nothing but almost getting arrested. And she wasn't convinced that Officer Hargrove—John—would truly let them off the hook.

Still, she couldn't disguise a longing look after John. Eleanor's intentions had been good—flighty and entitled, but good. Greta hadn't been alone with Oscar often, and while she'd grown up watching him as she accompanied her mother to the Boyds' residence at various times, Oscar had been on the dull side. He was always reading, or discussing business with his father, or poring over journals by D. L. Moody and other evangelists who spouted the relatively new dispensation-alist point of view. None of which Greta understood. She just remembered hearing Oscar go on about it once to a fellow associate and how she'd thought Oscar Boyd couldn't be more boring and unattractive than he was at that moment.

But that was then. This was now, and Oscar, for all his ho-hum, bespectacled mannerisms, had been the only one to step forward and believe her. To find Leo. To entertain the idea that perhaps not all was at it seemed.

Their shoes crunched gravel and sticks as they traversed down the lonely walk toward Oscar's motorcar. There were no stars, no moon to light the way.

"We will find Leo," Greta mumbled, more to herself than to Oscar, but it captured his attention.

"I pray that is so."

"I heard—" She bit off her words before her insistence at what she'd heard and seen tonight soured Oscar's opinion of her. She believed his faith in her was tenuous, if not a bit heroic.

"Your brother went missing a few days ago, but refresh my memory as to the last time you saw Leo." Oscar was calculating the timeline of events in his mind, Greta could tell. It would be good to discuss aloud, and she was thankful Oscar had prompted the discussion.

"I saw him the night before. The night that Officer Hargrove came to question me about the incident at Barlowe Theater."

"The infant falling?"

"Yes."

"Hmmm. And what was Leo's response to Officer Hargrove?"

Greta tugged her shawl around her as the cool night air rushed around her in a breeze. "He was defensive of me. We are trying very hard to remain together as a family, so any potential threat isn't taken lightly."

"Officer Hargrove threatened you?" Oscar sounded surprised.

"Oh no. No, but the insinuation that I had created a spectacle for no reason . . ." Greta let her words drain away. She didn't need to detail the events of that night. Leo had been there. It was common knowledge throughout Kipper's Grove that a young woman from the south side had somehow been granted entrance to the performance, created a scene, and now was being considered for possible ailments of the mind. "Since Gerard died, it's been . . . very difficult," she finished.

"I cannot imagine what your family has gone through." The sympathy in his voice made Greta draw in a shuddering breath. She wished she could confide in someone—even if it was Oscar Boyd—to share her darkest fears so they didn't curdle her stomach, keep her awake at night, and now haunt her daytimes with impending doom.

"Would you allow me to pay your debts to the Barlowes?"

Greta halted. She couldn't make out Oscar's features, but he'd turned and given her his full attention. A sudden warmth rushed through her, but then she answered, "No. I-I couldn't accept such a thing. Besides, I don't know what the debts will be or if they will even be substantial." They *would* be substantial, though, because even a few dollars made a difference to Greta's family.

"I could do it anonymously. That way, there would be no questions of impropriety."

Protecting her reputation as well? Oscar thought of everything.

"And," he added, "there would be no obligations to me. It would be a gift. To you and to your family, for the years of your mother's service in our home."

Greta was at a loss for words. His kindness and generosity had rendered her speechless.

Oscar took a step forward, most likely to better make out

her expression in the dark. "I feel at fault too. You would be relieving my conscience by allowing me to do this."

"At fault for what?" Greta breathed.

"For allowing Eleanor to place you in such a precarious position that night at the theater. While I fully support her having invited you to come along, unfortunately the social elite can be unkind when they realize someone is among us who has, in their eyes, not earned that position. I should have foreseen that someone would recognize you as—"

"A poor orphaned girl?"

He grimaced, drawing back. "Those are not the words I would have chosen."

"No, but it is the words they would choose."

His lack of response confirmed the truth that Greta had been correct.

Oscar seemed to consider his next words carefully. "Please, Greta, I am not so uninformed or aloof as to deny the realities you're facing." That he glanced in the direction of the poorhouse was no surprise, but that he would even broach the topic with her certainly was.

"Initially, Grove House was intended to help those in need—those who struggle with their health, with their minds, with supporting their families. But in reality we know it is a place of—"

"Trials," Greta inserted.

Oscar sighed. "Yes. It needs reformation. It's appalling a poorhouse even still exists in Kipper's Grove. They are obsolete in so many places now. An archaic form of pretending to care." He looked toward the south, where they were headed, and began walking again. "So much in Kipper's Grove needs to be reformed."

Overwhelmed by the magnitude of such an undertaking, Greta returned to the deepest trouble in her heart. "I just need to find my brother." She could hear the echoes of the pounding on the pipes in the theater. She could still recall the vacant, reverberating sound of a boy shouting. Even with the others being willing to investigate her claims, the theater had yielded nothing.

There was much to be said about convincing others that she was in her right mind and that she wasn't creating imaginary situations. But it was worse when one questioned one's own ability to differentiate between the real and the unreal. The lines blurred as grief and exhaustion overwhelmed, making it difficult not to wonder if it would be safer for all if they moved her to the poorhouse. Outdated institution or not, perhaps it would be more charitable in the end.

"You will consider my offer?" Oscar asked.

Greta didn't answer. She couldn't. She wasn't certain his offer was wise, and while it provided her an escape from the Barlowes' charges against her, it did nothing to resolve the long-term effects that being parentless, brotherless, and penniless had on her soul.

13

It was Virgil's cries that tore through Greta the following morning. After returning home to find the neighbors had left the boys there by themselves, Greta had aided them in preparing for bed, and they had collapsed onto their flimsy mattress in exhaustion. She didn't even remember if she had bid Oscar a proper farewell with gratitude for seeing her home safely.

But now another cry laced with panic sent Greta catapulting from her bed into a standing position. The daylight outside the window told her it was late morning and she had overslept. The boys had already risen and probably eaten a stale roll before going outside to play and roughhouse.

"Greta! No! Leave my brother alone!" Cecil's voice cracked as though already toying with changing into a young man's voice. But there was distress in his tone too, a defensiveness that heralded Leo's instincts.

Greta raced through the front room and onto the slanted porch. The front door was already open. The sun blazed above, making the maples and oaks along the street glow in their fall colors. Yet it was the men who were hauling Virgil and Alvin kicking and screaming toward a wagon that shoved Greta into action.

"Let my brothers go!" She stumbled down the steps. No, this

wasn't going to happen. They would not remove her brothers from her care!

Cecil, the eldest remaining brother who had not been snagged by a stranger, was launching toward her when a man with beefy hands jerked Cecil back by his arm. "Oh no, you don't!" he barked.

Greta was stopped by an older man dressed in a suit. Not an expensive one, but it was clear he wasn't from the south side of Kipper's Grove. His expression was a combination of severity and confidence that he was in the right.

"Miss Greta Mercy?"

"Let my brothers go!" Greta lifted her chin, daring the man to defy her.

"Miss Mercy," he tried again, moving to remain in front of Greta as she tried to skirt around him. Alvin and Virgil were crying now, while Cecil wrenched his arm away from the man who had grabbed him, glaring daggers at him.

"Please." Greta held up her hands. "Don't take my brothers."

"I am Mr. Clayton Flincheon—of the county board."

"I know who you are," Greta snapped.

"Then you know why I am here." He glanced beyond her toward their shack. "When your mother passed away, we gave you a strict set of expectations."

Oh, how she remembered! The county had wanted to split them up and have the boys placed in different homes. Gerard had fought them, however, guaranteeing he and Greta could care for the boys.

"We stated you could remain here and together so long as there was no reported trouble caused by the lot of you. We were to hear no word of the Mercy children, and as such, no action would be taken. That is no longer the case."

"Please, I'm of age to have guardianship—"

"This has nothing to do with your age, Miss Mercy. It is apparent you have lost control of your family since the death of your brother Gerard. My condolences, but the county board has since become aware not only of the current circumstances between yourself and the Barlowes but also of your inability to give your brother Leo the care he needs. Hence he has gone missing after trespassing onto private property, which is a misdemeanor. Explain to me how this negates the need for the county to step in, so that your family is properly cared for? To make certain that you are of sound mind?"

Greta frantically searched for an argument, one based on logic and reason. "Mr. Flincheon, please. One more chance, I beg you. I'm trying to find Leo. I know something awful has happened to him and—"

"All the more reason for our intervention."

"No, Leo needs me. Cecil. And Alvin and Virgil—we need to be together."

"Yet you leave the boys at the neighbors and unsupervised long into the night?"

Greta drew back. "You've been watching me?"

"Your neighbors want nothing to do with the care of your brothers." Mr. Flincheon's brows drew together. "There is support from the county, Miss Mercy, and we are here to offer that."

"Support, you say?" Greta gave a watery laugh. "That's not support, sir, it's condemnation. The poorhouse does not offer care to those in need! It's where you tuck away the unvalued, the unwanted, those whom you have determined to bring shame to the community."

"Miss Mercy, Grove House is a place where you and your brothers will be given food and a place to live until you find an alternative."

Greta didn't miss the more cultured use of the poorhouse's name by Mr. Flincheon. It was more palatable to refer to such a place in a way that made it sound like a respite, a house of charity.

"Grove House is filled with broken people. *Unsafe* people." Greta stifled a sob.

Mr. Flincheon appeared offended. "On the contrary, law and order are maintained at all times at Grove House."

Greta wouldn't bother repeating the horror stories she'd heard surrounding Grove House—a poorhouse filled with the needy, but also with those who abused and took advantage of one another. "Do not condemn us there, Mr. Flincheon. I promise to pack up the boys and leave Kipper's Grove. We won't be a burden on the county any further."

Mr. Flincheon closed his eyes in exasperation, then opened them and offered Greta a patronizing smile. "And you would leave your missing brother behind?"

Greta scrambled for a reason for Mr. Flincheon and the county to leave them be. She glanced at the movement to her side and saw her neighbors in their yards, staring, their faces grim. They took no joy in this moment.

"Mr. Flincheon," Greta began, "my brothers . . . please, don't take them."

"I don't believe you understand, Miss Mercy. I'm here for *all* of you. You are behind on your rent. You are unemployed. There is simply no cause for leaving any of you behind. I suggest you take a few minutes to pack up your things. We really must be going. Grove House is expecting you."

"'Over the hill to the poor-house, I can't quite make it
    clear!
Over the hill to the poor-house, it seems so horrid
    queer!
Many a step I've taken, a-toilin' to-and-fro,
But this is a sort of journey I never thought to go.'"

The elderly man's reedy voice followed the wagon as they rolled down the dirt lane toward Grove House. Greta held Virgil's head to her chest, her palm covering his ear as she glared at the old man. He stumbled alongside the wagon as if he were the Grove House's welcoming committee, reciting the poet William Carleton's popularized words. The men from the county, including Mr. Flincheon, ignored him.

Rheumy blue eyes looked up at Greta and met her narrowed gaze that was meant to warn the old man to be silent. Instead, he offered her a toothless smile, continuing with the popular song that had haunted almshouses for the last thirty years.

> "'What is the use of heapin' on me a pauper's shame?
> Am I lazy or crazy? Am I blind or lame?
> True, I am not so supple, nor yet so awful stout;
> But charity ain't no favor if one can live without.'"

"Oh, do be quiet!" Greta couldn't help but shout at the man.

"'Are ya able to earn your victuals?'" he cackled, quoting another line from the song. "'I'm willin' to and yet here be I! No one a-willin' to have me around!'"

"Shush, old man!" Mr. Flincheon ordered from his seat on the wagon. "Off with you now. Leave the woman and her brothers alone."

"Is she a fallen woman?" The man's voice rose into a higher octave that mocked her and the boys. "Then why're you here? Cain't pay your bills?"

"I said to be off!" Mr. Flincheon bellowed.

"Fine, fine." The man slowed his pace alongside the wagon and watched them as they rolled away. He lifted a hand and shouted after them, "I be Bart! They call me 'the feebleminded one'— how's that for insulting?" A wild laugh followed, and Greta felt Alvin shrink into her side. Cecil remained stiff, staring straight ahead, his chin lifted a tad. He was trying so hard to be strong.

"Do we have to stay here?" Virgil asked.

"It will be fine," Greta lied. Squinting, she could make out the rooftops of Kipper's Grove. Located just beyond the south side of town, Grove House wasn't far away, and yet Eleanor, Oscar, and Officer Hargrove seemed far beyond the reach of helping Greta and the boys.

Rolling to a stop before the looming structure, Greta and the boys stared up at it. From the outside, Grove House looked hospitable enough. It was made of brick, rising two stories with an attic window in the roof's peak. A wing jutted out toward the east, and a porch extended its entire length with whitewashed rails and balustrade and decorative arches. The lane leading to the building merged into a neatly laid brick drive that circled around to the front entrance. The patch of lawn that made up the center of the circle boasted a rock-bordered flower garden with rosebushes.

"See? It's rather pretty." Greta's words fell flat on the boys' ears, and she couldn't blame them. Pretty on the outside didn't mean living there would be pretty.

She caught sight of a woman, perhaps in her early thirties, ambling down a path just shy of the woods that bordered the property. She was dressed in drab clothes, her hair pinned away from her face but with loose strands. The woman didn't acknowledge Greta beyond a small smile. A sad smile. The weight of her life at Grove House seemed to communicate her apologies that Greta had arrived here.

Mr. Flincheon and his two men helped Greta and her brothers from the wagon. Then they scooped up the trunk Greta had hastily filled with their few belongings and keepsakes.

"If Leo is found, you'll make certain he's informed about where we are?" Greta pleaded.

Mr. Flincheon's "Of course" didn't at all sound convincing.

They climbed the porch steps, and the front door was opened by a stern-looking man. He looked Greta and the boys up and down, then offered a polite smile to Mr. Flincheon. "The Mercy family, I presume?"

"Yes, Mr. Taylor." Mr. Flincheon shook the man's hand. "Unfortunately, the other boy is still missing."

"Well then, our prayers will continue." There was no emotion in the man's voice, so Greta felt neither warmed nor encouraged. "Come with me, Miss Mercy." He motioned for them to follow.

Alvin and Virgil each took one of her hands.

Mr. Taylor tipped his head toward the men carrying Greta's trunk. "You may leave that in the vestibule. We'll have it retrieved shortly."

Greta and her brothers followed Mr. Taylor into his office. A curvaceous, prim woman stood by his desk, her hands folded in front of her.

"Mrs. Gaylord, this is Miss Mercy and her brothers, Cecil, Alvin, and Virgil," Mr. Taylor said.

She offered a half smile. "Welcome to Grove House."

Mr. Taylor eased into the chair behind his desk and gestured for Greta to be seated. "You understand that your being brought here is completely voluntary."

Greta coughed back a choke.

Mr. Taylor gave her a sharp look. His lips thinned. "Since the War Between the States and the passing of the fourteenth amendment, there is no longer 'involuntary servitude.' You have simply been given hospitality from the county due to your lack of funds to meet the rental agreement with your landlord and because of . . . *concerns* as to your welfare, your *mental* well-being, Miss Mercy, and that of the boys therein."

Greta swallowed hard, her throat aching from the day's events.

"We are not an institution," Mr. Taylor continued. "We are not state-funded. This is a county home and should be perceived as such—a home. Whereas you are free to come and go as desired, we strongly discourage it. Within the safety of these walls, many outlets are provided for you to contribute with your labors, as can the children, without returning to Kipper's Grove to seek out employment."

"So I am not to seek employment?" Greta asked. This seemed counterproductive to her.

Mrs. Gaylord interjected, "We only want the best for our residents." She avoided the question and moved on, ignoring Greta's confusion. "Now, the second floor of Grove House is for women. You, Miss Mercy, will find a bed there. We will issue the boys cots in the children's room at the far end of the east wing."

"No!" Alvin piped up. He straightened in his chair and sent a panicked look at Greta.

Greta reached for her brother's hand and leveled a firm gaze on Mr. Taylor. "My brothers and I are not to be separated."

"I'm afraid you have little choice in the matter. They are not infants, nor are they toddlers, nor are you their mother."

"I am their guardian. And as you said, I am free to go." Greta stood then, the boys leaping to stand beside her. Mr. Taylor rose as well.

"But you've nowhere *to* go, Miss Mercy. I find it difficult to imagine you would take your beloved siblings to live on the streets of Kipper's Grove. Unless perhaps you wish to emphasize the concern over your recent lack of judgment?" He waited. Greta didn't reply. "No? And if you did, the authorities would merely bring you back here out of the goodness of their hearts. You need shelter. The landlord will have already re-claimed the shack your parents rented, where you have been blessed to stay until now. You'll also need food. Your brothers are obviously underfed."

Mrs. Gaylord moved toward them, her skirts rustling against the hardwood floor. "Come now. Let me show you to your room." She extended her hand toward the boys.

"No!" Virgil flung his arms around Greta's waist. "I won't leave my sister."

Alvin joined his younger brother, clinging to Greta's waist with his scrawny arms. "Me neither." He glared at Mrs. Gaylord, who cast a helpless look at Mr. Taylor. Cecil joined them by placing his hand on Alvin's shoulder. His quiet, unspoken strength made Greta's heart break further. She had failed him. Failed *them*.

Mr. Taylor rounded the desk and crouched to face the boys eye to eye. He tried to sound kind, but Greta heard the underlying layer of steel. "Now, boys, you don't want to make this harder on your sister, do you? Be good little men and be strong for her. You will all be in the same building. We're not separating you but merely giving you your own places to sleep."

Virgil looked up with teary eyes at Greta and sniffed, silently weighing Mr. Taylor's words.

Alvin, on the other hand, lifted his chin and, with every defiant ounce of his soul, spit in the older man's face.

14

Kit

OCTOBER, PRESENT DAY

Mrs. Alpharetta Green's house was a simple white Victorian in the heart of downtown Kipper's Grove. The historical Barlowe mansion wasn't far away, and it was just across the street from the theater. Kit could see its magnificent brick form rising to its turreted glory. The Barlowes had always ruled over Kipper's Grove in one way or another. Strangely that hadn't really stopped, only they'd grown quiet over the decades. Working in the background, avoiding publicity, allowing people like Madison's grandfather to pick up the slack when it came to big business and small-town celebrity.

"Are you sure we're not getting in Detective Seamans's way?" Kit pressed as Evan drove the two of them to Mrs. Green's house. "I don't want to mess anything up in case he can find Madison."

"We won't get in his way. He has jurisdiction over Madison's case, but he won't be digging into the historical angles. There's no reason for him to—at least not with the evidence at hand."

"But he has the same evidence you do." Evan was muddling her already discombobulated mind.

"Right, but he's going to take the frontal approach to the investigation. He'll interview witnesses. He'll question Al Farrington—Madison's grandfather, right?" At Kit's nod, Evan continued, "Yeah, so Mr. Farrington will be high on the list. They'll do another round investigating the theater, see if there's anything they missed. The police have already put out a BOLO for Madison—a 'Be on the Lookout'—and everyone will call the station with any potential leads. You think Seamans will take the time to read Mrs. Green's book in which she tosses out rumors of tunnels beneath the historic theater?"

Kit nodded. Evan had a point. Or did he? "But there's literally nothing to connect Madison's disappearance to the break-in at the pantry. Or my accident."

"The police will agree with you. The only thing to link them maybe would be *you*. And you're irrelevant to her disappearance. *I'd* be more of a suspect than you are."

Kit hadn't argued further. Parts of Evan's theory made sense, while other parts sounded like fanciful speculation, content for the TV show. Although, come to think of it, they were remarkably absent one cameraman and one ghost huntress. She took a second to consider that.

Evan's SUV door slammed shut, and it jolted Kit back to the moment. She'd had a good night's sleep. Her headache was mostly gone, but her muscles were still sore, not allowing Kit to forget the accident from two days prior.

She exited Evan's vehicle, and he came around to meet her. He raised his brows and tilted his head in the direction of Mrs. Green's home. "You ready?"

"She's going to love this." Kit wasn't ready. She knew Mrs. Green by reputation only. The woman was probably as superstitious as Heather Grant. "Where *is* Heather?" Kit added aloud.

Evan shot her a quick glance as they approached the porch.

"She's recovering. It always takes her a good day or two after a walk. Especially when she gets sick."

"She's sick?" Kit didn't mean to sound rude. She just didn't understand.

Evan shook his head. "Remember she claims that negative energies—maybe a spirit supposedly—followed her back to her hotel. And it takes a while for her to expel them . . . or whatever she does."

"Exorcism?" Kit stopped and stared at Evan.

He faced her on the bottom porch step and laughed. "No. Those are for serious possessions—or so I'm told."

"A ghost following you back to your hotel isn't serious?" Kit challenged, not quite believing she was even discussing such a weird topic.

"Sure, assuming it actually happens. A ghost following you anywhere could be serious, I guess. But that's not what exorcisms are about."

Kit smiled. "Spoken like an expert."

"Heather would beg to differ." Evan winked, and for a second, Kit caught her breath. Evan scaled the rest of the porch steps in one leap, opened the screen door, and knocked on the main door.

Two narrow, stained-glass windows bordered each side of the entrance, and Kit saw movement behind one.

"Just a minute," a woman's voice called, tinged with the vibrato of age.

When she opened the door, Kit was surprised by how petite Mrs. Green was. She looked to be around five feet in height. Her brown hair was peppered with gray, permed into a Midwestern woman's hairdo that was meant to be easy to care for. Not fancy but presentable. Mrs. Green gave a pleasant smile as she dried her hands on a green dish towel. "You are Evan Fischer!" she announced.

"Guilty." He offered one of his own charming grins.

"I've watched your show, and I have to say, you bring up some good arguments, even though I don't agree with your attempts at debunking the paranormal."

"Why, thank you." Evan's response was paired with a chuckle.

Mrs. Green turned to Kit. "You're not Miss Grant, though, are you?"

Kit shook her head. "No, Mrs. Green, I'm Kit Boyd."

"Oh, so you're a Boyd! You're a longtime local, aren't you?" The woman certainly knew her Kipper's Grove history. "Your grandmother and I went to school together."

"Really?" Kit played along with the familiar small talk.

"We sure did!" Mrs. Green snapped her fingers, tucking the dish towel into the waistband of her pants. "She and I went to grade school together. How *is* your grandmother?"

"She passed away last year," Kit answered. "Uterine cancer."

"Oh!" Mrs. Green's face took on a look of pure empathy. "I am so sorry. You know, when you get to be my age, you hear about old classmates passing on, and it just . . . well, death becomes more real, I suppose." She paused, then recovered her happy self. "What can I do for you both today?"

Evan lifted the booklet written by Mrs. Green, the cover facing the elderly author.

Her smile stretched across her face. "It's been a while since someone asked me about that! Many years have passed since it was published."

"Your book is very informative," Evan said.

"Well, that was my intent." Mrs. Green waved toward the chairs on the porch. "Why don't you have a seat? It's such a lovely day, and the house is a mess. I'll bring out some water—or would you prefer iced tea?"

"Tea, please," Kit answered.

"Water is fine," Evan responded.

Minutes later, Mrs. Green settled into a chair across from them. She'd discarded the dish towel and donned a red sweater.

The chair creaked beneath her weight as she sat. "I assume this visit has to do with your show"—she directed her words at Evan—"but I'm surprised there are no cameras here for an interview."

Her hinting didn't influence Evan to give her the spotlight. "Perhaps we can schedule one in the future for that purpose. This is more of a . . . personal quest in the investigation."

"Mmm." Mrs. Green pressed her lips together and nodded knowingly. "I heard about Madison's disappearance. How awful! So you're helping investigate?"

"Well, Mrs. Green—"

"Call me Alpharetta."

"Alpharetta," Evan acknowledged. "We were with Madison when she disappeared. There are a lot of unanswered questions, both regarding our investigation of the theater's supposed ghosts and the welfare of Madison herself."

Alpharetta shook her head, catching Kit's eyes. Kit believed the sincerity in the woman's gaze. "I cannot fathom what could have happened to her. To just vanish like that? Really, in all my years leading tours of the theater at night, never did such a thing happen."

Evan lifted the booklet again. "I read in here there are tunnels that run from the Barlowe mansion to the theater, is that right?"

Alpharetta took a sip of her tea and swallowed, nodding. "The evidence is lacking, though. It has always been rumored, but never proven."

"No?"

"No. The original blueprints for the theater show nothing to indicate a tunnel or tunnels beneath it."

"Then why write about it in your book?"

She laughed. "Well, aside from it being a good story, I found it completely feasible. I even wonder if there are some who *do* know where the tunnels are but simply continue the secretive tradition! That theater is rife with story. From the moment they built it, nothing went right. It was as though it was . . . cursed? Riddled with bad luck?"

"Such as?" Kit slid to the edge of her chair.

Alpharetta took another sip. "Well, if you read the book, you'll recall there's the worker who was killed during the theater's construction, the woman in white and her infant who supposedly died in the theater, and of course the lost boys."

"Lost boys?" Evan cocked his head to the left.

"Sounds like Peter Pan, doesn't it?" She held up a finger. "But it has nothing to do with Neverland. No. Apparently, shortly after the opening of the theater, a couple of boys broke in and then disappeared there."

"Disappeared?" Kit perked up at the word. It was too similar to Madison's circumstances.

"Mm-hmm. And for the next week, some claimed they were hearing the boys—in the walls, beneath the floor. Banging on pipes. Hard to tell. It's such a maze beneath the theater."

"I've been to the basement. It's easy to find one's way around," Kit argued gently.

"Not the basement. No. The tunnels under the seats."

"I thought you said there isn't any proof of tunnels?" Evan interjected.

"Not to the Barlowe mansion, but there *are* tunnels under the theater seats. Mostly for heating. Ductwork, I suppose, although no one called it that. Rows upon rows of seats, rows upon rows of connecting tunnels through the floor and even the walls. Tunnels large enough for boys looking for trouble to get into, and dark enough for them to get lost in the maze. Not many people owned flashlights back in those days, and if they did, the batteries wouldn't have lasted long."

"But how could they not find the boys?" Kit was confused. "Wouldn't they just search the ductwork?"

"Considering it was 1915," Alpharetta responded, "there

were no camera systems, no heat-tracing devices, no electronic aid, nothing. They were going by the five senses, well, and common sense, and that was all. But the boys could get lost—and they did. Later, the banging stopped, the crying stopped, and no one ever found them."

"Never?" Evan asked.

"No. Never. They were just gone." Alpharetta snapped her fingers. "Of course, since then, people say they occasionally hear them. Crying. Shouting. Banging on pipes. Although it's ghostly now. The boys are long since dead."

Evan leaned forward in his chair. "Is there any reason someone today wouldn't want us looking into the rumors of ghosts and tunnels at the Barlowe Theater, the stories surrounding the place?"

Kit looked at him in surprise.

Alpharetta didn't seem at all bothered by the question. Instead, she shrugged and said, "Doubtful. Not now anyway. The Barlowes in decades past might have been. They always had their undies in a bunch. But now it's just Dean and Selma Barlowe, the great-grandchildren of the Barlowes who built the theater. And they're humble people, supportive of the historical preservation Madison is so passionate about. The only one who might be upset still would be Al Farrington, but he wouldn't go so far as to make his own granddaughter disappear!"

"Why is there such tension between Al and his granddaughter?" Evan asked, even though Kit knew he already had his own theories about that.

Alpharetta leaned back in her seat and crossed her legs. "Aside from their petty and dysfunctional family dynamics since before forever? Because Al hates any attention being given to the historical downtown district, while Madison is the queen of drawing attention to the district. Which attracts the activists and the history buffs, who crawl out of the woodwork and cause Al problems with his expansion efforts downtown. He's not interested in *preserving* anything. He's interested in the cheapest, most efficient way to build and make money." She looked at Kit. "Remember that apartment complex he built a few years ago overlooking the river?"

Kit nodded.

"Well, it overlooked the historic section of the river that runs through the old train yard and toward the park area, also historic. A lot of weddings take place there. Vintage photography. There's even the Spring Cotillion held in the park each year, just as it was back in the day. Having a lofty, contemporary complex looking down over the area and as a backdrop was not what anyone wanted. But it makes money, brings people to the area. Farrington is all about his business and boosting economics. To him, history stands in the way of progress and the future."

Kit winced. "I remember all of that."

"As to your original question," Alpharetta said, shifting her focus back on Evan. "Al would be the one to put up the biggest stink. But again, not at the risk of his granddaughter's welfare. The man may not have great business ethics, but he does have morals."

"Does he?" Evan challenged.

Alpharetta caught her breath and stared at him. "Well, I suppose we all have the potential to surprise each other, don't we?"

A photograph of Madison greeted Kit as she opened the coffee shop door, the little bell ringing overhead. It was a large poster, set up on an easel.

"Kit!" The watery voice shouted over the voices that echoed off the tile floors and vaulted ceilings.

Kit spotted a hand waving at her from the counter. Madison's younger sister, Avery. At nineteen, she was supposed to be out of state, attending college and earning her bachelor's in liberal arts.

"Avery!" Kit hurried toward the young woman, ignoring Evan, who stayed on her heels. Reaching her, Kit and Avery embraced, and she sensed the fear in Avery's body as she clung to Kit.

Sniffing, Avery pulled back, brushing her eyes with her fingertips to clear the tears. "I'm sorry."

"Don't be!" Kit wiped her own eyes. The sight of Avery was ghostly in itself. She was Madison's mini-me. Eight years apart, Kit remembered when Avery was born. She and Madison had been young girls who played mommy with Avery, stopping just shy of changing the baby girl's diapers. Now? Avery was willowy with long, highlighted blond locks, large blue eyes, and a porcelain complexion.

"You came home!" Kit moved in for another embrace. She had to. Avery was beginning to shake, and Kit was concerned that the woman would collapse if she didn't.

"Of course I came home," Avery hiccuped, her voice breaking. She pulled away and eyed Evan, who stood silently by. "You were with Madison? When she disappeared?"

Evan dipped his head in a nod. "I was. I'm very sorry."

"She's not dead!" Avery snapped.

"I didn't mean—"

"Avery." Kit put a calming hand on Avery's elbow, moving her gently away from her missing sister's poster. Another coffee shop customer stopped Avery for a brief hug and an offer of prayers. They moved along, and Kit convinced Avery to sit down at a square table with mismatched wooden chairs. "What about school?" she asked.

"What about it?" Avery's chin quivered, and she rummaged through her leather backpack for a tissue. Evan slid a clean one across the table toward her. Avery glanced at him, then looked sheepish. "Oh. Thank you." She took the tissue and directed her attention back to Kit. "School isn't important right now. I spoke with my adviser, and the university is giving me an extension on my assignments."

"That's good," Kit said.

Avery leaned forward, clutching the tissue in her hand. "Where is Madi? Where is she, Kit?"

"I don't know." Kit's voice wobbled.

Evan's chair dragged on the floor tiles as he pulled it out to sit down. "I take it there's no new developments?"

Avery shook her head. "It's been a few days now. Each hour that ticks by . . . well, I've watched enough TV to know what that means."

"No one is saying that a crime's been committed," Kit argued.

"What else could it be? Madi wouldn't just *leave*. Even our grandfather is getting anxious, and you *know* nothing upsets him. Nothing."

"How are your parents?" Kit reached for Avery's hand.

Avery clung to her fingers. "They're a wreck. Dad is flying in from Arizona with his new wife. Mom is popping her medications like they're candy." Their parents divorced when Avery was fourteen. Her mom blamed her attachment to her medications on the divorce. Her dad blamed the divorce on the medications. "Grandpa is going to put up a reward for any information on Madi's disappearance. The police aren't saying much, but Grandpa told me this morning they're confused as . . ." She stammered to a halt. "They're confused," she finished minus Al Farrington's notorious use of coarse words.

"It's not a typical abduction scenario," Evan supplied.

Avery finally took the time to look at him. "You're that guy from the show?"

"Yes."

"An ex-cop, right?"

"Detective."

"What do *you* think happened?" Avery shifted in her chair and leaned toward him. "You were there. What happened?"

Evan waited as the barista called out someone's triple soy caramel latte with an extra shot. "I have a lot of questions. There's no evidence of foul play. Why? She was there one minute, and the next was gone."

"You *all* disappeared for a bit," Kit reminded him.

"No," Evan corrected. "We were out of earshot. There's a difference."

"So what do we do now?" Avery leveled an expectant gaze on Evan that surprised Kit. "I mean, what would *you* do to find my sister?"

"We need to put the puzzle together. Starting with seeing what we can find out about the history of the theater that Madison was digging into. And see if there's any connection between Madison and the vandalism at the food pantry, not to mention the accident."

"What accident?" Avery looked between Evan and Kit.

Kit chose her words carefully. "I was in an accident two days ago."

"Oh my gosh!" Avery's hands flew to her mouth. "Are you all right?"

"A mild concussion, but it felt like I was plowed into by a semi. I'll be fine, though. Anyway, Evan thinks it's linked somehow to Madison."

"What? I don't understand," Avery said.

"I know. It doesn't have any grounds in logic, but—"

"Actually," Evan interrupted, "it does."

"How does that help us find Madi?" Avery's brows pulled together.

Kit looked to Evan. She wondered too.

"It may lead to nothing, but trust me, this is what I do."

15

Thankfully, her ants hadn't died. Kit shut her apartment door with her foot, anxiously peering into the ant farm. They moved about as if nothing had happened in the world outside their plexiglass-framed farm. After spending two nights at her parents' house, Kit was back home. Her place seemed still, closed up, and silent as she padded across the carpet, past the open kitchen and into the small living room.

Hours earlier, Evan had left her at the coffee shop with Avery. A meeting with his producer, he'd claimed, plus he needed to check in on Heather. It made sense. He wasn't in town to be *her* sidekick, but when he left, Kit hated to admit she felt the absence of his confidence, if nothing else. She'd finished her day with Avery, stapling posters to telephone poles and pinning them on bulletin boards. As if the people of Kipper's Grove, a small town, didn't know who Madison Farrington was and that she'd been missing. The looks she and Avery received from people were a mix of pity and sympathy as though Madison were already dead. Somewhere.

If she'd been abducted from a parking lot, it'd be easier to imagine such a scenario. Search teams would traverse grids of fields. Dogs would be out sniffing for Madison's scent. Maybe the FBI would be called in to help.

But this? Disappearing while on a ghost tour in the basement of a haunted historic theater? It sounded like a bad horror movie from the nineties.

Kit shoved her feet into slippers and flopped onto the couch, restless. She snatched up a throw pillow and turned on the TV. She maneuvered to the science channel, hoping for a documentary on insects. She'd even accept one on arachnids. Or canines. Any *creature*. There was a predictable chain of life and death in the world of insects and animals. It was predator and prey. Macabre and yet that's just the way it was.

Maybe that was why she was drawn to leggy creatures. Most people found them creepy, crawly, and everything gross. Kit found them relaxing. They had a mission, they went about performing that mission, and aside from cannibalistic spiders— which of course weren't insects—most were of the mind to care for their hive or grouping.

The documentary she was watching focused on the Sahara Desert. Kit settled back on the couch. She was fine with the Sahara. Anything but a show or movie that featured a beautiful heroine and a quirky best friend. She would give anything right now to be following Madison around, even if that meant Madison grabbed Evan Fischer's attention while Kit faded into the background.

Kit grimaced at her self-deprecation. Feeling more despondent by the minute, at home by herself, she shouted at her ant farm, "Talk to me!"

They didn't answer her, of course. She shook her head. She probably should have stayed at her parents' house.

Kit's phone rang and vibrated simultaneously, and she yelped. Wrestling it out of the pocket of her leggings, she answered it.

"Hello?"

The call either had cut off or simply wasn't connecting.

"Hello? This is Kit." She held the phone away from her face to look at the screen. She didn't recognize the number. Probably a spam robocall. It was *always* spam when there was a long pause after she answered.

"I'm hanging up now," Kit stated, moving to end the call.

"Don't."

The whisper sent chills through Kit.

"Who is this?" she demanded.

Labored breathing, but not obscenely. It was steady but heavy, reminding Kit of someone who suffered from asthma.

"Who is this?" she repeated.

"Don't."

"Don't what?" Kit sat up straight on the couch. "I said, don't what?"

More heavy breathing, followed by a low chuckle. "Don't," the voice said once more, and then the line went dead.

Kit began shaking. "Hello? Hello!" Nothing. She looked at the phone's screen to see the call had disconnected. The device trembled in her hand.

Without thinking, she dialed Evan's number. It was instinctive. He would believe everything she told him. He would know what to do. Except there was no answer.

Kit bolted from the couch, ignoring the remnants of pain that sliced through her head at the fast movement. She raced to the kitchen, searching for where she'd dropped her keys after returning home.

No way. No way was she staying here alone. Even though the call had nothing to do with where she was located and everything to do with the phone in her pocket. Hurrying to her bedroom, Kit tugged a sweatshirt from her closet, slipping it over her head for extra warmth. She kicked off her slippers and stuffed her feet into slip-on tennis shoes. She grabbed the stuffed cat she'd slept with since she was ten and jammed it in her pillowcase. Kit didn't care that she was nearing thirty and still slept with a stuffie.

She was going back to Mom and Dad's. Granted, she wouldn't

sleep at the end of their bed like she had when she was ten—
she had her stuffed cat now—but there was no way she'd stay
here in her apartment, alone, waiting for an ax murderer to
arrive at her door. And the way this week was going? It *might*
happen.

Within moments, she'd loaded a plastic laundry basket with
extra clothes, her bathroom necessities, and then, hesitating,
she retrieved her ant farm. It seemed cruel to leave them again.
Ax murderers probably got their start stomping on anthills.
Her six-legged pets were her only company, and somehow her
apartment felt violated now. Invaded. She would not leave her
helpless ants at the mercy of the evil, hoarse chuckler.

Her phone rang again, shivering against her leg. Kit froze,
the laundry basket and her keys in her hands. She'd jammed
her phone back into her pocket. She would have to set everything down to answer it.

Fine.

Resting the basket on the bed and dropping her keys, Kit
grappled for her phone. She looked at the screen.

It was the same number.

No way.

No. No. Never. No.

"You didn't call the police?" Kit's dad eyed her incredu-
lously as she deposited her laundry basket on the entryway
floor. She'd carefully wedged the ant farm in the basket so it
wouldn't tip over.

Her mom, Kris, closed the door behind her, and Kit noticed
she locked it as well.

"I didn't know what to do," Kit told her parents. "I just
wanted to get out of my apartment as soon as I could."

"Well, I'm calling the police," her dad stated.

"Ford, wait." Kris waved down her husband, but he shook his head sternly.

"This isn't something to wait on." He marched down the hallway toward their large kitchen and disappeared around the corner.

Kit looked at her mom. "I'm sorry."

"Oh, honey, that's what we're here for!"

"No, I'm sorry because I brought my ant farm with me." Kit pointed to it, carefully tucked among her clothes in the laundry basket.

Kris paled a bit. "Oh. Well. They may be the closest to grand-babies I get."

They laughed nervously, and her mother embraced her and held her for a moment longer than usual. "Let's get you settled back in your room."

Just minutes later, the doorbell rang.

"Kit!" her father bellowed from the first level of the house.

Kit and her mother exchanged looks.

"The cops were fast in getting here," Kris observed.

"I know." Somehow that didn't feel like a good thing. The urgency they'd put into coming to the Boyds' home was a little disconcerting.

Two officers stood in the entryway when Kit and her mom descended the stairs. After the introductions, and once Kit had answered the officers' questions to their satisfaction, a call was placed to Detective Seamans.

"This is a nightmare." Kit sat at the kitchen table as the detective arrived and shook hands with Ford. He then turned sympathetic eyes on Kit.

"I'm sorry this is happening," the detective said. "You've had a rough week." He slid out a chair and sat opposite her.

"Coffee?" Kris offered.

"Please." Detective Seamans drew in a deep breath, leveling a serious look on Kit. "You didn't recognize the voice?"

"No." Kit picked at a chipped thumbnail. "It was creepy."

"Male?"

"Yes. I think. Or maybe . . . did you see that movie where it was a girl murdering everyone, but her voice sounded like a guy's because she had a voice-box thing on her throat to alter her voice?"

Seamans cleared his throat. "Uh, no, I haven't seen it. About the call, we'll need to trace the number, although my guess is the person used a burner phone."

Ford leaned against their antique oak buffet, his arms crossed over his broad chest. His beard was trimmed but riddled with gray. His hair was thin on the top of his head, but his brown eyes were soft when they skimmed over Kit, only hardening with intensity when they landed on the detective.

"Do you think this is related to Madi's disappearance?" Kit asked.

The detective heaved a sigh. "I don't know, but a lot of this isn't adding up. Not with Madi, not with your accident, and not with the recent break-in at the pantry. Normally I'd say they're not related, but now? This call? It all seems to circle back to you."

Kit didn't like the idea that she was the common denominator. But if that were true, why would Madison be the one to vanish and not her? She decided to ask.

"Because she's close to you maybe?" Ford offered before the detective could answer.

"Could be." Detective Seamans nodded. "We just don't have much to go on at this point." He shifted his attention back to Kit. "What do you know of this TV show Madi invited here? What about its staff?"

"Not much," Kit answered. Her thumbnail was ripping under her incessant picking. She was too nervous to quit. "Like I said the night she disappeared, having them come was Madi's attempt to add value to the theater. So her grandfather would leave it alone."

"Did you do background checks on any of the people working the show?" Ford asked.

Kris placed a hot mug of coffee in front of Detective Seamans and shot her husband a look. "Evan Fischer can't be involved in this."

"He checks out," the detective confirmed. "Everyone did. I was just curious if you knew anything, Kit, that might point me in another direction."

She wished her mom had brought her a cup of coffee. Kit glanced at her, and Kris straightened, reading the request in Kit's eyes. "I'll get you a cup too, honey."

Kit nodded, then turned to Detective Seamans. There was no reason not to share Evan's theories with the man, so she quickly filled him in on the ideas he had about the secret tunnels and the possibility that everything was linked.

Detective Seamans took it all in without changing his expression. His index finger tapped on the ceramic mug emblazoned with deer antlers on the side.

Kris handed Kit her cup of coffee, and she wrapped her hands around it to warm them and keep them from trembling.

"He's got a good head on his shoulders," Detective Seamans observed. "And Evan is right. I can't go chasing down any so-called leads that might influence the case unless there's a clear reason to. What concerns me is that you're being specifically targeted. Does the caller's comment, *Don't*, mean anything to you?"

"No." Kit hadn't sipped her coffee yet. She was afraid it would splash over the rim because her hands were still shaking.

Detective Seamans blew out a breath. "Well, I want you to get ahold of us immediately if you receive any more calls like this. Anything that strikes you as suspicious."

"Do you think she's being stalked?" Kris couldn't disguise the waver in her voice.

The detective shot her a grim but comforting smile. He looked to Ford. "We can't be too careful."

Kit noticed the men exchange that unspoken vow to protect their own no matter what. It didn't make her feel any better. Well, it *did*. Having a father who cared so much had been a good argument against her fear of abandonment and had instilled in her a thin thread of belief that her value wasn't based on conditions. However, the threats coming from the caller, the accident, the food pantry, plus what had happened at the Barlowe Theater—they were real, lurking. And there was something dark and wicked about it all.

Like a silent, black shadow, whatever seemed to be lingering in the basement and behind the walls of the old theater, it was on the prowl, spreading toward Kit. It was hungry, wanting, needing. A curse that had remained dormant for too long in a building that held terrible secrets . . . until the curse could no longer be contained. It had devoured Madison, and it felt—at least in this nighttime moment—as though Kit would be next.

16

Greta

She woke up screaming. Thrashing at the sheet tangled around her. Moonlight shafted through tall windows opposite her cot, the panes resembling prison bars.

"Miss Mercy, Miss Mercy." A woman's voice urged her from her nighttime terror.

Greta gasped for breath, clenching her sweat-drenched nightgown. The image of the woman came into focus. It was the woman who had been walking outside of Grove House when they'd arrived. In the shadows of the night, her dark hair made her face almost ethereally white.

"She goin' to shut up?" a woman crowed from the far end of the room.

Greta noticed that she'd acquired an audience. It was her first night in the poorhouse. A few women had sat up in their cots. One was standing. The woman who had awakened Greta was sitting on the edge of Greta's cot, making the mattress dip.

"Go back to sleep. All of you," the woman instructed.

There was some grumbling. Some moaning. A sob came

from somewhere in the corner. A woman was crying, and it wasn't because of Greta's disturbance. There was hopelessness in her choked sobs as she attempted to stifle them.

"Are you all right now, Miss Mercy?" the woman at her side asked.

"I'm sorry," Greta whispered.

"Don't be. Everyone has night terrors here from time to time." Her eyes were sad, even by the light of the moon. "I am Alma."

"Greta." Night terrors made formalities unnecessary, it seemed. "Are you from Kipper's Grove?"

Alma gave a short shake of her head, then smoothed the braid that hung over her shoulder. She looked around as if to make sure the other women had settled back into their slumber. "You've had a difficult day," she observed. "The first is always the most overwhelming."

Greta felt her eyes burn with unshed tears. Alvin. Virgil. Cecil. She wanted her brothers so desperately that the pain was almost palpable. And Leo . . . her breath caught in a sob.

"There, there." Alma laid a soft hand on Greta's shoulder.

"I'm sorry." Greta sniffed. "My brothers—"

"You'll see them in the morning," Alma assured. "This isn't a fine establishment. There's no way around that truth. Mostly because the folks who come and go here are . . . different. But no one cares. Most of us are alone. You have your brothers, just in the other wing. Take heart in that."

"My brother Leo is missing," Greta confided in a hushed whisper of desperation. "And my brother Gerard died early this spring. My parents are both gone. I-I don't know how to keep us together. I need to find Leo."

"Shhh . . ." Alma smoothed back Greta's hair in a sisterly sort of way. Her sorrowful eyes never shifted away from Greta's. "Be thankful they didn't home out your brothers right away. Sometimes they do that. People needing boys for farming and such. Helps pay off debts, so that Grove House has free beds."

Horrified, Greta struggled to sit up. "Home out the boys?"

"Shhhh," Alma murmured again. "Don't fret. Not tonight. Just get some sleep, and the morning will come sure as the next night."

The mattress lifted as Alma stood. She looked down at Greta, her face unreadable in the shadows that stretched over it. "And don't wander—not till it's light out."

"Why?" Greta couldn't help but ask.

Alma glanced at the closed door to the women's ward, then rested her gaze back on Greta. "Sometimes people wander, and they don't come back. Grove House is a house, after all. Not a home."

Greta could not hold on to her brothers tight enough. They had raced down the hallway, ignoring the shouts of one of Grove House's aides and simultaneously throwing themselves into Greta's arms.

"It was awful," Virgil whimpered into Greta's shirtfront. He pulled away and looked up at her with his bright blue eyes. "There was another boy who kept coughing all night long, and then he threw up, and then a worker came and took him out, but only after he scolded the rest of us for being awake!"

"'Course we were awake!" Alvin countered. "Someone hacking up their supper makes everyone awake."

"Cecil?" Greta focused her attention on him. His hair was askew, shaggy and dirty. She had intended to have them bathe tonight—at home. Now . . . "Are you all right?"

"I'm fine." Cecil shrugged, not offering anything further about the previous night. He stood guard behind his brothers, his back ramrod straight.

Alvin scowled. "They're puttin' us to work!"

Greta drew back. She thought of Alma's comment during the night about homing out the boys. Staying in her crouch so she was eye level with Virgil and Alvin, she said, "Alvin, what do you mean, putting you to work?"

"Said if we're stayin' here, we gotta contribute," Cecil explained for his brother. "Guessin' they have wood needin' chopped and hauled for the winter."

"'Cain't have a Grove House without a wood house!'" Virgil said, his voice sassy as he mocked whatever staff member had recited it to them earlier. "I don't want to haul wood." Tears filled the boy's eyes.

"Did they say anything about sending you away?" She wanted to bite her tongue after seeing the fear that flickered in her brothers' eyes.

Cecil gave a curt shake of his head. "No. Nothin' about that."

"We'll be good," Alvin reassured her. "Won't give them no reason to send us away. I'll work hard."

Alvin would be a hard worker, that Greta knew. His reticence stemmed from the fear of the unknown. The authority of someone he'd never met. The separation from Greta.

She squeezed his shoulder and tried to smile bravely. "I know you will. But if you can be courageous, I will go find us another place to stay. Today. I'll see if I can get my old position back at the laundry or maybe find another place to work."

"Maybe working at the Boyds' house? Like Mama?" Alvin provided.

Oscar's and Eleanor's faces flooded her mind. It would horrify them to know she had ended up at Grove House. She also knew there had been no available employment at the Boyd mansion. Oscar might have offered to pay off her debts—whatever they were—to the Barlowes, but she couldn't expect him or Eleanor to rescue her and her brothers from this place.

"I'll see," she answered Alvin, wondering if it wouldn't hurt to ask the Boyds regardless. If it meant keeping her family together, loss of one's pride was a small price to pay for staying with the Boyds, perhaps working among their staff. She brushed his face with her fingertips, then Virgil's, then finally lifted her eyes to meet Cecil's. "I'll do my best. And I'm sorry."

"Not your fault." Cecil crossed his arms over his scrawny chest. "I'll watch the boys. You go on."

Leave the boys at Grove House? The idea was appalling to her, and yet, in spite of the miserable institution with its dour staff, crowded rooms, pitiable fellow inhabitants, and forced labor, at least the boys would be accounted for.

Greta stood slowly and gave her brother a nod. But as she turned her back to them, to face the unknown that awaited her in Kipper's Grove, she caught sight of Alma at the end of the hallway. Alma's body sagged with defeat and sorrow, but her eyes held an unspoken warning.

As Greta approached her, Alma leaned in and whispered, "Don't leave them here too long. They'll disappear."

Greta looked sharply at her. "You said at night—"

"Night. Day. Doesn't matter." Alma glanced over her shoulder. "Always something lurking here at Grove House. It's best to get out if you can."

17

Greta was sure someone followed her as she hiked into Kipper's Grove, but she never saw anyone. The trees waved their colorful fall branches, it seemed not so much in greeting as in warning. What had once felt like home, like a place where she and her family occupied a simple but secure position, now felt as though it had her cornered. She'd seen a mouse cornered once. A stray cat had toyed with it, batting it, flipping it into the air by its tail, wounding it, then playing with it some more. It was torturous to watch, and she had run for Gerard to come rescue the mouse.

"It's just part of life, Greta." His reasoning was sensible but also unacceptable.

It didn't seem right that some were the prey, always dodging and batting away at life, trying to escape its fangs, while others lounged with ease in the sun and in silks, indifferent to the suffering around them. Was it true that there was a limit to human kindness, that serving one's neighbor had little to do with Christian charity and more to do with merit and earning? If so, she had little control with which to leverage, and if asked of Grove House and the county, she had none whatsoever.

The almshouse looked down on Kipper's Grove from its mere two-mile trek outside of town. She made quick work of it, dodging the south side and avoiding people she knew. Her first stop would be her former place of employment. She'd known after her delinquency when Leo went missing that they would have terminated her employment. She hadn't gone back to check. It had been irresponsible, yet she hadn't been in the frame of mind to manage it all. Even now, as she hurried down the sidewalk toward the town's center, she could feel her nerves fraying.

Everywhere she looked, she hoped to see Leo. Maybe he was hiding behind a tree and waiting to jump out and frighten her. Maybe he'd simply gotten distracted and was going to be on the corner selling newspapers. Oh, how she wished he was so absentminded that he would have forgotten for well over a week now to simply come home!

It wasn't so. Barlowe Theater's domed roof jutted above the main street's other buildings, showing off its presence and beauty, its superiority. She hesitated in front of the drugstore, staring down the walk at the iron and glass marquee that advertised one of the first moving pictures ever to be seen in Kipper's Grove. *A Girl of Yesterday*, starring Mary Pickford. Greta didn't know who Miss Pickford was. She did know, however—because Eleanor had told her—that there was a rooftop room in the theater for the 597 pipes that were connected to the Wurlitzer organ in the pit near the stage. There was a toy counter in the same room with tambourines, Eleanor said, and bells and chimes and everything needed for the organist to add sound and effects to the silent films.

She would never see it. Never see a silent film.

"It's quite the sight, is it not?" A woman's voice at her shoulder startled Greta. She stepped to the side as the older woman, with her gray hair crimped and assigned into a perfect updo, looked at her with curious black eyes. Her hat was a shimmering peacock blue with a visor to shield her eyes from the sun, its side bent upward like a cresting wave. A green feather protruded past it and emphasized the green-embroidered trim of her elegant, sleek dress.

Greta was tongue-tied. She had never met Mrs. Frances Barlowe, but she knew this was her because she'd seen her before from afar. She had never *wanted* to meet a Barlowe again after her altercation and subsequent charge from Mr. Barlowe. His brutish person was intimidating.

Mrs. Barlowe offered her a grim smile touched with a bit of sarcasm. "When my husband, Rufus, got rich, he got boring."

Greta's eyes widened at the blatant statement.

Mrs. Barlowe laughed lightly and pointed to the marquee. "Do you see that? He spent thousands of our hard-earned dollars to, what, bring a picture that moves to the theater and enthrall over six hundred fools into watching the actress run around in a circle?" Her second laugh was musical, her powdery cheeks blushed with a pansy pink Greta doubted was natural. "Did you know there's a train coming all the way from the state's capital this Friday night for the Pickford opening? My husband always imagined besting the capital city, and now he's done it. They'll arrive in swarms on dinner cars, dine like drunken nitwits, and then tip their noses up so high that if it rains, I daresay they will drown."

A pointed look at Greta concluded Mrs. Barlowe's statement.

Greta remained speechless. It was too rude to walk away, and it was unheard of to respond. There was no safe response.

Mrs. Barlowe studied her for a moment. "You're the girl who made last week's performance interesting, now, aren't you?"

Greta choked, lifting her hand to her mouth to guard her lips.

Mrs. Barlow's shrewd smile was tinged with humor. "You made that evening worth remembering. While I'm thankful no *infant* was mortally injured, I do wish my husband would find the humor in it all. So dreadfully boring, he finds nothing of real life funny, and everything of film and performance, prestige and flaunting to be the epitome of life. Very dull indeed." Mrs. Barlowe adjusted the velvet strings of her purse that hung from her wrist. "Now, tell me, Miss . . . ?"

"Mercy," Greta supplied.

"Miss Mercy. How delightful. You look as though the Barlowe legacy of fame and fortune has hitched you to the back of our wagons and dragged you through the mud. Is that so?"

Greta wouldn't have minded had the ground opened and swallowed her. She glanced down the street. Pedestrians moved this way and that, everyone having places to go. Motorcars competed with buckboards and carriages for the right of way on the brick street. A horse was hitched to an iron lamppost, and a fine-looking lady looked on it with disgust. A child ran past them, his mother delicately hollering after the wayward child in hopes of stopping him, but to no avail.

"I see you've no wish to answer me." Mrs. Barlowe continued the conversation despite Greta's stunned silence. "I saw you standing here staring at the theater, and for a moment I felt pity for you."

Greta's head came up. "Pity?"

"Mmm, yes. Your brother went missing, did he not? In our theater?"

"Yes, ma'am."

"And I gather the search has all but been called off. Little effort is put into finding vandalizing hooligans who likely rushed home shortly after, whose families simply haven't reported them as being safely home."

"My brother has not come home," Greta said with conviction. It wasn't her place to speak her mind to Mrs. Barlowe, but the woman was being presumptuous. There was the loss, the brutal unknown that ate at Greta's soul.

Mrs. Barlowe turned to fully acknowledge Greta. She stood an inch or so taller than her, probably due to her heeled, patent-leather shoes. "We all endure suffering, my dear, silently or otherwise." She reached out with a gloved hand and patted Greta's cheek. Then she took Greta's hand in hers. "Silent suffering must be met with stubborn determination to survive."

Greta felt something cold press into her palm.

Mrs. Barlowe drew her hand back and reached into her handbag as Greta looked down in confusion at the key the older woman had left in her hand. A calling card was extended to Greta, who took it, knowing that questions permeated every line and crease in her face.

Mrs. Barlowe leaned closer and lowered her voice. "My card, should you ever need validation that you have my permission." And with that, Mrs. Barlowe proceeded down the walk toward the theater, the silk of her green dress shimmering in the sunlight.

Greta stared down at the key. A key for what? She looked at the calling card.

Mrs. Frances Barlowe
2 Pitchcock Lane
Kipper's Grove
Telephone: KG-28913

Why Mrs. Barlowe would choose to give Greta her calling card was a mystery. She owed the Barlowes restitution! Mr. Barlowe loathed her very existence. They had done nothing to help find Leo.

Bewildered, Greta clutched the key and slipped the card into the pocket of her dress. She could hardly assume Mrs. Barlowe meant to be any sort of benefactress. Still, something inside Greta made her dwell on the idea that she held Mrs. Barlowe's key . . . to something. Somewhere. And that maybe this *somewhere* held the answer to finding Leo.

"Greta! Oh, Greta!" Eleanor sang. She scurried after Greta, her shoes slapping against the walk as she chased Greta with as much ladylike decorum as she could muster.

Greta had come from the launderer, where she'd been sent away with a rude refusal to take into consideration her absence due to her brother's tragic disappearance. No matter, they had told her. Work had to be done, and if not, she could live out her last years in the poorhouse for all they cared.

Little did they know . . .

Greta ducked her head and tried to pretend she hadn't heard Eleanor calling her name. She had detoured from downtown to walk along a street lined with beautiful homes. Maples and oaks arched over the street. Fine greenery was beautifully manicured in the front lawns, porches were adorned with pots of ferns and chrysanthemums. It was a gentle street, the homes of families who were together, who shared a meal at the table, who felt their own personal worth in society, in their churches, in the circles of people around them.

"Greta?" Eleanor cried again. This time she was much closer, and Greta knew feigning not to hear would not only be unbelievable but also be unbelievably rude. She stopped and waited, turning and then wishing for the second time that day that the ground would eat her forever. Oscar trailed behind his impetuous sister, whose elbow stuck out in the air as she held down her sunburst yellow hat while she trotted.

Coming upon Greta, Eleanor released a breathless smile. "You're walking as if you're trying to get away from me!"

"Of course not," Greta lied and immediately felt the pang of guilt. It was becoming far too familiar now, this guilt. Guilt over trying to be more than she was worth had only emphasized how of little value she truly was.

She caught Oscar's eye as he approached. He smiled kindly, and she wondered if the kindness in his eyes would disappear if he learned of Grove House.

"You silly goose!" Eleanor huffed. "I've been trying to find you! If you only had a telephone—"

"Eleanor." Oscar's voice held a tone of reprimand.

She waved him off. "Oh, I know! I'm being rude. Still, Oscar wouldn't let me go looking for you at your home."

Greta glanced at Oscar, who looked down at his shoes.

Eleanor could barely contain her excitement. "We've paid your debt to the Barlowes!" She clapped her hands.

"What?" Greta's gaze flew up to meet Oscar's. He remained impassive, though his chest lifted in a stifled breath. Hope? Did he hope she wouldn't be offended by their charity? It was difficult not to feel a rush of relief course through her. Not that it would change their circumstances with Grove House, but it was a costly error she had made. Even though she was still certain of what she'd seen.

"Oh, do say something!" Eleanor pleaded, concern touching her face.

"I . . ." Greta struggled to find the words. Oscar *had* offered. A gift, he'd said. "I-I don't know what to say."

"Say thank you and leave it at that!" Eleanor bounced a bit as she concluded what to her was the end of a pleasant surprise. "Now, that house there"—she pointed—"belongs to the Jensons. I *must* stop and say hello now that I'm here. Will you wait for me?"

Greta noticed that Eleanor didn't invite her to accompany her, which was no fault of Eleanor's. Greta knew that she wouldn't be welcome. Her very appearance in her clean but worn cotton dress heralded the south side of Kipper's Grove at best. At worst . . . the poorhouse.

"I'll stay with Miss Mercy," Oscar said. "Don't be too long."

"I won't, I promise!" Eleanor bestowed her brightest smile on them and hurried up the walk to the beautiful white house with its green shutters and green scrollwork trim.

A moment of stillness was interrupted only by the rustling

of leaves as a cool October breeze filtered through them. Those leaves that had fallen skittered down the sidewalk. A squirrel darted across the street, its cheeks filled with nuts.

"I am terribly sorry if we offended or hurt you," Oscar said, breaking the silence.

Greta wanted to turn and flee. She wanted to run toward him too. For no other reason than that his gentlemanly kindness had broken through her stalwart facade. "I'm not offended," she answered softly.

"Or hurt?" he pressed.

Greta gave him a small smile. "So much of late hurts, I'm afraid I can no longer tell where it originates from."

Her admission startled her. She'd not intended to convey such honesty. Not to Oscar Boyd. His brows drew inward, and his eyes more concerned. "The police have told you nothing more of Leo's disappearance?"

"No." The key in her pocket felt heavy all of a sudden, as if it pleaded with her to take Oscar into her confidence to find out what it was for.

"That is balderdash." Oscar's frustration brought Greta's head up in surprise. "There should be no reason three boys are missing and no one is doing anything about it!"

"Three boys from south of Kipper's Grove," Greta added humbly.

"That shouldn't weigh into it."

"But it does."

"It shouldn't," Oscar insisted.

"But—" Greta felt her chin quiver, and she hated herself for her weakness—"it does."

Oscar glanced toward the Jenson home into which Eleanor had disappeared. He pushed his hands into the pockets of his trousers, his wool sweater vest tugged over the waistband. "There should be more urgency. After the other night . . . what you saw and heard . . ."

More urgency.

Oscar was right.

Here she stood fingering a key in the pocket of her dress. A key from Mrs. Frances Barlowe, no less, and she was hesitating with whether to inquire of Oscar for help? Even if he abandoned her later, for now he could serve the purpose of finding Leo.

She pulled it from her pocket and held it up for Oscar to see. "Mrs. Barlowe gave me this. Today."

Oscar frowned, reaching for the key. "What is it for?"

"I don't know. And she gave me her calling card and said if I ever needed her *permission*, I was to show that card on her behalf."

Oscar took the card and studied it. "Yes. It is hers. My mother has one of them." If he felt he needed to verify its authenticity, Greta couldn't blame him. It was beyond normal that she would have secured Mrs. Barlowe's calling card.

"What does it mean?" Greta felt helpless as she waited for Oscar to somehow interpret what she couldn't. To identify the key, the card, and the intent behind them.

He adjusted his glasses on his face and turned the key over in his hand. "I wonder . . ."

"Yes?"

"Could this be a key to the theater?"

Their eyes met in question, anticipation mixed with a bit of dread.

"But why would she give me a key to the very place from which I've been put out?" Greta asked. "Mr. Barlowe—most of Kipper's Grove, for that matter—thinks I have lost my senses. To give me a key to the most affluent building in town would be . . ."

Oscar's fingers closed around the key, and his expression grew decisive. "It would mean she wants you to find something in the theater. Something she dare not reveal herself, something she doesn't trust her husband with."

"Why me, though?" Greta pleaded for an answer that made sense, even as she realized there might not be one.

"Because she knows you will not stop until you find it. Until you find Leo. Until you uncover the secrets of Barlowe Theater."

18

Kit

OCTOBER, PRESENT DAY

The ringing of her phone would probably scare her to death for the next decade. Kit twisted in her spot on the barstool at her parents' breakfast nook and dug her phone from her pocket. Her mother stood frozen at the stove, spatula for flipping eggs lofted like a weapon against the foe on the other end of the line. Her father stiffened in his chair at the table to the right of her, lowering his morning paper. Kit lowered her eyes to her phone and the caller ID that lit up the screen. She released her breath in a *whoosh*. "It's just Corey."

"Thank God." Kris lowered the plastic spatula.

"I second that," Ford said. He pushed his glasses up his nose and returned to reading the paper.

Kit slipped off the stool, her feet landing on the hardwood floor. She put the phone to her ear. "Hey."

"Hey yourself, female." Corey was so weird sometimes, it was comforting. "I stopped by your place with coffee, but you weren't there."

Oh yeah. It was Friday. Corey always met her at her apartment

171

with a complimentary cup of his special home-roasted brew made in a pour-over concoction at his custom-made coffee bar in his too-nice bachelor pad. The man refused to spend a dime at the local coffee shop because, in his words, "That coffee is crud." So he'd deemed Fridays his day to rescue his "sidekick female."

"I'm sorry. I'm staying at my parents' house. Come over if you want. Mom brewed some canned ground stuff and it smells burnt." Her whine reached Kris's ear, and her mother scowled.

"On my way!"

She hung up and returned to her stool in the nook. A plate of scrambled eggs and bacon was waiting for her, along with toast. Kit noted the mug of hot coffee.

Kris pursed her lips in a mock look of annoyance. "Well, I tried. Apparently my coffee falls short of Corey's."

"You spoil me." Kit swallowed a bite of bacon. "Seriously, I never would've slept last night if I'd been at my place."

"And you shouldn't have slept there." Ford snapped his newspaper and then folded it. "Not with some nitwit out there harassing you. I'm not thrilled with the way things have gone this past week. And the fact that Seamans has nothing on Madison's disappearance? How is that possible? She was right there with you all that night."

"I know, Dad." Kit lost her appetite. It wasn't her father's fault. The reality of it all just kept repeatedly slamming into her. She should call Avery today and see if their parents had arrived yet. The Farrington family was going to be so overwhelmed and utterly destitute.

The front door opened, and Corey's voice filled the hallway. "Yo, yo, yo to the Boyd family diner!" He was used to stopping in and made his way to the kitchen, setting a thermos of triple-plated stainless steel in front of Kit. Without saying a word, he took Kit's coffee mug, rounded the nook, and poured the coffee down the sink drain—all while planting a kiss on Kris's cheek.

Kris laughed. "Corey, you need a wife."

He rolled his eyes dramatically. "I've tried for the last twenty years, ma'am, and God love your daughter, but I will not rob the cradle!"

"Thank you for that," Ford stated. He stood and tossed Corey a casual wave. "Please keep an eye on her at the pantry today. With everything going on right now, I don't want Kit to be alone. I'll let her fill you in about last night."

Concern was etched in Corey's face. "What have I missed? Not cool, Boyd, not cool."

"I know." Ford kissed the top of Kit's head, then moved to Kris for a quick peck. "I need to get to down to the church. It's men's Bible study, and unfortunately I'm leading it." He frowned.

"Unfortunately?" Kit scrunched her face.

Her father gave her a stern look. "I should be shadowing you all day."

"Dad. I'm an adult. I don't need a bodyguard."

"Age has zilch to do with safety, young lady. You call me if anything—*anything*—happens, you hear?"

"I will, Dad," Kit promised.

After Ford had departed, Kris excused herself from the kitchen.

Corey leaned against the sink. "Man, I would've given anything to have had parents like yours. You nailed it in the adoption department."

Kit nodded. Corey was right. There were so many times she felt guilty that even after all the years since being adopted into a loving home as a baby, she still felt that at any moment something could come along and make it all evaporate. Her parents would have reached the limits of their ability to give to her. And then it would just be Kit. Alone. The way she'd been the day the woman who had given birth to her left her at the hospital with the adoption facilitators instead of fulfilling the instinctive role of nurturer, protector, and fierce warrior over her child. Deep down, in the places she rarely voiced, Kit felt disposable. Even her faith was challenged by the idea that God too must certainly have His limits of grace.

"Yoo-hoo!" Corey waved at Kit.

She snapped to attention.

"You keep zoning out on me. What do I need to do to keep your attention? Make you more coffee?"

"I'm sorry." Kit offered Corey an apologetic smile and sipped the amazingness in the thermos before her.

Corey pushed himself off the counter and leaned on the nook. "So, today . . . we need to get in the orders for dairy. As you know, the truck will deliver on Monday, but with the break-in now, we're significantly short on eggs."

Kit froze. Orders. She'd forgotten it was Friday. "Did the volunteers do donation pickups today?"

Corey nodded. "Gwen took the van. She'll hit up the big-box stores. I'm guessing it'll be mostly bread and doughnuts, like last week. We're always short on produce this time of year."

"Gwen is a saint," Kit breathed in relief.

Corey snorted. "She thinks she is! This morning she asked if there was any way I could watch her kids when she went out tonight with her sister. Me? Watch kids? Has she met me? As if she deserves that sort of devotion for picking up banana boxes of doughnuts. No, thank you."

Kit laughed. "Hey, it's the food pantry. We're used to trading services."

"Not childcare!" Corey looked almost petrified in a comical sort of way. He grimaced and then got back to business. "Anyway, we should inventory dairy and then—"

"Um," Kit gnawed at her lip, and Corey's eyebrow drew upward in suspicion.

"What?"

"Avery is home."

"Madi's sister?"

"Yes. And, Corey, there're no leads on where Madi disappeared to. *Nothing.* It's been a week."

"Five days."

"Right, almost a week."

"Five days isn't almost a week—it's more like two-thirds of a week."

"Corey." Kit hoped the seriousness of the situation would bring his playful cynicism down a bit. "Madi is still missing. Avery said their parents are flying in, which will be a whole other set of issues—what with the divorce. And Al Farrington will insert himself right in the thick of it."

Corey frowned. "True, but it's not on you to sort out their family dysfunction."

"No," Kit agreed, "but you know I'd do anything for Madi. And she needs me now more than ever. I can't desert her." The desperation in her voice revealed more than she'd intended.

Corey took a sip of coffee from his own thermos and eyed her. "You have more of an abandonment hangover than I do, and I was a teenager before I had a permanent place to live."

She hated his observant nature.

Corey clicked his tongue. "Listen. You are fiercely loyal, Kit, because you know how it feels *not* to have someone stay loyal. It's the greatest fear of any adoptee whether we were a baby or a teenager. Sure, different implications and levels of emotional damage, and some don't believe it in the case of infant adoption—I know all the arguments. But seriously, just because you're afraid one of us will back out on you—which I've no intention of doing—doesn't mean you have to put yourself in danger for us. It doesn't prove you love Madi any more than you've already proven it in the past."

Corey waited patiently for Kit to respond. She couldn't. He'd hit the nail so hard on the head, her headache was coming back.

He continued, "The police are doing everything they can. If

175

they organize a search party or something, I'm all in. But until then, what can you do? I don't want to sound callous, but there are people—many people—depending on us too. At the pantry. For basic needs like food and toilet paper. Madi wouldn't want you to ignore them."

"But their lives aren't being threatened!" It hurt Kit that she had to argue this with Corey. She had wanted his support. His partnership. Like he always seemed to give her.

"We don't know that Madi's is either. There's no evidence anyone abducted or assaulted her. She legit just vanished in front of your faces."

"Not in front of mine," Kit snapped.

"Then maybe you should be more worried about this show and their ghost-hunting honchos."

"Corey."

"Fine." Corey stood, obviously displeased but attempting to understand. "I'll take care of things today. I get it. I do. I want to see Madi home safe too. But I want *you* to be safe. And, Kit, you were just in an accident! You're recuperating from a concussion. Someone vandalized the pantry! That's not a small list of things affecting *you*. You don't have to sacrifice everything to keep our approval—to keep Madi's approval. True loyalty isn't based on a scale, Kit."

His words stung, because while he had come to a healthy mental state of believing that was true, in her deepest places, Kit was certain the scale was there—it was just hidden really, really well.

Kit offered Corey an apologetic look. "I'm sorry. I'm so thankful for you. That you care. That you're willing to step up for me right now."

Corey rounded the nook and tousled her hair. His green eyes snapped with their familiar tease. "Step up, huh? You mean slop up. You should've smelled that rotting milk I had to mop after the break-in."

Kit slugged his arm.

Corey dodged it and pointed at his thermos as he headed for the door. "I want that back."

"It'll be empty!" Kit called after him.

"It better be!" he retorted.

The door closed behind him, and even though things had parted congenially, Kit still felt a flood of guilt. Her personal resources were being stretched. Her health, her emotions, her mental stamina, and now she was worried she was overburdening her friends and even her parents.

Kit closed her eyes and sipped Corey's coffee. Prayer would be a good way to start her morning. To center herself. To find strength. But at the moment, she hated to admit that things seemed to have slipped horribly and almost irrevocably out of God's control.

"I could do without another ghost walk." Kit eyed Avery, then Evan, and finally her gaze settled on Heather Grant, whose empathetic smile only served to make Kit like her more, not less.

"I know," Heather agreed, "but I'm sensing we may find some answers this way. For Madison's sake."

Kit cast Avery a desperate look. "Avery . . ."

"It's not what we'd normally do, I'll give you that." Avery shifted nervously on her feet. "But maybe this is God's way of providing answers."

God's way? Kit sincerely doubted it. Yet she needed to tread lightly because Avery was desperate to find Madison. *She* was desperate. But Heather Grant? The medium?

She sucked in a deep breath of fall air tinted with the scent of frying hamburgers from down the street at the bar. They stood just outside Barlowe Theater. Kit had gotten Avery's call to meet her here. She hadn't expected Evan and definitely not Heather.

Movement on her left snagged Kit's attention as Tom pulled into a parking spot. He shut the ignition off and opened the car door. "I brought the camera," he announced. "Annie called, and she wants footage sent over tonight. They need to piece together a timeline for—" He stopped at Kit's look. "What?"

"You're still *filming* this?" Kit's stare ping-ponged between the three-member team of *Psychic and the Skeptic*. For some reason, she had assumed they wouldn't be filming. Though in retrospect, it had been a foolish assumption considering who was here.

Heather stepped toward her. "Sometimes the camera helps. Tom can catch things that maybe don't stand out to me at the moment. And—"

"Anything we can do to find Madison," Avery interrupted. "If this brings awareness to the fact she is missing, why wouldn't we let them film?"

"Not to mention," Heather added, "it's what Madison wanted. She wanted to put the theater in the spotlight. To preserve its historicity. We can help accomplish that for Madison."

Kit blinked in amazement. Ghost hunts. Mediums. Television shows. The whole thing was a production, and it was Madison who was going to pay the price.

Evan held up his hands and pushed into the circle beside Heather. "Hey. Give me a moment, will you?"

Heather smiled in understanding. "Of course." She and Avery backed away and approached Tom, who was dumping camera equipment outside the theater's entrance.

"This is going to turn into a three-ring circus, Evan." Kit pointed to the theater. "You know this is a waste of time. You don't believe Heather's abilities, and frankly, I believe it's playing with fire."

"I don't disagree." Evan's hand touched her elbow, and Kit jerked away at his touch. He pulled back. "But if it gets us into the theater, if it gets us to where it all started, we might discover something, like maybe a detail, that'll help us find Madison. And now that we've talked to Alpharetta Green, we might see things differently. Tunnels. The heating vents below the seats. Has anyone looked there? Where those boys were supposedly lost back in 1915?"

Kit felt her shoulders drop in defeat. She wouldn't even fight this if she wasn't concerned that messing with the other world was dangerous at best and at worst a direct violation of her faith. Still, there were times even she questioned things. Questioned God. Or she simply questioned. And right now didn't feel like the best time to start a deep dive into theological debates on the afterlife. "Fine," she said.

"I'll be right there with you," Evan assured her.

Kit looked at him with skepticism. "Do you think this is dangerous?"

He shrugged. "Madison *did* disappear on our last walk."

"And you were with her then too." Kit stated the obvious.

His eyes darkened. "Yeah." It was all he said, and for the first time, Kit sensed an element of personal responsibility weighing on Evan. He had a history in law enforcement. Now he was chasing phantoms, and he hadn't been able to ward off whatever or *whoever* it was that had been the cause of Madison's disappearance.

"C'mon." Kit patted his arm in silent camaraderie.

It was time to hunt ghosts.

It was time to find Madison—or find the source behind the history of the theater that was swallowing their peace.

19

Silence was a thing of death. At least it seemed that way to Kit. Silence hovered around gravestones in cemeteries, hiding in the dark places and haunting the shadows. It toyed with one's senses. It had filled the historical Barlowe Theater with its presence. Not even the ticking of a clock could be heard.

The little red light on Tom's camera was blinking.

Avery stayed close behind Kit, and while it was only ten in the morning, it seemed as if were late at night, with the dead awakening inside the structure.

Evan stood shoulder to shoulder with Kit, a truce called between them given the mutually shared events of the week.

Heather led them past the nonworking marble fountain that rose from the checkered, black-and-white tile floor of the theater's lobby. The ornate glass doors that led into the horseshoe-shaped foyer surrounding the auditorium were closed. Heather opened them and slipped through, with Tom motioning for the rest to follow.

They'd been instructed to be silent. To listen and watch. The air felt oppressive the moment Kit's feet landed on the theater's red carpet. The electric lights had been dimmed, probably to add ambience as they filmed. The arched doorways into the auditorium were covered with heavy velvet curtains that

Kit knew were normally left open, the curtains tied back with golden tassels. The place was like a tomb, one that captured old memories, then suffocated them, refusing them as they drifted away to the land of the forgotten.

"What do you see?" Tom prompted Heather, who treaded quietly toward the curved stairs that led to the second floor.

She held up her hand and paused at the bottom step, cocking her head to the left, her eyes narrowing. She was watching something—someone.

Kit felt Avery's arm slip through hers.

Heather's voice broke the silence. She spoke in a low monotone, describing to Tom and the camera what she was seeing. Her eyes had taken on a strange sheen. Her pretty face seemed marred by the effects of the spirits she claimed were hovering in the air.

"There's a woman . . ." Heather took a deep, controlled breath. "She is dressed in a white evening dress."

"From what time period?" Tom asked. It seemed it was part of his job to inquire because Heather answered immediately and without irritation.

"I think late eighteen hundreds? Or early turn of the century maybe? It's long, sweeping, narrow at the waist, and fairly straight down in the skirt. I'm going to guess probably 1910, 1915? She says she's 'the woman in white.'"

Woman in white? Kit mouthed the name to Evan. He nodded, his eyes widening. In Alpharetta Green's book, the woman in white was an old ghost story that swirled around the theater. Kit hadn't paid it much mind, but she knew it was one of the stories Madison had used to entice the TV show to the theater in the first place.

Evan sidled up to Kit and lowered his mouth to her ear, whispering quietly, "Heather hasn't been told of the theater's history or legends. She wouldn't know about the woman in white." Kit could see the skepticism already brewing in Evan's eyes. "But she could've heard about the story from someone else." He turned back toward Heather.

Heather was slowly climbing the stairs, the red carpeting beneath her feet original to the theater, worn and threadbare now. Her hand skimmed the iron railing. "The woman is taking me up the stairs," she explained, "to the ladies' sitting room. It's where she goes to find respite."

"Respite from what?" Tom asked, making sure the camera was focused solely on Heather and then sweeping it in an arc to take in the stairs and the gaping doorway at the top that led into the sitting room.

"I don't know. She won't say . . ." Heather's face contorted into a confused expression. "She's mumbling and . . . crying. Softly. She keeps asking where her baby is. 'My baby, my baby,' she says. Over and over again."

Kit felt numb. It was too real, too dark, even though she couldn't see anything ahead of Heather to indicate there was any spirit communicating with them, any woman in white.

The legend was that a woman in white had accidentally dropped her baby from a box seat. Some argued it had actually happened, while others blamed a person in the crowd, a different woman who struggled with mental illness. Regardless, supposedly the woman in white still haunted the theater, searching for her baby. People had reported seeing her, shimmers of white, and sometimes even hearing the distant cry of an infant.

They'd arrived at the sitting room. This room was a mere whisper of its former elegance. The theater had poured what little grant monies it had into preserving the main auditorium and hall. Upstairs had suffered. The women's sitting room was where ladies in attendance had retired during breaks in the performance. At one time, mirrors would have adorned the walls surrounding the sofas and chairs, with giant potted palms gracing the corners near the two windows now shuttered from the view of the street and the marquee below. The wallpaper was stripped back on one wall. Three layers of it. The gold-embossed paper on top hid a floral rose beneath, and under that a faded yellow floral paper with emerald stripes, also faded by time.

Heather stood in the room, staring at the radiator along the far wall. Though the radiator was cold, at one point it would have heated this room, causing it to feel stuffy, together with the scents of ladies' Parisian perfumes, flowers from corsages, and hairpieces.

Kit could sense the distant past as it rose from the grave to meet them here. Avery clutched Kit's arm as though being pulled into the other, unseen world while not wishing to leave the seen world, that which was familiar. Kit's glance at Evan revealed his intense concentration focused solely on Heather.

"Boys," Heather stated bluntly.

Kit jumped.

Tom and the camera lens pressed close to Heather's face.

"There were boys." Heather took a few steps into a side room that was probably a bathroom at one time. Now it had cardboard boxes stored in it, an old lamp, and cobwebs. She placed a hand against the wall. "They're inside the walls."

"Who?" Tom asked.

"The boys," Heather answered without taking her eyes off the wall. She ran her hand along it, down to a vent in the floor. Crouching, she pushed her fingers into the cast-iron grate of the vent. "Like the one that followed me the last time. They're lost."

"Are they related to the woman in white's baby?"

"I don't know." Heather's face twisted into a look of worry. She wrapped her arms around herself and stood up, looking at Tom. "I don't like this. I'm hearing words. I don't like the words."

"What are the words?" Tom inquired.

"They're cruel. They're implying someone is suffering from mental instability. I-I don't know that . . . No, the woman doesn't want me to say them. I can't say them. She won't let me."

Kit couldn't help but take a step closer to Evan. And pray. She started to pray. Something was evil here. Something was darker than anything Kit had ever even attempted to approach, let alone entertain.

Heather whirled, her eyes wide and landing on Kit, but no— she was looking *past* Kit. "The basement. It's there. It's all there." She pushed past them with Tom close on her heels. A new urgency seemed to fill Heather, but also an intensity that set her apart from them all. "There's the boy," she whispered.

Hurrying, Heather scampered down the stairs, Tom in close pursuit.

"What does he look like?" Tom pressed as they walked.

Kit couldn't help herself. While Avery clung to her arm, she reached out and groped for Evan's hand. It was there. As if he'd been expecting her fear. His fingers wrapped around hers, and in another moment—in another world, it seemed—Kit might have admitted she enjoyed the warmth his hand offered. But not now. Now she just wanted his security.

Heather hadn't answered Tom. Instead, she led them down the narrow hallway, past archways and into the main part of the theater, then to the back stairwell that took them to the basement. It was the same stairs Heather and Tom had descended the night Madison vanished.

Coldness spread through Kit's limbs. She hesitated, but Evan tugged on her hand, and Avery urged her forward. At the bottom of the steps, a vintage floor-to-ceiling mirror still hung on the wall. It was the "final look" mirror used by the performers before they climbed another set of stairs onto the backstage.

Heather froze partway down the hall, in front of the door she and Evan had stumbled through after losing sight of Madison. She stared at it and pointed. "He went in there," she hissed.

"The boy?" Tom asked. His camera light cast a faint red glow across the wall.

"Yes. He ran through the doorway and disappeared." Heather took a few hesitant steps. "I see . . . Oh my." She entered the dark abyss, Tom close behind, and Kit regretting every step she took to follow them.

Blackness engulfed them. Kit saw Tom's form outlined by the dim light from the hall behind them. He fumbled for the wall with his free hand. No light switch.

"You bring a flashlight?" Tom whispered to Evan.

"Nope."

"Great." Tom fiddled with the camera's LED screen, and Kit noted the film went into night vision.

Now Heather looked like an apparition herself. Her skin pale white. Her eyes hollow and glowing. She stared into the camera lens. "I see blood. On the floor. And flower petals. The boys are playing in the flower petals." She tilted her head. "And there . . ." Heather took off into the depths of the basement.

Kit had never been beneath the theater. No one needed to go down here. The eleven dressing rooms were in the winged hallways behind them. This was the underbelly. Storage, she'd been told when she was younger. The furnace system. A network of pipes.

"We need to stay together," Heather mumbled. Only the light from the camera led their way forward.

Tom looked over his shoulder at them to see if they were following.

Avery pulled on Kit, who turned to see what she wanted. Avery shook her head wildly. "I-I can't do this."

"It's okay," Kit soothed, although she wasn't entirely convinced of that. "It's just the theater's basement."

"No. I need to get out of here. Now. Where there's daylight. Madison isn't down here, and I can't . . ." A sob caught in Avery's throat.

"I'll go with you," Kit reassured her. She could hear Heather muttering her observations to the camera. Evan had moved on a few steps, releasing Kit's hand, but now he waited in the dark.

"No." Avery backed away toward the door and the promise of light. "I'll be fine." She whirled and sped from the basement.

"Evan?" Kit's voice wobbled. She pushed her hand into her jeans pocket. Feeling her phone there, she pulled it out and played with the screen to flick on the flashlight.

A blessed shaft of light shone forth.

Evan was gone.

Heather and Tom had ventured deep inside the basement's cavern. She could hear Heather.

A pipe creaked.

Something overhead clanged.

A dank, musty smell permeated the air. Was it the same air as in the days when the woman in white was alive?

Kit spun around. Nope. She would follow Avery. Evan had gone ahead, so there was no reason to—

Ice-cold fingers wrapped around her wrist, the skin soft. Then nails like claws dug into her skin. Kit froze, flashing her phone's light in the direction of the hand, the pale-skinned arm that stretched from the dark innards of the theater's basement.

The hand released her.

The flashlight illuminated a maze of copper pipes, green at their joints, and a puddle of water on the floor beneath. Red water . . . like blood. Or was it just tainted with iron?

Kit felt the brush of something against her cheek. A brush of silk. Evening gown silk.

A white face flashed in her peripheral vision and then was gone.

Everyone was gone.

It was only Kit.

Alone in Barlowe Theater's basement, with the woman in white and the lost boy's pool of ghostly blood.

20

Greta

Officer John Hargrove jogged across the street toward Greta. His face was wreathed in a smile that deepened the long creases in his cheeks and emphasized his dark eyes. There was relief in his expression when he reached her side.

"You're all right then?" he asked without any small talk or greeting.

Greta surveyed her surroundings. She'd just exited the hotel next to Barlowe Theater through the back door into the alley. She'd inquired about employment, only to be turned away. Disheartened, weary, and dreading returning to Grove House with no hope to offer her brothers, she eyed John and answered, "I'm all right."

He leaned closer. "I know you were relocated to Grove House. I was worried when I heard the news."

A flush crept up her neck. She'd not told Oscar or Eleanor, and after she'd received a nod from Oscar solidifying their secretive plans for the key and the theater, Greta hoped she would meet no one else she knew. It was unfortunate that she should meet John. Unfortunate that he knew of her embarrassing circumstances.

John ushered her into an alcove in the alleyway, where a maple tree rustled in the breeze, dropping orange leaves around them. He swiped his officer's cap from his head. "I'm worried about you and your brothers."

"You needn't be." Greta smiled weakly. In that moment, she wished he *did* have reason to worry, that she and the boys were his responsibility. A law-enforcement officer, one known for his confidence and strength. Whoever ended up being wife to John Hargrove would be a blessed woman. She'd want for no other protector.

It wouldn't be Greta, that was for certain. With her recent move to Grove House, her dreams of a better life had spiraled downward. The very fact she lived there now would besmirch her reputation irreparably. The Mercy family would be viewed as those who lived among loose women, those too lazy to pay their offenses, as failures at life and work, men and women who were no longer in their right minds, some of them too old and as unclaimed by family as a stray dog. Grove House was filled with the unwanted, the unneeded, and the unwarranted.

"What can I do?" John asked.

Why he cared so emphatically, Greta did not know. "There is nothing you *can* do, John."

"I don't accept that. You don't deserve to live at Grove House. There must be . . ."

Greta shook her head. "The only way is for me to find the means to support my brothers and myself. To find affordable lodging—which is laughable since I couldn't afford to keep our previous place of rent."

"You're of age," John blurted, his countenance flushed. "Marry. Or—"

"Marry *whom*?" She didn't mean to challenge him so and regretted it immediately.

John, flustered, twisted his hat in his hands. "I-I don't know."

Her heart sank, even though it shouldn't. She knew that was not what he had intended to imply. His interest in her, though likely sincere, was coated in the unspoken reality of their stations in life.

"Just let me be, John." Greta tried to console him and thus relieve his embarrassment. "It isn't your duty to take care of me and my brothers. Do not concern yourself with my troubles. Merely do what your job requires and protect us from those who are intent on breaking the law—"

"Like your brother?" John interrupted.

Greta pulled back. "Pardon me?"

John's mouth was set in a grim line. "Your brother Leo broke the law when he trespassed into the theater with the other boys. As did you, Oscar, and Miss Boyd. Shall I arrest you? Should I say your brother had his comeuppance and cease searching for him?"

"I didn't say—".

"No." John smashed his hat back on his head, obviously agitated. "I'm sorry, Greta. I meant no offense. I am frustrated by everything of late. We've made no gains in finding your brother or the other boys, and . . ."

"And what?" Greta pressed. She ignored the wind that picked up, ruffling her hair loose from its braid.

John averted his eyes. He took stock of the alley, the theater's loading dock, the dirt ruts made by delivery wagons ladened with cargo.

"And what?" Greta asked again, unable to ignore the way her throat tightened with apprehension.

John met her pleading stare. "We've been ordered not to waste any more time investigating."

"Waste time?"

"Looking for the boys."

"But . . ." Greta's breath hitched. "But we have not found

them! If they are in the theater somewhere, trapped within the walls—"

"Only *you* heard them, Greta."

"So then, I am a witness to their cries! Isn't that evidence of something?" Desperation choked her.

"It's evidence that you see and hear things," John snapped back, not in anger but in frustration. "Don't you understand? They believe you *belong* at Grove House. That your mind isn't right. That your brother and his cronies are not missing but ran away, and you've concocted a story to draw attention away from your antics at the theater with the woman dropping her infant."

"I would never!" Greta stiffened, lifting her chin.

"Whether you would or wouldn't makes no difference. What they *believe* is what makes a difference, and no one believes that your brother and his friends are anything but rabble-rousers causing a stir. And you are only a—" He bit off his words.

"A what?" Greta lowered her voice.

"A disturbed woman."

"Do *you* believe that?"

"Does it matter to you what I believe?" John's words hung between them. A question unanswerable, and for a multitude of reasons.

"Why does it always have to be at dark?" Eleanor's whisper was far louder than Greta would have preferred. "We don't even know if the key will work."

"Then it won't matter if it's dark," Oscar mumbled under his breath, glancing this way and that. At midnight, the street lay deserted. The sky was both cloudless and moonless. A crisp chill blew through Greta's dress, dampening her skin and raising tiny bumps along her arms.

She felt conflicted by the impossibility of her choices. She was risking her brothers' welfare—one here at the theater, the others left behind at the poorhouse—by choosing one over the other. Trouble was sure to follow for her absence at Grove House. Trouble was sure to follow for trying to fit a key into the front door of the theater while praying no one saw them. Foolhardy, and yet once again Oscar and Eleanor had been pulled into the charade, like hopeful rich children used to being rescued by their daddy's money. It wasn't that way for Greta. There would be no one to rescue her. No one to pull her to safety. What to Eleanor was a fun game of espionage and intrigue was to Greta a matter of life and death.

"Hurry up!" Eleanor danced beside Oscar as he fumbled with the key. They'd tried it on the back alleyway door and on the new lock, a replacement to the one Oscar had broken the other night, all to no avail. It didn't fit. "Maybe the key isn't *for* the theater. There's no reason Mrs. Barlowe would even have a key to— Oh!" Eleanor's words ended with a tiny shriek as the theater's door opened under the click of the key.

Oscar and Greta exchanged glances.

He'd been right. Mrs. Barlowe had given her the key to the theater! Greta's hand slipped into the pocket of her dress. She felt for the calling card. If John found them—if anyone found them—it would be essential that she had the card with her. Of course, Mrs. Barlowe would be called upon to vouch for it and . . . What if this were a trap of some sort? If so, it would be a very elaborate trap and not one that—

"Greta, come!" Oscar whispered.

Startled, she realized he and Eleanor had slipped inside the theater. She hurried to follow them. He closed the door quietly, then locked it from the inside and slipped the key into his vest pocket. Light from the streetlamp outside streamed through the stained-glass windows at the front of the theater.

"Now what?" Eleanor's eyes widened. "What do we wish to accomplish that we haven't already?"

Oscar smoothed back his hair and met Greta's nervous gaze. He offered a calming smile. "Now that we know about the key, we must assume it's a veiled invitation from Mrs. Barlowe to investigate the theater further."

"Do you think she knows where the boys are?" Eleanor breathed.

Oscar shook his head. "Doubtful. My guess is she has suspicions. Or perhaps she knows of something Mr. Barlowe has been keeping to himself. We look for clues, then, that might aid us in finding Leo and the other boys."

"That sounds like needles in haystacks, Oscar," Eleanor whined. "Tell us what you're withholding."

Greta frowned. Eleanor knew her brother well, so if she felt he was withholding something, perhaps he truly was. Oscar locked eyes with his sister, who raised her brows to encourage him to speak.

"Fine." He sighed and pointed down the hallway toward the auditorium that was just beyond a set of glass doors. "I was able to acquire blueprints from the architectural firm that worked for Mr. Barlowe."

"You sneak!" Eleanor swatted her brother's arm.

"What would that tell us?" Greta felt suddenly sick. Cecil and Alvin would have worried over her absence at supper. Virgil would have cried. Now they would lie in cots, staring at a barren ceiling in a barren room, afraid to move.

"There are heating vents below each row of seats. If the boys crawled into this maze of venting, they would likely have gotten lost."

"Then it really could have been them I heard the last time we were here?"

Oscar gave Greta a little nod. "Perhaps. I talked with Father and—"

"You spoke with Daddy?" Eleanor squeaked.

Oscar held up a hand for Eleanor to remain calm. "You know

194

Father is friends with Mr. Barlowe. I didn't *tell* Father why I was asking; I was merely expressing my curiosity as I often do. My penchant for learning."

"Yes, yes?" Eleanor rolled her wrist to hurry up her brother.

"Father said Mr. Barlowe has been quite proud of the theater; however, during its construction there were . . . difficulties." Oscar looked at Greta.

She dared not think of Gerard now, her older brother, and his falling from the scaffolding, plummeting to the ground—

"Difficulties?" Eleanor said.

"Yes. Difficulties with the contractor that kept the job consistently behind. There were so many delays, they looked for shortcuts to make up time." Oscar frowned. "I don't know exactly what that means, but it might've had something to do with your brother's accident, Greta. And the vents below the seats might've been run differently from what's shown on the plans."

"I don't understand?" Greta was confused.

Oscar continued, "Father indicated there was one situation where the workers simply stopped running the vents. Some don't go completely from end to end or connect at all."

Eleanor leaned forward. "Which means what?"

"It means the boys—whether they went into the vents on a lark or for whatever reason—could have ended up lost between the floor, the joists, and the walls."

"Oh, dear heavens," Eleanor gasped.

"Leo is l-lost in the walls?" The image horrified Greta.

"Or," Oscar said, taking a deep breath, "they found a tunnel."

"Tunnel?"

"Father said there are rumors that Mr. Barlowe had a secret tunnel installed that ran from his home to the theater. This is what caused the delays because it was done in secret. And this is what—"

"The accidents were on purpose?" Greta's realization made

her legs weak. She grasped for something to hold on to. Eleanor linked arms with her and held her for support.

"We don't know that," Oscar clarified, "and we may never know. But Father suggested this could be why the strange difficulties began. Accidents because of the secretive work . . . and then a need to cover them up. There were several mishaps."

"Such as?" Eleanor's grip on Greta's arm tightened.

Oscar avoided Greta's eyes. "One contractor was fired and sent home. Shortly after he arrived back in Chicago, there was an altercation between him and an assailant, and the contractor was killed."

"And?" Greta bit her lip.

"Gerard may have been one of the workers assigned to the unprinted additions to the theater plans," Oscar admitted.

"And his scaffolding gave way," Greta supplied.

"Oh!" Eleanor snapped her fingers. "And there was that other situation with the worker who was hurt when a hot-water pipe burst. Burned, wasn't he? And they sent him to Milwaukee for medical care?"

Oscar held out his hands to stop Eleanor. "The fact is, everyone knows the theater's construction was not without accidents, shortcuts, and issues. *If* Barlowe had secret tunnels or anything *secret* built, it is *possible* he covered his tracks to keep it that way."

"But why so secretive? To lord it over all of us?" Eleanor tossed her head, as if offended that Mr. Barlowe would set himself above even the Boyds.

"That's what we are here to find out." Oscar had finally come full circle to answer Eleanor's original question. "These are all rumors, at least the secret passageways are. But if they're not . . ."

"Leo and the boys could be in it?" Eleanor straightened.

Greta followed suit.

Oscar nodded. "If the vents and the walls are wide enough

for the boys to get lost in, we can't ignore the possibility that they stumbled on to something Mr. Barlowe would never admit to—his secret tunnel."

"So we need to search for it," Eleanor determined for them all.

Oscar's smile was grim. "We need to search for anything that's hidden."

21

Kit

"You left me!" She couldn't help it. Kit slugged Evan's shoulder as he appeared out of the engulfing darkness into the shaft of light from her phone.

"Whoa! Whoa!" He held up his hands in surrender.

"What's going on?" Tom and Heather hurried into the same shaft of light, the camera still on and filming. Heather looked her normal self again, no longer in a trancelike state.

"Who grabbed me?" Kit demanded. She wasn't prepared for this. She'd rather be at home with her ant farm, watching documentaries about dung beetles, her feet in socks with bumblebees on them, drinking an average cup of coffee. Just like she always had. Before this. Before Barlowe Theater and the first ghost walk. Before Madison disappeared.

The other three basement occupants all looked at each other.

"None of us?" Tom offered her a stick of gum as some sort of peace offering.

Kit frowned and waved it away.

"Who did you see?"

Well, she had Heather's attention at least.

"It's not *who* I saw so much as . . ." Kit shoved her arm out, complete with the fingernail dents to prove she wasn't imagining things. "They grabbed my arm! Dug their nails into me. When I turned my phone light on them, they brushed by me."

"Did you see any identifiable features?" Evan reached out and gripped her wrist, examining the marks with his phone's flashlight. "Good idea, by the way." He indicated the light. "I never thought of my phone."

Kit ignored his thanks. "No, I didn't see any *identifiable features*." She was raw. She was snappy and mad. "If I had, would I be asking if it were one of you?"

"What *did* you see?" Heather squeezed in between Kit and Evan, making Evan drop Kit's arm. Heather touched Kit's shoulder in a comforting gesture.

Kit sucked in a steadying breath, focusing on Heather's eyes, illuminated by the phone lights that made the basement a bit more palatable.

"I didn't see much. I saw fingers. I saw white skin. I saw . . . well, something they were wearing brushed my cheek. It was white."

"The woman in white." Heather's statement was followed by a direct look into Tom's rolling camera.

"Oh, for heaven's sake!" Kit rolled her eyes. She was more than over the paranormal. "It wasn't a ghost. Ghosts don't dig their fingernails into human skin!"

"Actually—" Heather began to correct her.

Evan edged in front of Heather as though they were vying for Kit's attention. "Okay. Enough. Let's get out of the basement. We didn't find anything anyway."

"But—" Heather's protest was silenced by a very firm glare leveled on her.

Evan nudged Kit, who shrugged him off and headed out of the basement. She didn't need prodding. She was more than happy to leave the basement *and* the theater.

"Kit!" Evan shouted after her. She took the stairs two at a time, raced down the curved hallway that skirted the auditorium, and burst into the daylight-filled lobby. She charged for the front doors and doubled over to grab her knees once she'd hit fresh air.

Evan jogged up behind her. "Hey." His hand touched her shoulder, and Kit shrugged him off, hiking down the sidewalk away from him. He followed her. "Are you okay?"

Kit spun on him. "I was grabbed by someone in that basement!" she hissed.

"No one's saying you weren't," Evan insisted, his blue eyes reflecting a sincerity Kit wasn't expecting. "But let's talk about this."

"I'm going to the cops. I'm letting Detective Seamans know— whoever grabbed me probably abducted Madison."

"And did what? Took her where? How come the rest of us didn't see this person?"

"I don't know!" Kit's voice rose. "The basement is big. It spans the theater. They could've gone anywhere."

"Listen." Evan approached her like he would a nervous cat. Hesitant, careful, calculated. "Kit . . . let's take a minute to breathe."

"Breathe?" Kit pressed her lips together and stared at him.

"Yeah. Breathe. It's what people do."

"I know that."

"So do it."

"I *am*!"

"Actually, you're gasping. You're going to hyperventilate. Get more oxygen to your brain and you'll be able to think more clearly."

"I *am* thinking clearly." Over Evan's shoulder, Kit noticed

Tom and Heather emerge from the theater. They glanced their way and then headed toward Tom's car.

"What's your mom's name?" he asked.

"Kris." She glowered. She knew what he was doing. Focus on reality. Bring her back to earth.

"And your dad's?"

"Ford." She took a few deep breaths.

"Okay. And your middle name?"

"Elizabeth."

"All right." Evan nodded his encouragement. "Tell me about your first pet."

"I had a rat." She remembered the white-and-brown rat with its naked tail. "None of my friends would hold it. They thought I was weird."

"What was his name?" Evan prompted.

"*Her* name was Rosie." Kit was breathing normal now. She nodded. "Okay, you win. Way to divert my attention. I'm calm now."

Evan's grin transformed his face. He should smile more often, though Kit wasn't about to tell him that. "All right. Let's give it a rest for now, get you some water. Your head is still recuperating from the accident too. You need to sit down and rest for a bit. No one is questioning what happened."

"But Detective Seamans needs to know—"

"I'll tell him. But first let's take care of you."

Kit curled up on the sofa, tugging the fleece blanket Avery handed her around her legs and waist. "I'm not helpless," she protested weakly. Yet Evan had been right. She could feel the onslaught of a headache, which was exacerbated by her concussion.

Avery handed her a cup of peppermint tea, her blue eyes—so

much like Madison's—worried. "Drink this." She turned to Evan. "I'm glad you brought her here. I've been trying to calm down since *I* left the theater earlier. That place is creepy and awful, and I can't . . ." Her voice caught, and she didn't finish whatever she was going to say.

Evan sat at the other end of the couch from Kit. He motioned for Avery to sit and relax in the recliner opposite them. "Kit said your rental house was close by."

"Yes," Avery replied. "My parents are arriving tomorrow. I didn't want us at Madison's house, it's too . . . anyway, my grandfather would make our lives miserable." She looked around the stylish living room of her vacation rental. "It's the biggest place I could find in town. Mom can share the first level with me, and Dad and his wife can—" She stopped and grimaced. "Sorry, you don't need to know all the family details."

Kit sipped her tea. It was hot and comforting. She gave Avery a reassuring smile. "I know it'll be tough when your parents get here."

"I just wish Mom and Dad could learn to coexist." Avery swiped at her eyes. "Anyway, would you like some antibiotic cream for those marks?"

Kit looked at her arm. The fingernail marks hadn't split the skin but just dented it. "No, thank you. I'm okay."

"I called Detective Seamans," Evan said. "They're going to sweep the theater again. I don't expect them to find anything, though."

"That's unfortunate." Kit sipped her tea.

Avery cleared her throat and sniffed. "I'm sorry I ran out."

Evan nodded. "It's not easy visiting the place where a loved one disappeared."

"No. It's not." Avery paused as if debating something in her mind, then pushed up with her hands on her knees and stood. "I need to show you both something."

After a few minutes, she returned with her tablet and took a seat between Kit and Evan on the couch. A whiff of raspberry shampoo and vanilla lotion drifted off Avery. She swiped the tablet, and the screen came to life. "I was able to access Madison's video journal last night." She looked up at them. "I figured out her password. And I found her last entry. She filmed it the day she went missing."

Evan scooted forward, his curiosity piqued. Kit didn't feel nearly so excited. Madison's beautiful face was frozen on the screen. Her eyes sparkled. She was wearing the same red blouse she'd worn the night they walked through the theater. Her blond hair, like corn silk, was pulled back into a high pony with a pearl wrap to make it more elegant. Determination emanated from her expression.

That was Madison.

Avery hit the play button, and Madison started to speak.

"Hey, future me, remember this day when you're old, all right? I hope it doesn't backfire on you. Grandpa Farrington is such a behemoth, and he's going to be furious. Anyway, tonight's the night. Heather Grant and Evan Fischer from the TV show *Psychic and the Skeptic* will be here, and the tour will commence."

Evan met Kit's eyes. His reflected the same level of concern for what they were about to hear. Something felt . . . off.

Madison continued. "I'll be interested to see if Heather says anything about the woman in white or the lost boys. Everyone local knows about them, but whether she'll make contact or not—who knows? I hope she does. Maybe we'll find out if that story about the woman in white actually happened. I hope Evan Fischer has a fit and tries to prove her wrong. It'll make the show more entertaining and get viewers up in arms to preserve the theater."

Avery pressed the pause button.

"Does she say anything more?" Kit wasn't sure why Avery paused it.

Avery swallowed hard as though swallowing secrets. Instead, she answered honestly. "Yes. And this is where it gets weird."

"Weird?" Evan's brows rose. "Why?"

"Just listen." Avery hit play again.

Madison's voice flooded the room. "So when I was reading the pieces of Greta's journal I found in the storage area—"

"Wait." Kit held up her hand.

Avery pressed pause.

"What does she mean, Greta's journal?" Kit looked between Avery and Evan.

"Yeah, who's Greta?" Evan asked.

They both turned to Avery. She winced. "See what I mean? Weird. Keep listening." She hit play on the screen, and Madison's voice filled the room again.

"Greta wrote something about a tunnel. She confirmed the rumor that was floating around at the time that the Barlowes had constructed a secret passageway from their house to the theater. Greta is writing about the lost boys, and it's obvious she's related to one of them. Which means the story of the lost boys is true. Just as I suspected." Madison grinned into the camera, her white teeth and full lips highlighted by a pale pink lip gloss. "Which is great news."

"Why is it great news?" Kit frowned.

Madison went on, answering the question she had no idea Kit would be asking of her recording days later. "Because it adds credibility to what I've been telling Grandfather all along. The theater is filled with historical secrets. It must be protected. And after tonight," Madison added with a smile, "it will be." She leaned forward. The recording stopped.

Evan sat back on the couch. "Why is Madison so passionate about the theater?"

"Its history. She loves anything historical," Avery supplied.

"But why the theater specifically?"

"Because," Avery said, giving a small laugh, "it's the *pièce de résistance* of Kipper's Grove. And because our grandfather has plans for the downtown area. But it's more than development versus preserving the historical. Our grandfather has always been on our dad's side. He covered for Dad. His affairs. The way he stepped out on Mom. Madison hates Grandfather Farrington for it, and she always tries to undercut him. It's why she's been raising money for the pantry and helping bring in volunteers. It hurts the Farrington pride. And the theater is icing on the cake."

"Madison sounds a bit vindictive," Evan said.

"She's not vindictive," Kit interjected sharply in defense of her friend. "How would you feel if your grandfather all but helped your dad cheat on your mom and made excuses for it?"

"And your mom?" Evan asked Avery, not answering Kit's accusatory tone. "How has she handled the strained relationships?"

"She's like me," Avery replied. "We just want everyone to get along. Mom can hardly stand Dad, but she plays nice—usually. She's not hurtful like Madison can sometimes be. At least to Dad and Grandfather."

Kit had never considered Madison to be mean, just protective. Of her mom, of her family, of the parts of Kipper's Grove that represented family and heritage. To Kit, Madison was a warrior trying to preserve the theater, while Al Farrington with his incessant need for progress and economy was a model for those willing to abandon something precious in exchange for what better suited their selfish agendas.

"Do you know where this journal Madison found is?" Evan looked between Avery and Kit. "Or anything about this Greta who wrote it?"

"I've never heard of it," Kit responded.

"I don't know where the parts are that Madison had," Avery

answered, "but I found a note card Madison had left on her table." She powered off her tablet, explaining as she did so. "She'd written something about 'the rest of the journal' and Alpharetta Green's name."

"Alpharetta Green." Evan nodded and looked at Kit. "Looks like the woman is going to get some camera time after all."

22

Greta

It was too familiar. The skulking through the theater in the dark of night. Her fear that she'd become separated from Oscar and Eleanor or that someone would catch them in the act of trespassing. But was it trespassing when the owner's wife had given her the key to the theater's entrance? It was also too familiar to exit the theater under cover of darkness after having found nothing.

The disappointment was so palpable that it hurt physically. She felt nauseated as she anticipated hearing Leo's cries for help, this after spending the last hour with Oscar and Eleanor, feeling along the basement walls for cracks, levers, indentations, anything that might lead them to a hidden passageway.

"That was fruitless." Eleanor heaved an unladylike sigh. Her hair was unkempt and slipping from its chignon. Her navy blue dress shimmered in the moonlight. "We've found nothing."

Greta didn't know what to say. She wanted to express her gratitude to her friend. Flighty and entitled, Eleanor had more than proven her loyalty and her friendship by just being here.

209

Now, as Greta saw the frustration on Eleanor's face, she realized that in spite of Eleanor's initial excitement over the adventure, it had turned into a true hope that Leo and his friends would be found.

"Something is not right." Oscar kicked at a stone. It was the first outward sign of emotion that Greta had seen in him. He pulled his foot back and cast her a sheepish look as they huddled in the shadows of the back alley. "I'm sorry. I truly thought . . . this shouldn't be so difficult."

"It isn't your fault," Greta whispered hoarsely around tears.

Eleanor's arm slipped around Greta's shoulders in a tender embrace. "Oh, Greta, we'll find Leo. We'll put Mr. Barlowe to shame in whatever he's hiding. We'll—"

"Don't make promises," Greta shushed her friend. "We're the only ones looking for Leo and the boys. The police can't be bothered to do anything about their disappearance any longer."

"Says who?" Eleanor drew back.

"Officer Hargrove." Greta couldn't help but look at Oscar. He was watching her, yet his face remained impassive when she mentioned John. Greta didn't know why it mattered what Oscar thought. That she was beginning to lean on his quiet strength didn't slip past her, though.

"Well, that is sheer poppycock!" Eleanor frowned. "We must get Daddy involved, Oscar. We must."

Oscar gave Eleanor a patient smile. "Father can do nothing, and he's certainly not going to break into the theater with us."

"Oh, he'd be horrified if he knew we were here!" Eleanor held her fingertips to her mouth as she realized the truth of what she said. "Mama would lock me in my room."

"We'd best get you home," Oscar concluded. Eleanor's words were beginning to sink in, it seemed. The reality of the risks the Boyd siblings had taken in trying to help Greta. He shifted his attention to Greta. "We shall walk you home first."

"No!" Greta squeaked. At Oscar's frown, she hurried to explain, "I-I need the time alone to . . . to think."

"That's understandable," Oscar said.

"Yes, but we can't allow you to walk home alone!" Eleanor added.

"She's right." Oscar stepped from the shadow of the theater and into the alleyway. He extended his arm in a gentlemanly gesture Greta felt she hardly deserved.

She backed away. "No, really. I'll be all right on my own."

"It's unseemly," Eleanor insisted. "Oscar, don't allow Greta to walk home alone. Not to the south side!"

Greta gave a sad laugh at her friend's naivete. "I grew up on the south side, Eleanor. I know it well."

"But you could be ruined," Eleanor protested.

Greta ached at the fact that what would ruin someone of Eleanor's status would merely go unnoticed by those in her world. Being alone without a chaperone was more common than the social elite realized. And not all young women faced violence, nor did they experience their reputations being ruined. Instead, their ruination came from poverty or from the lack of marriageable men willing to take on a wife and potential children. They were faced with places such as Grove House, which awaited her. A place where neither Oscar nor Eleanor knew she now lived.

"Please." Greta moved away from the Boyds. "I will see myself home. Thank you both for your willingness to help me, but you must return to your normal lives. There is nothing but trouble here if you continue. After all you've done for me, such as paying my debts to the Barlowes, I could not live with myself should you be forced to sacrifice more."

With that, Greta spun on her heels and hurried down the dark alley, away from the light and hope that simply being with Oscar and Eleanor brought to her. But mostly away from Leo, and the place she believed he had been lost. A place where he would be lost forever.

Her words of bravery had been spoken without thought to the actual walk to Grove House. Trees that were fast shedding their leaves bordered the road, their scraggly branches grasping at the sky like bony arms and hands. The half-moon kept hiding itself behind clouds, plunging Greta into blackness until she could scarcely make out a stone on the road. Then the moon would taunt her as it peeked out and cast its rays with just enough light to make the world around Greta one of fearful images and shadows.

A bat swooped across the road in front of her. Greta tugged her shawl around her shoulders and increased her pace. She'd left Kipper's Grove behind, moving swiftly now toward Grove House. She could see the outline of the building on the hillside. It was gray, cold, and unfriendly.

The wind picked up, whipping Greta's hair around her face and falling free from the braid she'd twisted and pinned up. Now it slapped at her as if in warning, urging her to go back to Kipper's Grove. To Leo . . . But she couldn't go back, not with Cecil, Alvin, and Virgil ahead at Grove House.

Greta darted a look over her shoulder. The road, the trees, the sky were all dark—a blue-black darkness that caused a shiver to race through her. She stumbled over a tree root in the road. The ground rushed toward her, and she tried to catch herself with her palms. Her hands struck the dirt and pebbles, scraping her skin. Tears of panic burned in her eyes as she realized she was being followed. Someone was behind her. She clawed at the ground, pushing herself up on her knees. Her foot caught on the hem of her dress. It ripped as she tried to stand. With a cry, Greta plummeted forward a second time.

Greta grappled with her dress, pulling it up above her knees so she could stand and run. A hand closed around her elbow, its grip unyielding. "Let me go!" she screamed. Her hair had plastered itself over her face, and with tears blinding her, she lashed out with her hands. They connected with a firm chest. "Let go!" she shouted again.

"Greta!"

Twisting, she kicked the man's leg.

"Ow! Greta! Stop, it's me!"

"Leave me alone!"

· Her assailant grabbed her other forearm, holding both her arms up, bent at their elbows. "Greta, please stop!" The man's glasses reflected the moonlight for a moment. His hair hung around his face, no longer neatly combed off his high forehead.

"Oscar?"

"Yes. It's me, Oscar."

Greta stopped struggling. She squinted in the darkness to better see him. Oscar loosened his grip. Greta's breaths came in gasps, her chest heaving. The wetness from her tears had caused her hair to stick to her cheeks. She reached up, free now from being held, and raked it away.

"Oscar, what are you doing here?" She was relieved, angry, and wanted to throw herself into his arms all at the same time.

Even with his wiry and angular stature, in this moment his presence appeared strong, rugged, even authoritative. His shirt had come untucked from his trousers, the tails hanging below his sweater vest. He ran a hand through his straight hair that fell into his eyes.

He stepped closer to her. "What are *you* doing here, Greta?"

Greta could read concern, doubt, and even . . . was that hurt in his eyes?

"I took Eleanor home and then hurried to catch up to you. I didn't feel it safe for you to . . ." He broke off, then continued, "You are past the south side, Greta. Why are you here?"

Greta could tell that Oscar Boyd had already surmised her answer, but he merely wanted to hear the truth from her lips. She refused to look away. The wind caught her words, and

Oscar leaned closer. Greta tried again. "You know why I'm here, Oscar."

"Tell me." His brows drew together. "After all we have done for you, the least you can do is be honest with me."

"After all you have done?" Greta shook her head. "I should have known your payment for my debts would come with a price. You will hold it over my head and guilt me into telling you what is not your business to know?"

"That's not what I meant!" Oscar shouted over the wind.

They stood in the middle of the road, staring at each other, with Grove House looking down on them. Its presence mocked her, laughed at her.

"What did you mean then?" Greta challenged.

"I meant . . ." Oscar waved his arm toward Grove House. "I thought I had earned your trust, Greta. Why would you hide this from me? From Eleanor?"

Greta couldn't formulate a response. She felt her nostrils flare against the emotion she was holding back.

"Where are your brothers?" Oscar demanded out of concern. "Are they at Grove House? Alone?"

"They're not alone," Greta choked out. Although the boys' supervision was being carried out by strangers. Strangers who had already determined it was their right to decide the Mercy family's future.

"How long have you been living at Grove House?" Oscar asked.

"It all happened so fast," Greta said, finally admitting it. Frustration and failure plagued her thoughts. The dreadful *knowing* that she had let her brothers down. Let Leo down. What would her parents and Gerard say if they were here? "They came for us two days ago. I didn't have a choice."

"You could have asked us for help!" Oscar insisted.

"What would you have done? The risk of telling you was greater than that of not!"

Oscar reached out and held her shoulders. The wind swept her skirts around his legs, embracing them both. "What risk was there in being truthful with us?"

Greta couldn't speak around the lump in her throat. What could she say? The risk of losing them? Were Eleanor and Oscar even hers to lose? They weren't her family. They could never *be* family. They were worlds apart, and yet they were the closest she had to kinship.

"What risk?" Oscar said again, this time with a little shake of her shoulders.

"Losing *you!*" she cried.

Oscar looked taken aback. His grasp on her shoulders loosened.

"I mean . . ." Greta scrambled to explain. "Eleanor. You—"

Oscar dropped his hands.

Greta's breath came in short shudders, pressing down on her. Every regret filled her with shame. She'd exposed not only her growing reliance on Oscar to Oscar but also to herself. It stunned her. Embarrassed her.

Oscar raked his hand through his hair again. Agitated. He looked over his shoulder toward Grove House, then back to her. "Let me walk you home," he stated simply.

Greta searched his eyes. He didn't avert his attention, and together they expressed the questions, the anxious awareness of their circumstances, and the unspoken words that would have to remain that way. Unspoken.

23

Kit

Alpharetta's front porch was delightfully arranged with orange-and-rust throw pillows, antique flowerpots with freshly planted mums, and lace doilies draping off the side of a wicker table that held a pile of old books artfully displayed. Alpharetta herself was dressed in a tailored pair of gray slacks with a floral blouse of navy and red, finished off with a hand-knit maroon cardigan. Her makeup was perfect, her permed hair styled impressively.

Alpharetta Green was in her glory.

Kit gave her own style a once-over. Canvas tennis shoes, blue jeans, a T-shirt that sported *This or That* with a choice between a ladybug or a butterfly, and a zip-up hoodie. Okay, so maybe she needed to take style tips from the older woman, who was practically posing in front of Tom's camera.

Evan had explained to Kit earlier that their producer wanted candid filming for most of the footage they gathered. He felt it could be a *Psychic and the Skeptic* episode unedited, which would engage even more viewers. A special showing. It was nauseating to Kit that the show was benefitting from Madison's disappearance.

"Have a seat!" Alpharetta gazed into the camera.

Evan sat down, seeming not to care that Tom was moving around to get a better shot of them both. Heather wasn't with them today. Evan had explained to Kit earlier that this segment of filming would be focused on his attempts at debunking Heather's claims about seeing the woman in white and the lost boys.

Kit leaned against the porch railing. She was used to being inconspicuous. Alpharetta wasn't interested in Kit or her plight to find Madison. She was eager to share what she knew best, and that was ghosts.

"Tell me what you know of the story of the woman in white," Evan began. He'd assumed the professional voice of a TV interviewer.

Kit wasn't sure she liked it. It made him seem more distant from her. She startled at the thought. More distant? She'd known the man all of a week. The dependence she was starting to develop bugged her. He was attractive, definitely. Self-assured, horribly. Opinionated beyond words. But he also felt safe. In a weird, untested, but instinctive sort of way. Kit hated it when she was drawn to people that way. A craving to trust and build friendship and loyalty made her a sponge where instead she should be building walls.

Alpharetta's chortling grated on Kit's nerves and brought her back to the present. The older woman leaned forward and patted Evan's knee in camaraderie over whatever joke she'd just shared.

Evan smile patiently. For the camera. Kit could see that inside he was already becoming impatient—it glowed in his bright blue eyes.

"Anyway," Alpharetta continued, "the woman in white is mostly a mystery. No one knows who she was or *if* she was.

As the story goes, she dropped her infant over the rail of a box seat, and after the ruckus, there was no baby to be found." Alpharetta offered a conspiratorial smile. "And there are locals who believe she still haunts the theater. I've spoken to several of them. During a recital even as recent as last year, the choir instructor was wearing an in-ear monitor, and he claims to have heard a baby crying. When he took the monitor out, there was no crying baby. No one else had heard a thing. Another time, one individual heard the woman crooning through the monitor. In fact, it's since turned into a superstition that performers at the theater wear in-ear monitors only when absolutely necessary, so the woman in white and her baby cannot jinx the performances."

Evan didn't appear impressed. Instead, he allowed for a pause, then asked, "No one has any record of the woman's name?"

"None," Alpharetta acknowledged.

"Have there been any investigations of the woman in white?"

"Ghost hunts? Of course!" Alpharetta crooned. She leaned back and crossed her leg over her knee, cupping it with her hands. "Many. Since they became a thing. Paranormal teams like yours have brought in equipment to try to connect with the dead. A few have, but without avail as to identifying her. You see, many spirits, once they've passed on, are lost in more ways than you may think. Some have forgotten their own identities. So while they know their deathly circumstances, they claw at trying to recover who they were. Where they came from. Some don't even know they're dead. Those are the pitiable ones, truly. Can you imagine being dead and not knowing it?"

"Mmm." Evan nodded. "What historical evidence do you have that is tangible in regard to these stories of hauntings?"

Alpharetta seemed taken aback. "Tangible?"

"Yes," Evan said. "Recordings, videos, documents, diaries, eyewitness accounts—that sort of thing."

"Oh!" Alpharetta grinned, then reached down to pick up a canvas bag leaning against her chair. She'd come prepared apparently but was too engaged in the dramatics to realize Evan would be unaffected by the stories and lore. She pulled out a few folders and rested them on her lap. But before she opened them, Alpharetta eyed Evan. "You really don't believe in the paranormal, do you?"

Evan looked unfazed by her bluntness. "No. I don't. Anyone can walk through a building and concoct visions and stories of what they're seeing. But without evidence, they're just that. Stories."

"That's very insulting to Heather, the woman you work with." Alpharetta's voice grew a tad colder. "And to me, if I'm being honest."

"I could say the same about both of you. Shouldn't my own beliefs be given the same respect? Is there a reason I'm denied the request for physical evidence?"

"I gather faith is not important to you?" Alpharetta challenged.

Evan gave a half smile, almost as if he enjoyed the banter. "Of course it is. But even God offers evidence to accompany the demand for faith. I find the paranormal to be all about emotional experiences."

"Emotional experiences," Alpharetta repeated. "So you think an entire industry, including your own show, is based on concocted stories, emotional instability, and deceptive tactics?"

Kit was surprised by Alpharetta's shrewdness. Her smile was turning less friendly, her demeanor more defensive. She obviously didn't appreciate Evan's skeptical approach.

Evan softened a bit. "Mrs. Green, I respect who you are, and I'm happy to listen to what you have to say about the paranormal. I only ask for the same in return. I do believe there's a spiritual world; I'm just not convinced it's what many think it to be. For centuries the devil himself has been portrayed as a liar and an illusionist. Do you argue with the ancients that he might well be duping us into seeing what we want to see instead of what truly is?"

"Which is what?" Alpharetta tossed back.

"Something much darker than a dearly departed person from the past," Evan stated baldly.

"You believe in the supernatural then?" Alpharetta frowned in confusion.

"I believe in two things, Mrs. Green," Evan said. "I believe that for many of the stories of paranormal activity, there's an explanation involving humans—those still living, that is—or one involving physical science which has manipulated the explainable into something else. The rest, while unexplainable, is subject to God and a world we cannot fathom—a world God himself has warned of the dangers of dabbling in."

"Well then," Alpharetta said, refixing an eager smile on her face. "For the sake of your show, let me extend this to you, and you can do with it as you will. But I will always argue on behalf of those who linger, who want their stories to be told."

"Fair enough." Evan reached for the folder Alpharetta offered him. She held on to the folder for a second longer as he tried to take it from her.

Kit noted the glint of warning in the otherwise exuberant woman's eyes. It seemed Alpharetta Green would defend those spirits to the death.

Tom aimed the camera at Evan and Alpharetta, a lollipop stick protruding from his mouth. He shot Kit a look she couldn't quite interpret, though it appeared he'd grown tired of the philosophical debate going on.

Evan opened the folder to find sheafs of paper covered with writing, all of it in pencil.

"That's part of a journal written by a young woman in 1915. Greta Mercy."

Evan didn't look her way, but Kit had a feeling that if the camera wasn't filming, he would have. This had to be the same journal Madison's video blog had referred to.

"And how is Greta Mercy related to the story of Barlowe Theater?" Evan asked.

Alpharetta lifted an old photograph from another folder on her lap and handed it to Evan. "This is Greta. Her story is woven through that of the lost boys and even a bit of the woman in white. Most people aren't aware of Greta's part, though."

Evan took the photograph, studying it. Kit cautiously moved to see the image of the woman, trying not to make undue noise with the camera rolling. The woman was young, a few years younger than Kit perhaps. She sat primly in a chair, her hands folded in her lap. It was an unadorned photograph. Kit could tell by the dress Greta Mercy wore that she hadn't been wealthy. Her dress appeared to be simple cotton, maybe a dark gray. Her hair was probably light brown. If the photo were colorized, Kit imagined Greta would have had more tawny-colored hair, like Evan's. It was difficult to tell what shade her eyes had been. She was pretty, but the part Kit noticed the most was how sad she appeared in the photo.

Alpharetta's next words added to Kit's observation. "Greta Mercy lived in Grove House. It was the poorhouse of Kipper's Grove at the time. Most poorhouses in the United States by the early twentieth century were owned and managed by the counties. They weren't federally funded, and they were slowly transitioning from being a place of forced inhabitance to one that was optional. For those who hadn't anywhere else to go and no one to support them. Which, the records state, were the circumstances Greta Mercy found herself in at the time."

Evan's thumb stroked the image of Greta in the photo. Then

he set it down in exchange for a sheet from Greta's journal. "Was she a widow?"

"No." Alpharetta looked genuinely sad on Greta's behalf. "By the time Barlowe Theater was built, Greta's parents had both passed away. Her older brother was one of the construction workers killed while building the theater."

"*One* of the workers?" Evan looked up.

"The theater had its share of accidents and issues while being constructed."

"I see." Evan focused again on the photograph. "What did Greta have to do with the theater after that?"

Alpharetta pressed her hair back as the breeze ruffled it. "Her brother Leo was one of the lost boys. After he went missing, she and her other three brothers ended up at Grove House."

Kit bit back a myriad of questions that piled in her mind. Why did Madison have only a part of Greta's journal, and Alpharetta the other part? Whatever happened to Greta and the lost boys? Could this have anything to do with Madison's disappearance over a hundred years later? If so, how?

"I believe," Alpharetta continued, "if you browse Greta Mercy's journal, you'll find she was uncovering quite a lot of hidden things meant to stay hidden. Her search for her brother and his friends was not welcome by Rufus Barlowe. His wife, however"—Alpharetta offered a knowing smile—"was another piece to the puzzle altogether."

Evan appeared only casually interested, and Kit wanted to strangle him. Ply the woman with questions! Stop trying to look all cool and thoughtful for the camera!

Tom must have sensed her angst. Without shaking the camera, he'd reached into his pocket and extended a cherry lollipop behind him toward Kit. She snatched it. Fine. She'd remain quiet. Unwrapping the treat, she stuffed it in her mouth and tried not to bite down on it to make the lollipop crack. The flavor of cherry filled her mouth.

223

"So, Greta Mercy was the sister of one of the lost boys. Has the woman in white ever been identified?" Evan asked.

"No," Alpharetta answered. "As I said before, no one knows who the woman in white was. Or who started the rumor of her infant falling from the box seat but never being found. If I hadn't seen the woman in white myself, I'd almost believe it was folklore and not a haunting."

"You've seen the woman in white yourself?" Evan didn't bother disguising his skepticism.

"Oh, yes. What more tangible evidence do you need, Mr. Fischer, than an eyewitness?"

"Eyewitnesses can lie," Evan said without apology.

Alpharetta gave a small laugh. "You truly *are* a skeptic, aren't you? But even Greta Mercy wrote of the woman in white. She saw her. The woman in white was real. The lost boys were real. No matter how much evidence you try to collect to finish their story and put it to bed and refute the idea that they still wander through Barlowe Theater, even Madison knew they were real. It's why she invited you, isn't it? To prove that the theater *is* haunted. And by allowing her grandfather, Al Farrington, to deface the historical elements surrounding it, he will disturb more than just their spirits. He will awaken the past and its secrets, which were never meant to be awakened."

"What secrets?" Evan wanted to know.

Alpharetta's eyes slid half shut as her smile thinned. "Ohhh, we all know Rufus Barlowe had secrets, and that the theater held his secrets. And it seems he died with his secrets. What were they?" She leaned forward, her stare at Evan intent, and then she swung her head around to look directly into the camera. "Secrets are meant to stay that way or old curses come to life. Nobody wants that."

24

Kit trudged down the sidewalk away from Evan and Tom, who were loading Tom's camera into the back of their rental car. Corey had called, and Kit wished she could clone herself.

"She's going to drive me up a wall, Kit." Corey wasn't prone to whining, but if anyone could push him there, it was Gwen, the donations-pickup volunteer.

"Gwen is just trying to help." It was sure to be a late night. Kit had just told Evan she'd go with him to the Barlowe mansion to see if the Barlowes would be willing to talk.

"She brought her *kids*," Corey added.

The cardinal sin. Kit bit back a smile. "You and Gwen are vying for the spot of favorite coworker, aren't you?"

"Stop." Corey sounded half serious. "I know we couldn't manage without her, but she just suggested we skip the pickup this week."

Kit frowned. "You mean donation pickups?"

"No, I mean giving out the food to the people who need it."

"That doesn't sound like Gwen."

"Precisely. If you don't come now, Gwen will actually post the signs. She likes to think she's your replacement when you're not here. I think it makes her feel important."

"She does do a good job, Corey."

Corey's voice squeaked. "She plays Spice Girls on the stereo! Spice Girls!"

"So tell me what you want?"

"Funny."

Kit could see Corey rolling his eyes.

"I want you here, Kit. You know that. But I get it. Madison is more important right now."

She couldn't tell if he meant that or was only saying it to make her feel better. Kit heard Evan coming up behind her. "Look, I'll come in later tonight," she promised. "Tell Gwen I'd rather she not cancel this week's offerings to the community. Let her know people are relying on us."

"Oooookay." Corey didn't sound convinced. "I'll do that. I'm also going to tell her that you said 'jazz only' on the speakers."

"I hate jazz."

"But I don't."

"Fine. Jazz."

"Thank you." Corey sounded a tad smug. "Hasta la vista, baby."

"Later, Schwarzenegger." Kit had to admit, she was missing the food pantry. Missing the banter with Corey. Missing Gwen's bullheaded ability to volunteer herself right into being irritating. The world needed more passionate volunteers like her. And Kit needed the food pantry. The routine. The world around her being predictable. Not all this mystery.

"Everything okay?" Evan asked as she turned to face him.

They stood on the sidewalk a few houses down from Alpharetta Green's. Kit realized she'd walked away from it all without explanation when Corey called.

"Yes." She slid her phone into her pocket. "Just stuff at the pantry."

"You're able to take this much time off without a problem?" Evan inquired.

"Yes and no. I'll need to go in tonight."

"By yourself?"

Kit shrugged. "I guess I hadn't thought that far ahead."

"Want me to help?"

The offer took her aback. Kit searched for something to say and came up blank. "I, uh—"

"Hey, I do more than interrogate people."

Kit chuckled. "I figured as much, but I—"

"Seriously, probably best not to be there on your own. Not now anyway."

"You're right," Kit acknowledged, even though she didn't want to. "What did we accomplish today in talking with Alpharetta?"

Evan glanced over his shoulder at her house, then back at Kit. "We learned more about Greta Mercy. We confirmed the lost boys are more than just a legend. Now we need to dive into who Greta Mercy really was and approach the remaining Barlowes here in town, see if they'll talk with us."

Frustration welled inside Kit. She crossed her arms over her chest. "And how is that going to help us find Madison?"

"I don't know." Evan turned and waved at Tom. "We'll catch up with you later," he called.

"What are you doing?" Kit frowned.

Tom waved back and got in the car, pulling out and driving away.

"What do you mean?" Evan asked, turning back to her.

"I mean, why did you send Tom away?"

"Because you need a little TLC." Evan took her gently by the elbow to steer her down the sidewalk half covered in autumn leaves that crunched under their feet.

"From *you*?" Kit eyed him.

"Ouch." Evan let go of her elbow and jammed his hands into his pockets.

227

"Sorry." Fine. She could feel the guilt of someone with human decency and recognize that had sounded hurtful.

Evan didn't look hurt, though. He looked as confident as ever. Sure of himself.

"Aren't you ever afraid people are going to just stop liking your spot on the show?" Kit blurted out. "It's not like you play the endearing one who tries to empathize with dead people. You're practically on a mission to shut them all up."

"Assuming they're actually speaking." Evan shrugged, unaffected by her question.

"But aren't you worried you'll come across too harsh? That the show will cut you out?"

"I think that's why the show is popular. Heather and I counteract each other. Drama, tension, and all that." Evan waved jazz hands at her.

"But what if—?"

"Why do you care?" Evan stopped and looked down at her.

"Well, I . . ." Kit realized he was quite taller than her. She'd not noticed that before. Of course, she was only five-foot-four, so even a guy of average height would seem tall to her. She hadn't meant to bring up the topic of rejection. But boy if it wasn't eating at her! Corey and Gwen were bound to get frustrated soon with her lack of attention at the pantry. But if she stopped searching for Madison, it would leave Avery on her own with her dysfunctional family, and Madison's safety was top priority. If she'd been abducted, if she'd been—

"Kit?" Evan's voice was softer this time.

She looked him in the eyes. "Yes?"

"You need to cut yourself some slack. You can't be everywhere and everything for everybody. No one can."

"I can try." Her voice sounded small, even to her.

"Sure you can, but you'll fail. You know that, right?"

"Yes," she admitted. Evan's question was more personal than she preferred to answer.

228

"Look." Evan started walking again. Kit followed, catching up until they were shoulder to shoulder. "I don't expect to be on the show for the rest of my career. Life doesn't work that way. Things change. People come and go."

"But why?"

Evan stopped again to look at her. "What do you mean?"

"Why do they come and go? What about loyalty? Why must there be conditions and so much change and . . . running out of capital with people?"

"Like Monopoly?"

"Yeah. But not the game. I mean monopoly with others. People have only so much to give and then they're finished. They mortgage their loyalty and move on to another game."

"Or life just moves them in different directions."

"Sure, but what about the ones who leave because they're done with you?"

Evan studied her for a long moment. "Are you afraid you've lost Madison?"

Kit started to shake her head, then stopped. "Maybe, I don't know. Madi disappeared—she didn't just *leave* me. There's a difference."

"But you're afraid she did," Evan stated.

Kit stared at him. He was voicing a scenario she hadn't yet considered, let alone put into words.

"You're afraid that something as nefarious as an abduction is too extreme maybe? Same as something paranormal influencing Madison's disappearance."

Kit rolled her eyes. "Well, I never actually thought a ghost ran off with her."

"No, but we're acting under the assumption she disappeared against her will."

"She did," Kit asserted.

"Okay. Then what are you afraid of? Why the worry about being left behind?" Evan would not let up.

"Because it's just what people *do*, Evan Fischer." Kit threw up her hands in exasperation. "It's what people do when they're tired of you."

An orange maple leaf drifted down between them, floating back and forth on the heavy silence.

Evan's eyes were stormy, more so than she would have expected from him.

"What?" She crossed her arms in self-defense.

"I thought you were a woman of faith."

"I am." That was brutal, and Evan knew it. Kit glared at him.

"Then act like it. God hasn't abandoned you yet, has He?"

"No."

"Then you're not abandoned. You don't need anyone else but Him. That's why I'm not afraid. Not afraid of losing my job, not afraid of people leaving me. Human nature is conditional. *People*, unfortunately, are conditional for good or bad reasons. But *God* is not. So you trust Him, you step out in faith that others will care for you in His strength and grace, and you realize that sometimes people make mistakes. They leave you. Or they betray you. Or life just sends you in different directions."

Kit looked deep into Evan's eyes, searching for something to be angry at. She hated his truth. Hated the way he'd stated it so bluntly and plainly, and yet he was right. There was no sympathy in his voice, not even empathy, but neither was there any cruelty or hardness in his expression. To Evan Fischer, it was just that simple.

"Anyone who puts all their faith in another person is bound to get hurt," he finished.

Somehow, his words didn't make Kit feel any better.

Dean Barlowe was a tall, wiry man in blue jeans and a light blue polo. His hair was sparse, his glasses framed kind, brown eyes, and he seemed altogether unsophisticated for being a Barlowe. His wife, Selma, was petite, with an equally friendly smile, her olive complexion and dark eyes a pretty complement to Dean's simplicity.

They welcomed Evan and Kit into the Barlowe home without any fanfare. The three-story brick mansion with its curved driveway and arched overhang was imposing. At its peak was an octagonal window, and Kit remembered as a little girl she was always afraid to stare at the attic window for fear she'd see the ghost of Rufus Barlowe peering down judgmentally at her. That was another Kipper's Grove rumor—Rufus Barlowe's ghost.

After the introductions had been made, Dean and Selma led Evan and Kit into the conservatory, which overflowed with ferns, palms, spider plants, and other greenery Kit couldn't identify. It was an insect's paradise.

"It's beautiful," she murmured, aware she was looking for six-legged cuties. Yet she knew this wasn't an insect conservatory. It wasn't as though the people of Kipper's Grove were never allowed access to the Barlowe mansion. At one point in its history, when Kit had been in elementary school, they'd offered paid tours. So she'd been here before, although that was years ago.

But she'd never been to the attic window, where Rufus Barlowe was said to appear on occasion and judge Kipper's Grove below.

Dean pointed to a gold-framed watercolor on the wall. "Selma painted that!" He gave a proud smile, showing the gap between his two front teeth.

Selma nodded shyly.

Evan studied the painting, a hummingbird hovering over a red flower. "It's beautiful," he said.

Selma laughed lightly. "It's all in the eye of the beholder."

Dean stuffed his hands in the pockets of his jeans. "Barlowes past would roll in their graves if they saw Selma and me. We like to frequent art fairs and craft shows and flea markets. Nothing pompous or lofty like the late Barlowes."

Kit felt herself relaxing in their presence. Just the name Barlowe brought with it an element of historical impetus that was intimidating. Had she met Dean and Selma at a craft fair, she would never have pegged them to be part of the distinguished Barlowe family.

"I'm guessing you want to see the basement?" Dean asked.

Evan looked surprised, and he shot Kit a quick glance. "I, uh . . ."

So the self-assured Evan Fischer *could* be at a loss for words! Kit reveled in this for the brief moment that it came and went.

Dean looked between them expectantly. "I assumed so, what with the show you're filming and then Madison Farrington's disappearance. I half expected the cops to come here, but they haven't yet."

Selma swatted her husband's arm. "I told you that you should call them."

"Do you know something about Madison?" Kit felt a twinge of hope rise within her.

Dean haphazardly waved toward the hallway just past the sliding pocket doors of the conservatory. "Not specifically, no. But it's no Kipper's Grove secret that my great-grandfather Rufus Barlowe is said to have built a secret passageway between this house and the theater."

"Did he?" Evan flat-out asked, and for once, Kit didn't mind his bluntness.

Selma tucked her dark hair behind her ear and answered, "We honestly don't know."

"I've wondered myself," Dean admitted. "I've even gone over the old blueprints for the place. Spent some time knocking on the walls in the basement to see if I heard any hollow spaces. And with Madison just vanishing the way she did, it sure did get my curiosity going again."

Selma offered Dean a loving and patient smile. "He's been down there the past several days, poking around, trying to see if we can put this family mystery to rest once and for all."

Dean reached over to pick off a dead leaf from one of the plants. "And to see if we can help find Madison," he added. "She's always been a champion of my family's theater and the history of Kipper's Grove. Considering her grandfather is Al Farrington."

"You don't like him?" Evan inquired.

Dean dropped the dead leaf into an empty pot on the floor. "Oh, it's not that I don't like him. He's a businessman, and I can't fault him for that. Honestly, he's not much different from my great-grandfather Barlowe. To progress, you typically have to step on people to get there."

"Or on history," Selma provided.

"Or on history." Dean nodded. He then snapped his fingers. "Now, let me show you what I've been doing in the basement."

With a glance between them, Evan and Kit followed Dean and Selma from the conservatory, along a back hallway, and down a wooden staircase that led to the basement level.

"I think I'm beginning to really not like basements," Kit murmured as she stepped onto the cold floor. The cinder-block walls were cool to the touch. The air smelled as if history had been trapped here and decaying for over a century.

"We got a new water heater and furnace installed about two years ago." Dean pointed to the appliances as they passed. "The spot I've been checking out is over here." He led them through a long empty room that looked like it might have once stored coal, then on into another cavernous, windowless room.

Selma gestured toward the wall that had a wooden framework built against it. "We thought perhaps that structure was shelving at one time designed to disguise a hollow area."

"The entire wall looks like it's made of block?" Evan squatted near it to get a closer look.

"That's what it seems," Dean agreed. "A few years ago, we brought a GPR down here to see what we could find."

"A what?" Kit asked.

"Ground penetrating radar," Selma said.

Dean continued, "It's like an X-ray machine that can take photos of the layers of earth. If there's an anomaly, it will show on the picture by way of a gap, shadow, or even a coloration. A GPR is often used to locate unmarked or lost graves."

"Archaeologists like to use them," Selma added.

"Did you find anything?" Evan didn't appear too hopeful, and Kit assumed if they had, Dean would have led with that.

"That's the odd part," Dean admitted. "There was a section behind the wall that appeared as though it might've been a void at one time. But it wasn't large enough to be a tunnel. It was more the size of where my great-grandfather Barlowe housed a vault."

"We never went any further to investigate," Selma explained, rubbing her bare arms against the damp chill of the basement. "While it intrigued us, there wasn't any motivation to demolish the wall."

It would have been enough of a motivation for Kit! She didn't express her thoughts out loud, however. But a hidden vault? Why not tear down the wall?

"But I got to thinking just yesterday," Dean went on, "what if the vault was like a decoy for the passageway?"

"How so?" Evan frowned.

"If there was a vault, one wouldn't think to look beyond it. But what if we were to get inside—assuming that's what the void area is from the GPR—and we find that the back of the vault's wall is false?"

"You mean the entrance to a passageway?" Evan pressed his lips together and nodded. "It's not unrealistic."

"No. It's not."

"But if that's the case," Kit couldn't help but interject, "and

Madison somehow got sucked away into this supposed secret passageway, then the only way for her to get out is the way she came in. Through the theater. Since this wall is blocking any old entrance."

"And?" Selma pressed gently, sensing Kit was leading somewhere with her train of thought.

"And that means Madison is trapped inside the passageway for some reason, or she's not in it to begin with."

"If she's trapped inside—" Evan began.

"She's starving to death," Dean finished. "Assuming there's enough oxygen flow in and out."

Kit's body tensed. This whole scenario sounded farfetched and ridiculous. "But for Madison to have been abducted, whoever took her somehow had to get her out of the basement without any of us seeing or hearing it. Impossible," Kit concluded.

"Unlikely," Evan corrected.

"Okay. So assuming this *passageway* exists," Kit continued, "the other option is that someone shoved her inside and locked her in. Yet no one's found any evidence of the entrance to the theater, which means Madison has been in an underground tunnel that goes from the mansion to theater for more than a week now?"

"What would that someone's motive be?" Dean questioned.

"Motive?" Kit squawked without intending to. "Who cares about a motive? We're talking about Madison being trapped in an old secret passageway like some Nancy Drew novel, only in this real-life story she's without food and water. And we can't find her!"

"Kit." Evan stood from his bent position by the wall.

She could feel the panic and the disbelief coursing through her. She wanted to grasp on to reason, only there was nothing reasonable about this theory. In fact, it was a load of poppycock—if she could steal an old-fashioned word to replace a more current expression. "Don't *Kit* me!" She scowled at Evan.

Dean and Selma had grown respectfully quiet.

Evan approached Kit, and she lifted her hands in warning. "Don't," she commanded.

Evan reached for her.

"I said *don't*. Don't touch me, Evan." Kit shrugged him off. "A human being doesn't just vanish into thin air. If Detective Seamans is right, someone took Madison or else she ran off herself for some odd reason. If you all are right"—Kit swept her arm around the room—"then Madison is stuck in a *wall*! She's probably dead by now. Or almost." Kit's words cut off in a gasping sob. "How is this helpful to Madison? To anyone? How do we find—?"

The sob that sucked the words from her cut off her breath as well. Evan didn't hesitate to wrap his arms around her, pulling her to his chest.

Kit wasn't prepared for the show of tenderness. She wasn't prepared to feel Selma's comforting hand rubbing her back.

Evan's embrace was too nice of a place to be. The comfort he sought to give her was empty considering what Madison was potentially suffering.

Kit tried to pull away. Evan let her step back, but he kept his hands on her arms, drilling his blue eyes deep into hers with a familiarity she wasn't sure he had earned in the short time they'd known each other.

"Deep breaths, Kit, deep breaths," he coached.

Selma hadn't stopped rubbing her back, and for a weird moment, Kit was thankful for her presence. It was calming.

"This is why we came here," Evan reassured Kit. "To find answers."

"I don't like these answers," Kit whimpered, wiping at the tears that stained her face.

"None of us do," Dean asserted. He went over and picked up a sledgehammer leaning against the wall. "So let's get to work."

25

Greta

Mrs. Gaylord had the appearance of a woman who'd sucked on a lemon and then been assaulted by a flock of pigeons. At least that was how Alvin had described Grove House's head mistress to Greta that morning at breakfast. Now, as Greta followed Mrs. Gaylord to Mr. Taylor's office, she had to admit that Alvin hadn't been that far off.

Breakfast that morning had been a harried affair. After hugs and tears from the boys, Greta offered them as many empty promises as she could to reassure them that they would be leaving Grove House soon. Only Cecil had the wherewithal to look unconvinced. Today the boys had been ushered along with other children to "do their duty" in earning their keep at Grove House, while Greta had been summoned for who knew what. Only she had a feeling she knew exactly what.

"In here, Miss Mercy." Mrs. Gaylord extended her arm toward the open office door.

A whiff of tobacco drifted through the doorway. Greta hesitated only a moment before deciding that facing Mr. Taylor couldn't be much worse than facing Mrs. Gaylord.

She was wrong.

Rufus Barlowe stood at the window, his broad back and large form a massive deterrent to any possibility of hope. He turned as she entered, his right hand gripping his pipe. His muttonchops framed his wide face, and his handsome features were hard and not at all welcoming.

Mr. Taylor stood behind his desk as Greta entered. He gave a nod to Mrs. Gaylord. "Thank you," he stated.

Mrs. Gaylord made quick work of shutting the office door, which made it very apparent that Greta was trapped in a room with two intimidating men. That Mrs. Gaylord hadn't remained for the sake of propriety concerned Greta. It didn't bode well if proper etiquette was considered unimportant.

"Sit," Mr. Barlowe commanded with a tip of his head to one of the chairs opposite Mr. Taylor's desk.

Greta obeyed. The chair was not welcoming either, as she could feel springs in its seat poking her bottom. She twisted to find a more comfortable position.

"I expect you know why you are here?" Mr. Taylor sat down, folding his hands on the desktop and looking at Greta with censure in his eyes.

She opted to remain silent.

"Of course she knows," Mr. Barlowe groused. He puffed smoke into the room, then strode over to the desk and leaned against it, crossing his beefy arms over his chest and staring down at Greta. "You trespassed into my theater. Again."

Greta's breath caught. How did he know? She wished Oscar would somehow burst into the room and rescue her from this moment.

"You also left Grove House and didn't return until past midnight. We have a curfew, Miss Mercy," Mr. Taylor said.

Mr. Barlowe waved the man off. "Be that as it may, I'd like to hear what you have to say."

"I . . ." Greta faltered. What should she say? Dare she show him Mrs. Barlowe's calling card? She hadn't expected to have to use it with him, for he was sure to accuse her of stealing the card.

"I-I-I," Mr. Barlowe repeated, mocking her. He leaned toward her and pointed his pipe at her. "I should have you arrested. You have been nothing but trouble, and somehow you've wheedled your way into the good graces of the Boyds' offspring. I had a visit from his son, Oscar, who wrote me a personal check to pay off your debt. This is how you repay me for accepting it? This is how you repay the Boyds for their generosity? You trespass into my facility, sneak around under cover of darkness, and dare to insinuate that your brother and his cronies are lost in my theater?"

"I never—"

"Your very presence implies as much and makes me appear to be an uncaring snollygoster!"

"A what?" Mr. Taylor inserted, confused.

Mr. Barlowe ignored him. "How did you get into my theater? I want to know. I *demand* to know."

Greta swallowed hard. She had no intention of mentioning Oscar or Eleanor. She had no idea how Mr. Barlowe even knew she had been in the theater last night. "I-I had a key." Mrs. Barlowe had extended her the grace of her calling card, and now Greta prayed that it would be sufficient.

"A key?" Mr. Barlowe let loose a guffaw that startled both Greta and Mr. Taylor, whose hand twitched and knocked over his teacup. He dabbed wildly at the remaining drops of tea that scattered across his papers. "And where," Mr. Barlowe continued, "did you receive a *key* to the theater?"

"From your wife, sir."

His eyes narrowed. "My wife, you say."

Greta pulled the calling card from her dress pocket and extended it to him. Mr. Barlowe took it, studied it, then slid it into his coat's inner pocket. He still leaned against the desk, but he took a moment to look out the window and watch as a Grove House occupant meandered by across the lawn. When he was finished watching, he turned back to Greta. "And that key is where exactly?" he asked.

Greta fished it from her pocket and placed it in his hand, hoping he didn't choose to believe she had stolen that as well.

Mr. Barlowe's jaw worked back and forth. His agitation was palpable.

Mr. Taylor's thumb tapped a rhythm on the desk.

The clock on the fireplace mantel ticked.

Tick. Tock. Tick. Tock.

"I will say this only once." His tone was so deep, so grave, that Greta could feel a murderous chill in it. She was almost certain that if Mr. Taylor hadn't been there, if Grove House wasn't occupied, or if they were somewhere secluded, Mr. Barlowe would have wrapped his hands around her throat and strangled her. Be rid of her. Instead, he was left to deal with her civilly.

"If you ever come near my theater again, it will be the last time you see your brothers. I will have you institutionalized."

Greta sent a shocked look in Mr. Taylor's direction. Surely he would step in and intercede! Such a threat was uncalled for with no evidence of—

"And the incident at my theater with your claim of a baby falling through the air is all I'll need to prove your incapacity to care for yourself or your brothers. Your brothers would be sent away to work, and our community be rid of you all. Do I make myself clear?"

Ice filled Greta's veins. She felt frozen to the chair. Mr. Taylor hadn't spoken a word for or against her. Mrs. Barlowe's calling card had done little for her defense. Numb, Greta gaped at Mr.

Barlowe, the horror of his threat becoming more real with each passing moment.

"Leo" was all she could whisper. To obey Mr. Barlowe meant to give up on Leo. On the other boys.

Mr. Barlowe shook his head. "Leo is dead, Miss Mercy. Or he has run away. Accept that fact and move on or suffer the consequences." A muscle in his jaw twitched. "Understood?"

Greta was tongue-tied.

"Do you understand?" Each word was delivered in staccato.

Greta nodded.

"Good." Mr. Barlowe drew back and took another long puff on his pipe. He turned his attention to Mr. Turner, who, quite pale, remained as silent as Greta and equally as cowed. "I expect you to better serve the occupants of this benevolent house provided by the county and make certain they're not free to run willy-nilly about the countryside after dark. It isn't safe, Mr. Taylor, nor would it please the county if your residents suddenly went missing."

"Oh, absolutely not. I-I agree, Mr. Barlowe." Mr. Taylor's stammered acquiescence would have made Greta sick had she not just experienced Mr. Barlowe's threats herself.

"Then I believe we are all clear on the matter." Mr. Barlowe straightened, tugged at his lapels, and offered a chilly smile to Greta. "Miss Mercy. Mr. Taylor." He strode toward the office door, his threats remarkably conveyed.

"Well, hello!" It was the squeaky voice of the old man who had dogged the wagon on Greta's first day here. He stood in the doorway, smiling up at Mr. Barlowe, who had just opened the door to take his leave. "You be the grand master of this place?" he cackled.

"God forbid," Mr. Barlowe growled. He placed his hat on

his head, his pipe balanced in the corner of his mouth. "Pardon me," he said with intent to move past the elderly man.

"Pardon me, Your Highness!" The old man cackled but didn't move. "That's a fine pipe you got there, sir. I'm Bartholomew Hepburn, but you can call me Bart."

"I'd prefer that you simply got out of my way," Mr. Barlowe insisted, impatience lacing his voice.

Greta was still immobile in the chair, her body trembling from the confrontation with Mr. Barlowe, her mind trying to encapsulate all that he had threatened and what it meant for her, Leo, Cecil, and the two smaller boys.

"Oh, Alma!" Bart shouted as he turned his attention down the hallway, not moving from his position blocking the doorway.

Mr. Taylor seemed to find his balance, and he pushed from his chair. "Bart, please step aside for Mr. Barlowe."

"Alma! C'mere!" Bart waved wildly.

Greta twisted in her chair to better see the scene playing out in the doorway. Bart reached out and snagged Alma's arm, jerking her to his side. The sad woman yelped, looked up at Mr. Barlowe, her face blanched, and she focused on her shoes.

"Alma, don't you like his pipe?" Bart's insistence she look at Mr. Barlowe was emphasized by his shaking her arm.

Greta glanced at Mr. Barlowe. His thunderous expression had tempered into a wary glare. "Do move, sir," he ordered.

Bart danced to the side finally, but in doing so, he pulled poor Alma directly into the path of Mr. Barlowe. "My father smoked a pipe," Bart said. "Did yours?" he asked Alma, who kept her eyes downward. "Did he?"

"No," Alma answered quietly.

Mr. Taylor hurried around his desk, shooing Bart away. "Be off with you. You've work to do outside."

"I do?" Bart's eyes widened. "Ohhhh, so I do!" He laughed and danced crookedly down the hall.

Alma seemed as frozen in her spot as Greta was in her chair.

Mr. Barlowe gave Mr. Taylor a side-eyed glower. "*That* man should be institutionalized."

"Bart comes here every winter, Mr. Barlowe," Mr. Taylor explained, even though it was obvious Mr. Barlowe wanted no such explanation. "Like some of the old folks of Kipper's Grove who haven't any family. With the winter being so long, Grove House is where they can get properly cared for until they move home in the spring."

"Blasted county system." Mr. Barlowe sneered. "Free care for the indolently poor and the mad." He eyed Alma. "And what are you still standing there for?"

She lifted her eyes for a quick moment. Greta noticed two rosy spots on her cheeks. "I-I'm sorry, sir."

"Go to the kitchen, Alma, and see Mrs. Gaylord about your duties." Mr. Taylor seemed like an utter angel compared to Mr. Barlowe.

Alma's eyes met Greta's with concern, and then she hurried away.

Mr. Barlowe cursed under his breath, then strode after her, his footsteps echoing down the hall.

Finally, it was only Mr. Taylor, Greta, and the open door of his office. It appeared he wanted to save face for whatever reason. Mr. Taylor cleared his throat. "Miss Mercy, Grove House is a place of charity. I do hope you remember that as we move forward from today."

"Yes, sir." She was too frightened to say anything else.

"Mr. Barlowe is a benefactor, and we . . . appreciate his generosity outside of the funds the county provides us."

She needed no explanation as to why Mr. Taylor was under Mr. Barlowe's thumb. It appeared most of Kipper's Grove was as well.

"Am I safe in assuming there will be no more, uh, kerfuffles caused?"

"Yes, Mr. Taylor," Greta said.

"Good. Good. Let's keep it that way, and then neither you nor I will have anything to worry about."

26

"What are we gonna do?" Cecil and Greta sat on a bench in the backyard of Grove House. Alvin and Virgil played hopscotch with a few other children, giving Greta the opportunity to speak to Cecil. She didn't want to burden her brother, but the day had left her shaken. Not just shaken, but hopeless.

"I don't know what we *can* do, Cecil." Greta picked at her fingernail that was chipped and worn. Nothing at all like Eleanor's beautifully manicured hands. "I can't risk having Mr. Barlowe send you boys off to only the Lord knows where. We'd never see each other again!"

"He's gotta know you ain't lost your senses, Greta." Cecil's face was dark with anger, but he handled it in his quiet way. "He's scared of ya."

"Scared of me?" Greta drew back, staring into her younger brother's bright blue eyes.

"Sure." Cecil nodded. "Seems like you're snooping in places he don't want you. Same as Leo. You know Leo only went to the theater to find out what happened with that lady and her baby. Then he disappears? It don't make no sense."

Greta wanted to persuade Cecil that he didn't know what he was talking about. But there was truth in the boy's words, and Cecil was perceptive and "smart as a whip," as Gerard used to call him.

"Do you think Leo is . . . ?" Greta couldn't finish her question.

Cecil's countenance darkened further. "Dead? Maybe. Or maybe Mr. Barlowe took him and Fred and Teddy and shipped them off somewhere to get them out of the way."

Greta's eyes widened. She'd heard of awful things done to poor boys who were destitute. But not in Kipper's Grove! That sort of thing was reserved for big cities like New York or Chicago, places like that. And how did Cecil even know such evil existed? Selling boys into labor was pure wickedness. Yet it happened all the same.

"I think Mr. Barlowe's up to something. I think that theater is his place to do business." Cecil snapped his fingers. "And he's gonna get ya if you get too close."

Greta drew a shuddered breath. She looked around to make sure no one was walking by the bench on which they sat. The children playing hopscotch laughed and shouted. Virgil tossed a rock into one of the squares and started his turn.

"I can't just abandon Leo." Her voice wobbled.

Cecil straightened his thin, twelve-year old shoulders and summoned his best man-of-the-house expression when he said, "It's time you let him go or we're all goin' to lose each other." Sure enough, there was still some little boy left in Cecil. Tears brimmed, and he blinked rapidly to hide them. "Leo wouldn't want ya to lose us, Greta."

She stifled a sob and lifted her eyes to the sky. Clouds floated in autumn puffs of white against a gray sky. A few birds swooped overhead. God was nowhere in sight.

"What should I do?" she whispered, wishing God would not only hear but also answer. Any way she looked at her circumstances, it was a losing battle, and she wasn't even sure what she was fighting.

"Mr. Barlowe is a bully," Cecil concluded. "A big one."

It was a simple description, but Greta knew Cecil was right.

An image of Mrs. Barlowe flashed across her mind. Why the key? Why come alongside her randomly in town and press her calling card into Greta's hand?

Greta thought of the look on the woman's face. It had been placid, almost unreadable. There was no fear, no panic that she was feeling oppressed by her husband. There was no insinuation that she knew where Leo had gone. And yet there had been an unspoken understanding that she wanted Greta to search the inside of Barlowe Theater . . . but to discover what?

And it couldn't be Leo. Mrs. Barlowe had no investment in Leo or his friends. So it was something else. Something deeper, darker, more concerning. So concerning, in fact, that Greta wondered if Mrs. Barlowe had learned to be impassive to it, while knowing deep within herself it needed to be exposed, brought into the light.

Whatever it was Mrs. Barlowe wanted Greta to find in the theater was precisely why Mr. Barlowe wanted Greta to leave well enough alone.

And somehow woven through everything was the person who had started it all. The woman in white with her petrified expression as her infant fell over the railing of the box seat.

It had happened.

Greta knew what she'd seen.

The floor creaked beneath the weight of someone. Greta rolled onto her side, the pillow flat and useless beneath her head. She opened her eyes, willing them to adjust to the dark. A woman farther down the room was snoring. Another woman breathed heavily, congestion in her nose and chest creating a wheezing sound in her sleep.

Greta heard the floorboard again. She pushed herself up onto her elbow. There, a few cots down, a woman was sulking across the room. Her hair hung long around her shoulders. Her nightgown reached her bony ankles. Her feet were bare.

It was Alma.

Greta waited as Alma drew closer and finally neared the end of Greta's cot.

"Alma?" Greta whispered. "Are you all right?"

Alma didn't answer. She kept walking, her shoulders stooped, her steps leery and hesitant.

"Alma?" Greta whispered louder so as not to disturb the other women in the room.

Alma ignored her, or she didn't hear her, Greta wasn't sure which. Instead, Alma reached the door that was shut firmly.

"Don't wander. Not till it's light out."

Wasn't that what Alma had warned her against? Stay in bed. People who wander don't come back?

Greta sat up fully. The room was not so dark that she couldn't make out the outline of Alma's hand as she reached for the knob to open the door. There was a slight stick as the door protested opening, humidity having swelled it in the doorframe. A scrape, the squeak of hinges, and Alma's silhouette was clear in the doorway. The hall loomed beyond her. Though Greta had walked that hallway just after dinner, after sitting with Cecil and her brothers outside, she felt now that it was nighttime, somehow the hall was much more than just a way to get from one place to another in the house. It felt like a passage to a horribly frightening place.

Alma stood still in the doorway.

Worried, Greta swung her legs from her cot. She stood, intent on approaching Alma to see what she needed. To ask if something was wrong.

Alma started forward, slinking down the hallway, her fingertips running along the wall. Greta paused at the border between the room and the hall. If Alma was sleepwalking, it wasn't right to leave her alone. She could fall, could hurt herself. The fact Alma hadn't responded to Greta convinced her that she must be unaware.

"Alma?" Greta tried again. She stepped a tentative foot from the room. "Alma!" Her call came out in a hiss.

Alma was already most of the way down the hall. She'd reached the corner where the stairs would descend to the main level. She dragged her hand along the wall and stopped. Turning toward Greta, Alma stood. Frozen.

Greta beckoned for Alma to come back. A silent, frantic wave with her hand. She didn't know if Alma's warning from the other night had merit, but now, after Mr. Barlowe's threats and Mr. Taylor's acquiescence, Greta wasn't convinced that Alma had been telling tales. If Mr. Barlowe was profiting off child labor, who else might be disappearing from Grove House? A place for the poor where no one would bother checking on the welfare of those who vanished here.

Alma stepped around the corner and out of sight. Greta hesitated to follow. If Oscar had been here—even Eleanor—she would have been emboldened by them just as she had at the theater. But now? Alone? With Alma clearly not registering that it had been Greta she'd looked directly at? No. She had looked *through* Greta, as if Greta hadn't been standing there waving for Alma to come back.

Greta breathed a prayer and hurried after Alma. While she was scarcely a friend, she had been the only person who'd shown her kindness at Grove House. Her warmth had endeared her to Greta.

At the top of the stairs, Greta looked down to see Alma already crossing the entrance, her fingers grazing a side table, then a hall tree, then coming to rest on the gleaming brass doorknob that reflected the moonlight through the window.

Alma turned the knob, and the front door opened. Cold

night air swept up the stairwell, across Greta's bare feet, and up her nightgown to her bare legs. The mist that settled over the earth greeted Greta with a warning. Greta tiptoed down the stairs after Alma, who had already moved onto the front porch of Grove House, leaving the door open wide behind her. Alma started down the porch steps and was in the drive when Greta reached the front door.

The wind blew a chilly gust of air through Greta's gown. It lifted Alma's hair from her shoulders and twisted it around as it breathed on them. Cold breath. The ominous vow of winter to come as October prepared them for the onslaught of snow.

"Alma!" Greta tried again, this time speaking just above a whisper.

Alma walked down the driveway. It was as though she were being called and it was critical that she answer. Finally, Greta increased her pace until she reached Alma's side. Stones on the driveway bit into the bottoms of her feet. She took Alma by the arm. She could feel the woman's cold skin beneath the thin cotton of her nightgown.

"Alma, wait," Greta pleaded.

Alma paused. She looked down at Greta's hand, then lifted her eyes to Greta's. Her gaze was vacant. The sadness that had etched itself in the lines of her face was gone now, and in its place was a solemn acceptance. Resignation perhaps.

"Where are you going?" Greta asked. "Please, come back with me."

"Did you know, when I was a little girl, I would sing a duet?" A smile touched Alma's lips. An eerie smile that told Greta Alma was far away in her memories. "'Little birdie, sing your song. Little birdie, it won't be long. Tweet a chorus and chirp a line, dear little birdie, won't you please be mine?'"

The tune was off-key. Alma's voice shook as she half sang, half whispered the words to whatever song it was she recited.

"We used to sing that for Papa," she said.

"Alma, let's go back inside. You can sing it for me again once we're back in our room," Greta urged.

"Papa didn't like it." Alma's voice turned cold. "He didn't like our song."

"Alma—"

"Go home." Alma traced her fingers tenderly down Greta's cheek. "Go now, dear girl, before he comes. When Papa comes, you will disappear. Don't disappear, Emily. Don't disappear."

Greta stared after Alma as she turned and walked away into the night.

Why had she called her Emily? Who was Emily?

Greta started after Alma, then stopped. Her brothers. She dared not leave them behind again. She watched as Alma wandered away until the darkness and the mist swallowed her whole.

27

Kit

Evan had stayed for dinner. Dinner with *her parents*. Rather than being in her late twenties, Kit felt as if she'd been transported back to high school, hoping her dad liked her new boyfriend. Except Evan wasn't her boyfriend—not to mention she hadn't really dated much, or ever. Walking in Madison's shadow did that to a girl.

Her dad, sensing Kit's emotional day had her insecurities rising to the fore, opted for her favorite activity to round out the otherwise tumultuous day. A campfire in the backyard's fire pit, complete with s'mores. And of course her mom had invited Evan to stay.

Considering the interview with Alpharetta Green and then the afternoon's foray into bludgeoning the basement wall of the Barlowe mansion, Evan didn't seem worse for the wear. At some point, he'd run back to his rental, checked in with the show's producer, left notes with Heather, and changed into a pair of jeans and a hoodie. He was safely platonic in his typical tailored trousers and oxford shirt for the show. But this Evan

253

Fischer? This was a completely different side of him, and Kit wasn't prepared for the onslaught of emotions that catapulted through her. Especially when he plopped into a camp chair next to her, smelling of smoke and Old Spice.

He stuck two marshmallows to the end of a s'more stick. "Want some?" His blue eyes raked her face.

Kit shook her head and looked away. Into the fire. The fire that danced and played in the crisp night air. Sticks sparked and snapped. Smoke swirled in plumes toward the darkening sky, where stars were beginning to pinprick their light through the atmosphere.

Evan held out his stick so the marshmallows could brown. "It's an art," he stated.

"Hmm?" Kit turned her angsty attention to the marshmallows that lofted over the orange-and-blue coals.

"Making a s'more. It's an art." Evan's chair squeaked as he adjusted himself so he could position his stick a little bit closer to the coals. "A slow turn. Hold it above the coals just enough for the heat to saturate it and make it gooey. Toast the outside. You don't want to burn it."

"I always burn it," Kit countered, drawing her knees up into the extra-large canvas chair she sat in and pulling a blanket over her lap that her mom had brought out. Her parents were in the house pouring hot coffee into thermoses. Hot chocolate for Evan because apparently he was a sociopath and preferred chocolate.

"Why?" Evan turned his stick.

"Because I like to watch the sugar puffs burn." What else was she supposed to say? That she was too impatient to wait for the marshmallow to brown to perfection? That she liked the taste of the charred layer of sugar before biting into a semi-cold marshmallow center?

Why were they talking about marshmallows anyway? They should be in the Barlowes' basement, busting down the wall.

Trying to find that vault—if that's what it was. They should be drilling a hole and inserting one of those police cameras that were like snakes, so they could see inside—see if Madison lay there, wasting away. Trapped.

"We shouldn't be here." Kit's statement was emphasized as a chunk of wood in the fire snapped.

"The Barlowes control what we can and can't do. They had plans tonight." Evan turned his marshmallows again as one side gave off its warning signal of smoke and before it burst into flame.

"What plans are more important than Madison? They heard our theories. They were *part* of it! I thought Dean had a sense of urgency, but—"

"Kit." Evan pulled his sweet lumps of toasted fluff from the fire. "We could demolish for hours before we find anything. And then it could be nothing. The odds of Madison being trapped in a passageway—sorry, but I just don't buy it. Maybe there is one, and maybe she found it. I think if we can uncover the answer to that, it'll help us find her. Still, I don't think she's trapped between the Barlowe mansion and the theater in an underground tunnel. I believe the tunnel, if it exists, is only part of the answer."

Kit pressed her lips together. It was unacceptable. This campfire, this lounging, this . . . She jumped to her feet, startling Evan.

"What are you doing?" He pressed his marshmallows between graham crackers and chocolate.

"I'm going to Avery's place. I'm not going to stop until we find Madison." She looked around on the ground for her water bottle and phone. She bent to retrieve them. "I'm going to call Detective Seamans and see where the investigation is at. I'm going—"

Evan was standing in front of her. He'd set his s'more on a paper plate on the ground.

Remembrance flooded Kit at the same moment Evan opened his mouth to speak.

"And I need to go to the pantry!" She'd promised Corey she would get work caught up. Everything was pressing in on her. She couldn't sit around and relax, making s'mores by a campfire. Spinning away from Evan, Kit started toward the house.

"Kit!" He chased after her. "Wait up."

"What?" She stopped and faced him.

"You're not going to the pantry alone."

She raised her brows in defiance. "I'm my own person, Evan. You don't need to follow me around town. Go. Film something." Kit gave him a flippant wave of her hand.

"Hold on!" Evan shouted after her as she trotted away. "Kit!"

He couldn't understand. There was too much waiting around for a miracle to happen. Waiting for the police to find something about Madison. Waiting for Avery to call her and tell her Madison had shown up and was okay. Waiting for direction? And all while harboring her own doubts that she didn't want to admit. Didn't want to tell anyone.

What if this *was* something far more nefarious? What if Barlowe Theater's stories of hauntings and spirits had their roots in something real?

She reached the car she'd borrowed from her parents and opened the door. A hand on her shoulder stopped her.

"Kit."

It was her father. Fabulous.

"If you're going to go, take Evan with you," he instructed with that fatherly tone that brooked no argument.

"Dad."

"I'm serious, Kit. After that call the other night? You really think it's wise to go to the pantry at night to work alone?"

"Nothing's come of it." Kit jammed her water bottle in the holder in the car. "Nothing's come of anything—that's the problem."

"We have to pray that the Lord will—"

"You think I haven't been?" Kit cried. "I've prayed that we'd find Madison. I've prayed that all this would just go away. I feel like everything is out of control. Everything is spiraling down, and nothing is going to be resolved. Not Madison, not the break-in at the pantry, not that stupid phone call."

Evan came up behind her father. He directed his words to her father. "I'll go with her."

"Thank you." The men shook hands as though Kit had nothing to say about it.

And apparently she didn't.

Evan skirted the front of the car and climbed into the passenger side seat. He looked at her. "Well? Let's go before you pitch another tantrum."

At the moment, Kit wanted to pitch him and all his handsomeness right out of her life.

The pantry's outdoor motion lights turned on and flooded the parking lot as she pulled into her space. She'd been silent the entire way here. On one hand, she felt petty and temperamental. On the other hand, Kit saw reason in Evan's coming with her. She really didn't want to be alone at the pantry. But she could've called Corey. He would've been more help than Evan.

Hiking to the door, she punched her code into the lock. It was easier to ignore Evan than to acknowledge his presence behind her. She tugged on the door and entered, turning on the florescent lights that flooded the large room with its metal shelves.

"This place is old." Evan surveyed the room, the rafters overhead, the plaster walls.

"Mm-hmm." Kit was tired, and if she was tired, then wherever Madison was, Madison had to be exhausted. She made her way to the shelves of canned goods. Pleased to see Corey had stacked and organized them by vegetable, fruit, and beans, she moved around the corner.

Fabulous.

Boxes of cookies and crackers lay in piles on the shelves and on the floor. She would need to organize them before they could be given out. Plus she'd need to do inventory. Count the categories. Identify what might have been damaged in the vandalism versus perhaps misplaced, and then—

"Does anyone think this place is haunted?" Evan interrupted her assessment.

Kit shot him a look. "No."

"I guarantee you, if Heather came here, she'd say she saw someone."

"I'm sure." Kit bent to pick up a crushed box of vanilla wafers. She wasn't even angry at whoever had trashed the place. She was just defeated.

"This place used be the old poorhouse, right?" Evan asked, poking his head into nooks and crannies that would reveal nothing but more food and supplies that had been donated for those in need.

"Yes. A county home. They shut it down in the 1930s. Then it became a school, and then it was abandoned until the 1980s when someone bought it. It's been offices and such since then. The food pantry was started here about ten years ago. The board hired Corey and me to manage it, and the rest is run on grants and donations."

The lights went out.

"Hey!" Kit spun, trying to see Evan in the instant darkness that had enveloped the room. "Evan?"

"Kit?" She heard him call from the far end of the room.

"Turn the lights back on!" It wasn't funny. Nothing was funny tonight.

"Where are they?" Evan called back.

"You didn't turn them off?"

"No."

Kit felt along the shelf as she made her way toward the wall and the door where the light switch was located. "Hold on."

Her toe hit a cardboard box. Empty, it skidded across the wood floor and hit something she couldn't identify. Everything loomed like shadows before her. Evan's earlier remarks about hauntings suddenly gave her the creeps, and she was glad Heather wasn't here.

"Kit?" Evan called again. "You okay?"

"Yeah, I'm just trying to find the—" Her words were cut off as an arm wrapped around from behind her, tugging on her throat and pulling her back against another body.

She couldn't breathe. Kit clawed at the arm around her neck as it tightened around her throat.

"Kit, I can't find the light switch." Evan was clueless as to her struggle in the darkness.

She tried to elbow her assailant. The person was strong but had a paunchy gut. The arm around her throat was covered in a coarse shirt, the hand gloved in leather. She felt the gloved hand pressing against her jaw.

A light at the opposite end of the room snapped on. In a quick second, her assailant released her, shoving Kit forward into a pile of cardboard banana boxes. They toppled on top of Kit. She heard her attacker run, the back door slam open, and then there was silence.

More lights flooded the pantry.

Kit coughed violently, trying to clear her airway. She rubbed her throat as she rolled onto her side, kicking away a box that fell onto her leg.

"Kit!" Evan charged toward her when he saw her on the floor. "Are you all right?" He dropped to his knees, assessing everything, from her to their surroundings.

"Someone was here . . ." She choked. "They . . ." It hurt to talk, to breathe.

Evan helped her sit up, and she had no qualms about leaning against him. The softness of his sweatshirt felt comforting as she pressed her face into his shoulder. Kit felt his muscles shift as he fumbled for his phone, yet he still retained his hold on her.

"I'm calling 911."

She didn't argue. She couldn't think.

Evan explained the situation to the dispatcher, then adjusted his position from his knees so he could sit down and she could fully lean into his embrace. He tucked his chin against the top of her head. "I got you," he mumbled into her hair.

For now.

He had her for now.

But what about tomorrow, and the next day, and the days following when this oppressiveness hadn't lifted, Madison hadn't been found, and it was time for him to pack up and go home?

28

"Are you kidding me?" Corey's stringent voice echoed through the pantry as he burst into the main storage area. The police were outside, and Kit could see the flashing lights of their squad cars through the windows. The EMTs had rushed here too, but she'd refused an ambulance to the hospital. There was no point. She could breathe okay. Her throat was a little sore and bruised, but the damage overall was minimal.

Corey slid to a halt next to her chair, his eyes grazing Evan. "What happened?"

The police must have alerted Corey, as he was the second emergency contact for the pantry next to her.

"Someone was here when we arrived—at least it seems that way. They assaulted Kit." Evan had hold of her hand, and Kit had no desire to let it go. She knew it was platonic, but it gave a sense of security that would have left her completely abandoned had Evan pulled away.

Corey didn't seem to care that Evan answered for Kit. He crouched in front of her so he was at eye level. "Are you okay?"

"I will be." Kit sniffed. Gone was her anger, her irritation. Urgency had returned, only it was married to fear now. Outright fear. She could reason away a fluke car accident. She could remain numb to a creepy one-off phone call. But she couldn't reason away a full-on attack. And the attacker had been so quiet! Like a ninja. If Evan hadn't found the lights when he did . . .

"What if it was the same person who took Madi?" Kit rasped out with her hurting throat.

Corey exchanged looks with Evan. "Honey, let's hope not." He patted her knee. "If that's the case, then I'm signing you up for self-defense classes until you're so good you could kill me with your pinky finger."

Kit smiled weakly. "I don't want to kill you."

"That's good." Another pat to her knee. Corey then turned to Evan. "So, do the cops know who it was?"

"No. And Kit didn't recognize them."

"I didn't *see* them," she said, adjusting her hand in Evan's. He loosened his grip, but when she didn't pull away, his fingers closed back around hers.

"They came up from behind?" Corey's brows rose. "If I were here, I would've drop-kicked them into next year."

"No, you wouldn't have." Kit's laugh was watery with tears.

"You're right," Corey agreed, "I wouldn't have, but I sure would've wanted to. Thank God you weren't here alone." His look of gratitude to Evan relieved Kit a bit. While there had never be anything between her and Corey, she didn't want Corey feeling jealous or even replaced.

"I'm pretty sure the police will connect this to Madison— and the car accident."

Evan's statement brought Kit's eyes to his. "Why?" She didn't quite see the connection.

Evan rubbed the back of his neck with his free hand. "Because there's too much stacking up with you and Madison at the center of it all. The different events have got to be connected somehow. There's a point where there's too much coincidence to ignore."

"Suspects," Corey blurted. "Let's name them."

"I don't have any," Kit whimpered, and this time she didn't bother to second-guess leaning over and resting against Evan.

"I'll bet you it's Al Farrington, Madison's grandfather." Corey's eyes widened as Kit opened her mouth to argue. "Ah, ah! Don't say he would never do anything to his granddaughter. Anyone who knows the man wouldn't put it past him to do whatever it takes to protect his interests."

"I'm sure Detective Seamans has already vetted Al Farrington and ruled him out as a suspect," Evan said.

"You're probably right." Corey nodded and sniffed. "Well, if I need to, I'll camp out here at the pantry. And I'll take them out if they come back."

"You're so tough." Kit rolled her eyes and gave a small laugh.

Corey slapped his bicep, which really wasn't all that impressive. "You better believe it. Anything for my girl."

It wasn't fair that when she was at the end of herself, there was a handsome man to half carry her into the house. She should be walking herself in. That was fair. Being exhausted and emotional made her vulnerable.

Evan stopped by her apartment with Kit, helped her pack a few more items, and was now leading her into her parents' house.

Ridiculous. She should've stayed at her apartment. She should've done so many things. What, she couldn't pinpoint. Not at the moment. Not when she was this tired and emotionally drained.

Kit leaned against Evan as he helped her to the living room. It was past midnight, and her parents would have no idea what had happened at the pantry with her getting assaulted. With all the commotion, Kit had neglected to call them. She collapsed onto the couch, her hand snagging Evan's hoodie pocket accidentally. It tugged him down next to her, causing the couch cushion to sag and throwing them together at its lowest point.

"Sorry," Kit mumbled, feeling a blush creep into her cheeks.

Evan reached over and removed her glasses, placing them on the coffee table. He kicked off his shoes.

"What are you doing?" Kit tried to scoot over so she wasn't half sitting on his lap.

He leaned back on the couch, propping his feet on the coffee table. In a swift and easy move, his arm slid around her and pulled her into his side. "You've already used my shoulder for half the night—might as well finish it out there." His gruff observation sent Kit's emotions into a whirligig ride.

"I'll be fine," Kit tried to convince herself, and yet she didn't move away from him.

"It's okay, Kitty-cat. Anyone and their brother's mother can tell you don't want to be alone tonight."

"My parents are here," she protested, but there wasn't much conviction in her voice. How could there be? Evan Fischer was practically heroic, even though all he'd proven himself good at was being contrary, sleuthing through history, and of course holding her. He was *really* good at holding her.

And he smelled good.

"Are you smelling my sweatshirt?" he asked, quietly laughing.

The living room was dimly lit, the gas fireplace flickering.

"I'm not . . . Okay, fine, I was smelling your sweatshirt," Kit mumbled into his shoulder. Her eyelids felt heavy. Her heart was . . . so sore. So confused.

"Glad I washed it then." Evan's free hand came up and gently pushed her hair from the side of her face. "Go to sleep, Cat."

"It's Kit," she murmured.

"Sure."

The clocked ticked.

Then it chimed.

One, two, three . . .

She stirred.

. . . six, seven.

Kit bolted upright, pulling away from Evan, where she'd been sprawled across his chest. His head was back and to the side, a light snore emanating from his mouth. She sensed movement, and Kit jerked her head up to see a man standing over them. Ford Boyd.

Her dad was staring down at them, a coffee mug clutched in his hand, his gray eyebrows raised. "Soooo . . ." he started.

Evan stirred, opened his eyes, and then stretched as if nothing was out of the ordinary. "Wow. I was out hard."

"It's seven in the morning!" Kit sprang from the couch like a guilty teenager.

"Yes, and the coffee is brewed." A smile played at Ford's mouth.

"I—"

Ford held up a hand. "It's fine." Then he grew serious. "I got a call from Detective Seamans this morning. He was checking in to see if we wanted a protective security detail on the house."

"No." Kit wiped her hands down the front of her jeans, trying to get her bearings.

Evan remained on the sofa, looking up at them as if he belonged there.

"We don't need a security detail." She wasn't on a hit list. Well, she didn't think she was anyway. Kit played with her hair that felt like it was a bit out of control. "Everything's fine."

Ford sipped his coffee, then looked her in the eye. "I beg to differ."

"So do I." Evan pushed off the couch, stretching his arms over his head and yawning. "I have a kink in my back to prove it." He brushed his finger along the base of Kit's neck. "You have bruises."

Kit ignored him and reached for her phone that she'd left on the coffee table. "Three missed calls from Avery."

"I'd call her back then," Ford said. "And do *not* go anywhere alone."

"She's with me," Evan stated affirmatively.

"You didn't ask me—"

"In this case, he doesn't have to," her dad interrupted. Ford gave Evan a nod. "You have *my* permission."

She'd barely had time to grab the thermos of coffee Mom offered her before racing to her car with Evan. He stuck out his hand for the keys, and Kit gave him a side-eye. She scurried to the driver's side and slid in behind the steering wheel. "My car, I drive."

Evan didn't respond. Instead, he climbed in, and within seconds they were on their way. He still sported his hoodie and blue jeans, but now he also wore a scruffy face and hair that stuck up all over the place.

"Avery was crying so hard I could hardly understand her." Kit sped up.

"Yeah, but let's not die before we get to her. Slow down." Evan's direction made sense.

Kit eased her foot off the gas pedal. The messages Avery left had each grown in frantic urgency. When she'd called Avery back, the young woman had begged Kit to come to the theater as quickly as possible.

"What exactly did Avery say?" Evan asked as he thumbed through his phone.

Kit gripped the wheel tighter. "Something about her grandfather coming over. Her mom was a wreck. The police found something—about Madison."

"Sounds like they haven't found her, but they've come across new evidence."

"Or she's dead." Kit's words caught in a gulp. This was surreal, like a dream. There were so many moments she'd robotically gone through her day, even though her best friend was missing. But now? If they arrived at the theater and Madison was—

"Deep breaths, Cat."

Kit didn't even bother to correct him this time.

A few minutes later, she drove around the one-way block and pulled into a perpendicular parking spot outside the theater. She could see inside through the glass doors beneath the marquee. Avery's blond ponytail bobbed as she talked with animated hands to a shorter woman, who Kit recognized as Avery's mom, Carol.

She and Evan exited the car simultaneously. The theater doors opened, and a police officer waved them inside. Raised voices filtered onto the street, but there was no crying, no heartbroken sobs. This was good news potentially, with the hope that Madison could still be alive. It was bad news as to the state of mind of the theater's inhabitants.

"How *dare* you accuse me of this!" Al Farrington boomed. His son, Madison's father, stood in front of him, veins popping on his neck.

"Then what is this?" He waved a piece of paper in front of Al's face, which looked like a photocopied page from a spiral notebook.

"I don't know, *Dan*!" Al glared at his son. "What is it?"

"Everyone, that's enough!" Detective Seamans's command superseded the others, and they rumbled to a conversational halt.

Avery looked up and noticed Kit. She flew past her mother and fell into Kit's arms. "Oh my gosh, I'm so glad you're here!"

Detective Seamans caught Kit's eye. It was clear he expected her to be silent also. Evan hung back by the door, but the detective spotted him.

"No cameras?" Seamans drilled Evan with a stern look.

"No cameras," Evan affirmed.

The detective nodded. "All right, everyone, settle down. Finding the note isn't proof of guilt of any one person."

It was obvious that the situation had gotten out of hand, courtesy of texting and phone calls among the Farrington family before the police had time to corral the ones they needed to corral.

"What note?" Kit whispered to Avery.

Avery's eyes filled with tears. "It's a piece of paper in Madison's handwriting. Notes about Grandfather and some potentially illegal activity with his investors. The police found the note downstairs on the theater's boiler room floor."

Kit frowned. They'd been in the boiler room recently, and the police had combed the area multiple times. But no one found any note. Why would it suddenly show up now?

"I am *not* involved in illegal practices!" Al Farrington bellowed. He waved his arm in the air. "This accusation from my granddaughter is paranoia at its worst. She wants to undermine me, and this is stooping very low to accomplish her goal!"

"How dare you accuse Madi! Your granddaughter is missing!" Carol, Madison's mother, said with a shrill wobble in her voice.

"I know that!" Al shouted back to his ex-daughter-in-law.

"What did you do to Madison?" Carol leveled a fierce look on Al.

Al snatched the photocopy from his son Dan's hand and balled it up in his fist. "Madison has been trying to undercut my efforts to run an effective enterprise in Kipper's Grove since the moment she went to the university. She and her benevolence are sickening because she makes me out to be a complete cad."

"You *are* a cad." Avery's one-liner went unheard by all but Kit.

Al remained focused on Carol. "I've given generously to charities and good causes and have done a lot for this town. We all know this is a personal vendetta of Madi's against me for what happened between you and Dan."

"How dare you!" Carol scowled, her eyes welling with tears. "*You* covered up Dan's affairs for years before I found out!"

"He's my son." Al glanced at Dan, who had tightened his lips in silence. "What was I supposed to do? Break up your marriage myself? And yet somehow you *both* managed to turn it into being my fault, and you turned my granddaughters against me."

"It's not only that," Carol argued. "You know Madi's passion for preserving historical places, while you've shown nothing but contempt for preservation."

"They're not all worth preserving!" Al roared.

"They *are*!" Carol wailed.

"They're not!" Al shouted. "The hotel we tore down last month that had Madison all worked up was filled with asbestos and black mold. Not to mention the foundation was so weak, the place was going to collapse soon and kill someone."

"Well, that's not the case here," Carol said, indicating the theater.

"People!" Detective Seamans tried to regain control. "Do not make me have to detain you all."

"There's motive for taking Madi. Right there." Carol pointed in Al Farrington's direction.

The older man's jaw tightened. His gray hair hung over his forehead, evidence he'd been raking his hand through it in agitation.

Detective Seamans ordered two of his officers to take positions closer to Mr. Farrington and Madison's mother, Carol. Dan Farrington, Madison's father, kept his mouth shut.

Avery clung to Kit's arm.

"Now," Seamans began, "The note we discovered in the basement of the theater was *not* there in previous sweeps. However, we have verified that it does indeed seem to have been written by Madison herself. That being said, we are not placing anyone under arrest." He turned to Carol, and she visibly stiffened. "Mr. Farrington here, as the note states rather emphatically, is being accused of certain illegal practices, and a proper investigation will take place. Meanwhile"—the detective held up his hands again as he sensed the room preparing to erupt—"the rest of you are to stay away from each other. We don't need your family distracting from the primary issue at hand, and that is finding Madison."

"Does finding the note mean she's still alive?" Kit couldn't help but ask.

The detective's expression turned softer when he saw her. His eyes seemed to register the bruises on her throat. His tone was gentle. "We don't know how it got there."

"Why were you even looking down there again?" Dan Farrington inquired.

Detective Seamans glanced at Evan. "We were following up on a few leads."

"Like what?"

"I'm not at liberty to talk about them right now."

Kit looked toward Evan. He met her eyes. Had he been talking with Detective Seamans on the side?

"I just want this all to be over." Avery's teary voice filled the lobby of theater.

"We all do," Dan Farrington said, the man's tired eyes revealing his anxiety. Kit noticed the tightness of his jaw as he clenched it. He glanced at his ex-wife and then at his dad. "If there's anything either of you know that will help us find Madi, please say so."

"I don't know a thing!" Carol was quick to say. Her glare

was one of animosity that anyone would think she might be holding back something about Madison's whereabouts.

"Dad?" Dan eyed his father.

Al·Farrington's eyes turned steely. "If I knew anything to help find Madi, I would move heaven and earth." Dan paled a bit at his father's emphatic statement. "I don't try to ruin her the way she tries to ruin me."

29

Greta

She should have opted to follow her cautionary self and stayed at Grove House. She shouldn't have been lured away from the porch by Alma's hypnotic hold over her. She should have worn shoes. The stones in the dirt road bit into the bottoms of Greta's cold feet as she followed the woman. "Alma, please." Something was not right with Alma. The sad woman Greta had known so briefly at Grove House seemed to have drifted away in her mind. She was intent on a destination that only she knew, and Greta's pleas had done nothing to dissuade her. "Alma?"

"Come, Emily. Papa's waiting." Alma tilted her chin up, ignoring the chilly wind that whipped through the trees along the road as they made their way toward Kipper's Grove.

She should leave Alma and return to Grove House before she found herself in trouble. Mr. Barlowe's threats hung over Greta's head. The umbrella of security she'd hoped Mr. Taylor would offer as overseer of Grove House now held little comfort. Not that it had held much prior. For Mr. Barlowe's invisible

273

reach seemed to extend everywhere in Kipper's Grove. Even including the county.

"Emily?" Alma paused, looking back at Greta, waiting for her to follow.

"I'm not Emily," Greta corrected. Surely Alma could see that.

"Come." Alma held out her arm. "Don't leave me alone." Alma's appeal tore at Greta's soul. The responsibility to look after those who needed her warred with her duty to be there for her brothers.

The brutal truth was that she cared more for her brothers than for Alma. But to turn her back on Alma was to be everything Greta most hated. A betrayer. Someone who refused to be there when needed. When circumstances required too much sacrifice, they ran away.

Greta could not do that.

She reached out and took Alma's cold hand. The woman, older than her by maybe five or ten years, smiled her sorrowful smile. "I'm sorry," she said.

The wind picked up and whipped their nightgowns around their legs. What a frightening sight they must make! Two lonely women, pale in the night, dressed in shifts, their hair blowing this way and that. Holding hands as though at any moment monsters would emerge from the woods to devour them like the wolves of fairy tales.

Kipper's Grove became more populated the farther they walked. The south side was familiar with its dilapidated homes. Alma continued to trudge forward. Greta found herself limping as they went. Where they were going was a mystery, and the farther she walked, the more she regretted accompanying Alma.

She held back, tugging on Alma's hand. "We must go back."

Alma shook her head, the whites of her eyes bright in the night. "No. Papa will have tea. And we can sing 'Little Birdie' for him. Maybe he will like it this time!" Alma had the hopeful look of a child wishing for their father's approval, together with the nagging doubt that it would be given to them.

"Alma—"

Greta's words cut short as out of the shadows a familiar form strode toward them. Officer John Hargrove. As he approached, she shrank away, aware of the indecency of her nightdress and bare feet. But there was nothing she could do to shield herself or Alma.

"Greta?" John looked to Alma and then back to her, his eyes raking her form that was shivering from the cold. "What are you doing? Where are your shoes, and why are you dressed like that? It's the middle of the night."

Greta linked arms with Alma to reassure her. Alma hunched her shoulders and looked away from John. Greta was tongue-tied, lost for a good explanation.

"I'll see you home," he declared.

"Please don't!" Greta started. She quickly tempered her reaction. "I mean, no thank you. I-I can see Alma home." In the state she was in, she wanted to get as far away from John as possible. It was mortifying and embarrassing what Grove House was turning her into. Had God no mercy at all to shield her from such shame?

"Take them." A gruff voice broke the thickness between them.

Greta jumped as another man stepped from the shadows, stalking up behind John. It was another officer, but this man was stockier with a round face and a thick neck.

John turned, his back guarding Greta and Alma from the other man. "Ambrose, I'll take care of this."

"Tarnation, you will!" The other officer—Ambrose—tried to step around John, but John blocked him.

Greta backed away a few steps, taking Alma with her. There was something about Ambrose that had heightened her caution.

John gave Ambrose a slight push of warning. "Back away."

Ambrose cocked his head. "You're going to put your hands on me, Hargrove? Do you think that's smart?"

John lowered his hands, though he was still trying to reason with Ambrose. "I said I'll take care of this. Leave them be."

"That's not the order, and you know it." Ambrose sidestepped John and came toward Greta and Alma. His shoulders were beefy, and he held a stick in one hand, slapping it against the other. "Miss, I'll need you to come with me."

Greta gave John a questioning look, hoping he would do something. When he didn't, when instead he looked at the ground, she realized he was not going to intervene further.

"Sir, we've done nothing wrong. Please, allow me to take my friend home. She's sleepwalking." It was a better explanation than anything else Greta could come up with at the moment.

"Sleepwalking, eh? That's the first time I've ever heard that pinned on Alma before." Ambrose chuckled darkly.

Greta looked between the officers. "You know Alma?"

"'Course we know Alma." Ambrose approached her and bent to look up into Alma's downturned face. "Don't we, Alma?"

Alma hastily looked up, whimpered, and then directed her eyes back toward the ground.

"Time to go home now." Ambrose took hold of the arm that Alma didn't have linked with Greta's. "Your daddy said if it happened again . . ."

Alma's head came up. "He wants me?"

"He does indeed." Ambrose's reply was patronizing. As he started to lead Alma away, she slid her arm from Greta's. "Bring her," Ambrose instructed John, tipping his head in Greta's direction.

John stepped up to her, his face apologetic. "I'm sorry, Greta."

"John?" She was confused by what was happening.

"I need you to come with me."

"Where?"

"Please." He didn't add the words that might have made Greta feel better. There was no *Trust me*, no *It's okay, there's nothing to worry about.*

She obeyed, having little choice as his hand stole around her arm in a commanding grip, but every part of her fought against him. Against a man she thought she could trust, but now was terribly frightened had become her enemy.

"Where are you taking us?" Greta began to struggle against John's hold as he urged her from the vehicle they'd transported the women in. His aggressiveness didn't match what she knew of him from before, his kindness. Though she didn't like it, she was too stunned to form a proper response.

As Alma walked obediently alongside Ambrose, Greta pulled back, staring through the night's effervescent glow at the outline of the looming mansion in front of her.

The Barlowe mansion?

"John?" Fear dripped from the question in Greta's voice.

John didn't look at her. He tugged on her again. "Come."

Greta stumbled as he led her around the back of the mansion, through shrubbery along a narrow path, following Ambrose and Alma.

"Why are you doing this?" She pulled her arm against his grip. "Let go, John, please. What are we doing here? John—" Greta stepped on a sharp stone, and she cried out.

John paused, allowing Greta to regain her balance. She limped forward, then stopped. "John, please. Let me go. I need to go home. My brothers need me."

John's jaw worked back and forth. He shook his head. "It's

too late for that." He led her forward again, a little slower this time. "You're too involved now. You know too much."

"Know too much? About what? I don't know anything!"

John didn't answer her. He didn't look at her. His handsome profile became less so the closer they came to a side door tucked into an alcove of the mansion. The door was partly open.

John pushed the door the rest of the way open, urging Greta inside before him.

The room was plain, the light dim. Its walls were made of brick, and the floor was of stone, cold beneath her feet. It appeared to be a workroom of some kind, evident by the brooms, dusters, rug beaters, and other household tools stored here.

Alma stood in the middle of the room, her arms wrapped around herself. She was shivering. When Greta noticed her friend's condition, she realized that she too was numb from the cold and shivering.

Ambrose leveled a dark look at John that indicated some sort of warning. Then he left them, climbing a short flight of stairs and disappearing around a corner.

Greta sidled next to Alma. "Are you all right?"

Awareness had returned to the woman's eyes. "I'm so sorry," she mouthed.

Footsteps alerted them, and Greta lifted her face to witness Mr. Barlowe descending the same stairs Ambrose had just taken, who was directly behind Mr. Barlowe now.

Mr. Barlowe's countenance was surly and unpleasant. That he was angered was evident in the odd little light in his eyes. A warning type of light that only increased when he saw Greta.

"You didn't tell me about Miss Mercy," he said, turning to Ambrose.

Ambrose gave a little shrug. "I blame Hargrove for that."

"Me?" John retorted. "I was going to let her go back to Grove House."

Greta felt John's hand on the small of her back. Maybe he

meant to offer her some security, but she stepped away feeling betrayed and abused instead.

Mr. Barlowe snorted. "Back to Grove House? Use your head." He leveled his attention on Alma. "So. You decided to come home. Again." It was a statement, not a question, and he looked extremely displeased.

Home? Stunned, Greta eyed Alma, whose hair hid her face from them all. Alma stared at her feet.

"I told you to control your episodes."

"I'm sorry, Papa." Alma's voice was small and childlike for a grown woman.

"I'm sorry, Papa," Barlowe mocked. He waved Ambrose and John away. "Go. Both of you."

The men did as they were told, John hesitating as he met Greta's terrified eyes. "I'm sorry—"

"Get out, Hargrove! You're worthless!"

Greta followed Alma's example, focusing on her bare toes, allowing her hair to hide her face.

Mr. Barlowe was Alma's father? Greta had seen no evidence of that at Grove House earlier today when they'd met face-to-face. But perhaps that was what had catapulted Alma into her muddled state of mind. She had reverted for a while to being a child again.

Barlow came up between them, grabbing hold of each of their arms. Alma whimpered. Greta flinched against the pinching of her skin beneath his hand.

"You know where you go," he growled at Alma. "Now you get to have a friend there too." Barlowe kicked open a door that revealed a staircase that led down into the basement. "It's what I get for having a half-wit for a daughter." He spat in Alma's direction.

Greta dared not say a word as her bare feet met with the cold stairs.

30

Kit

OCTOBER, PRESENT DAY

"You told Detective Seamans about the possible hidden passageway?" Kit asked as she and Evan hiked their way from the theater toward the Barlowe mansion on the other side of the street.

"Of course. I said Seamans wouldn't have either the time or a reason to investigate it. I never said I was hiding anything from him. I would've been irate if I were the investigator and wasn't kept aware of what was going on."

Kit hurried to keep up. "That makes sense. But did you know they'd found that note from Madison?"

"No." Evan's feet hit the sidewalk in front of the Barlowe mansion. "I'd just filled him on what we found with Dean and Selma Barlowe. The growing possibility that there might be a passageway after all. He said he planned to go back to the theater and look into it again."

Kit put out a hand to stop Evan. "What about Heather and Tom?"

"What about them?"

281

"Aren't they supposed to be filming this? Finding Madison? Won't you get in trouble with the show?"

Evan grimaced. "Don't worry about the show, Kit. Heather's a big girl. The producer can work with her just as much as I can. She doesn't need me there to film everything. Right now, I don't have any desire to be near her or the crew."

"She wouldn't like to hear you say that."

"Then we won't tell her, will we?" Evan started for the mansion again.

Kit followed, adjusting her glasses that had slipped down her nose. "Why are we going to the mansion?"

They'd reached the vast porch of the mansion with its brick pillars and heavy stone planters, red impatiens and vinca vines trailing down their sides. Evan climbed the stairs toward the ornate front doors.

"Dean and his crew have been working all night to try to expose the vault—assuming his theory is correct."

Kit pulled back. "Evan, wait. You said they had a prior engagement, which was why we left yesterday evening and didn't keep excavating."

Evan had the decency to look sheepish. "Detective Seamans felt it was best if you weren't there. You realize you've hardly slept or eaten this week? You needed rest."

"So you lied to me?" Kit stared at him.

Evan shook his head. "No. I . . . ." He reached for her, but she sidestepped him.

"Yes, you did. While they were trying to find Madison, you had me relaxing by the campfire?"

"I was trying to help you, Kit. I was following Seamans's orders. I was—"

"It's not your place to protect me." Kit's throat was thick as tears threatened to spill over. She knew Evan could see them in her eyes. She remembered waking up against his chest. The smell of his sweatshirt. The feel of his protection last night at the pantry. But as was typical with most people, there was a limit to their loyalty. "Loyalty doesn't include lies," Kit stated.

"We just wanted to keep you safe and help you rest," Evan said helplessly. He didn't apologize. He offered justification instead.

Kit gave a little laugh. "Well, that backfired on you both. Instead, I got assaulted and almost strangled to death."

"Not funny." Evan's expression darkened. He heaved a sigh and took a few steps toward the mansion's door, then stopped and turned to face her. "Look, I overstepped. I see that now."

"Yeah. You did." Kit pressed her lips together to keep the tears at bay. "I'm not Heather. I'm not a show. I'm not a ghost. I don't need debunking, Evan Fisher, and I don't need you to prove me wrong or step in and direct the course of events. Between you and my dad, I feel like I'm back to being a juvenile who can't make her own decisions."

"Okay. Yeah. You're right."

"Thank you." Kit lifted her chin and moved to pass him.

Evan's voice halted her. "So how does a guy protect a woman he cares for if he can't stop her when he sees her careening toward danger because he'll be accused of being heavy-handed or dominating or a liar?"

Kit stared at him.

Evan stared back.

"My delivery might be off, Kit, but doesn't the intent of the heart mean anything? Doesn't the fact that I'm trying my best to keep you safe mean anything?"

His words sliced into her with a truth that hurt. "You barely know me," she whispered.

Evan nodded. "I know, but that doesn't mean I don't care, that I don't want to help and protect you. Remember that. Please," he added. Then he lifted the iron knocker on the door and brought it down.

"You lied to me."

Before Evan could reply, the door swung open, and Selma beckoned them inside. Her eyes were bright with anticipation and excitement. "Come in! Come in!"

"How's it going?" Evan's ability to shift from the tense conversation to a polite friendliness as they followed Selma's petite frame into the mansion both impressed and unnerved Kit.

He wasn't entirely wrong in his assessment. The current culture wasn't fond of men who took leadership over a woman. *She* wasn't fond of men who assumed such leadership, and yet part of her wanted that. That hero to step in and navigate difficult circumstances for her. At the same time, she felt the need to hold men—even her dad—at a distance to protect herself. From them. From *loving* them. Not that she even remotely loved Evan, but still—he was someone she could potentially see herself with, and that thought terrified her. It was the ultimate vulnerability, the relationship between a man and a woman. Two separate people with separate minds and wills and roles. So did Evan have the right to mislead her in order to protect her? No. But his intentions of protecting her spoke of something she was almost more afraid of. Being cared for. Being led. Because if he cared, she could easily sink into that offer of security. Her roots had taught her security was tenuous at best. What happened if and when he misled her? What happened if she lost her identity in him and then lost him altogether? She would be who she was at birth. Without an identity, without someone to depend on . . .

She would be lost.

She was better off alone. She could forgive Evan's errors in judgment, but she was still better off alone.

Selma was leading them down a hall, and her talking jerked Kit from her tumultuous thoughts.

"We're almost through the wall. The team had to shore up the foundation before we could completely break through," Selma explained over her shoulder.

"The *team*?" Kit inserted.

Evan had obviously been affected by their conversation on the mansion's porch. His reply was softer, more sober. "Detective Seamans wanted some of his men here."

"And your film crew is here too," Selma inserted. "I'm not sure about your cohost . . . Heather? And Dean and I asked some of our friends to help out."

Selma gave Kit a bright smile, unaware of the churning in Kit's gut.

All night. All night they'd been working on the wall while she'd been kept away.

Evan motioned for her to hold back. He caught Selma's attention. "We'll be right behind you. Can we have a minute?"

Selma looked between them and nodded kindly. "Of course." She stepped away, leaving Evan and Kit at a standoff.

"I'm sorry. I didn't know the film crew was here. I wasn't hiding that from you too. But really, I'm sorry."

They were the words she'd wanted to hear.

Evan continued, "But I'm not sorry for wanting to keep you safe. For wanting you to rest so you don't relapse. You'd been assaulted, you're still dealing with a concussion, and your parents were worried. They told me you don't slow down. Detective Seamans said the same. I was—"

"You were everyone's tool to get me to rest," Kit said.

"I don't know if you see it, Kit, but there are a lot of people who care about you. You give your all to the ones you love, but have a hard time receiving the same in return."

"Because I'm afraid it's not going to stick," Kit answered before she realized what she'd said.

Evan frowned, studying her face. "Kit—"

"It's okay." She pressed her fingertips to his arm in a gesture of truce. "Let's just . . . move forward."

"Yeah. Forward."

She pushed ahead of Evan, feeling his eyes on her back.

Selma was around the corner waiting, and she led them to the basement, this time going a different way through a back room that housed cleaning supplies and shelves with paint cans and odds and ends. She opened a door to a narrow flight of stairs and started to descend, Evan and Kit close on her heels.

Kit took quick stock of the room they'd entered. Plastic sheeting hung from the ceiling to deter the flow of dust. Two men in dirt-encrusted jeans and boots worked alongside Dean. The television crew had set up a strategic light for filming. Tom and another camera operator were manning cameras. Heather wasn't there, but another man from the show, obviously in charge, stood off to the side and motioned for Evan the minute he caught sight of him.

Dean's voice echoed through the basement. "Okay, we're going to bust through!"

The next few moments were dusty and loud, and then silence enveloped them all.

"Holy cow," Selma breathed beside Kit.

Dean stood with his hands at his waist, elbows out as he turned wide eyes toward his wife. "We found it."

Beyond the debris, a vault was framed into the wall. Its door was cracked open about an inch and sagged on hinges that were rusted from years of neglect.

"Barlowe's vault," Dean declared. He blew out a controlled breath of anticipation and glanced at Evan. "Here we go." Pulling on the vault door, it groaned a metallic protest. Even the hired workers leaned forward to see what was inside. Selma stepped toward her husband.

Kit moved beside Evan merely because it would give her a better line of sight. He glanced at her, and she looked away. She'd figure out how she felt about everything later.

Tom edged up next to her, camera positioned in his hands.

Dean snapped on a flashlight and flooded the inside of the vault with light.

"It's empty," Selma announced.

"Wait." Dean aimed the flashlight. "Are those ledgers?" He leaned into the vault and pulled out a stack of black books. Selma held the light as Dean gingerly opened the cover of the book on top, its binding crumbling a bit. He skimmed the first page. "They're transactions, I think. Varying amounts of monetary exchanges for . , ." He lifted shocked eyes. "Uh, looks like Barlowe was involved in some serious smuggling."

"Liquor?" Selma asked.

"Maybe. Lots of illegal things, it seems." Dean flipped to the back of the ledger. "There's a list of names here. Probably buyers or sellers. Most of them are out of Chicago."

"What year did Barlowe build the theater?" Evan asked.

"Back in 1915," Dean supplied. "It would've been before the height of gangsters like Capone, but there are historical records in Kipper's Grove that Capone stayed in town a number of times."

"Barlowe could've been involved in that type of thing later," Evan concluded. "This could have all been the beginning."

"Could be." Dean handed Selma the books and swung his light back into the vault. "There's nothing else in here." He ducked to step inside, raising the beam of light into the corners and around the back of the vault. "Hold on. What's this?" Dean waved for Evan to come inside.

Evan glanced at Kit, and she avoided his eyes.

"What'd you find?" Evan asked as he entered the vault, his voice echoing in the box.

Dean was shining his light along the back wall of the vault. "See there? There's a thin crack all along the top and sides. It's not a seam—it's definitely a crack."

"Vaults don't have cracks," Evan said.

"Exactly." Dean handed Evan the flashlight. "Which means, if my theory is correct, this back is moveable." He tried pressing on different parts of the wall, pushing with his shoulder to see if it would give way.

287

"What about this?" Evan reached up into a corner and out of sight of Kit.

There was a loud clank, followed by a cloud of dust. Groaning of metal on metal echoed through the basement, and those outside the vault took an instinctual step back.

Once again, there was a moment of stunned silence. And then Dean's exclamation ripped through the group huddled outside the vault. "And that, folks, is what a secret passageway looks like."

"You're gonna want to see this." Evan's words were directed at Kit, who held up her hand in front of the cameraman. He was far more intrusive than Tom with his handheld. The show's manager tapped the guy on the shoulder and motioned for him to step back.

Dread filled Kit like none she'd experienced before. She should be excited, intrigued, if not a little exuberant. But every pore in her body was petrified to step foot in the century-old tunnel—and not because she was afraid it was going to collapse with age. No, she was afraid she was going to find Madison, and not in the way she hoped to find her friend.

"Hold on." One of Dean's hired hands stopped her. He was a few steps into the tunnel. He looked back at Dean and Evan. "We need to make sure this tunnel is sound. The last thing we want is it collapsing. We don't know how well it's supported."

Okay. That was it. Enough was enough. Kit pushed her way in between Evan and Dean. Her feet landed on hard-packed earth and ahead of her was a tunnel just high enough and wide enough for a full-grown man to traverse. Some pipework ran along the edge, for what she had no clue. Every several yards or so there appeared to be a structural support.

"I'm not waiting any longer," she stated. "If Madison is in here, I'm going to find her."

"Kit!" Evan barked after her as she started into the tunnel. She heard him scrambling in behind her.

A light shone ahead of her, which jolted Kit into awareness that her impulse was iffy considering she'd charged into the tunnel without a light. She looked behind her. Evan was following. The workman had stepped back into the vault and was arguing with Dean about anyone being allowed in.

Kit paused because, frankly, she needed Evan and his light. He glared at her with frustration, then turned to address Dean. "Just give me a minute with Kit and—"

The back of the vault, which had turned out to be a hinged door that opened out and into the tunnel, suddenly shifted. Due to its heavy weight, the door swung back toward the vault. Dean shouted. The workman reached out to stop it. There was a scream from Selma, and then the door slammed back into place.

Evan launched toward the door, looking for a way to open it from inside the tunnel. "Hold the light!" He waved the flashlight at her.

Kit grabbed the flashlight and held it as Evan examined the door. There were no latches, no levers on this side.

"Dean!" he shouted.

They could hear Dean from the other side, a distant echo, but they couldn't make out the words.

"Twist the bolt and lever at the top right of the wall!" Evan shouted, then pressed his ear against the vault.

Kit looked behind her down the passageway. It smelled earthy and old. Spiderwebs swooped from the ceiling along the edges.

Evan cursed and slammed his palm against the vault. "The bolt, Dean! The bolt!"

"Why isn't it opening?" Kit was already starting to feel claustrophobic.

Evan shot her an intense glare. "Because *I* was the one who opened it. There are bolts on the inside of the vault that appear to be part of the structure. One of them twists when you push on the frame just so, and it releases the latch."

"So Dean can—"

"I didn't get a chance to show him. He wasn't watching me when I opened it."

"If you figured out, they can figure it out." Kit tried to reassure herself as much as Evan.

He gave her a dark look illuminated by the flashlight, his face a bit ghoulish. "Let's hope."

"Do we just wait then?"

"You want to wait now?" The irony in his words were thick. "You charged ahead without thinking, Kit."

He was right, but she didn't want to admit it. Then he'd make the point that this was exactly why he'd done what he'd done last night. To protect her—because she didn't protect herself.

"I'm sorry. I just don't appreciate people making judgment calls on my behalf."

Evan's exasperated expression summed up what he had to be feeling. "You're a concussed, half-strangled, exhausted woman. Exhibit A, we're trapped in an underground tunnel. So really? You're thinking clearly?"

She had the flashlight. He didn't. Kit hesitated a moment, then started down the passageway.

"Kit, hold on!"

"What if Madison is in here? We need to find her!"

"Just go easy." Evan was right behind her, and she could feel him as he brushed against her shoulder.

They headed slowly down the tunnel. The flashlight shone ahead and disconcertingly revealed an area of earth that had collapsed and partially blocked the way forward.

"See?" Evan's comment was unnecessarily smug.

Kit didn't answer. She squeezed around it while hearing Evan stammering behind her.

"Evan—" She stopped. She'd caught sight of color ahead. There wasn't supposed to be something that looked red in a tunnel over a century old.

Kit increased her pace, her heart pounding.

"What is that?" Evan had caught sight of it too.

"Madison?" Kit called, breaking into a jog. Her foot caught a rut in the ground, and she almost catapulted forward. Evan caught her around the waist, pulling her back against him.

His breath was warm against her ear. "Slow down, Cat. You're gonna cause an accident."

"But Madison—"

"Kit. If that's Madison . . ." His words hung there, and Kit caught on to their meaning.

"Madi!" Kit cried. She launched forward, tearing from Evan's hold. The flashlight bobbed ahead of her, catching the color of red near the ground. Madison was lying prone. She had to be.

Except as Kit drew closer, it quickly became apparent the red was merely cloth. No person. No body. Just a shirt. Brilliantly red, in a remarkably black passageway.

Kit bent, shining the flashlight to study the cloth. Evan kneeled behind her. She could hear him breathing, and it matched hers.

In. Out. In. Out.

All the nervous anticipation melted into disappointment and then, as Kit reached for the shirt, morphed into utter horror.

"Evan?" Kit turned toward him in her cramped position, holding the shirt out. She met his eyes and knew he knew the moment he saw it. She didn't have to say it, but she did anyway. "It's Madison's shirt. The same one she wore on the night she disappeared."

31

Greta

The basement of the Barlowe mansion was dank. Crates filled with who knew what were stacked against the walls. There was a half-empty bottle of whiskey perched on top of one of the crates. Leaning against the crate was a rifle. What kind, Greta had no idea, but she eyed it, wondering if she were to get hold of the rifle, if it were loaded, would she even know what to do with it?

Mr. Barlowe urged them ahead of him until they stopped at the door of a large vault. The black iron looked unfriendly, and when Barlowe began to turn the mechanisms, Greta's breath caught in her throat.

If he locked them in the vault, they would die! There would be no air!

"Please, Mr. Barlow," Greta begged. "Please let us go. I promise I won't say anything—"

"Shut up!" he growled.

Alma caught Greta's eye and gave a tiny shake of her head. Her face was void of color, her body sagged with resignation,

293

and the sorrow that was always part of her countenance seemed deeper, more poignant.

The vault door gave way, and Barlowe motioned impatiently. "Get in."

"Mr. Barlowe . . ." Greta procrastinated as Alma obediently stepped into the vault.

The man pressed his face up to hers, and she smelled alcohol on his breath. "Get. In."

Tears escaped her eyes. Barlowe shoved Greta into the vault, her whimper turning into a hollow echo once inside. There was a piece of art leaning against the far wall of the vault. A few money bags. Some liquor. A pile of ledgers.

"You know the rules, Alma."

She nodded, holding her fingers to her lips as if to stifle her crying.

The door swung shut, enveloping them in darkness. Greta crumpled to the floor. Alma slid down the wall, and Greta felt the woman's hand take hers.

"Shhhh. Papa will come back. He always does." Alma's faith in him was far greater than Greta's.

"Why?" Greta felt that word encapsulated far more questions than she could put in words.

Alma didn't answer. Her body shifted, and she settled in. "Just wait, Miss Mercy."

Greta lost track of time as the minutes ticked by. Her eyes could not adjust to the blackness of the vault because there was simply no light at all.

After a while, she sensed Alma shift, moving to her feet.

"Alma?" Greta ventured.

Alma didn't say anything. Greta heard her moving along the back wall of the vault. Alma grunted, and then a scraping sound commenced. A latch giving way. A small crack of light invaded the vault, coming from the back wall.

"Papa doesn't know that I know," Alma said. "When we were

little, Papa would send us to the vault as punishment. The rules were no crying, no screaming, and no playing with his things. But he didn't know that we figured out the secret."

Greta pushed to her feet. She could barely make out Alma's form in the faint light as the back of the vault swung out into a passageway. A lantern hung from a beam that stretched across the low ceiling. The walls and the ground were of earth, shored up and secured by a wooden framework. A pipe ran along the ground. Alma pointed to it.

"That pipes air into the tunnel," she explained. Alma began to transform in front of Greta as she led the way toward the lantern. She reached up and unhooked it, holding the lantern out so it shed light farther down the tunnel. Alma turned to Greta and smiled. "Come." Her expression had lost all signs of sorrow, and in its place was an odd look of anticipation

Greta followed, her bare feet against the cold earth. Alma made her way with a familiarity that told Greta she had done this many times before. The tunnel twisted to the right, and they continued. Soon another light shone at the far end of the passage.

Greta squinted, trying to focus on what lay ahead. An opening. Smaller than the vault. Barely wide enough for someone to fit through and perhaps a crate the size of what Mr. Barlowe had stored in his basement.

As they neared the opening, Alma's excitement heightened. "Emily." The whispered name floated through the air, escaping from Alma's lips. She reached the opening and lifted her leg to crawl through it, and then she was gone.

"Alma!" Greta hurried to catch up, her reticence giving way to terror of being left alone in the passageway. She climbed through after Alma, her feet landing on lumps of coal. She ducked, for the box she found herself in wasn't high enough for her to stand. It stank of dirt and oil. Coal dust swirled around her. Greta crawled a few feet farther until the box opened into a room. She maneuvered her way out of the box, the floor cold against her feet.

Pipes creaked around her. A boiler was positioned at the far end of the room. There was barely enough light to see.

"Alma?" Greta whispered loudly.

There was no reply.

She explored deeper into the room and spotted a doorway with light coming from beyond. Moving toward it, Greta noticed a short hallway, and beyond that a series of rooms, unlit and unused. Frowning, she followed the shaft of light. The sound of feminine voices came from up ahead.

Greta ran her hand along the wall as she tentatively explored the hallway. She turned a corner and reeled backward, clapping a hand over her mouth. A woman stared back at her, eyes wide, hand over her—

Wait.

Greta's breath came in short gasps.

It was her reflection in a tall mirror at the end of the hall, where a set of stairs climbed to an upper level. The light came from the top of the stairs.

Greta tiptoed toward them, ignoring the reflection of herself that only served to frighten her more. At the bottom of the stairs, she looked up. "Alma?"

Alma spun around, and her smile swiftly faded into a panicked expression. Beyond her was a face, then a flash of white as a woman fled into the shadows.

"Greta, please, no." Alma held out her hand to make Greta stop.

But Greta had seen the woman in white just before she disappeared, after leaving behind in Alma's arms an infant swaddled in a blue blanket.

"This is the theater." Awareness seeped into Greta as she climbed the stairs toward Alma, who clutched the baby to her breast. "Who was that woman?"

Alma shook her head. "No, no. You mustn't . . ."

Greta reached the top landing, her feet momentarily relishing the feel of the velvety red carpet of the theater. "That's the baby," she realized aloud. She stared at the quiet bundle in Alma's arms. "The baby I saw fall from the boxed seat."

Alma backed away, up the slanted floor of the hall that wrapped around the auditorium and main theater with its row upon row of empty chairs. The houselights were off, making the hand-painted domed ceiling and its magnificent chandelier impossible to see.

"Is the baby all right?" Greta tried to approach Alma, who looked at her as though Greta might steal the babe from her arms. "Alma? The baby, is he all right?"

Alma spun and hurried up the corridor, holding the infant so tightly that Greta feared she would crush it. Greta ran after her, reaching the foyer, the stairway to the upper level ladies' room, and the box seats rising out of the darkness on her left. The double doors to the main lobby of the theater were before her. Greta knew from the nights searching the theater with Oscar and Eleanor that she was mere steps away from freedom.

Alma stood stock-still, staring at her from farther down the lobby toward the far side of the horseshoe hall that bordered the auditorium.

"Alma?"

"Go," Alma said.

Greta saw her shift the bundle in her arms. "Alma, the baby—"

"Please go." Alma's arms lowered, the infant lowering with them.

Greta started. Alma was going to drop the baby! She launched forward as Alma flung the infant from her chest. Spinning, Alma sprinted away, her bare feet silent on the carpet, her nightgown a flash of gray.

The baby fell to the floor with a sickening thud. Greta cried out. She'd seen it fall once from the boxed seat. How was it no one else had? How was it plausible the infant could live only to be thrown again?

Greta fell to her knees beside it. She reached for the blanket, flinging it off the infant. Her breath caught in her throat.

Bright, glass eyes stared back at her.

The white face of a hairless doll made to imitate a baby. The torso of the doll was clothed in a white nightdress, tied with silken thread at its neck.

The baby didn't blink. It didn't cry.

It couldn't because the baby wasn't real.

32

Greta pounded on the door to the Boyd residence. She didn't care that she was barely clothed in her nightgown or that her hair hung in dirty strands around her face. There was nowhere else to flee. The police were untrustworthy. At any moment, Mr. Barlowe would discover she was no longer locked in the vault in his basement. Her brothers were back at Grove House and unable to offer any aid. She was fleeing from a tyrant. A ghostly woman in white. Alma who, it was clear now, suffered from a broken mind. And a doll. A doll that had started it all after plummeting from a boxed seat in the theater.

Greta pounded again.

A light flickered on from inside.

"Coming! Coming!" a man bellowed.

Latches clicked. The door gave way, and Mr. Boyd stared out at her through his spectacles. His beard was mussed, his lean face an older version of Oscar's. He wore a velvet smoking jacket, which was the same color as his slippers. "Who on earth are you?"

"Greta Mercy, sir. Please let me in."

"Who?" He scowled, searching beyond her as if looking for a better explanation.

"I'm friends with Eleanor. Please, sir." Greta started to push her way past him, but his arm shot out and blocked her entrance.

He glowered at her. "How dare you!"

"Father!" A deep voice shouted from the top of the stairs behind him.

Greta ducked under Mr. Boyd's arm and flew toward Oscar, who rushed down the stairs. She barreled into his chest, sobbing as his arms came around her with a strength that promised not to let go.

"Oscar, what is the meaning of this?" Mr. Boyd demanded.

"Greta? Greta!" Eleanor hurried down the stairs in a flurry of lace and yellow nightclothes. "Oh, Father, we must get her inside where it's warm!"

"She *is* inside." Mr. Boyd, exasperated, shut the front door with a firm thud. "Now be quiet or you'll wake your mother."

"Too late, Henry," a sleepy voice, rather musical in nature, filtered down the stairs.

"This is a literal congregation of madness." Mr. Boyd marched to a room off the entryway and flicked on the electric lights. The pale green warmth of the sitting room enveloped them all in light. "Bring her in here," he commanded.

Oscar pulled back, cupping Greta's dirty face in his hands. His lentil-colored eyes were filled with concern for her welfare. "Are you all right?"

"She's not all right!" Eleanor answered for Greta. "Look at her. I would mistake her for a phantom. And her feet are bleeding!"

Mrs. Boyd half floated down the stairs, wrapped in a heavy housecoat of deep burgundy. "Oh, dear," she said as she took in the sight of Greta. "You're Greta Mercy. Jane's daughter."

"Jane?" Mr. Boyd scowled.

Mrs. Boyd flung him a look that stated he really should know these things. "Jane Mercy. I employed her here for several years before she passed. Remember? Greta is her only daughter?"

"I don't recall." Mr. Boyd turned to stoke the coals in the fireplace. "This is all quite out of the ordinary."

"Eleanor." Mrs. Boyd snapped her fingers. "Go get the young woman a housecoat. This is unseemly!" Her pursed lips were directed at Oscar, who had refused to let Greta go and now seemed to realize he held tightly to a woman clothed only in a cotton nightgown.

"Yes. A housecoat. Fetch a blanket too," Oscar directed, not being swayed by the impropriety of the situation. He looked at Mrs. Boyd, who was waiting for him to let go of Greta. "For heaven's sake, Mother, she is trembling. If I let her go, she'll fall to the floor."

"Oh, dear." Mrs. Boyd pressed her fingers to her lips.

Within moments, Eleanor flew back down the stairs, a violet housecoat that smelled of rosewater in one arm, and a quilt draped over her other.

Oscar released Greta as he gently turned her. Eleanor helped her into the housecoat, tying it at Greta's waist.

"Oh, Greta, what happened?" Tears sprang to Eleanor's eyes.

"Summon Bertie." Mrs. Boyd seemed to have regained her posture with Greta fully clothed. She reached for a ribbon on the wall and rang the bell herself. "When she arrives, we need hot tea with sugar. And have her bring some crackers."

"Yes, Mama." Eleanor hurried into the hall, intent on greeting their housekeeper halfway to save time.

Oscar led Greta to a sofa near the fire. He lowered her onto it, and she knew she should let go of Oscar, but she couldn't get her hands to cooperate. She clung to him, so he sat next to her as Mrs. Boyd draped the blanket around her shoulders.

Mr. Boyd stood over them, his hands at his waist. "Now, explain yourself, Miss Mercy."

Mrs. Boyd swatted at his arm. "You're going to frighten her, you brute. Sit down and let the poor girl catch her breath."

A shocked look fluttered across the man's face. He blustered, then obeyed his wife, sinking into a chair opposite Oscar and Greta.

"Who is she to you?" He directed his question to Oscar.

Oscar looked up, and Greta noted his expression never wavered. "She is Greta."

"Greta? First name? I see." Mr. Boyd clicked his tongue.

Greta knew she needed to say something. Alma was still in the theater, along with the woman in white. She'd left the horrible doll on the floor when she'd fled. Goodness knew what would happen to Alma if Mr. Barlowe found her.

"We must summon the police," Mr. Boyd concluded.

"No!" Greta sat up straight, pulled from Oscar's hold. "No, please don't."

"Whyever not?" Mr. Boyd frowned.

"I-I . . ." Greta shifted her attention to Oscar, pleading that he believe her. "Officer Hargrove and another officer, Officer Ambrose—they took Alma and me to the Barlowe mansion."

"Alma?" Mrs. Boyd interjected. "Who is Alma?"

"For pity's sake, Edith, let the girl speak," Mr. Boyd said.

Greta continued, relaying all that had transpired. As she did so, Mr. Boyd and Mrs. Boyd grew solemnly quiet. Oscar's face darkened.

Eleanor hurried into the sitting room, leading a plump older woman, also dressed in a housecoat, who held a tray of tea and crackers.

"Leave it on the table, please," Mrs. Boyd instructed. "And thank you, Bertie. You may go."

The servant bustled away.

Eleanor moved to pour the tea, but Mr. Boyd held up a hand to stop her, his attention solely on Greta.

She shrank into Oscar, who, thankfully, did not pull away.

"Your charges are severe, Miss Mercy. And you're accusing the most influential man in our town."

Greta's throat closed in panic. If Mr. Boyd didn't believe her, the retribution from Mr. Barlowe would be traumatic.

Mr. Boyd stood from his chair and strode to the front window, pushing back the curtain. He peered into the night, paused, and then turned. "You say it was two officers who took you to Barlowe's?"

"Yes, sir," Greta replied.

Oscar's took her hand in his. His palm was warm, his grip strong.

Mr. Boyd didn't seem to notice his son's movement. He crossed his arms over his chest. "I never trusted Barlowe."

Hope surged through Greta.

Mrs. Boyd leaned forward in her seat. "Well, I like his wife. Frances is quite amenable."

Mr. Boyd nodded. "Poor woman. Marrying him after his first wife died. I always pitied her."

"Mrs. Barlowe isn't his first wife?" Eleanor piped in.

"No," Mr. Boyd answered. "He married his second wife when you were a wee thing."

"His first wife died of consumption. They say," Mrs. Boyd added. "Mr. Barlowe sent her away some time before her passing. To an institution somewhere out east. It was quite sad."

"And Mr. Barlowe remarried the current Mrs. Barlowe, who is probably more spirited than the man bargained for." Mr. Boyd gave a short laugh.

Mrs. Boyd smiled primly. "It's why I like Frances. She can keep the man in line."

"Or can she?" Mr. Boyd's countenance darkened.

Oscar cleared his throat. "She gave Greta a key to the theater."

Mr. Boyd raised an eyebrow.

Oscar admitted their midnight escapades into the theater, their hopes of finding Leo, and the communication from Officer

Hargrove that the police were no longer searching for the lost boys.

"There's a tunnel that runs from the mansion to the theater," Greta said.

Mr. Boyd didn't appear at all moved by her statement. "So it's been rumored."

"No." Greta looked at Oscar. "I was in it—tonight. Alma knew all about it. She kept calling Mr. Barlowe 'Papa.'"

Mrs. Boyd gasped, holding the teacup Eleanor had given her inches from her mouth. She stared at Greta.

Mr. Boyd's expression was stunned surprise. For a long moment, no one said a word.

Then Eleanor broke in, "The Barlowes have a child?"

"Henry . . ." Mrs. Boyd's shock was fast clearing in exchange for an awareness of something that suddenly made sense.

"It's not possible," Mr. Boyd muttered.

"What's not possible?" Oscar slid forward on the sofa, not releasing Greta's hand. "Father?"

Mr. Boyd hefted a sigh. "They had children, Barlowe and his first wife. But they passed away shortly before he sent his wife back east."

"Children?" Eleanor's head popped up from where she was stirring sugar into tea for Greta. "The Barlowes have no children."

"Not his current marriage to Frances, no," Mrs. Boyd assured. "But with his first wife . . . why, they would be over thirty now."

"They?" Eleanor tipped her head to the side. "There was more than one Barlowe child?"

Mr. Boyd had removed his spectacles and was cleaning the lenses with a handkerchief. He stopped abruptly and looked directly at Greta. In that moment, she knew he believed her. Mr. Boyd believed the preposterous nature of her claims. He believed the trauma that she had been enduring. He turned to address Eleanor with the truth. "Barlowe had two children. Daughters. They were twins."

"Twins?" Eleanor's shock matched Greta's.

Mrs. Boyd sipped her tea delicately, then inserted, "They were supposed to have perished—Mr. Barlowe and his wife had a funeral for them. They are buried in St. Mary's Cemetery."

"How did they die?" Eleanor breathed.

Oscar's hold tightened on Greta's hand.

Mr. Boyd answered with a grim expression, "The girls took ill and passed away."

"But apparently," Oscar concluded, "one of them *didn't* perish. She survived."

"Alma," Mrs. Boyd responded.

Greta gratefully took the tea that Eleanor offered her, though her eyes were set on Mr. Boyd. "And Emily," she whispered.

Mr. Boyd looked a tad bewildered. "Emily?"

"Alma kept calling me Emily. Quite by accident, I'm sure."

"That was her twin sister's name," Mrs. Boyd said.

Greta and Oscar looked at each other. Eleanor set the teapot on the silver tray with a clunk. "Is anyone thinking what I'm thinking?" There was a playful intrigue in her tone that seemed a bit inappropriate for the revelation of the moment.

"The woman in white," Oscar said.

"Who?" Mrs. Boyd asked.

"Emily." Greta nodded. "That's why Alma insisted on returning. Emily *is* the woman in white."

33

Kit

"She was here." Kit clenched Madison's shirt in her hand. "Madison was here. It's how she disappeared!"

Evan pushed past Kit, hiking farther down the tunnel. "Bring the light," he instructed.

Kit followed, hurrying to keep up.

"If the legend is true, the tunnel runs from the mansion to the theater." Evan pointed to the ceiling, supported by old beams. "Which means the street is somewhere above us, and we're probably getting close to the theater."

"The tunnel isn't that long," Kit said.

"A block maybe? I doubt Barlowe had it built just so he could attend his theater in style and avoid the crowd. This looks more like a tunnel for smuggling things."

"It would make sense that the lost boys disappeared in here." Kit shone the flashlight ahead of them.

"It's possible." Evan pointed ahead. "See? The passage ends there."

307

"Are we at the theater?" Kit grazed the end wall with the beam from the flashlight.

"I don't know yet." Evan ran his hand along a metal plate bolted to the wall. "It's a hatch of some sort. Not a door."

"Can we get out that way?" She really didn't need to get claustrophobic on top of everything else. Kit stuffed down a wave of panic.

Evan fumbled with a metal bar that held the hatch shut. He lifted the bar, then tossed a quizzical glance at Kit. "That was almost too easy." The hatch door opened, and Evan extended his arm behind him. "Can I have the light?"

Kit pressed the flashlight into his hand. Evan shone it through the hatch.

"Whoa." His voice echoed.

"What is it? The theater?"

"It's the coal bin. In the boiler room of the theater."

"What?" Kit squeezed in next to Evan. "Then this for sure was not a fancy way to arrive at the theater."

"No. It was meant to stay hidden. Hold on." Evan crawled through the hatch into the empty coal bin. "This would have been filled back in the day." His words bounced off the interior of the bin. "I don't even know how Barlowe would've used it without shoveling coal and in and out to make room."

Kit crawled after him. "Maybe they didn't fill it completely."

"Maybe." Evan offered his hand to Kit as she made her way from the tunnel. Once clear, they exited the coal bin, landing on the boiler room floor. Evan dug into his jeans pocket for his phone. "I need to call Dean since there was no signal in the tunnel. Let him know we're okay."

"What about Madi?" Kit held up Madison's shirt that she'd refused to leave behind.

"I'll get word to Seamans too." Evan strode from the room to get a better signal with his phone. Kit followed, entering the hall. The dressing rooms lay just ahead of her. Decades ago, entertainers filled these rooms, applying makeup and donning costumes as they prepared to go onstage. It was either live performances or silent movies when Barlowe Theater first opened. Now it was just silent. No one entertained here any longer. It was now a coffin of old memories and legends. Stories and spirits of people who had been left behind to—

"Kit!"

Kit yelped and spun. Heather Grant exited one of the dark dressing rooms. She moved toward Kit with a relieved smile on her face.

"I'm so glad you're all right!" She motioned behind her. "Tom texted me and said you and Evan were locked in a tunnel?"

Kit held Madison's shirt up for Heather to see. "Yes. And we found this."

Heather's gaze flew up to meet Kit's. "That was Madison's!"

Kit nodded. "We know she was in the passageway. We just don't know where she is now." She clung to the hope that Madison was alive. But who had forced her into the tunnel? Who had trapped her there, and where had they taken her?

Heather opened her mouth to say something, then clamped it shut.

"What?" Kit pressed.

Heather smiled hesitantly. "I'm not sure how much credence you put into what I see. Evan is thrilled to try to disprove me."

Kit didn't want to dissuade Heather from sharing her own theories. Even if Kit didn't believe in the paranormal the same way Heather took stock in it, there *were* elements of Heather's sightings that had come to fruition.

Heather glanced behind her as though someone were standing there. "I keep hearing the lost boys. One of them calls himself Leo."

"Leo?" Kit had heard that name before, yet it didn't register clearly as to how it might apply here.

Heather continued, "He keeps saying 'the woman in white' over and over again to me. He wants to jump me—to become a part of me—so he can communicate" Her eyes widened.

Kit took a step back. The air grew thick between them. "Heather . . . what does that mean?"

"It's when a spirit tries to take over someone else—someone living. By doing so, it enhances the spirit's ability to express themself. You know, by using me as a conduit."

"Don't do that." Kit took another step away. She held up the hand that wasn't clutching Madison's shirt. "Seriously, Heather, please don't."

Heather sucked in a deep breath. "Your parents."

"My what?"

Heather's eyes grew big as she stared through Kit, looking beyond her to something unseen. "Leo and your parents. There's something about them. I don't know . . ."

There was pounding on the stairs, and Evan came charging down. "Kit!" he called.

Heather jumped, snapping out of her trance.

Kit whirled, the feeling of being caught amid something dark, something evil, curling in her soul.

Evan noted Heather, then Kit.

"Evan, I . . ." Kit reached for him without hesitation, wanting to distance herself from the aura surrounding Heather. He extended his hand, taking hers and tugging her toward him, away from Heather.

"Let it be, Heather." Evan's stern reprimand raised the woman's eyebrow.

Heather turned on Evan with disdain in her eyes. "You always shut me down. Just when I can help."

"Is that what you think you're doing? Helping?"

Heather crossed her arms over her chest and cocked her head to the left. "I don't know, Evan, why don't you ask Kit's parents."

310

Detective Seamans had taken Madison's shirt into evidence, and the police had cordoned off the tunnel, both in the Barlowe mansion and in the theater. Now Kit sat in the front passenger side of her own car, this time allowing Evan to drive her home. Heather and Tom rode along in the back seat, Tom's handheld camera rolling.

That Evan looked infuriated was an understatement.

"I had to let them come," Kit muttered.

"Why?" Evan glanced at Heather in the rearview mirror. "You're the one who was upset we were going to film after Madison disappeared. Now you're going to let the show exploit your parents' good graces?"

"Heather said they knew something," Kit said, feeling wobbly, not at all convinced. "If Heather can help them—"

"So you're going to believe a medium?"

"No, I . . ." Kit pushed her hair behind her ear, aggravated that it was tickling her face. "I just want to get to the bottom of this. Madi believed in the story of the lost boys and the woman in white. It's why she invited your show to come in the first place. I want to go back to where it all started. With those stories. Just like you said. And now that we found the tunnel . . . well, Madi stumbled onto something from the past that has a legitimate influence on something today. It's probably why she was taken."

Evan's knuckles were white on the steering wheel as he pulled into the driveway of the Boyds' home. Kris and Ford stood outside, waiting. Ford looked none too pleased.

Kit eyed Evan with censure. "You called my parents?"

He didn't bother to gauge her reaction. "Yeah, 'cause I don't like good people getting blindsided."

"I don't blindside people," Heather interjected from the back seat. "I tell what I see and that's all."

"Sure." Evan killed the engine and hopped out.

Kit didn't know if she was angry at Evan again or if he'd shown wisdom in giving her parents a heads-up.

Ford frowned, and Kris didn't look particularly happy.

"Honey, what is going on?" Kris asked her daughter as Kit approached.

"I just need to ask some questions and—"

"Evan told us you were trapped in Barlowe's legendary tunnel?" Ford interrupted. "Now you're bringing a medium to our home?"

"Hello, Mr. Boyd, Mrs. Boyd." Heather smiled, attempting to make friends.

"*Dad*." Kit gave him a be-nice look, but Ford's response was swift.

"Don't 'Dad' me, Kit, you know what I think about messing with the spirit world. It's not safe, and it's not wise."

"Who is Leo?" Heather interrupted.

"Who?" Ford's frown deepened.

They stood on the blacktop driveway outside the house. The sun was strong, but the fall breeze cool. Leaves skipped along in front of Heather's feet, and she tightened her beige cardigan around her body. "I was asking who Leo is."

"I don't know any Leo," Ford answered. He offered her a thin smile, an attempt at politeness. "While I respect you and your beliefs, I ask that you—"

"Leo?" Kris stepped forward.

Kit's gaze swung to her mom. "You know of him?"

Kris looked to her husband. "Wasn't your father's uncle named Leo?"

"Great-uncle," Ford supplied, not taking his eyes off Heather. "I met him once."

"So there *is* a Leo in your family?" Heather concluded.

"And?" Ford crossed his arms.

"Can we go inside and sit down?" Kit asked.

"No," Ford replied emphatically.

Kit knew her dad was probably praying for God to build a hedge of protection against what he believed to be a form of witchcraft. She, on the other hand, believed that God needed to intervene somehow. Could He use other means? Somehow the thought made her feel guilty. No, God didn't need mediums to communicate with the dead. The realization came to her, clearly and swiftly.

Kris cleared her throat. "Leo was Ford's great-great-uncle, the brother of his great-grandmother." She was trying to keep the peace by reciting the Boyd family tree. "Great-grandmother Greta was—"

"Greta?" Evan piped up.

Kris was stunned silent for a moment by his reaction. "Yes. I remember because I was helping Ford's mom put together the Boyd family tree. Greta Mercy. Mercy was her maiden name—"

"Greta Mercy." Kit and Evan said the name in unison, their eyes meeting.

"The journal," Kit added.

"Alpharetta and Madison both had pieces to a journal written by Greta Mercy. She was the sister of one of the theater's lost boys," Evan explained.

Heather nodded, releasing a deep breath of satisfaction. "Mmm, that makes sense now. Leo is who I saw in the theater. He's a lost boy." She looked directly into Tom's camera, which was recording everything. "A lost boy who keeps telling me we need to identify the woman in white."

"Wait." Kit lifted her hands. "Hold on. If Leo was a lost boy, then . . . he wasn't lost."

"He couldn't be," Kris acknowledged. "Not if you met him once." She looked to Ford.

Ford hefted a sigh. "No one ever mentioned Leo was one of *those* lost boys." He eyed Heather.

"This isn't Heather saying it." Kit urged her dad to listen.

313

"This is your great-grandmother saying it. Greta. In her journal."

"But how did they find Leo then? Were the lost boys not really lost?" Evan mused aloud.

"Maybe we would know if we found out who the woman in white truly was?" Heather turned to Kit. "You saw her, didn't you? In the theater's basement. She left marks in your arm? You know she's real, so who was she? She's trying to get a message to us."

Kit saw her father whip his head around to look at her. "Kit?" He took a protective step toward her.

She hesitated. What did she really believe? If that had truly been the spirit of the woman in white . . . But if it wasn't, then it had been human. Like an old *Scooby-Doo* cartoon where the ghoul tore off his mask and—

"Where is Madison?" she said, leveling her attention on Heather.

"I have no idea." Heather drew back, surprise etched on her face.

"*You* were the woman in white," Kit accused.

"What? No." Heather shook her head. She gave Tom a desperate look. "No, I was with Tom, I promise you. Tell her, Tom."

Tom nodded and spoke around his camera. "She was, Kit. I can vouch for Heather."

"Then where is Madison?" Something was becoming clear to Kit. Her fear of abandonment all these years had always left room to question. To question her faith in other people. It was time to let her doubts rise, despite the outcome she dreaded. "Where did you put Madison?"

Heather stammered.

Evan stiffened.

Tom kept the camera rolling.

34

Greta

It was all moving so quickly. Morning dawned as Mr. Boyd gave them instructions. Everyone was to get dressed.

Eleanor ushered Greta to her room, where she rifled through her wardrobe for a dress. "Blue? No, green would suit you."

Greta hardly cared. "I need to get back to my brothers. If Mr. Barlowe—"

Eleanor turned, holding a lovely green frock to her chest. "Trust my father. He will take care of everything."

Oh, to have the blind and loving trust Eleanor was so fortunate to give her father! Never had Greta felt her father had the wherewithal to resolve all that life served up to them, and when he died, life only continued to prove that sort of comfort was reserved for another class of people, those quite different from the Mercy family.

"You *do* trust him, don't you, Greta?"

Greta met Eleanor's question with a solemn nod. It was what Eleanor wanted to see, but was she to be honest, Greta would shake her head and cry that she trusted no one with the welfare

315

of her brothers but herself. And even in that, she had failed. She had failed Leo. She had failed all the boys.

"Hurry then." Eleanor laid the dress on the bed. "Let's get you cleaned up. Off with that filthy nightgown."

They spent the next several minutes hurrying to make Greta more suitable for the day. Were she not almost certain Barlowe would abduct her if she left the Boyd residence, Greta would have refused to follow this ridiculous regimen of getting dressed in exchange for racing back to Grove House to protect her brothers.

Mr. Barlowe would go after them, of this she was certain. And he would be right when he made the assumption she would be there waiting, willing to fight on behalf of Cecil, Alvin, and Virgil. Only now she was in a new sort of trap. The Boyds' home. Being persuaded to trust them, to have faith that somehow all would be resolved. But there could be no satisfactory resolution. Any way the day was to go, it would end in tears and heartache. This Greta knew, and she prepared herself for it as Eleanor buttoned the back of the dress.

Finally suitable to Eleanor's standards, which she declared "haphazard" and "will have to do," the young women returned to the main floor.

Greta froze as she witnessed Mr. Boyd and Oscar in conversation with two police officers. Panicked, Greta scanned their features. It was not John, nor was it Officer Ambrose.

"Miss Mercy." Mr. Boyd extended a hand toward her when he saw her and Eleanor in the doorway. "Please come."

Greta entered hesitantly, looking to Oscar, whose eyes pleaded that she trust them and cooperate. She didn't release his gaze as she approached, and it was only when Mr. Boyd began to speak again that Greta broke eye contact with Oscar.

"This is Detective Patton." Mr. Boyd nodded toward one of the men. He was an older gentleman with gray sideburns, understanding gray eyes, and a thick mustache. Mr. Boyd continued, "I fully trust Detective Patton. He and I have been friends since our youth. It is why I summoned him specifically."

Detective Patton gave a little bow. "Miss Mercy, may I assure you that I will treat this matter with the utmost importance."

She doubted it. There was little chance that an officer of the law would put more stock in a woman from the poorhouse than he would a leading citizen of Kipper's Grove like Rufus Barlowe.

"Detective Patton and Officer Trent have been told the details of last night's events."

Patton focused his attention on Greta. "You say you saw Alma and Emily Barlowe, correct?"

Greta glanced at Eleanor, who smiled a bright smile of encouragement. Greta turned her hesitant gaze back to the man in front of her and his blue uniform with brass buttons. "I saw Alma. She is my friend from Grove House. I don't know who the other woman is."

"And there was a tunnel?"

"Yes." Greta nodded. "Please, sir, I need to get back to my brothers, who are staying at Grove House. If Mr. Barlowe gets to them first, he promised he would—"

"Would what?" Oscar's question was heavy with concern.

Greta's lips quivered. "I don't know. But Alma told me that if you leave your room at night, you may disappear. And Mr. Barlowe said that if I caused more trouble for him, he would send my brothers away to work."

"He would what?" Detective Patton reared back.

Greta nodded as hot tears trailed down her cheeks. "I don't know what that means."

"We are too close to Chicago, that's what that means," Mr. Boyd declared. "I've heard of this before, and Chicago is a hub of such activities. Selling orphans and poorhouse folk in trade for goods. They're sent to work in mines, sold to farmers for cheap labor, and such things as that."

Eleanor's gasp was cut short as she pressed a hand over her mouth.

"But Barlowe?" The detective looked genuinely perplexed. "I seriously doubt that he would—"

"His daughters are alive!" Oscar intervened. "If he faked his own daughters' funerals, what more is he capable of?"

"We don't know that they're alive." Detective Patton's disbelief confirmed Greta's fear. He was already questioning. Finding loopholes and ways to convince himself that she was an unreliable lower-class female with false allegations.

"There is one way to find out," Oscar said, his expression resolved. "And if you won't do it, I will."

"Son." Mr. Boyd put his hand on Oscar's shoulder.

Detective Patton nodded. "All right. We will look into it."

"Now." Mr. Boyd's demand carried with it the weight of another influential leader of Kipper's Grove—himself. "You will look now."

"Yes, yes." Detective Patton nodded quickly. "Of course. We'll head to the theater straightaway."

Kit

Another car pulled into the driveway, interrupting the standoff between Kit and Heather. It was obvious Heather had no intention of admitting to anything regarding Madison.

Avery scrambled out of her car.

"Kit!" She skidded to a halt when she saw everyone standing there.

The front passenger door of Avery's car swung open, and a figure slipped out.

"Madi!" Kit shoved past Heather and Tom, launching at Madison and pulling her friend into her arms instinctively. "Thank God! Oh, thank God!" She stepped back, verifying it truly was Madison she held. Yes. It was! Her blue eyes shone with tears. Her blond hair was gathered into a perfectly messy bun. She had on a button-up blouse, cuffed blue jeans, and a tailored jacket. She even wore her signature perfume.

Kit couldn't believe she was here. Whole. Alive. Well taken care of. Fresh and vibrant and . . .

She pulled away, her recent suspicions returning.

Madison's eyes had overflowed now, and a few tears rolled down her face.

"Madi?" Kit didn't understand it, but she knew something was terribly and horribly wrong. She looked to Avery, whose expression was sheepish. Then Avery diverted her gaze to the ground.

Ford stepped forward. "Madi, we're glad you're all right."

Evan had moved toward them too. As had Tom, his camera lens aimed solely at Madison.

Heather slapped his arm. "Shut it off, Tom." She batted him again. "Shut it *off*!"

"But—"

Heather silenced him with a glare.

Tom stopped the recording and lowered the camera.

"Madi, what's going on?" Kit heard the wobble in her voice and then recognized it in Madison's eyes. Guilt. "Avery?"

Avery stared at her. An awful silence ensued. And then Avery whispered, "I'm sorry. It went too far. I didn't know. It went too far!" She spun and ran for the house, her hand over her mouth and her sobs drifting through the air.

"I'll talk to her," Kris said, heading after Avery.

"Madi, what is Avery talking about?" Kit was afraid she knew. It was what had been impressing on her since the beginning. That fear that the ones closest to you were often the ones who betrayed you—who abandoned you. Or to put it in less dramatic terms, the ones closest to you were the ones who could hurt you more than anyone else in the world.

"We should go," Heather announced. She turned to Tom. "C'mon," she said and gave him a little shove.

"Wait." Evan's voice sliced through the moment. He looked between Heather and Madison, who were suspiciously avoiding each other's eyes. Then he pointed at Madison. "You're not alone in this, are you?" Evan spun toward Heather. "Heather?"

"Sorry, Evan, but we need to get back."

"To where?" he challenged.

"Can someone tell me what's going on?" Tom asked.

"It *was* a ruse, wasn't it?" Kit voiced her fear with absolute conviction.

Madison looked away.

"To get publicity? For the theater? You kidnapped yourself, didn't you? You'd found the entrance to the tunnel in the coal bin, and you hid there." Kit couldn't help that her voice was rising. She felt her dad's hand on her shoulder, but she shook it off. "The woman in white, the lost boys . . . you used the story to create interest for the show, and then you, what, disappeared? You *planned* this whole thing!"

"I thought you would understand," Madison managed to say.

"Understand?" Kit laughed in shock. "Why would I understand?"

Madison's face pled with Kit to listen, to comprehend. "You've shared my struggle against my grandfather and his machine of a company. And when I put together that the lost boys were part of your own family's past, I assumed—"

"You assumed I'd support you? In the ruse? To film some amazing special episode for *Psychic and the Skeptic* where the historian disappears and leaves a medium behind to miraculously see things? So I'm supposed to get on board when I am suddenly *enlightened* by Heather that a lost boy was part of my family tree? Is that it? You banked on me being okay with this because it involved my family's history?"

Madison's helpless expression indicated to Kit that everything she'd just said was true. Kit swallowed back a sob. "You knew it all, didn't you? You'd figured out the whole story of the lost boys, the woman in white, and you were feeding the facts to Heather, who would then slowwwwly reveal them"—Kit dragged out the word—"and sloowwwly make us all more horrified by the fact that history was repeating itself and had taken another person, Madison Farrington, the new lost girl of the theater. I suppose next you were going to miraculously be found and claim the woman in white rescued you. Like she did the lost boys, apparently."

"The woman in white didn't rescue the lost boys. She took them." Madison's defeat was palpable. She seemed frustrated that her plan was dissolving before her eyes. "The woman in white was Barlowe's daughter Emily. He had twin daughters, with a history of mental illness from his first wife's family. He tried to manage it by placing one daughter in Grove House, Alma, who wasn't as poorly off."

"The Grove House that is now the food pantry building?" Evan's inquiry wasn't friendly in tone.

Madison nodded at him. "Yes. The other daughter, Emily, showed many signs of distress. He kept her secluded in the mansion until she was uncontrollable. She found the tunnel, and the theater became her stomping grounds. When the lost boys were sneaking around the theater, she trapped them in the tunnel."

"And you found all this out how?" Evan drilled Madison.

"Research. Lots of exploration. Same thing you do for every episode of *Psychic and the Skeptic*. You were already well on your way to figuring it out."

"Yeah," Evan said, "we were. And you told Heather so she could *see* things."

"I *did* see things!" Heather protested.

"Convenient when you have the local historian feeding you details of the past."

Tom's camera hung by his side. "Why? Why would you . . . ?"

Heather rolled her eyes and waved toward Evan. "Because every show he tries to make me look like a storyteller. I want my own show, without a skeptic. This was supposed to make that happen. If my sensitivities could lead you all to finding Madison, I would—"

"You would be a hero, and you would discredit me," Evan finished for her.

"Yes." Heather sneered in disgust. "Only it didn't work out that way."

"Because we used history and evidence. Like I always do," Evan concluded.

Madison toed a dandelion that stuck up through a crack in the driveway. "I'm sorry, Kit. I honestly never meant for things to get so out of hand. When Avery came to town, I knew I needed to come forward. I didn't intend for my parents to fly in. I'm sorry for the fear I caused everyone. That night, after she showed you my video blog, I came clean with Avery. She thought we should keep up the charade."

"You planted that note in the boiler room?" Tom was piecing it all together.

Madison nodded.

Heather looked away in disgust.

"And the woman in white?" Kit smiled thinly at Madison. "That was *you*. You clawed me. You kept the whole charade going just to, what, save the theater and the downtown from your grandfather's plans for the area?"

Madison's voice was helpless and pleading. "It made sense at the time. You don't know what my grandfather is like."

"You have the police investigating your grandfather for *illegal dealings*!" Kit cried, stunned that Madison could be so foolish, so selfish, so . . . "Did you ever stop to think that maybe *we* were worth more than a stupid theater to you?"

"Kit." Madison reached for Kit. "I do care about you. You're my best friend. I didn't think it would all blow up into something this big."

"And you thought you'd drag the food pantry into it too. Why, because it was the old poorhouse back in the day? To recall the struggle between the rich and poor?" Kit, angry and feeling betrayed, taunted Madison. "Parallel their story with your story of a girl against a rich grandpa."

"What are you talking about, Kit?" Madison looked confused. "I was only trying to help you."

"By having someone break in? Was that you? Did you stay with Heather at her hotel and sneak out at night to make body outlines out of bacon on the pantry floor?"

"Seriously, Kit, I have no idea what you're talking about. When I found out about the Boyds and the poorhouse, I—"

"Boyds and the poorhouse?" Evan interrupted.

Madison looked his direction and nodded, confusion now mixed with regret reflecting in her eyes. "Yes. About twenty years after the boys went missing in the theater, Oscar Boyd, Kit's great-great-grandfather, purchased the poorhouse from the county after the county decided to shut it down. But the records weren't made public and must've gotten lost. My grandfather has been making bids to buy the property from Kipper's Grove. The town has overseen the management of it for decades. That's when they found out the original owner was the Boyd family—not the town. So the food pantry building actually belongs to you, Mr. Boyd." Madison looked to Ford, whose shock was apparent. "Why then would I arrange for it to be vandalized? I wouldn't want to hurt you by doing that, Kit."

Madison's words were the epitome of hurtful irony. Kit backed away from her. "I need a minute to think." She started toward the street.

"Kit, wait." Madison followed.

"No." Kit shook her head. "Leave me alone."

"Kit!" She heard Evan call after her. But all she could see was the fruition of her worst fears. That a loved one was willing to sacrifice her for their own personal gain, that she was expendable. Her feelings and her loyalties were taken for granted.

"I don't know what she's talking about," Kit heard Madison urgently saying to the others behind her. "I had nothing to do with the food pantry break-in."

"Kit!" her father shouted.

This time, Kit had no intention of listening, of giving second chances, or of choosing to believe the best in the ones she loved. It was just as she'd always believed. There was always an end to one's loyalty, and this time it would be hers.

35

Greta

"This is preposterous!" Mr. Barlowe's glower probably would have been enough to cease the war overseas were he shipped to the front lines.

Greta shrank behind Oscar, praying that God would end this nightmare she had been swept up in.

Detective Patton cleared his throat, obviously intimidated by Barlowe's mannerisms as he unwillingly unlocked the doors to the theater. "We just need to have a look inside."

"To validate *her* story?" Barlowe's black eyes speared Greta.

She shouldn't be here. She needed to return to Grove House and check on her brothers. They must be worried sick by now. Greta wasn't convinced that Mr. Barlowe didn't have his own lackeys already paying her retribution by spiriting her brothers away at this very moment.

"The charges are quite serious." Mr. Boyd leveled a frank stare on his peer.

Mr. Barlowe turned to Oscar's father. "I would have expected more loyalty from you, Boyd. Siding with this . . . this *chit*? You realize she comes from Grove House. She's probably after

325

your money—your *son!*" Barlowe swept an angry arm toward Oscar. "You're being manipulated by a liar, and we all know she isn't in her right mind! The debacle at my theater was what started all this."

"And no infant was found," Detective Patton added, which was very unhelpful.

They entered the theater with Mr. Barlowe leading the charge. He stopped in the lobby, his voice echoing off the ceiling with the cherubs gleefully smiling down on them. "Here. Have your way with it all. You'll find nothing. No one. You'll see this woman's accusations are false, meant to discredit my good name."

Detective Patton ducked into the theater's hall, the vibrant hues of red welcoming him with the impression of elegance and class.

Barlowe followed, Mr. Boyd behind him, who turned and addressed Oscar and Greta. There was warning in his eyes. "I'm not sure what we will find. Regardless, Miss Mercy, you are here at the behest of Detective Patton to identify Alma or Emily—or both—if we find them. I recommend you stay silent until questions are asked of you."

Mr. Boyd's tone was stern. Greta could see the tenuous ledge he was tiptoeing merely for her sake and on the word of Oscar and Eleanor. If they found nothing, if Alma and Emily weren't here in the theater . . . Greta hated to conjure what that would mean. For her. For her brothers. Even for Oscar and Eleanor and Mr. Boyd.

Entering the hall, Greta immediately noticed the doll Alma had thrown at her was no longer lying on the floor. She bit her tongue. She wouldn't point that out, yet the mere fact added to the dread within her.

Detective Patton had confronted Mr. Barlowe at his mansion. But if Barlowe had already uncovered that she and Alma had escaped via the tunnel off the vault, there was a strong probability that he had already gained control over Alma—even Emily, assuming she was the woman in white—and had moved them somewhere else. Greta's accusations would fall flat. Even if the tunnel were exposed, without the presence of the other women, there would be no credence given to Greta's claims. Her abduction, the abuse, the crookedness of Officers Hargrove and Ambrose . . . none of it would ring true.

"Fan out." Detective Patton motioned left and right to the officers with him. "Search everywhere. If you happen to see someone, proceed with caution. We don't want to scare them away."

"Bah!" Mr. Barlowe barked. "Scare away? Trust me, you won't find anyone!"

Ignoring Barlowe, the detective asked Greta, "Where's this tunnel you spoke of?"

Oscar gave Greta an encouraging nod. She summoned the willpower to answer, "Down in the boiler room."

"Let's go then!" Mr. Barlowe's scowl burned proverbial holes into Greta. He pushed ahead of Detective Patton and led the way. "Secret tunnels. What utter foolishness!"

Greta wasn't sure how Mr. Barlowe planned to convince them there wasn't a tunnel when she could lead them straight to its entrance. A foreboding in her spirit warned her that with Mr. Barlowe, anything was a possibility.

They reached the basement, skirted the dressing rooms, and entered the boiler room.

"Where is this so-called tunnel?" Mr. Barlowe demanded of her before anyone else had the chance to ask.

Detective Patton held out a hand level with Barlowe's chest. "Please, Mr. Barlowe, I ask that you allow me to conduct the investigation." He directed his next question to Greta. "Where did you find this tunnel, Miss Mercy?"

Greta pointed to the coal bin that was perhaps five feet in height and boxed in by walls and a door. "I came out of there. You'll find a hatch at the back of the bin."

Detective Patton moved to the coal bin, pulling open its door.

Greta's heart dropped.

Coal was piled high. Too high. The hatch was well covered and out of sight. Detective Patton exchanged looks with Mr. Boyd, who turned to Greta expectantly. "You're certain you came through the coal bin?"

Greta nodded, although she could sense the thin thread of hope she still clung to unraveling by the second.

"You expect us to believe you pushed your way through coal?" Mr. Barlowe jeered. "Impossible!"

"Detective?" An officer hustled into the boiler room. "We've checked the theater. There's no one here."

"See?" Mr. Barlowe's fury was palpable. "I want to press charges. I want this woman jailed for defamation of character and for trespassing. I know you have an officer on your force who can testify that Miss Mercy has indeed broken into the theater before."

"Miss Mercy?" Detective Patton swung around to address her.

Oscar stepped forward. "She wasn't alone."

"Oscar," Mr. Boyd snapped.

Greta put her hand on Oscar's arm and shook her head. This wasn't his battle. He and Eleanor had sacrificed much on her behalf. Their loyalty and their devotion were more than Greta could have ever asked for or expected. She would not allow them to further damage their futures when hers already lay in ruins. "I merely wanted to find my brother Leo. After the evening here when I thought I saw an infant fall—"

"*Thought* she saw!" Mr. Barlowe snarled.

"Mr. Barlowe, please." Detective Patton held up his hand again. "Go on, Miss Mercy."

"Leo was only trying to clear my name. To prove that I wasn't making up stories. I saw an infant fall, but now I know it was a doll. I'm sure of it. And the woman who dropped it was . . ." Greta bit back her accusation. It would do no good to claim that Emily Barlowe, who had been buried in the Kipper's Grove cemetery, had somehow grown into a woman, only to toss a doll from a box seat. It was preposterous.

"Was *who*, Miss Mercy?" Detective Patton pressed, though Mr. Boyd had already explained the theory prior. The detective appeared to be calculating the evidence to warrant any further investigation on his part.

Greta lifted her chin, dismissing the concept of being convincing. Tell the truth. It was what she'd been taught as a youngster by her parents. It was what she and Gerard had tried to foster in their younger brothers. Integrity. Loyalty. Sacrifice for one another and others. She thought of Alma. Sweet Alma who wobbled between her adult mind and that of a child. Simply wanting the love of her father, regardless of the abuse he had put her through. Alma needed Greta to fight for her. Perhaps Emily, the woman in white, did also.

"Alma and Emily Barlowe." Greta spoke the names with clarity, though even she could hear the nervousness in her voice. "Alma was with me at Grove House. I believe Emily has been here at the theater, going back and forth between here and the Barlowe mansion. I don't know why. But I do know—because I experienced it myself—that Mr. Barlowe locks Alma and Emily in his vault."

"That is preposterous!" Mr. Barlowe shouted. "How dare you? My daughters have lain buried for well over a decade!"

Detective Patton had heard this before, at the Boyds' residence, but now, in front of Mr. Barlowe, he appeared to be gauging his response to Greta's accusations.

"And the vault has a door that opens into the tunnel," Greta added.

"There's nothing illegal about having a tunnel," Barlowe protested.

Detective Patton sharpened. "So there *is* a tunnel?"

Mr. Barlowe hesitated briefly before admitting, "Fine. I have a vault. There's a space behind it. For privacy's sake. That is all."

"And if we empty the coal bin?" Detective Patton led.

Mr. Barlowe's face was growing red, the veins in his neck bulging. "You'll have an empty coal bin," he retorted.

Detective Patton snapped his fingers at his officers. "Empty the coal bin," he commanded.

Greta drew against Oscar in surprise. She'd not expected the detective to lend even the slightest credence to her story in the wake of Mr. Barlowe's arrogance and prominence.

Footsteps outside the boiler room snagged their attention—shuffling, as though someone was being pushed and prodded against their will.

"I can walk myself!" a man's voice declared, just as another officer shoved him into the room.

Mr. Barlowe stiffened.

Detective Patton exchanged looks with Mr. Boyd.

Oscar's hand went to the small of Greta's back, and proper or not, she was glad for the reassuring touch. She was most certain the next few minutes would be the last she spent under any semblance of Boyd protection.

Officer John Hargrove blustered. He stopped when his eyes met Greta's. Instant shame filled his, a silent plea and apology. Then he noted Mr. Barlowe, and he straightened.

Detective Patton took a step toward his officer. "Tell me, Hargrove, what do you know about last night's events?"

Kit

October, Present Day

She'd never squealed her tires before today. Granted, she was driving her parents' car due to the accident, which now she furiously questioned if somehow Madison had been behind as well.

Had she attempted to kill Kit? That seemed outlandish, even for Madison. But everything was murky now. Grimy and icky. While she was thankful Madison was okay, in some ways it was worse to know that Madison had coordinated these events. Plotted them. Overseen them. And Heather Grant was part of it. Well, that made sense, but it didn't spear through Kit like Madison's actions had.

To fake her own disappearance, to have an entire town—her own *family*—worried sick that in a few weeks they would be planning a funeral? It was beyond belief! And for what, a historical theater? To prove her grandfather was a money-grubbing monster? If anything, Madison's actions would discredit all her efforts now. Had she failed to calculate the high cost of what would happen if her cover was blown?

Kit adjusted her grip on the steering wheel, driving to the one place she should have been investing her energies. People like Madison were entitled. They grew up with everything they needed. A solid family history, parents—dysfunctional maybe but parents by birth—a sibling, a good education, enough money to support them so they could pursue their activist dreams. Madison thought she could play with people's emotions, manipulate them into doing what *she* thought was best.

For the first time, Kit wondered if maybe Al Farrington wasn't the bad guy after all. Maybe he knew something about the buildings he wanted to renovate or tear down. It had been proven in the past that some old historical places posed more of a danger than a benefit to people. Like the historical factory six counties over that proved to have had residue from chemical waste contaminating the water supply. Surely a community shouldn't try to preserve a historic place that hurt people.

But maybe that was too simplistic. Kit eyed the orange-and-yellow trees that whizzed by as she drove to the food pantry, to what used to be the poorhouse. Grove House, they'd called it. The hardworking, dedicated folks of Kipper's Grove—the town's foundation—how many of them found themselves there at Grove House? Tossed aside by the county.

Those folks who'd been dealt a hard blow by life should've experienced the grace of God through the actions of sharing and service. This was why Kit worked at the food pantry. And it belonged to the Boyd family? The idea sank in slower than her anger and hurt allowed, but she recalled Madison's explanation now. Not that she believed anything Madison said anymore.

Her eyes brimmed with tears until she struggled to see the road clearly.

There had to be a balance in life. It couldn't all be so black and white. There was beauty in a place like Barlowe Theater. A rich story and a legacy left by people who'd made a difference in Kipper's Grove. But there was also beauty in a place like Grove House, now the food pantry, which helped legacies to survive by helping people survive. And then there were people like Madison, whose missions became warped, and by . . . people like her who forgot where her true focus should be. Kit bit back a sob.

She didn't regret her devotion to finding Madison, but until that first walk at the theater when Madison vanished, she'd been slowly rerouting her attention to *Madison's* passions. To *Madison's* convictions. Kit Boyd had become the epitome of a heroine's sidekick. So much so that she'd lost the essence of who she always knew she was supposed to be.

Kit Boyd.

Adoptee.

Fighter for the underdogs.

Someone who saw value and precious worth in the people society too easily ignored. The human family was diverse, with broken people in every category and group within the caste system. People were what mattered most. Not buildings. Not even history. The here. The *now*. The souls whom God let cross Kit's path to be impacted *today* so that in the future, their legacy would speak of healing and not brokenness. Of hope and not destitution. Of God and not a world alienated from its Creator, who wildly loved *all* people.

36

Kit punched the code into the combination lock for the pantry door. When it gave way, she tugged it open with purpose. She needed to call Corey and explain to him her revelation. To apologize for putting so much on his shoulders the last several weeks as she'd followed Madison around, intent on pleasing one friend while not realizing what she'd done to the other.

She was reaching for the light switch when a shrill voice stopped her.

"No. *You* listen."

"Please," an unfamiliar voice drifted her way. "Let's just talk about this."

"Talk? *You* got me into this mess. *You* better figure a way out of it."

Kit snuck down the aisle of cookies and treats. She pressed her hand against the metal shelving and peeked around toward the front desk. She saw Gwen, who was seated in the desk chair, the light from the computer monitor illuminating her face. Her expression was focused. She stared directly ahead at the one who stood in front of her. A man. Average height. Indistinct in appearance from the back.

Kit frowned, then started to step out to say something when

the man's hand came into view. Kit froze. The intruder held a handgun in front of Gwen.

"You were supposed to deal with Kit—and the paperwork!" He slammed the gun on the desk, his hand covering it, the barrel pointed squarely at Gwen.

"I—" Gwen had gone pale, and her hand shook as she went to remove a cigarette from its box. "I did what I could."

Gwen. Oh, this was bad. Kit ducked back behind the shelving unit, fumbling for her phone. She needed to call 911 immediately. She should have listened to Corey, his complaints about Gwen. About how she tried to *be* Kit when Kit wasn't around.

Her phone wasn't in her pocket, and Kit stifled her annoyance. She'd left it in the car. She could see it in her mind, lying on the passenger seat where she'd tossed it in her hurry to get away from Madison.

"All you had to do was get Kit out of the way. Between Madison and the accident and the vandalization here, there should have been no reason for you not to get to the copies of the paperwork and destroy them."

Kit could tell Gwen was trying to keep calm, but the unlit cigarette bobbled nervously between her lips. "I couldn't find where Madison put the paperwork," Gwen said. "And you didn't tell me that Madison was going to disappear! We could've just *asked* her."

"I didn't know what Madi had up her sleeve!" The man shifted, rubbing his face while holding the gun haphazardly. "She didn't tell me she was up to her own shenanigans. Besides, she never would have told us where she put it. She wouldn't do that to Kit."

Kit backed away. There wasn't anything she could do to stop the strange man without endangering Gwen further—not that Gwen deserved her loyalty. If she could get to her car, then she could call the cops. Kit turned as quietly as she could toward the door. Her elbow caught the edge of a box of cookies sticking out on one of the shelves. It fell to the floor, taking another box with it.

"What was that?" Gwen's cry catapulted Kit into a run.

She had to get out of the pantry! She had to—

"Kit Boyd!" The unidentified man's shout stopped her.

Kit turned slowly, her hands raised high so they could see she wasn't doing anything that deserved getting shot for. She froze when her eyes connected with the stranger. "Dan?" Her voice echoed in the pantry. Dan Farrington, Madison's father, appeared almost as jittery as Gwen, even though he was the one with the firearm. "What are you—?"

"Come here!" Dan waved the gun. "Come sit next to Gwen."

"Gwen—" Kit started.

"No." Dan stopped Kit. "You sit there." He kicked out a metal folding chair that was against the wall, the gun still aimed at them.

Kit could tell Dan wasn't accustomed to holding a firearm. He kept adjusting his grip on it, as if questioning what he was doing as he did it.

"Dan, what's going on?" Kit tried to get him to explain. Her confusion was compounded by Madison's recent appearance and her horrid admission to scheming.

Gwen's expression was grim. "Kit, I'm so sorry, I—"

"Oh, stop." Dan laughed. "You were fine doing what I asked as long as you got paid."

"But I—" Gwen tried to protest.

"It doesn't matter." Dan raked his free hand through his hair, agitated. "All I needed you to do was get Kit out of the way, then get the paperwork and—"

"What paperwork?" Kit inserted. Somehow she and Gwen had to overpower the man.

Dan Farrington blew out a huge breath and tilted the gun toward her. "Madi called me and let me know that in all her historical digging, she found out your family owns this building."

"Okayyyyy . . ." Kit dragged out the word, unsure what that had to do with Dan Farrington becoming unhinged.

Dan's exasperated look was her reward. "My father was trying to buy this property. Millions, Kit. Millions in revenue if we could build industrial buildings here. The dairy farm corporation that my father invests in? A milk production and packaging plant, right here, would bring in *millions*. But then Madison finds the paperwork and calls to tell me like she's some sort of Midwestern Indiana Jones! She had *no idea* what she had. She would have been thrilled to sabotage her grandfather that way, but instead she had already dreamed up her cocka-mamie idea with the theater." Dan gave a shout of incredulous laughter, shaking his head at Kit. "Can you believe what she did? I wasn't planning to fly here myself. I figured Gwen here could get you out of the way, find the documents, and that'd be that. Dad could buy the property, and we'd be able to keep on with our plans."

That the Farrington family was dysfunctional had been un-derstood by Kit for years. Dan's affairs. The broken marriage. Carol's influence on her daughters. Madison and Avery against their grandfather and even their father. But it had never oc-curred to Kit that Dan Farrington would take sides with his father, Al.

"So Al doesn't know . . ." Kit faltered.

Dan grimaced. "What Dad doesn't know won't hurt him."

"The illegal dealings Madison was trying to expose Al for were—"

"Doesn't matter *who* was behind them. You screwed it all up, Kit. Actually"—Dan whirled toward Gwen—"*you* screwed it up. Where else would Madison have hidden those documents?"

"I don't know." Gwen coughed back a sob. "I looked every-where here. I looked in Madison's house after she disappeared. I've looked *everywhere*."

"Gwen, did you tamper with my car?" Kit asked.

"I did, yes . . . but I didn't want you hurt. I figured the tire would wobble and you'd feel it. It was meant to scare you and that's all. The threatening phone call, the vandalizing . . . I thought they'd distract you enough so you weren't here all the time. Madison made it sound like she'd filed the documents here. She was going to surprise you with the news your family owns this property. But then she disappeared, and you got h-hurt and . . ." Gwen collapsed forward onto the desk, burying her face in her folded arms.

Kit blinked. Remorse? From Gwen? She remembered the first day Gwen volunteered at the pantry. She was smiling, happy. She quickly caught on to driving the pantry's van around to do donation pickups. She was that volunteer you could count on when others dropped out. She was a mother, for heaven's sake! Never had she ever given off a vibe that—

"For a single mom, a chunk of money is all the motivation needed to help out," Dan said. He paused and shook his head. "But now I'm so deep into this . . ."

Kit held her hands up, palms out. "Dan, together we can figure this out."

Dan's expression was grim. "How? I've already lost Madison—as soon as she finds out what I did. My father will be furious. He may appear cutthroat, but he's on the up-and-up, wants everything to be legal. He'd have just walked away and allowed the documents to be presented and the property be returned to your family. So that leaves me facing criminal charges." Dan shrugged, the gun still swinging between Kit and Gwen. "I tried to put an end to—"

"It was you who attacked me here in the pantry that night," Kit said.

Dan furrowed his brow. "I've lost my way, Kit. It's what happens when your family falls apart, and all you have left is money. Business. Legacy. Do you know what it's like to be a Farrington? Do you?"

Kit shifted her weight to her left foot, and Dan leveled the gun on her. "Don't, Kit. I'm not happy with how things have developed. But I can't lose anything more."

Without hesitation, Kit launched herself toward Gwen. Dan shouted.

Kit yanked Gwen down behind the desk. "Stay here and keep your head down!" Kit whispered.

"I'm sorry, Kit—"

"Not now," she breathed. She patted Gwen's hand as Dan hurtled over the desk. Kit jumped up, running for the shelves and diving behind them as Dan yelled.

"No!"

There was no gunshot as Kit expected. She sprinted for the door. For freedom. For Gwen. For herself. For those who had gone before and those who would come after, who believed they weren't worth fighting for. When truly they were.

Greta

OCTOBER 1915

John told them everything. Mr. Barlowe swore retribution as they hauled him away.

"I'm so sorry." John kept shaking his head, his dark eyes begging Greta for forgiveness. "I didn't mean to get so deeply involved—"

"No one ever does," Detective Patton interrupted. He motioned for the other officer to lead John away.

Greta sagged against Oscar. Stunned and only a bit relieved, she was grateful for his support, but hesitant when Mr. Boyd turned toward her. There was resolution in his eyes.

"Show us the hatch, Miss Mercy."

Two officers had been busy emptying the coal bin. Greta left Oscar's side, feeling the immediate absence of his strength. She would need to get used to that. Once this was all over, she was certain Oscar Boyd would never associate with her again. Even if he wanted to, no friendly acceptance emanated from his father.

Greta ducked to poke her head into the coal bin. She pointed. "There. The hatch is in the back corner."

An officer squeezed in past her, the remaining coal in the bin making his journey to the back unsteady. The coal crunched under his shoes. His flashlight lit the innards. There was a scraping sound as the officer kicked away coal from the corner, a metal *clang*, and then, "Found it!"

Greta stepped aside as Detective Patton pushed his way through. "You see it?"

"Yep. There's a tunnel back here just like she said—big enough for us to squeeze through." The officer's affirmation brought Greta a little relief.

Between John Hargrove's confession of guilt that he was working on Barlowe's payroll and the tunnel now revealed, Greta knew at least part of her own testimony had been proven.

Minutes later, Detective Patton had left his officer to explore the tunnel while they made their way through the theater and across the street to the Barlowe mansion.

Mrs. Frances Barlowe was waiting for them, a thin smile on her lips. The same expression as the day she'd slipped the theater key into Greta's hand. "I'm guessing you're here to see my husband?"

"Unfortunately, I've already seen him," Detective Patton said firmly. "We need to see inside your house."

"Of course." Mrs. Barlowe stepped aside.

Patton hurried past her, followed by two of his men.

"Mr. Boyd," Mrs. Barlowe acknowledged.

341

"My apologies, ma'am." Mr. Boyd swept his hat from his head. "I'm sure this is all quite unexpected."

"Quite not, actually," she sighed softly. Mrs. Barlowe looked at Greta. "In fact, I expected this very thing."

"Why?" Greta whispered. She couldn't speak louder, for her throat was clogged with tears.

Mrs. Barlowe's eyes glimmered with emotion. "Living with a man like Rufus is, well, it takes planning to—"

She was interrupted by a flash of white. Then came a cry of fear, followed by a series of wails.

Mrs. Barlowe whirled away from them. "Stop! Please stop!"

Mr. Boyd, Oscar, and Greta hurried after her.

Mrs. Barlowe knelt in front of a sofa, a woman in a white dress curled into its corner. "Emily." Mrs. Barlowe attempted to soothe, but her voice was strained by a lack of patience. "Please, Emily, stop this!"

Greta stared. It was Alma, wasn't it? No. No, it wasn't. Alma pushed past Greta in the doorway, giving her a sad smile. She hurried to her sister and knelt alongside Mrs. Barlowe.

"Emily, it's all right. Here. Here is your baby." Alma pushed a doll into Emily's arms. "Hold it. Rock it. It needs you," Alma crooned.

Emily calmed, her hand stroking the hairless head of the doll. She adjusted its blanket while fixating on her identical twin sister, Alma. "My baby," she cooed.

Alma and Mrs. Barlowe exchanged looks, and Mrs. Barlowe struggled to her feet. She tried to collect herself, running her hands down her skirts to smooth any wrinkles. "Now you know. This is what I've been forced to endure for years. My husband's secrets."

Alma, still crouched on the floor by the sofa, pressed her forehead against her sister's leg. The twin women became lost in their own world, both mothering the lifeless doll on Emily's lap.

"Mrs. Barlowe, I-I hardly know what to say." Mr. Boyd's response was reflective of all of them.

Oscar stood a fair distance from Greta. She sensed his absence but realized even now that he was beginning to draw the lines as to the future. Yes, Greta had not been lying or seeing things. Yes, she had been correct. Yes, things were getting rectified. But no, she would not need his assistance much longer.

It was the last part that kept her full relief imprisoned in the reality of grief and loss that never seemed to release its hold. When all was said and done, she would still be at Grove House, still worrying over her little brothers, still aching to find out what had happened to Leo.

"Don't say anything, Henry." Mrs. Barlowe dispensed with formalities. "My husband had no qualms about committing his first wife to an institution, seeing as it was for her medical benefit. But his daughters? He wanted no one to know of their condition. Unfortunately, Alma has been far easier to manage than Emily. Emily has her father's wits, and though she has no concept of reality, she is very smart. She's manufactured ways to keep my husband on his toes these last years."

"The infant?" Oscar stepped forward. "Is it—?"

"It's just a doll," Mrs. Barlowe said, "and nothing more. No sordid tales of lost babies." She redirected her attention to Greta. "That was perhaps Rufus's worst evening ever when Emily snuck into the box seat for that performance and tossed her doll over the edge." Mrs. Barlowe's laugh was almost musical. She clutched her throat lightly, shaking her head. "If it wasn't for the doctor, who is good friends with Rufus, Emily would have outed Rufus then and there. But the doctor was able to whisk the doll away, and you, poor dear, took the blame for it."

"How many in Kipper's Grove are . . . ?" Mr. Boyd cleared his throat.

"On my husband's payroll?" Mrs. Barlowe smiled. "I have a list. I'll gladly relinquish it."

Greta felt weak. All over. She fumbled for a chair and found one, sinking into it.

"Yes, do sit down." Mrs. Barlowe glanced at the twins, and while there was no motherly love in her expression, there was empathy. Or perhaps it was pity. "I've spent years knowing of my husband's secrets, but outside of his own flesh and blood, they never so directly affected another person. At least not that I'd personally witnessed. Frankly, I was appalled."

"And that's why you gave Greta the key?" Oscar inserted.

"Yes, but to bring a man like my husband to his knees, it takes more than his wife spreading stories about him. No one would believe me. It all needed to come out. Every bit of it. The tunnel, the girls, the fact that he'd faked their deaths years before so he would no longer need to answer for their illness and how it would tarnish his name and reliability. I don't know what all my husband is involved in, but I know it's not good. And I know his cohorts would not take lightly the accusations of . . . shall we say, instability in the family?"

A few steps brought Mrs. Barlowe closer to Greta. She looked down at her with a sort of elegant tolerance that made Greta like her and feel small all at the same time.

"I'm sorry I had to use you to expose the truth of this family. All will be made right now."

Greta wished Mrs. Barlowe was telling the truth. But all couldn't be right. The Barlowe secrets had cost Gerard his life. They had stolen Leo from her. They had ruined the lives of two beautiful women, who with some care and love could more than likely have blossomed. Or perhaps at least known some sense of happiness and acceptance.

No. It would never be all right.

An officer burst into the room, startling them all. Emily shrieked, curling her body around her doll. Alma flung herself over her sister as if to guard her.

"Come quick!" the officer panted, out of breath.

"Where? What is it?" Mr. Boyd demanded.

"Come. Now." The officer spun on his heel and raced from the room, leaving them but one option, which was to hurry after him.

"We found something!" the officer shouted over his shoulder. "And not just the tunnel!"

Greta was never so thankful as to feel Oscar's hand wrap around hers as they ran.

37

Kit

Evan caught her by the waist as she burst from the food pantry.

Kit grabbed at him, not bothering to ask how he'd gotten there or why. "Dan Farrington—" Kit tried to catch her breath. "He's inside. He has a gun. And Gwen—she's in there too."

Evan motioned to the two squad cars already pulling into the parking lot. "I called the police. When I found your car here, I knew something was up."

"Evan, I-I . . ." Kit struggled for words as Evan pulled her away from the pantry.

For several minutes, chaos ensued. Kit huddled against Evan, a safe distance away. Shouts. Pounding. Then, to Kit's relief, a police officer pushed Dan out the door, his hands in cuffs, his head hanging low.

Gwen followed, one of the officers escorting her to a waiting squad car.

Corey's truck pulled into the lot. He jumped from the driver's seat, and Kit broke away from Evan and ran toward him.

She threw herself into Corey's embrace. Her friend returned the hug, then held her back from him, his hands on her shoulders.

"I'm so sorry, Kit. I had no idea about Gwen. I—"

"Well, now you don't have to listen to the Spice Girls or get asked to babysit," Kit said, half sobbing and half laughing.

Corey looked to the sky and then back to her. "Kit, I am *so sorry* I didn't see that part of Gwen. That I didn't know. Why? Did she say why?"

"It was Madi's dad. He paid Gwen to get me out of the way. Apparently, Madi hid documents here that say my family *owns* the land and the building."

Awareness flooded Corey's face. He looked past Kit to Evan, who had come up behind her. "*That's* what those documents are?"

"You know about them?" Kit straightened.

"Yeah." Corey's stunned expression matched his tone. "Madi gave me some documents a few weeks ago. She said to keep them safe, and she'd ask for them back later. I didn't think much of it at the time."

Kit swiped her tears away. Madison. Trying to bless Kit at the same time she'd used her and abused her emotionally.

"The authorities will need to see those documents," Evan interjected.

"Of course." Corey nodded, then turned back to Kit. "Are you all right? I've got only pieces of the story of what happened, but it sounds messed up, Kit."

"I'll be fine." She gave him a watery smile.

Corey exchanged glances with Evan, then leaned close so he could catch Kit's gaze. "Honey, you just remember that we're surrounded by broken people, and we always will be. Love gets twisted with ambition and spite and selfishness. But then there are others that by the grace of God will choose to be a true friend. To stick by you, to care for you, and to protect you. We're here, Kit. Don't allow this to ruin your faith in what God gifted you with when you were a tiny little girl in a diaper."

Kit laughed, though the tears flowed unchecked, and she could feel Evan's hand rest gently on the small of her back. Not possessively but in a caring way.

Corey chuckled. "You are loved. And your parents, I, and others"—he glanced at Evan—"will fight the good fight and stick by you. Because you're worth it, Kit. You're worth it."

Greta

OCTOBER 1915

Three pairs of eyes stared at Greta from the dark corner of the basement. Their faces were covered in coal dust, their clothes filthy, their bodies gaunt.

Mr. Boyd reached out and caught Greta as her legs gave way to shock.

Leo surged forward, grabbing hold of Greta. Together they sank to the floor, Mr. Boyd releasing Greta. The other two boys, Fred and Teddy, were quickly ushered from the basement with officers talking excitedly about contacting their parents.

"How? Where?" Greta cried, not caring that Leo's filth was wiping on to her. He smelled like dirt and coal. He felt bony and small. Her strong, cocky brother clung to her with a desperation she'd never felt from him before.

She looked up to Detective Patton for answers.

The man's face was alive with a beaming smile of satisfaction. "We found the boys down here in another part of Barlowe's basement."

"Let me guess, his coal bin?" Oscar sounded none too impressed.

"Yes." Detective Patton nodded with the right amount of displeasure toward Barlowe. "Apparently, the night they went missing, Miss Emily Barlowe locked them in the tunnel. When Mr. Barlowe found them, well, there wasn't much he could do without exposing his own sordid life."

"So he kept them locked in his basement's coal bin?" Mr. Boyd's words sent shivers through Greta.

Leo pulled away from her, addressing the detective. "He said he was goin' to send us west. He was just waitin' for some men from Chicago or somethin'."

"Oh my goodness!" Greta pulled Leo back into her arms. She wasn't going to let him go. Not now. Not ever.

"Greta, you're squeezing too hard." Leo coughed and laughed.

Greta released him with her own teary laughter. "The boys—they'll be so happy to see you."

"I wanna go home," Leo said and wiped the tear tracks from his cheeks. "I'm done here. I was just tryin' to prove what you saw at the theater! That's the only reason I left."

"I know, I know." Greta pushed Leo's hair from his face. "It's okay. We're at Grove House now, but we'll be together. It's all right now. We can be together."

"I don't care where we stay . . ." Leo's voice broke.

Mr. Boyd cleared his throat, grabbing their attention. They all looked to him, and he directed his question to Detective Patton. "Does Mrs. Barlowe know the boys were locked up down here?"

The detective shook his head. "There's no evidence she did. Leo here stated that they never saw Mrs. Barlowe. Only Mr. Barlowe and Emily. Of course, we can't hold Emily responsible. In fact—" he hesitated, glancing at Greta and Leo—"there could be a big comeuppance for the Barlowes when this gets out. It could be tough for Alma and Emily. A lot of folks won't understand just 'cause . . . well, the women aren't right in their minds."

Realization spread through Greta. The awful stigma of illness would not garner the girls much empathy from those who would judge them for their actions, not their hearts. "What will happen to them, Detective?"

"Mrs. Barlowe will more than likely not want responsibility for them. They're not her daughters. Alma cannot return to Grove House—it wouldn't be good. They need proper help and care. There are places—*good* places—that can provide them a happy life. But not if this hangs over their heads."

"What are you saying?" Mr. Boyd's tone made it clear the outcome might not be palatable.

Detective Patton's gaze included everyone in the room. "It means we help protect the Barlowe daughters by not involving them. Mr. Barlowe was the one responsible for holding the boys. Emily and Alma were not. If we keep them out of it, no one will know of them, and they can continue to live their lives unaffected by their father's transgressions."

"But you'd have to convince Fred and Teddy's folks too?" Greta said.

Detective Patton nodded. "Yes. But to be honest, the hard fact is that the ones who will be believed are—"

"You and the Boyds," Greta finished, fully understanding. Even in the wake of Mr. Barlowe's misdeeds, the word of those with little influence also held little weight.

"We're willing to do all we can to protect the Barlowe daughters," Mr. Boyd stated.

"That's right," Oscar added.

Leo's next words encompassed the gravity of what had happened. "There are more victims than just me and the boys. That lady never did anything to harm me. She was just trying to take care of her baby doll."

351

Her baby doll . . . "But what about the banging on the pipes?" Greta asked. "And I heard a baby cry."

"Yeah," Leo said, "there was one night Fred got out to the tunnel and then hid under the stage. Then Mr. Barlowe's lacky—that Ambrose fella—caught him again. As for any baby ya heard, that woman who first took us, she does that. Bawls like a baby. She scared me, Greta."

His admission reminded her of the trauma Leo and the other two boys had experienced. It would take weeks, months probably, for them to heal. In the end, Greta couldn't help but squelch the sorrow that coursed through her. A woman's baby doll had begun it all. A beloved item that to one innocent soul, Emily Barlowe, was her entire world. Just like Greta's brothers were to her.

38

Kit

The campfire in her parents' backyard snapped and shot sparks into the night air. The crisp autumn evening had brought with it a kind of peace, one that Kit had no intention of taking for granted.

Mom and Dad were in the house, having retired hours ago, and now Kit sat alone in silence. It was after midnight. There was something beautiful about being alone. Just her, God, and the crickets.

Kipper's Grove had become a different place to Kit from what it was before. So many curtains had been pulled back on the lives of people she thought she knew. With Dan Farrington and Gwen in custody, Al Farrington had issued a public apology on behalf of the Farrington family for the actions against Kit Boyd and her family, as well as the irresponsible and costly actions of his granddaughter, Madison.

The town of Kipper's Grove had begun the process of straightening out ownership of the land the poorhouse once stood on. Apparently, Oscar Boyd's attempts to close the poorhouse had taken years and ended with his claiming the area as Boyd land so it could never be revived. Kit's dad, Ford, had been floored at the news, and Kit's parents were already making plans to partition the property so the food pantry could be made owner of its own plot and building.

Madison was over her head in trouble, both with the law and with the Friends of Barlowe Theater Guild, not to mention with her family and grandfather. Kit knew it was going to be a long and drawn-out saga. Avery had her own issues to deal with too, after she'd joined Madison in the deceit. Overall, Madison's goal had been accomplished. The theater was safe, as was the downtown's historic district surrounding it. But she and Madison would never be the same. Their friendship had been broken by dishonesty, and yet part of Kit longed to extend a hand to Madison simply because of Madison's desire that the land be granted to the Boyd family, its rightful owner. It was convoluted. But as Corey had coached her, love was convoluted. Only it could at times, he'd shared later over coffee, become toxic. Distance wasn't a bad thing; sometimes it was healthy. It could bring healing, or if not healing, new direction.

Kit picked up a stick in the yard and tossed it into the circular fire pit. It snapped as it hit the coals, reminding her of the helplessness in life and how the heat of trouble could consume. Though it wasn't a pleasant thought, it was reality. The flames would come, and they would test you. There was no getting around a trial.

Evan's image flashed through her mind. It'd been two weeks since he had left. A goodbye, a platonic hug, and shared phone numbers. He'd not texted. Not once. The pang of that was more poignant than Kit wanted to admit. There was no reason to expect anything different. Their lives had crossed through a traumatic experience, that was what had bonded them, but now it was time to return to their own lives.

The *Psychic and the Skeptic* crew had cleared out of town

almost immediately after the debacle with Madison was revealed. Somehow Heather was getting away scot-free, with the exception that her contract was voided after the current season. Evan hadn't shared how he felt about that. Without Heather, the show would end. Kit wondered if through the entire weirdness of the situation, Heather actually believed she'd seen what she claimed or if she'd fabricated it for the sake of personal benefit.

Kit resigned herself to not knowing.

Not knowing. A person never really knew who would weave in and out of their lives. After reviewing her family tree with her parents, they'd uncovered that not only had Leo been one of the lost boys but Greta Mercy had donated her journal of memories to the founder of the Friends of Barlowe Theater Guild. It was an effort to keep the theater's history intact. The good and the bad. Apparently, Alpharetta Green had found part of it, and Madison the other, all while sifting through the theater's archives over the years.

Kit had visited Dean and Selma Barlowe to see if they had any information as to story of the lost boys of the theater. They said they only knew what Kit knew, that Greta Mercy's journal revealed the lost boys had indeed existed. Apparently, however, they had been recovered—unlike popular legend. As for the woman in white, they would have to accept that mystery would never be solved. Had there been a real woman in white? Had there been an accident with an infant? No one knew. Kit was okay with that.

She smiled, poking at the fire with her s'more stick. She would like to think that someday she'd wear an in-ear monitor and maybe hear the ghostly voice of the woman in white, crooning to her infant in the shadows of the box seat.

"There's an art to toasting a marshmallow."

Kit jumped at the voice, twisting in her chair. A warm wave rushed through her as Evan strode across the lawn, his hands stuffed into his pockets.

"What are you doing here?" Her question fell far short of the euphoric excitement she felt. "After midnight no less?"

Evan smiled, easing onto the ground beside her camp chair. "I collaborated with your parents. I needed a vacation. The show has imploded, and I could use some R and R."

"So you came here?" Kit asked.

He shrugged. "I missed you." He didn't even bother to look at her. Instead, he grabbed a stick and started poking at the coals in the fire pit.

Just like that.

I missed you.

And yet more had been expressed in those three words than in any others he could have said.

Kit studied his profile, his jawline, his hair, his strength. He was a friend. One she'd not expected. And he was here. For her. With no expectations, conditions, or even promises.

That was how loyalty began, though, wasn't it? Walking through trials together and then coming out the other side of them . . . together.

Kit turned her eyes to the glowing embers of the fire. "Yeah," she breathed. "I missed you too, Evan."

Greta

OCTOBER 1915

She would never stay there again. Not at Grove House anyway. It hadn't pained her or the boys to leave it behind, and after the emotional reunion with Leo, not to mention the inquiry beginning with Mr. Taylor's questionable association with Mr. Barlowe and Grove House, they were glad to be rid of the place. A small house had been donated—supposedly—by an anonymous benefactor to the Mercy family. It was in a pleasant little section of Kipper's Grove. Greta had gently confronted Eleanor regarding the generosity of the Boyd family acting anonymously, but Eleanor had insisted that they'd had nothing to do with it.

Now, as Greta swept the front porch, her eyes settled on a motorcar that wound its way down their quaint little street. There was a woman in the back seat. Prim and wearing a placid expression. Her gloved hand lifted in a small wave, which Greta returned. Then she knew.

Mrs. Barlowe.

The house was her way of extending her gratitude, but also expressing her apologies.

Greta leaned the broom against the house and stepped off the porch onto the stone walkway lined with rosebushes.

Was it possible to endure so much and come out of it with peace? They were together. The boys would be able to attend school next quarter. Greta would find work, thanks to the letter of recommendation from Oscar and Eleanor's mother.

Greta gazed up at the maple trees, swaying in the wind, dropping more leaves and becoming more barren as October quickly made its way to November.

"You're happy then?"

Oscar's voice drifted down the sidewalk toward her, and Greta turned a pleasant smile in his direction. They'd not spoken much since the events unfolded. It seemed everyone needed to fall back into their places, into some semblance of order. Yes, Greta had accepted this would keep her separated from Eleanor, and yes, from Oscar too. She was working class, while they were part of the social elite. Those two worlds weren't meant to bond beyond cordial acquaintance, and if Greta were so blessed, friendship.

Oscar approached her, his feet kicking piles of unraked leaves from his path. His hands were in his trouser pockets, his shoulders relaxed. He wore a deep brown sweater vest, and his round, gold spectacles made his lean face even more handsome. He looked toward the Mercy house, then settled his warm, lentil-soup eyes on Greta.

"You're happy here." It was an observation of truth.

Greta nodded. "I am. We are."

Oscar mimicked her nod. They stood face-to-face.

"My father said that Mr. Barlowe has been linked to some shady dealings in Chicago."

"Yes, I heard."

"Mrs. Barlowe is going to keep the theater open," Oscar continued. "Although I'm not certain I will ever attend again."

"It's a beautiful place," Greta said, "in spite of it all."

Oscar cleared his throat. "Greta, I know it is bold of me to ask, to assume, or even hope . . . but I was truly wishful our acquaintance didn't have to end now that a resolution has been acquired."

He was so formal.

Oscar straightened his angular shoulders.

Greta was certain in that moment, her heart melted—as hearts were often wont to do when hope was given the opportunity to grow. "I will most likely be employed somewhere as household staff," she replied, letting Oscar know that his offer, while unbelievably kind and perhaps hinting of more, would nevertheless be impossible for her to accept.

"So?"

Greta frowned.

Oscar gave her a rather bewildered expression. "I don't see what your employment has to do with my hope of continued friendship."

Must she explain it? Greta fumbled for words. "Well, there is the matter of where I've come from, and though everything has been settled, some still eye me and my brothers as . . . I mean, we're not a part of your world—"

Oscar stepped forward and took a gentle hold of her shoulders, engaging her focus with his earnest one. "Has it never been clear to you that I am not of that world either?"

"But you are," she whispered.

Oscar made a face and tipped his head to the side. "A bank account might be a ticket into the elite, but one must also possess charm and wit, strength and athleticism, and I—"

Greta laughed lightly.

"Yes!" Oscar laughed with her. "Let's be honest and admit I am none of that. I love books. I have a mind for theology. Logic is also beneficial. I may work with my father in business, but I am rarely invited to the young people's social engagements merely because I am boring."

Greta turned serious. "I don't find you boring."

"And I don't find you beneath me."

She stood there at a loss for words as the leaves drifted softly to the earth around them. But then no words were necessary. Had they ever been necessary? Greta knew in her soul that Oscar had always been near, off to the side watching her as she grew up with Eleanor. Escorting her and Eleanor with the proper care of a doting brother. Now she saw the truth of it— Oscar had always been there.

Oscar cupped her chin in his hand, urging her to lift her eyes. To look into his. To see her worth in the reflection of his love.

"You *do* know," he whispered, his lips hovering so close to hers that she could sense their warmth. "I have never kissed a woman before."

Greta's instinct was to turn away, but his tender grip held her steadfast, eye to eye with him. She whispered her deepest fears. "Perhaps you haven't set your hopes high enough, and instead you're merely settling with me." Tears sprang to her eyes. The kind that hurt from months of sorrow, the kind that would always be lurking just beneath the surface. Wondering if she would be unworthy or if truth would finally reveal what she was most anxious to believe but frightened to hope for. That Oscar Boyd was more than she could have ever had the courage to pray would one day be hers. And if God was indeed gifting him to her, then surely she was loved.

"Perhaps," Oscar said, his thumb tracing her jawline, "I was just waiting for God to bring you to me." His mouth brushed hers, whisper soft and hesitant. He pulled back just a little, looking deep into her eyes. His smile was strong, gentle, and he shook his head in wonder and disbelief. "That you could even be mine . . . the miracle of that."

His awe stunned Greta. Oscar saw it written on her face, and he shook his head again. "Greta, don't you see? I have never been on any woman's list of eligible men to wed. I'm not strong or handsome or heroic or—"

She pressed her fingers to his lips. "You are all of that and more," Greta whispered.

Oscar kissed her fingers, then pulled her hand away. "Then we must spend every moment in amazement that truly there is love that exists with no conditions, no limitations, and no expiration."

"No expiration . . ." Greta repeated his words, savoring them.

Oscar leaned toward her, and just before he finally kissed her in full, with fervor and with a possessiveness to match his declaration, he stated, "Till death and forever after."

Author's Note

Writing the story of Barlowe Theater took me to the shadowy places of the theater in my hometown. Many of the facts you read about Barlowe Theater are based loosely on the Al Ringling Theater in Wisconsin, which was erected by one of the brothers of the Ringling Bros. Circus. It's a beautiful masterpiece of architecture and comes with its own ghost stories. In short, there have been "sightings" of a woman in white who supposedly did drop a child from one of the balcony seats and who is still looking for her infant today.

The idea of the lost boys is based on the story of a few boys who supposedly got lost in the maze of a below-floors, behind-walls tunnel system. As the legend goes, the boys were never found, though you can still hear them clanging on pipes and shouting for their freedom long after the theater has been closed for the night. I'll leave it to you, the reader, to determine if this tale is true, but it definitely provided the inspiration for the story you just read.

I also wanted to take a moment to address the *believability* of the adoption/abandonment struggle that Kit faces in this story. We often hear of abandonment struggles in children who have been adopted in their later years or who have gone through the foster-care system. Less frequently do we hear of the elements of abandonment and anxiety that develop in those who have been adopted shortly after their births.

When one studies the impact of the immediate bonding of an infant to its mother and father, imagine an infant being taken instantly from its mother and transferred into foster care until the adoption process is completed. Granted, today more adoptions are including the adoptive parents in the actual birthing process, and the gap from birth to bonding is much shorter. But in the past—and in my own personal story—this was simply not the case. Infants were transferred from person to person until a few weeks after birth or perhaps a few months and they were finally "home" with their adoptive parents. What this has done to infants like me was to create a gap between bonding and security, thus instigating an innate sense of insecurity, instability, and the underlying belief that relationships are temporary and conditional.

Kit's struggle that she will eventually run out of value and therefore become expendable was taken from my own personal hours of therapy and self-realization. Therefore, I felt it was important that this aspect of infant adoption have awareness brought to it. Adoption is a beautiful process and has changed and impacted my life for the better. I hope at some point, your life will be touched by its beauty, and that you can help an adoptee realize the permanence of your love and devotion.

Questions for Discussion

1. In this story, a distinct division exists between lower- and upper-class citizens in the town. What are current parallels to this division?

2. Kit's struggles with the fear of abandonment stem from a background of adoption and the belief that eventually people run out of grace and will take their leave. What other life experiences could cause an individual to struggle with that fear? How could such a concern affect one's behavior toward others?

3. Greta's deep sense of loyalty to her family propels her into situations she wouldn't otherwise have found herself in. Do you express loyalty by rushing into a circumstance regardless of the consequences? Or do you tend to be cautious in your approach when defending a loved one? What are the pitfalls of both responses?

4. While poorhouses were employed to shelter impoverished individuals through much of English history, few people are aware that this construct was also a part of America. How are poorhouses from the past similar

to the ways in which society now responds to issues of homelessness and underprivileged families?

5. Barlowe Theater was loosely based on an actual theater built in Wisconsin by Al Ringling of the Ringling Bros. Circus. In what ways did the theater's design, structure, and state of maintenance lend themselves to the spooky elements of the story?

6. Which scene or scenes in the story added unexpected twists for you and kept you guessing?

Acknowledgments

As usual, writing a book takes an army, and this one was no different.

I would like to thank Walmart for creating online grocery shopping. The hours your ordering system has saved me will be a foundation of time this book forever stands on.

I would also like to make sure there's a shout-out to Coffee Bean Connection, my local coffee shop, and yes, to Starbucks, because without either of you, I'd be writing complete horror novels with no happy endings, and that just wouldn't be acceptable.

To my family, it gets old eating cold cereal and frozen pizzas, but hey—we manage. And kids, your father did not marry me for my homemaking abilities, so there's that clause you should know about by now.

The cats. Always the cats. You may not be the most popular of pet options, as dogs seems to take first place in most of American society. But I will say the fact that you are independent and yet loving is the true example of a loyal animal. Even if you would eat me after I was dead.

Then there's the list of people who influenced this novel in one magical way or another. As always to my team at Bethany House, I issue you all imaginary trophies simply for allowing me to put words on paper. My agent, you are and always will be the champion knight who rides ahead into battle—not that there's actual battles, but you get my drift. To the friends who put up with my midnight memes, my ridiculous texts, and my endless number of cancelations on social events because "I have a deadline": Tracee Chu, Ashley Russ, Jerilyn Finger, Sue Poll, and Angi Nichols.

Christen Krumm, you are my coworker in pretty much everything now. To Paul Wolter and the Al Ringling Theater, thank you for the tours and for preserving the rich theater history that brightens our hometown.

Finally, to the "Table Tribe." I may be an extrovert masquerading as an introvert most of the time, but one of these days I'll make good on my intention to have dinner with you all.

Turn the page for a *sneak peek*
at another exciting read
from Jaime Jo Wright

NIGHT FALLS
on
PREDICAMENT
AVENUE

Available in the spring of 2024!

Keep up to date with all of Jaime's releases at
jaimewrightbooks.com
and on Facebook, Instagram, and Twitter.

SHEPHERD, IOWA—1901

It was terrible. That moment when you stared at a behemoth in the dark and knew you'd beheld a monster.

Effie James hadn't an ounce of resistance left in her. Terror had evolved into a ghastly stillness. The kind that choked her, like bony fingers wrapped around her throat, squeezing with a methodical joy as it watched the life drain from her eyes.

"Effie."

It was an awful feeling, the realization that the mound of dirt beside the cavern in the ground was meant to cover you after you were dead. Like a cold blanket.

"Effie."

There would be nothing left to fellowship with but the creatures that burrowed through the ground and eventually through her remains. A terrible—

"Effie!"

Effie jerked from her thoughts, her shoulder bumping into the tree against which she huddled in the darkness. The whites of her sister's eyes were bright in the moonlight. The house loomed ahead of them, silhouetted in the midnight moon's stare.

"What's *wrong* with you?" Polly persisted. Her form was more petite than Effie's and was swallowed by the man's shirt she had buttoned to the collar and stuffed into trousers they'd stolen from their brother's dresser drawer.

Effie shook her head to clear her wandering thoughts. This was what they did on a regular basis. Unwieldy and disobedient thoughts that rambled and raced into blocks of words and images that weren't happening anywhere else but in her own mind.

It didn't help that only a few yards from the house's back

porch rose gravestones that inspired imaginative musings, lonely sentinels of memories. The oldest gravestone dated back to the early 1800s.

"Effie!"

She startled again and stared through the night at Polly.

Her sister released a sigh of loving annoyance and shook her head. "Effie James, you're doing it again. Where did you go this time?"

"I've been here all along." Effie tilted her chin up a bit.

"Mm-hmm." The disbelief in Polly's response was evident. But there was humor in her voice when she added, "Do try to stay attentive."

Effie sucked in a stabilizing breath. "I'm always attentive."

"Of course you are."

The sisters stared ahead into the night. Graveyard on one side, two-story house on the other, the backyard between with its gazebo. From the roof dangled a pulley and a bucket.

The James sisters had passed by 322 Predicament Avenue countless times. Everyone in Shepherd had. It was the strangest, most mysterious place in the entire town. A place of transients who came and went. Or died. People in Shepherd weren't certain what happened to those who stayed at 322 Predicament Avenue, just that they would come and then they would disappear.

On occasion, dirt in the cemetery looked to have been trifled with, giving way to rumors that perhaps the unknown occupants of 322 Predicament Avenue had arrived but had never really left. They'd just *moved* to a different location on the property—a permanent one.

Effie and Polly weren't the first to sneak onto Predicament Avenue in the dead of night. It was a rite of passage for the young. Except Effie and Polly were supposed to be the obedient *adult* daughters of Reginald James, the town's bank president.

Until tonight.

At twenty, Effie should have been the voice of reason for her sister, who was two years younger, but trying to cage Polly was like trying to keep dandelion fluff from blowing in the breeze. Polly was a free spirit, and while Effie was the cautious, bookish one, her fierce sense of loyalty meant she would follow precocious Polly anywhere. Even to 322 Predicament Avenue. At midnight.

"Now," Polly whispered in Effie's ear, "tradition states we must plant both feet on the back porch and kiss the iron doorknocker's lion head before we leave."

Effie stared at her sister. This wasn't the first time she'd heard the rules of Shepherd's miscreant tradition. She just never fathomed she'd be partaking in it. But what Polly wanted . . . well, Effie couldn't say no.

Polly's eyes sparkled with a mixture of moonlight dust and eagerness. She was thrilled, passionate. Effie, on the other hand, shifted her attention back to the run-down, hopefully empty house. It was a monster. A monster of stories that swirled with rumors of murder and death, and if they survived tonight and returned home safely to their beds, why, it would be a miracle.

"Are you ready?" Polly whispered.

"For what?" Effie couldn't help but ask another question to avoid the inevitable.

Polly gave a stifled giggle. "To kiss the iron lion, silly."

"Hardly." Effie shifted her feet, the maple tree she was hiding behind offering minuscule cover. "Polly, you *do* realize how juvenile this is?"

"Of course!" Polly chirped. A flash of teeth meant her pretty face was beaming. "Charles has done it, and so has Ezekiel."

The mention of their younger brothers only reinforced Effie's argument. "Yes, and they're fourteen and sixteen—not of marriageable age with reputations to protect."

"You sound like Mother. Come on, let's go!" Polly tugged on Effie's shirtsleeve.

The next few seconds were a flurry of feet pounding on the grass as the two ran across the patchy yard toward the house.

Shutters hung askew from the house's windows, leaving dark voids to appear like ghouls glaring at them. The back porch tilted to the side where its foundation had settled, the fieldstones holding it up having sunk into the ground.

Polly gripped Effie's hand, and Effie felt little reassurance at being half dragged toward the house.

One never knew when someone was living at 322 Predicament Avenue. Tonight could be the night they'd come face-to-face with some nameless occupant. A hobo. A shamed woman of the night. A criminal hiding out. Goodness knew *who* might be living there. There had been petitions to knock the place down to eliminate such issues. All of them had failed. This was private property, after all.

Effie's toe caught a divot in the lawn, and she stumbled.

Polly hauled her to her feet. "We're here," she said in a conspiratorial whisper. "The bottom step. Look!" With a gleeful toss of her head, Polly hopped onto the bottom step. "Two feet!"

"On the step," Effie said, her uneasiness growing. "We're supposed to be on the porch."

"Yes." Polly nodded, then let go of Effie's hand, and even with the night's meager light, Effie could see the delight in Polly's eyes. "Here I go."

Polly hurried up the final two steps, landing with a quiet thud onto the porch. She shifted so her foot wouldn't go through the hole of a missing floorboard.

"Polly!" Effie couldn't find the courage to lift her foot to the bottom step, let alone follow Polly onto the porch.

Polly ignored her, pulling on the dilapidated screen door, whose hinges squeaked.

"Shhh!" Effie hissed.

Polly waved her off and ran her fingers over the lion's head.

Its fangs formed the portion made to strike against the base of the door knocker.

"Hurry up!" Effie glanced nervously over her shoulder.

A scream ripped through the night.

Polly froze, her lips pressed against the lion's head.

Effie felt a chill pass from her head through to her toes. The breeze became still. The trees didn't dare rustle a leaf.

Another scream came from inside 322 Predicament Avenue, this time with a gargled, strangled, "Nooo! Please—"

Polly hurtled down the steps toward Effie, grabbing at Effie's arm. Horror replaced fear as Effie spun around, following Polly back across the yard—away from the graves, and away from the horrid house.

Jaime Jo Wright is a winner of the Christy, Daphne du Maurier, and INSPY Awards and is a Carol Award finalist. She's also the *Publishers Weekly* and ECPA bestselling author of three novellas. Jaime lives in Wisconsin with her cat named Foo; her husband, Cap'n Hook; and their littles, Peter Pan and CoCo. Visit her at jaimewrightbooks.com.

Sign Up for Jaime's Newsletter

Keep up to date with Jaime's latest news on book releases and events by signing up for her email list at the link below.

FOLLOW JAIME ON SOCIAL MEDIA

Jaime Jo Wright   @jaimejowright   @jaimejowright

JaimeWrightBooks.com

More from Jaime Jo Wright

In 1865, orphaned Daisy Francois takes a housemaid position and finds that the eccentric Gothic authoress inside hides a story more harrowing than those in her novels. Centuries later, Cleo Clemmons uncovers an age-old mystery, and the dust of the old castle's curse threatens to rise again, this time leaving no one alive to tell its sordid tale.

The Vanishing at Castle Moreau

In 1910, rural healer Perliett Van Hilton is targeted by a superstitious killer and must rely on the local doctor and an intriguing newcomer for help. Over a century later, Molly Wasziak is pulled into a web of deception surrounding an old farmhouse. Will these women's voices be heard, or will time silence their truths forever?

The Premonition at Withers Farm

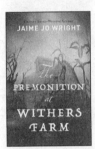

Wren Blythe enjoys life in the Northwoods, but when a girl goes missing, her search leads to a shocking discovery shrouded in the lore of the murderess Ava Coons. Decades earlier, the real Ava struggles with the mystery of her past—all clues point to murder. Both will find that, to save the innocent, they must face an insidious evil.

The Souls of Lost Lake